REGENCY
Seduction

Lucy
Ashford

D1392224

MILLS
BOON

First Published in Great Britain 2017
By Mills & Boon, an imprint of HarperCollins*Publishers*
1 London Bridge Street, London, SE1 9GF

REGENCY SEDUCTION © 2017 Harlequin Books S.A.

The Captain's Courtesan © 2012 Lucy Ashford
The Outrageous Belle Marchmain © 2013 Lucy Ashford

ISBN: 978-0-263-92378-0

52-0317

Our policy is to use papers that are natural, renewable and recyclable products and made from wood grown in sustainable forests. The logging and manufacturing processes conform to the legal environmental regulations of the country of origin.

Printed and bound by
CPI Group (UK) Ltd, Croydon, CR0 4YY

A REGENCY

Collection

The Captain's Courtesan

Lucy Ashford studied English with history at Nottingham University, and the Regency is her favourite period. She lives with her husband in an old stone cottage in the Derbyshire Peak District, close to beautiful Chatsworth House, and she loves to walk in the surrounding hills while letting her imagination go to work on her latest story.

You can contact Lucy via her website: www.lucyashford.com.

Chapter One

Spitalfields, London—February 1816, 8 p.m.

'The Temple of Beauty?' echoed Captain Alec Stewart, lifting his dark eyebrows as he eased his foil into the nearby sword rack. 'How old are you, Harry—twenty? And still wet around the ears, my young pup. The Temple of Beauty is nothing but a den of harlots, take my word on it.'

For the last half an hour, this dusty old hall at the heart of the east London mansion known as Two Crows Castle had echoed to the click of gleaming blades, to the muttered curses of Lord Harry Nugent, and the curt admonitions of his tutor. Now the fencing lesson was over and Harry collapsed on a bench to mop the sweat from his brow and make his plea once more.

'Oh, Alec, do *please* say you'll come! It's my birthday after all. And the girls are as sweet a bunch as you'll find in London!'

Alec laughed aloud. 'Trust me, they're whores.' Pouring out two brandies, he handed one to his pupil. 'I'm not coming. But—happy birthday all the same.'

Harry Nugent, inordinately rich and a truly hopeless

fencer, sighed and sipped just a little of his brandy, which
was rough. He let his gaze rove with a certain amount of
trepidation around this lofty hall, where the chill February wind rattling at cobwebbed windows sent shadows
from the candles leaping across the smokestained rafters.
Then he glanced at his fencing master, who, tall and loose-
limbed, looked as though the exertions of the past half-
hour had affected him not one jot.

Harry took a deep breath. 'Alec!'

'Hmmm?'

'It's really not right, you know, Alec, that you should
live in a wreck like this and make your living by running
a sword school. You're a war hero, man!'

Alec shrugged. 'War hero or not, I've scarcely sixpence
to scratch with, Harry. Anyway, I quite like it here.'

Harry watched as his fencing tutor idly pulled another
fine rapier from the rack and tested its balance. Alec was
one of the best swordsmen in London and used to hold an
enviable reputation as a captain in the Light Dragoons.
Once, they said, he was light-hearted, never serious, even
on the night before battle. London's ladies used to adore
him; he'd had his pick of the *ton*'s heiresses, and for a
brief while was betrothed to one. But now... Now, he was
a stranger to London's social scene and his once-merry
brown eyes were etched with cynicism.

'Even so, to live like *this*!' Harry couldn't stop himself
blurting it out. 'You should take up the matter with your
father, you really should! Everyone says so!'

Alec made a gentle feint with his rapier. 'Do they indeed say that?' he asked softly. 'Do you have fun discussing me with your friends around London's clubs and
watering-holes, Harry?'

'No!' protested Harry Nugent, rather flustered. 'Well,
we say nothing we wouldn't say to your face, Alec!' He

spread out his hands in entreaty. 'You needn't actually—
you know, *do* anything with any of the girls tonight. Just
join us at the Temple for a bit of fun! And perhaps,' Harry
went on innocently, 'a night away from this place would
do you good. Your brother said—'

Alec's well-shaped, flexible fingers suddenly went very
still around the hilt of his rapier. If Lord Harry Nugent
had fought at his side at Waterloo, he'd have known to be
wary of that look.

'When, exactly,' said Alec in a deceptively soft drawl,
'did you see my esteemed brother?'

'Why, it was mere chance, at Tellworth's tables in St
James's last night!'

Still in London, then. 'And what in particular did he
say?'

'He said…' Harry hesitated '…he said you are a little
too fond, like all former soldiers, of the brandy bottle—
which we all know is a lie!—and that is why, he says, you
tend to avoid decent company.'

'Decent company, eh? And will my delightful brother
be at Tellworth's again tonight, do you think, my fresh-
faced, intriguingly honest Harry?'

'Not as far as I know…' Suddenly Harry's face brightened. 'I say, Alec, are you thinking of making your peace
with the fellow? That's surely what your father wishes,
ain't it? Now, that really *would* be capital!'

Alec reached across and ruffled the younger man's fair
curls. 'Make my peace?' he echoed. 'Harry, let me tell you
something. If I come across my brother tonight, I shall take
very great pleasure in slicing whichever expensive coat
he's wearing into precise, inch-wide strips.' The rapier in
his hand gleamed as he thoughtfully practised a *coup de
pointe*. 'I don't much care for his taste in clothes, you see.'

'Oh, Lord,' muttered Harry. 'Oh, Lord.'

'No bloodshed, though. For which my brother should be profoundly grateful.' Decisively, Alec put the weapon away and started to propel Harry gently towards the door. 'Enjoy the Temple of Beauty, my young and innocent friend. And if you really consider there'll be any girls there who *aren't* whores, then you're an even greater gudgeon than I thought. Now, here's your...' he blinked at the wide-brimmed creation '...I think it's what you'd call a hat. And your coat.'

'Very well.' Harry nodded. 'Same time next week, Alec? And Alec—do you think I'm making progress?'

Silence. Then, levelly, 'Your technique, Harry, never ceases to amaze me.'

'Oh. Oh, I say.' Harry left, looking rather pleased. Alec shut the door on his departure a little too hard and brushed the ensuing shower of ceiling plaster from his shoulders.

The damn place was falling to pieces. Rather like his life.

Alec was the younger son of an earl, and had served in the army for seven years. He'd returned home with a reputation for gallantry, and his future should have been bright indeed.

But here in London, the very air was tainted. Tainted by his own *brother*.

'Beg pardon, Captain!' A small but tough-looking man with a black patch over one eye had entered the hall. 'I've got three fellows here, wantin' to speak to you.' Hovering behind Garrett were some men who were plainly ex-soldiers, though their uniforms hung in rags from their half-starved bodies. And—they saluted Alec. That got him. In spite of their pitiful condition, they saluted him.

'They're old 'uns from the Fourteenth, Captain,' Garrett explained. 'Want to know if we've got any room to spare.'

Two Crows Castle was full to bursting. Alec sucked in a deep breath. 'Garrett, I really don't see how we can—'

'We could squeeze some extra pallets in the top attic, Captain!'

'Right.' Of course. How could they turn away these brave men, any one of whom might have fought at his side on the bloody battlefields of Spain? 'Right,' he repeated, 'see to it, Garrett, will you?'

'Straight away, Captain!' Garrett saluted and turned smartly to escort the ex-soldiers to their new quarters up-stairs. 'Look sharp now, lads!'

'God bless you, Captain!' they were trying to say to Alec. 'You're one of the very best! A Waterloo hero and more!'

Alec waved them away. Then he sat down and raked his hand through his dark hair.

A hero and more? In his father's opinion, far from it.

'My own son.' The Earl of Aldchester had looked stricken—no other word for it—as Alec had stood be-fore him a year ago in the luxurious drawing room of his Mayfair mansion. 'Alec, I cannot believe you have come here to try to destroy my new-found happiness with the woman I love!'

Alec had been in his uniform, the famous blue jacket and white breeches of the Light Dragoons. It was February 1815, and all the army's senior officers had been quietly warned that the Emperor Napoleon was bent on escape from Elba, but Alec had other matters on his mind, for he'd just heard that his father was planning a June wedding.

'Please believe me, sir.' Alec had stood very straight, hating every minute of this interview. 'It's your happiness that I wish to preserve…'

The Earl had got slowly to his feet, suddenly looking

every year of his age. Once, Alec knew, he'd dreamed of a military career for himself, and historic paintings of famous British victories a hundred years ago—Blenheim, Ramillies, Malplaquet—were hung around the walls of his beautiful house. He would await Alec's brief periods of leave from the army with almost painful eagerness. 'Ah, this fellow Wellington!' he used to say. 'At this rate, my son, he'll be snatching the Duke of Marlborough's title as the greatest British general ever!' He used to listen to Alec's accounts of Wellington's campaigns with his eyes full of pride.

But he hadn't been so proud though on that ominous encounter last February.

'You surely realise,' the Earl had said heavily, 'that I used to live for the times you came home to me. For your news of the war. But—to come to me instead with scurrilous *tattle*...'

'Father,' Alec had said quietly. 'Father, I only wanted to ask you if you have *known* her for long enough. If you are sure that she can be trusted, in every way.'

'Trusted?' The Earl looked wretched. '*Trusted?* Oh, Stephen warned me, so often, that you were jealous of my marriage and that you were afraid of losing my favour!'

'Sir, that is not so, believe me!'

'Enough.' The Earl sat down again abruptly. '*Enough.* You must see that what you have just tried to say to me means that I can no longer receive you in this house as my son.'

Fateful words. Irretrievable words. And his father had sounded quite broken as he uttered them. Indeed Alec's voice betrayed his own emotion as he replied, 'Sir, I am sorry for it. And please believe me when I say I will always hold you in the deepest esteem. But I must beg you, one last time, to listen—really *listen*—to what I have to say! Sir, this marriage must not take place!'

His father had stared at him. Almost dazed. 'I just don't *understand*. Perhaps if you were to meet her. Meet her properly, I mean, and talk to her.' He was on his feet again, pacing to and fro. 'Yes, that's it. And then you would realise for yourself how badly you have misjudged her.'

'I will not change my mind, sir. I'm sorry.'

The Earl sagged with despair. Then his eyes grew hard. 'Very well. So be it. One last thing, then. My future wife requires a London base for her mother. She once mentioned that the Bedford Street house I've let you use for the last few years would be suitable. And now I must ask you to vacate it, as soon as possible. Needless to say, your allowance will cease forthwith.'

Alec stood very straight, his face expressionless. 'There's the matter of the home for old soldiers in Spitalfields, sir. I trust, however sorely I've displeased you, that you'll continue with your plans to fund it?'

'Do you know,' said the Earl, his voice breaking a little now, 'I'm beginning to think that it's associating with men of that kind that's made you lose all sense of family duty!' He gazed at his younger son in utter anguish. 'I suggest that you run it yourself, since you obviously care more for your—your lowly battle comrades than you do for me!'

'That is not so, sir—'

'Enough!'

Alec, his jaw clenched, had given a curt bow and left.

His brother had his wish at last. This was a breach between son and father that surely could not be healed.

Soon afterwards had come Alec's recall to duty, for Napoleon had escaped from Elba, and under his leadership the swelling French army had swept northwards to meet the allies in the last and bloodiest battle of the long war: Waterloo.

Then Alec had come home. Only he had *no* home, of course. His father had married in the summer while Alec was away fighting, and Alec's new stepmother's relatives had delightedly appropriated the smart house that he had once occupied.

So Alec had made the decision to move into the home for old soldiers in Spitalfields himself. It had once been a grand mansion, built by a rich Huguenot silk weaver called Ducroix, but the house, like the district, Spitalfields, had fallen on hard times; the name the locals had given to Ducroix's pretentious home—Two Crows Castle—seemed more than ever like an ironic jest.

Before their estrangement, it had been his father's idea to buy it and refurbish it. 'I cannot enjoy my wealth when I see injured and destitute soldiers begging at every street corner,' he'd explained to Alec.

The Earl had bought the lease, but the refurbishments had never started. And now it was up to Alec to try to keep the crumbling mansion habitable by using the money from his army pension, together with a small inheritance from his mother and the income he earned from fencing lessons. Quite simply, he felt he owed it to these men. They had given their all for their country and were left with nothing, often not even their health.

Alec had not heard from his father since that day of their terrible argument and refused all invitations from the *ton*. He had built a new life for himself and in a way he was content.

Or would have been, had he not got his damned brother to deal with.

* * *

Garrett's return broke abruptly into his abstracted thoughts.

'That's them sorted up there, Captain,' Garrett said with satisfaction. 'Makes six lads in the attic now, bit of a squash, but they was all in Spain, so they'll have plenty to talk about.' He eyed Alec warily. 'And I've some more news for you.'

'Yes?'

'Apparently,' Garrett went on in a rush, 'that brother of yours was seen in the Park this afternoon, large as life in his fancy curricle. And he had a lady with him.' Garrett hesitated again. 'A prime 'un, Captain. Dark hair, blue eyes...'

Alec felt an ominous pulse throbbing in his temple. *Steady, now.* 'Do you know,' he said softly, 'I feel a sudden urge to speak with my brother, Garrett.'

'So I thought, Captain. That's why I asked around about his lordship's intentions for the rest of the day. And he's decided, all of a sudden it seems, to visit some place in St James's tonight. The Temple of—the Temple of...'

Alec went very still. 'Not the Temple of Beauty?'

'Aye, that was it. The Temple of Beauty, in Ryder Street. Now, I know he's got that grand house of his barricaded against you like a fortress, but he's likely to be heading to this Temple place alone...'

And he would not be expecting to meet his younger brother. Alec did not hesitate. 'I'm going out, Garrett. Expect me when you see me.' He was already pulling on his greatcoat.

'Sure you don't want company, Captain?'

'Quite sure.' Alec was flinging open the door when he came to an abrupt halt, for outside in the passageway a large, golden-haired dog was watching him expectantly.

Alec swung round, eyes ominously narrowed. 'Garrett, do you know what this creature's doing here?'

'He's been hangin' about outside for days, Captain. No food, no 'ome. Thought we might manage to fit him in.'

Alec raked his hand through his dark hair. 'Do you realise how much dogs this size eat?'

Garrett remained imperturbable. 'He's nowhere else to go, Captain. His name's Ajax.'

'Ajax. Then, Garrett, you'll oblige me greatly by *finding* Ajax somewhere else to go!'

'Very well. Gently now with that door, Captain!'

Too late. As the door slammed shut after Alec's rapidly departing figure, flakes of ancient plaster pattered down from the ceiling. Garrett, with a sigh, fetched a broom to sweep them up, then ruffled the dog's head. 'Blasted place is fallin' to bits… Don't worry, lad. Our Captain's all heart. Most of the time.'

Ajax gazed up at his new friend and wagged his tail happily.

Chapter Two

The Temple of Beauty, Ryder Street, St James's
Later that evening

The first-floor dressing room was crowded and smelled of cheap perfume. Rosalie Rowland edged her way towards the nearest door and opened it a few inches, hoping for a breath of cooler, fresher air.

Oh, fiddlesticks. She shut it again quickly.

Men. Dozens of them, queuing from the ground floor all the way up the staircase. Men, tall and short, rich and poor, plump and thin, all filling the air with the smells of tobacco and strong drink. Men, queuing to see—amongst others—*her*. On stage tonight, in the upstairs hall of the notorious Temple of Beauty.

Rosalie fought down a renewed wave of panic. If she didn't catch her death of cold in this—costume that was as flimsy as a bride's veil, she'd catch something horrible from the dirt. Not that such a minor detail bothered the proud proprietor, Dr Perceval Barnard, or his wife. Or the other girls, who chattered and giggled as they clustered to paint their faces in front of the looking-glasses hung askew on the walls.

'On stage in ten minutes, Greek goddesses!' squawked Mrs Patty Barnard. 'Make sure you're all looking ravishing, now!'

'Think she means—ready to be ravished,' drily put in dark-haired Sal close by. Within minutes of Rosalie's arrival here earlier today, kind Sal had promptly taken her under her wing. And people to watch out for, Sal told her, most definitely included Patty Barnard, a shrill, domineering forty-year-old, whose dyed red hair dazzled the eye.

Mrs Barnard didn't hear Sal's comment, but her sharp eyes shot to Rosalie. 'You. New girl. Pull your gown lower. Our gents haven't paid to see a bunch of Vestal Virgins!'

Rosalie kept her expression demure. 'Certainly it's the last place on earth they'd expect to find any, ma'am.'

The rest of the girls sniggered. Mrs Barnard looked at her, frowning, uncertain, then swung round to the others. 'Girls, stop squabbling over those Grecian arm-bracelets. There should be sufficient for you all… Charlotte, my dear, what a truly exquisite Aphrodite you make!'

And the normal hubbub of chatter and preparation resumed.

The Temple of Beauty was, Dr Barnard liked to declare, a gentlemen's club. But there were no rules for membership, merely an initial payment for the evening's entry, after which the clients could indulge in the usual pursuits of dining, drinking and gaming. Many other clubs in London offered the same. But here, at the stroke of ten, all the patrons moved as one to join the queue for the upstairs hall, because the Temple of Beauty was known throughout London for its classical *tableaux* featuring scantily-clad girls in costumes who posed in what Dr Barnard called 'attitudes' for around ten minutes while the gentlemen in the audience, already mellow with food and wine, feasted their eyes.

'I have an exclusive clientele, my dear, most of them highly educated in the Greek and Roman myths,' Dr Barnard had earnestly assured Rosalie yesterday morning when she'd called about a post. 'And I pride myself,' he went on, 'on my own knowledge of those ancient times of glory!' He'd waved an expansive hand towards his crowded bookshelves, though his lecherous appraisal of her face and figure had rather spoiled the effect of his lofty words.

Rosalie had dragged her eyes from an oversized volume called *The Myths of Apollodorus* and gazed back at him brightly. Now she looked anew round the crowded dressing room. Greek goddesses? Well, the chief of his girls, Charlotte—'the star of our firmament!' was how Dr Barnard had introduced her to Rosalie earlier—looked more like a Covent Garden street-walker than a heavenly deity. Tonight, as Patty Barnard adjusted Charlotte's dyed locks fondly, Sal hissed to Rosalie, 'D'you think our Mrs B. would find Charlotte quite so exquisite if she caught her romping in bed with 'er husband whenever Mrs B.'s back's turned?'

Rosalie felt laughter bubbling up. But it faded, as she glanced at herself in the mirror and thought, just for a moment, that she saw another face—pale, wistful—gazing back at her.

Her sister. Oh, her sister might have stood here. Might have looked into this very mirror...

She jumped as Mrs Barnard's harsh voice rasped in her ear, 'You, girl. Take that ribbon off!'

Rosalie's fingers flew up to the pale blue ribbon with which she'd tied back her silvery-blonde hair. 'But I thought...'

'Do you think,' went on Mrs Barnard, 'that the Ancient Greeks tied back their hair in that fashion, my girl?'

Rosalie rather suspected they did and was prepared to argue the point; Sal stood heavily on her toe.

As it happened, Rosalie was now quite happy to let her long hair hang free. It meant she could hide behind it. And heavens above, looking at this garment they'd given her to wear, she'd need to.

When she'd first seen her dress, laid across Mrs Barnard's plump arm, it had looked perfectly respectable. She was Athena, the goddess of wisdom, after all, so a long white-muslin tunic girdled with a turquoise cord seemed appropriately demure. 'The turquoise will match your eyes, my dear!' had simpered Mrs B.

Up until now, Rosalie had never really considered that she had much of a figure to hide. She was twenty-one years old, of medium height, and rather too thin; her legs, she considered, were too long and her bosom decidedly undistinguished compared to the voluptuous figures that were on display around her. Besides, she'd always made a point of dressing to deter any roving male eye. She'd never in her life up till now worn her hair loose and tumbling to her shoulders, had never worn a gown remotely like this one. Demure? That was before she got it on. It was sheer, it was clinging... For heaven's sake! How could she go out on stage like *this*?

She'd done her very best to adjust the ridiculously low neckline by quickly threading a turquoise ribbon through the scalloped lace that edged the yoke and pulling it together into a bow just above the curve of her breasts. But Sal, who was busy powdering her own extremely well-displayed plump bosom, turned to her, powder puff in hand. 'Ma Barnard will never let you get away with *that* cover-up, darlin'. Not in a thousand years.'

Rosalie protested. 'I've no intention of going out there *half-naked*!'

'What did you expect, in Dr Barnard's Temple of Beauty? Gawd, dearie, I wish I had your looks. Your face and figure, that gorgeous hair of yours—'

'My figure? My hair?' echoed Rosalie.

Sal sighed. 'Own up, now. You ain't done nothing like this before, ever, have you?'

'Well, no. Not exactly...'

'Not on the run, are you, from the law, or some cross husband?'

'No! Not at all, Sal! And anyway, I don't suppose that any of them will be paying much attention to me. Will they?'

'New girl at Dr B.'s Temple of Beauty? Course they'll be lookin' at you!' Sal drew closer. 'And after the show— did Mrs B. explain? There's a bit of music in what they call the Inner Temple on the next floor up, and it's there that the gents pay to come to dance with us.'

'*Just* dancing?' Rosalie enquired rather faintly. She had already discovered that this place was like a rabbit warren, with five floors of rooms and various twisting staircases.

Sal winked. 'Just dancin' to start with. Then—who knows?—you might end up with a nice rich lord to milk for a while, if you just shut yer eyes through all the grunting and heaving. But watch out, gal. If they promise love, they're lying through their teeth.'

Rosalie nodded, her heart sinking. She knew that. But so many didn't.

Rosalie, I'm in London. I'm in trouble. Please help me. That was all that was in Linette's pitiful letter last October. Nothing else—no address, no other clue—except that Rosalie knew Linette had always wanted to be an actress.

Now emotion squeezed at Rosalie's throat like a necklet of iron when she thought what had become of that dream, and a touch of fear also; Linette had been only two years younger than Rosalie, and though Linette's blonde locks were more luxuriant and her figure more shapely, the sisters did bear a resemblance. At the interview yesterday, Rosalie had worried that Dr Barnard might spot it.

But his gaze had been one of cursory approval. 'Oh, they come and they go, our girls!' he'd said airily, when she asked him why he had vacancies. 'A world of opportunities awaits them, after all!'

Opportunities. Anger, as well as despair, surged through her. Then the door flew open and Danny, the lad who helped backstage, burst in. 'Three minutes to go, *lay-dees*!' He looked straight at Rosalie and winked.

'Dirty little rascal,' said Sal amiably. 'Always hopes he'll catch us with nothing on. Here—have some rouge.'

'No thanks.' Rosalie turned to face her. 'Sal, how long have you worked here?'

'Feels like a lifetime, but I've been here all of six months! What with Mrs B.'s sharp tongue and her hubby docking our pay at any excuse, no one sticks it more than a year.' Sal was piling on more rouge. 'Why are *you* workin' here, gal? Standin' about on stage in next to nothing isn't what you was brought up to, anyone can see that! You're clever, you speak like a lady. You could have bin a governess or something, surely!'

'I have a child to care for,' Rosalie answered simply. 'Governesses with children don't get hired.'

Sal looked at her quickly. 'How old's your little one?'

'Two. She's just two years old.'

'Ah, bless! She's lucky, then, havin' you to watch over her,' said Sal wistfully. 'Me, I was put on the streets by my ma when I was ten. To think I'm playin' Hebe, the virgin goddess— Lord knows I can hardly remember bein' a virgin meself. But I've learnt lessons. I know the ways of the so-called gentry like the back of my hand. And remember, the best way to make life comfortable for yourself and your little 'un is to open your legs to a rich man—but get his money first, you hear me?'

'Ladies!' shrieked the boy Danny, flinging the door wide open. 'Ready to go on stage!'

'Here we go.' Sal grinned.

Here we go indeed, echoed Rosalie silently.

But not before Mrs Patty Barnard, inspecting every goddess as they filed through the door, ripped open the bow securing the neckline of Rosalie's bodice and tugged it down to show the curve of her breasts. 'Told you before, Athena. Think you're in a damned nunnery?'

Rosalie pressed her lips firmly together, but a faint flush of defiance rose in her cheeks.

With the curtains still closed, all the girls hurried to take up position on stage. Charlotte was carefully seating herself on a damask-covered throne and preening her dyed golden locks, while the others clustered around. Now Rosalie could hear Dr Barnard standing in front of the stage and announcing to the gathered audience, 'For your delectation, my honoured friends! A scene of exquisite and ennobling artistry—the Greek goddesses!'

Rosalie had kept as far to the back as she could. *Oh*, she wondered, the breath hitching in her throat, *what had she let herself in for?*

The heavy curtains were gliding back.

There must be nigh-on a hundred men out there.

She felt rather sick. For Linette, her beloved sister. She would see this through, for Linette—and for Linette's child, Katy.

Chapter Three

'Dear Rosalie, why on earth are you asking me about such a place?' had been her friend Helen's startled response when Rosalie mentioned the Temple of Beauty two days ago. They were in Helen's printing shop, and all around them were heaps of freshly printed broadsheets. 'From what I've heard,' Helen went on, 'that Temple is nothing but a glorified brothel!'

'Bwothel,' little Katy had lisped. 'Bwothel.'

Quickly Helen turned to the two children, who were drawing stick men on some scraps of paper. 'Toby, darling, take Katy to the kitchen and get her a glass of milk, will you?'

'And a treacle bun?' Six-year-old Toby, always hungry, asked the question hopefully.

'And a treacle bun each, yes, if Katy wants. Look after Katy, now!'

'C'mon, Kate.' Holding out his hand, Toby had valiantly led the toddling two-year-old past the for-once silent printing press towards the kitchen. Katy was still lisping, *'Bwothel. Bwothel...'*

Rosalie watched them go with a catch in her throat, then said quietly to Helen, 'Toby's wonderful with Katy. I'm so very grateful to you for letting us stay here with you, Helen. I wish you'd let me pay you for our food, at least!'

'And I wish *you'd* take my advice and stop going round these dreadful places on your own.' Helen had sighed. 'Men who visit the Temple of Beauty have only one thing on their mind! Are you going because you've heard that Linette might have been there?'

'Exactly. You know how Linette always talked of being an actress? Well, now I've found out she may have worked at this Temple of Beauty, three years ago.'

'That place! Oh, poor, poor Linette!'

Helen had been a teacher at the little school in the village where Rosalie and Linette grew up, then she'd married and moved to London, where her husband ran a small publishing press in Aylesbury Street, Clerkenwell. But a few years later he'd abandoned Helen and their little son, Toby, for a singer from Sadler's Wells. Helen had always kept in touch with Rosalie by letter, and after her husband's departure she wrote to her young friend that she'd resolved to make a success of the publishing business on her own. When Rosalie's search for Linette brought her to London last autumn, it was to Helen that she turned.

'I will pay you, Helen, for my accommodation,' Rosalie had insisted when she arrived outside Helen's door.

'Nonsense.' Helen had hugged her warmly. 'I'll do everything I can to help you find your poor sister. As for payment—well, how about writing for *The Scribbler*?'

'*The Scribbler*? Helen, what's that?'

And Helen had gone on to explain.

The Scribbler was a weekly news sheet Helen produced, a round-up of London events and advertisements, which Helen also used from time to time to denounce the greed of the rich and the plight of the poor.

All this Helen had told Rosalie as she'd unpacked her

bags last October. 'What I really need,' Helen had said, eyeing her former pupil thoughtfully, 'is someone who'll write a weekly diary of London life. Something light, about the theatre, for example, or an amusing commentary on the latest women's fashions... How about it, Rosalie? You have talent—I realised it when you were my pupil.'

'But I've never thought of writing for *publication*!'

'Why not? I remember you write with such charm, such humour—just try it, please?'

Helen's suggestion certainly paid off, because Rosalie's weekly articles—published under the pen name of Ro Rowland, a fictional young man about town—had become resoundingly popular. In other circumstances, Rosalie would have revelled in her new life. She'd come to love this little Clerkenwell printer's shop with its ancient hand press that rattled away merrily in the front parlour. But Helen could be stubborn, and every so often Rosalie had to make clear what she was after. What her purpose was.

'All I want is to find out the truth about Linette,' Rosalie had repeated steadily in the face of Helen's objections. 'I thought we'd discussed this. My sister might have met *him* at the Temple of Beauty and I cannot leave any stone unturned.'

'Then...' Helen had hesitated '...it might just help you to know that Dr Barnard keeps a secret register of clients. Names, addresses, the dates they visited, that sort of thing. I only heard about it because once I was offered the chance to publish some of it by a man who worked for Dr Barnard and showed me some pages he'd copied. I refused, of course—I'd have made too many enemies. But I learnt that Dr Barnard keeps this register—he calls it his green book—in his office, hidden inside a hollowed-out copy of a big old book called *The Myths of Apollodorus*. And since you know, roughly, the dates that Linette was there, it just might help you! It's such a tragedy that you don't know the name of her villainous seducer—'

Rosalie cut in, giving Helen's hand a squeeze. 'Thank you for the news about the register. You are such a good friend.'

Helen shook her head, sighing. Though over thirty now, she still looked just like the village schoolteacher she once was, with her brown hair pinned up tightly and her eyes behind her spectacles shining with intelligence. 'Just look after yourself, my dear, won't you? Get out of that "Temple place" just as soon as you can. *Men.*'

'Men don't worry me, since I've got a foolproof defence, Helen,' Rosalie said lightly. 'I'm simply not interested in them. Though we mustn't forget that there are some good men in the world!'

'Not that I've met lately!' snapped Helen.

Rosalie put her head on one side mischievously. 'What about your friend Mr Wheeldon?'

'Francis! Oh, well, he's different.' Helen was busily putting the latest copies of *The Scribbler* into piles for distribution. 'And you certainly wouldn't find *him* at Dr Barnard's Temple of Beauty!'

True. Rosalie had chuckled at the thought of the kind, middle-aged churchwarden Francis Wheeldon visiting such a place. She picked up a *Scribbler*. 'Shall I take some copies of this to the news vendor in the Strand for you, Helen? You usually sell quite a few there, don't you?'

Subject changed. But Rosalie hadn't wavered in her resolve to visit the Temple of Beauty. If appearing on stage for a night was the only way to get further in her quest, then so be it. That register could be a breakthrough—because Rosalie had lied to Helen. She *did* know the name of the man who had ruined her sister. But she was keeping it to herself, for she had no doubt that he was not only hateful, but dangerous.

Now Rosalie was looking down from the stage at all these lecherous *roués* in fresh disbelief. How could her darling sister have fallen in love with someone who came to a place like *this*?

'Athena!' Mrs Barnard was hissing at her from the wings. 'You, new girl, stop glaring down at our guests like that! And pull your bodice lower, or I'll come out and do it myself!'

Rosalie muttered a retort under her breath and dragged down her bodice just the tiniest fraction. Sal winked at her. It was going to be a long ten minutes. Lifting her chin, deliberately staring at a fixed point at the very back of the hall, Rosalie mentally started composing a piece for *The Scribbler*. *'Tonight your fellow about town Ro Rowland took himself to the well-known Temple of Beauty. And there he observed that a large number of the male spectators, being over fifty years old, were alas too short-sighted to fully enjoy the beauteous goddesses on display...'*

Suddenly, the door at the back crashed open. A latecomer strode in and halted abruptly. He looked around, not up at the stage, but at the men in the audience, some of whom had turned in irritation at the slam of the door. Rosalie caught her breath.

He was not an old, fat lecher. He was tall and dark-haired, thirty at most. He was quite unmissable.

'Now, there's a sight for sore eyes,' Sal murmured appreciatively at her side.

Rosalie nodded mutely. Most of the men in here favoured the current fashion for fancy tailcoats in blue or bottle-green superfine, padded at the shoulders and adorned with ridiculously large silver-gilt buttons that would lend themselves to the cartoons of Cruikshank or Gillray. But he—her man—was dressed casually, almost roughly, in a long grey overcoat that hung open to reveal a rumpled linen shirt and a horseman's tight buckskin breeches tucked into worn leather riding boots. Instead of a high starched cravat, he wore a simple white neckerchief knotted loosely at his throat.

He looked angry, determined, and—absolutely gorgeous. His wide-set eyes smouldered with fiery challenge beneath jet-black brows. And his careless attire served only to emphasise the masculine perfection of his body—that broad chest, tapering downwards to lean hips and muscular thighs... *I'm sorry to let you down, Helen, but perfect is the only word for it.* Fascinated, she let her gaze rove back up to his face, noting how his untamed dark hair lent dramatic emphasis to those lean, sculpted features and that amazingly sensual mouth.

His firm jaw was shadowed with at least a day's stubble. He looked as though he didn't give a fig for the company he'd disturbed. An aura of danger emanated from him, together with the cynicism of a man who'd already seen rather more of life than he should.

Yet—you only had to look at him to imagine being in his arms. To imagine doing things a well-bred girl shouldn't even be thinking of. What was he doing here? *You know the answer to that, you fool.* Yet somehow, he—her man—looked as if he hated all this just as much as she did.

Don't be an idiot, Rosalie. She could just imagine Helen proclaiming with a snort of derision, 'Of course, a man prefers to pay for a woman, because the act of purchase means he can discard her the minute he's had enough of her!'

Just for one incredible moment, his gaze met hers so

searingly that she felt as if he was undressing her with his eyes. The warm colour suffused her skin. Then he turned his back on the place with a shrug of scorn and walked out. She felt, ridiculously, a sense of loss. A few minutes later the curtains were gliding shut and the girls, chattering avidly, were being shepherded off the stage. Back in the dressing room Rosalie put her hands to her flushed cheeks. Sweet heaven, who *was* that man?

And then Sal came over, and was digging her in the ribs. 'Isn't he just about the most gorgeous creature you've ever seen? Don't try to deny it. I saw you staring!' She chuckled.

Rosalie's heart plummeted. 'Does he…come here regularly, then?'

'Lord alive, never seen him in here before, more's the pity. Shouldn't think *he* has to pay for his pleasures, should you?' Sal put more powder on her nose. 'But I've just heard one of the girls saying he teaches sword fighting to the gentry and is known as the Captain, because he was in the army for years.'

Never seen him in here before. Rosalie was already scraping her long hair back into a tight coil. That was as well. Because she could just imagine Linette—anyone—going off with him at one beckoning glint from those wicked, slanting dark eyes.

Then she reached for the everyday clothes she'd arrived in and started towards the changing room. Sal jumped in front of her. 'Now, just a minute. What are you doing, gal?'

'Going home,' answered Rosalie calmly. *Just as soon as I've paid a quick visit to Dr Barnard's office.*

'What? You're not stayin' on?'

'I was only hired to do the stage show, I made that quite clear… Whatever's the matter, Sal? You look worried!' In fact, more than worried—Sal looked almost frightened.

'Dr Barnard spoke to me about you earlier,' Sal whispered, glancing round to make sure they weren't overheard. 'He said I had to make sure you stayed on for the dancin', see, even if it's just for a bit!'

'But *why*? I told him I'd appear on stage and nothing further, at least for the first night!' In fact, Rosalie didn't have the slightest intention of coming back here at all if she could help it.

Sal bit her lip. 'Dr B. was hopin' that perhaps you'd change your mind. New girls are always a draw, see, especially ones as pretty as you. And—' her fingers knotted together nervously '—if you don't show upstairs, I get the push, Rosalie.'

'Oh, Sal…'

'But it's all right,' went on Sal bravely, 'you go, it's not your fault—it's a lousy place, this!'

Rosalie was desperate to get at that secret register. If not tonight, then she'd come back tomorrow and endure the stage show yet again; there was nothing else for it. But to go upstairs, on offer to all those men…

'Well, look at little Miss Prim and Proper!' It was Charlotte, sneering at Rosalie's drab cloak. 'So you're disappearin' already, are you? Of course, you won't want to face the fact that nobody out there is going to be in the slightest bit interested in paying out good money for *you*!'

'That's as well, isn't it?' answered Rosalie calmly. 'Since I never wanted them to.'

Charlotte glared. 'I told Perceval—Dr Barnard—you was too high in the instep for this place! He's just doin' his accounts, down in his office, but soon as he arrives up here, I'll tell him you ain't nothing but a stuck-up troublemaker!'

Down in his office. Botheration. Rosalie put down her clothes and shook her hair loose. 'Actually, Charlotte,' she said, 'I've changed my mind. I *am* staying.'

Charlotte's mouth opened and closed. Sal swung back to Rosalie. 'Oh, my Gawd, girl, don't do this just for me! You said you were dead set against joining the dancing, and I understand, I really do...'

Rosalie set her chin stubbornly. 'Sal, how long does Dr Barnard usually take to do his accounts?'

'Oh, ten minutes or so, that's all, then he's eager to mingle with his gents upstairs!'

'Well, I'll go upstairs, too,' declared Rosalie. 'Just long enough to make sure he sees me there, then I'll slip away. Will that do?'

'Won't it, just!' breathed Sal. 'Thanks, gal, for savin' my job here. But...' she patted Rosalie's cheek '...put some rouge on, eh? You got to look as if you mean it!'

Sal hurried off upstairs. Slowly Rosalie dabbed on a little rouge, hating it. Once more, now that she was on her own, she remembered that terrible winter night two months ago, when she'd received the message from Helen. *Rosalie, I'm so sorry, I've found your sister.*

Memories of a spring morning came back to her unbidden. She had been a small but leggy ten-year-old and Linette just eight. There'd been a storm in the night, with the wind and rain howling around the oak woods that surrounded their village, and at first light she and Linette had raced down to the stream at the bottom of their garden to see how the moorhens' nest they'd been watching for days had fared.

Linette had been entranced by the newly hatched chicks, huddled in their sprawling mound of twigs that was lodged precariously against a small island in the centre of the river. But the morning after the storm Rosalie saw that the high waters had loosened the nest and any minute it might be dragged away, chicks and all, by the muddy brown flow.

Hitching up her skirts and pulling off her shoes, Rosalie had waded in, while little Linette, so pretty even then, had watched from the bank, her hands pressed to her cheeks. Rosalie, up to her knees in water and challenged by the mother moorhen squawking its outrage, steadily placed stones and twigs around the unwieldy nest full of open-beaked chicks until it was firmly anchored again in a cleft of the leafy island.

'Oh, Rosalie! You've saved the babies!' Linette had been ecstatic.

From the top of their garden, Rosalie and Linette's mother, not well even then, had been watching, too. As they ran back up to her, she'd hugged her girls tightly to her. 'My brave darling Rosalie,' she'd said in her broken English. 'And Linette. You are both *mes petits anges*, my little angels!'

That was when Rosalie had noticed the bucket and brush by the wall of the house and realised that their mother had been crying. And then she had seen the words, painted on the side of their outhouse, that her mother must have been trying to scrub away when they came running up from the river. *You don't belong here, French whore.*

Later that morning at the village school Rosalie had shown her new teacher the story she'd written about a bird in its floating nest travelling far downstream and finding a new life.

That young teacher was Helen Fazackerley and she had read Rosalie's story with absorbed attention. 'This is wonderful, Rosalie,' she had said quietly. 'Is this some-thing you would like to do? Travel and discover new places?'

Rosalie had looked steadily up at her teacher. 'If we went somewhere else, would they be kinder to my mother, Miss Fazackerley?'

On, on flew Rosalie's memories, to the December of last year. A cold evening, a bitter evening, in damp, bleak London. Rosalie had by then been staying with Helen for two months, searching all the daylight hours and more for Linette; asking at the theatres, the opera houses, everywhere she could think of for her sister; following clues that too quickly went cold. *Rosalie, I'm in London. I'm in trouble. Please help me.*

But it was Helen, who regularly went out at night with a group of her church friends to take soup and bread to the hungry in some of the worst districts of London, who found Linette at last.

Rosalie had been reading little Toby his bedtime story when she'd received Helen's message. Biddy, their good young neighbour, had come in to look after Toby, while Rosalie, with one of Biddy's brothers, hurried to meet Helen at the address she'd give her—a rubbish-strewn attic off the Ratcliffe Highway. There, on a dank mattress beneath a broken skylight, lay her nineteen-year-old sister, her once-lovely face pinched with grief and illness, while at her side a beautiful little girl with dark curls gazed up at the newcomers, clutching a battered rag doll and whispering, 'Mama. Mama.'

Rosalie's search for her sister was at an end.

Helen had immediately taken the crying infant to her house in Clerkenwell. In the meantime Rosalie had fought hard to conceal not just her grief, but her overwhelming rage as she'd held her sister in her arms and stroked back her hair from her forehead. 'Take me to him,' Linette had whispered as she clutched her sister's hand.

'Who, Linette?' Rosalie had tried so hard to keep her voice steady, though the pain in her heart had threatened to choke her.

'He has a castle. A wonderful castle. Take me to him, please...' Linette had been struggling to speak by then. Faintly she'd breathed his name—then died, moments later, in Rosalie's arms.

Since then, Rosalie had redoubled her efforts to find Linette's destroyer, working her way round every London theatre, high and low. Not asking outright, for that brought danger; but pretending she was looking for a lost friend. And a few days ago, fast running out of hope, she'd visited a seedy little theatre off the Strand.

The greasy-haired manager, Alfred Marchmont, had said curiously, 'I remember a girl called Linette. Linette Lavalle, that was it—pretty, she was, well spoken, with fair hair...'

For a moment she could hardly breathe. Emotion twisted her insides. At last she nodded. 'When was she here?'

'Well, she came for an audition—it would be, oh, spring three years ago; I've a good memory for faces and names.' Marchmont looked at her curiously. 'She was pretty, as I said, but she moved on after a couple of months to Dr Barnard's.'

Three years ago. 'Does this Dr Barnard run a theatre, then?'

Marchmont had hesitated. 'He runs a stage show. Of sorts.'

So now, at Dr Barnard's famous Temple of Beauty, Rosalie prepared herself to endure the company of the half-drunken *roués* upstairs. But as soon as Dr Barnard appeared and observed her there, she would slip down to his office to see if his secret book went back to the summer of 1813, when Linette might have worked here—and met Katy's father.

Chapter Four

'Look, lads, it's Captain Stewart! He was one of Wellington's officers at Waterloo!'

Alec Stewart was all set to leave the Temple of Beauty. There was no sign of his brother; Garrett must have been wrong. But now these friends of Lord Harry Nugent's had clustered around him in the smoke-filled bar, blocking his exit.

Alec made a half-hearted effort to answer their eager questions, but he was tired of battle talk. He wanted to point out to these young blades that war was a damnable business, then get the hell out of here. But then Harry himself appeared and accosted Alec with delight.

'So you decided to come after all, Alec! Weren't the girls just wonderful?'

'They were about as I expected, yes,' said Alec steadily. This wasn't the place or time to explain to Harry that actually he thought they looked greedy and desperate. Though not quite *all*. His eyes had been tugged reluctantly back to the stage by just one of the goddesses—Athena—the slender one who tossed her long fair hair and looked almost angry, as though she hated being there amongst those plump, painted courtesans…

For God's sake, man. She has to be a courtesan, too!

'Must go, Harry,' Alec said. But Harry was babbling in his ear, to make himself heard above the general din.

'You're not leaving yet, are you, Alec? You *must* stay for the dancing upstairs.' Harry was pointing eagerly to one of the many winding staircases that threaded through this tall, ancient building. 'You could have your pick, if they knew who you were!'

'Really not my style.' Alec clapped the curly-haired young man lightly on the shoulder. 'I only came because I thought my brother might be here—and he's not. Enjoy the rest of your birthday and don't let yourself be fleeced too badly, will you?' Alec started towards the exit.

'But, Alec, your brother *is* here!'

Alec ground to a halt. 'What?'

'He was too late for the show, but he went straight upstairs to the Inner Temple to take a look at the girls on offer there... Alec? Alec, if you're going up there, too, don't forget you'll have to get a ticket first!'

Alec, already making for the stairs, swung back. 'I'm not going to be paying for my pleasure, believe me.'

'But you need a ticket to get in! Look, you can buy one over there!'

Damn. Alec could see the queue snaking along one of the passageways. But—Stephen was here. And this was a matter—a *family* matter—that could not be put off any longer.

'And so, you see, sir,' Rosalie was saying earnestly, 'that the education of young women is absolutely *vital* to the future of social enlightenment, wouldn't you agree? By education, I mean, of course, not just needlework and a little French, but a full grounding in mathematics, the sciences...'

The young buck who'd waited so eagerly for a dance and possibly more with the extremely striking new blonde goddess was beginning to look distinctly alarmed. He muttered hastily, 'Just remembered. There's this fellow I've got to see...'

With narrowed eyes Rosalie watched the man hurry off across the crowded room towards the door. Five customers had so far bought tickets from the footman at the door to dance with her. Five customers had beaten a rapid retreat as soon as they decently could, thanks to her unexpected—and unwelcome—topics of conversation. Rosalie held up five fingers to Sal and mouthed, 'Enough?'

Sal, busy coping with the attentions of a drunken admirer in a loud plum coat, nodded and whispered back, 'Certainly is—thanks!'

Rosalie heaved a sigh of relief. She'd got Sal out of trouble and had managed to scare all her admirers to death within moments. Now all she had to do was wait for Dr Barnard to appear, then she could change out of this ridiculous outfit, slip down to his office, check his green book and get out of here. Mrs Barnard shouldn't be a problem; the old harridan was still playing the pianoforte with clunking determination, while couples waltzed and groped their way around the floor. Though Rosalie decided to move out of her line of sight, into an alcove away from the light of the candles, just to be on the safe side.

But someone was blocking her way. 'Oh!' Her hand flew to her throat.

For a fleeting moment, some faint physical resemblance made her think of the Captain. But even as her pulse started to race, she realised this man was older and not as tall, with a fleshier face and just a hint of a weak chin. And his clothes were—expensive. His coat was of bottle-green kerseymere, his cuffs were edged with lace and a diamond-studded silver pin nestled in the folds of his cravat. The rather strong scent of citrus cologne clung to him.

'My dear girl,' he said, 'I do apologise if I startled you—that wasn't my intention in the least. I wonder, would you do me the very great honour of dancing with me?'

'As a matter of fact,' she said quickly, 'I was just about to leave.'

A shadow of something—was it anxiety?—crossed his face. 'And I respect your wishes wholeheartedly, but might I mention that there could be a slight problem?'

'A problem?'

'Indeed. You see, I was talking to your Dr Barnard on the stairs only a moment ago. He's just returned to his office for more tickets for his doormen. But he'll be arriving here any minute; since I've paid him personally for a dance with you, he would be a little angry, I fear, to discover that you'd slipped away.'

Rosalie's heart sank. *So it still wasn't safe to get into Dr Barnard's office—bother.* She swallowed. 'Yes. I see…'

'I'll tell you what,' offered the man. 'Instead of dancing, I'll fetch you a glass of wine, shall I?'

'I would prefer lemonade,' she interrupted quickly. 'And I really cannot stay long.'

'I am honoured to be given even a few minutes of your time,' he said softly. 'You can't believe how eager I am for this chance to get to know you.'

Alec frowned as the footman took his ticket and waved him into the Inner Temple. The candle-lit room was filled with gaudy splashes of colour, thanks to the cheap gowns of the women and the scarlet and mauve wall-hangings. In one corner an older woman with red-dyed hair played the piano with more determination than skill and a dozen or more couples moved around the floor in a manner that clearly hinted at more intimate encounters. The odours of stale perfume and tobacco assailed his senses.

And there—Alec's square jaw tightened—there was his brother, Stephen, dressed to the nines as usual and talking to someone Alec couldn't quite see since Stephen's back blocked his view.

Alec walked with deceptive nonchalance across the room. People moved out of his way, as they tended to.

'Stephen,' he said softly at his brother's shoulder.

His brother swung round, the blood leaving his face. 'You,' he muttered. 'Always *you*. What in hell are you doing here?'

'I've come to speak with *you*, Stephen.' Alec gazed thoughtfully at his brother. 'Since you're too scared to let me into your house, I thought we could have a pleasant little chat right here.'

'This is hardly the place or time to discuss private business!'

'Believe me—' and Alec's voice was suddenly harsher '—I take no pleasure at all in having to step anywhere near the dungheap of your *private business*. But you give me little option.'

Stephen's eyes darted round. Quite a few people were watching; some couples had actually stopped dancing to stare. Stephen turned to the person at his side. 'My dear,' he said, 'I do apologise for this gross intrusion.'

And for the first time, Alec realised who Stephen had been talking to.

He cursed under his breath. He hadn't wanted her to be here. Blue eyes, as he'd thought: turquoise blue. He absorbed the slender delicacy of her figure, the perfect outline of her profile, the way her silver-blonde hair trailed down the silken white column of her graceful neck...

Athena. He felt, for one wild moment, the overwhelming desire to haul her over his shoulder and carry her out of this tawdry place.

Then he realised she was wearing fresh face paint. Rouge, badly applied. Disillusion flooded him. *She is a whore, you fool.* Alec's gaze locked again with his brother's. 'Pay her off,' he said. 'This is just between you and me.'

He saw the girl whiten beneath that rouge as if he'd struck her. But at that very moment Stephen touched her shoulder. 'Listen, my dear,' Alec heard him murmur. 'If you will just wait for me over there, I'll be free in a moment, I promise you...'

'I said—pay her off,' interrupted Alec. 'Or I will.'

Stephen flushed and dipped into his pocket, then thrust some coins in the girl's hand. 'Here,' Alec heard him mutter. 'And there'll be more, if you'll wait for me...' He bent to whisper something.

Alec expected Athena to give Stephen an enticing smile, perhaps, or a curtsy of promise as she left.

But her blue eyes flashed scorn. Two spots of colour burned in her cheeks; then the girl just let those damned coins clatter one by one to the floor as if they scorched her. The noise interrupted the pianist, who stopped playing. And the girl stalked off without a backward glance, blonde head held high. Stephen clenched his fists and looked after her. 'Damn it, I needed to talk to her!'

'Wrong, Stephen,' Alec shot back. 'You need to talk to me.'

'Not here.' Stephen sounded quite feverish. 'For God's sake, not here, in public!'

This time Alec's voice was like a whiplash. 'You make it impossible for me to hold a conversation with you anywhere else. Now, I think you were about to explain to me why you were seen today by the whole of society driving in the park—and you were with her again. Then you come whoring, here. You are—unbelievable.'

'I had my reasons for coming here! A matter of unexpected business—'

'*Business?* Listen, Stephen. Don't you think it might be a good idea if you suddenly found some unexpected business to take you out of town, for a week, or two, or even longer?'

Stephen moistened dry lips. 'Are you attempting to threaten me?'

'If you think I'm merely attempting it, then I'm obviously not making myself clear enough. Let me put it this way. It would be as well for you, brother—it would be *very much* in your interests—if you disappeared from London for a while.'

'Damn you! You will not interfere like this!' Stephen looked round quickly at the avid onlookers who gathered closer. 'You know, I hold some cards, too, Alec. Push me too far and I'll play them, I swear!'

Alec gave a lethal half-smile. 'Then play them, brother mine. Damn well play them. Unlike you, I have nothing whatsoever to lose.'

'If you think—'

'For our father's sake, Stephen,' broke in Alec warningly, 'I'll expect news of your departure in the next day or so.' He looked around the room and its occupants with scorn. 'Now, my God, I'm out of here.'

'Back to your old soldiers,' muttered Stephen.

Alec swung round on him. 'My old soldiers smell sweeter than this sewer of a place.' And he strode off, the crowd parting to make way for him, the door crashing shut after him as he left.

The murmuring rose to excited chatter. All eyes were

now fastened on Stephen, who, still flushed with anger, walked quickly towards the ante-room where refreshments were being served, looking, looking all the time. *That girl*, Stephen swore under his breath. Thanks to his damned brother, that girl, who looked like the other one, had got clean away.

In fact, Rosalie was still there, pressed into a shadowed alcove. She saw that slowly the room was returning to normal. Dr Barnard had arrived and, suspecting there'd been trouble of some kind, he spoke curtly to his wife, who began to play the piano again extremely loudly. Dr Barnard called out that the wine was on the house and a cheer was raised; couples started returning to the dance floor.

But Rosalie's pulse rate showed no sign of calming.

Something had happened to her when the Captain drew near. It wasn't just that he was so handsome. It was because he was so *different* from all these other men. It was as if he was some kind of rebel, walking alone and unarmed into an enemy camp, quite heedless of any consequences. And close up, she'd been able to see even more clearly how his overlong dark hair, his ill-tied neckcloth, the shabby long coat that moulded itself to the powerful muscles of his shoulders and chest, only added to the hint of danger that blazed in those emotion-packed eyes.

He was, quite simply, devastating. And he thought her a whore. *Pay her off—or I will.*

She shivered. She saw that the man Stephen was now talking in a low voice to some footmen at the door. She didn't want to see any more of *him* either, and the sooner she was out of here the better...

'Ros. Ros? Thank God I've found you, girl.' It was Sal, tugging at her sleeve. 'Now listen, you've done me a favour, so I'll do you one, right? Dr Barnard, he's after you.

Someone's said to him you've got some connection with a London gossip rag.'

Oh, no. Rosalie caught her breath and tried to laugh. 'Ridiculous—what on earth makes him think that?'

'No use trying flummery with this one, gal. Our Danny-boy's told Dr B. he's seen you out deliverin' news sheets. And soon as he's got everyone back and busy on the dance floor, Dr Barnard is going to be huntin' for you, see?'

Oh, Lord. Rosalie was already on her way, hurrying through the crowd to the back staircase.

Down to the office first, for that all-important book of clients. Then—she'd be on her way.

Alec was walking steadily down the stairs. His brother would do as he'd said and clear out of town for a while, no doubt of that—Stephen's knees had actually been shaking. Though whether Stephen's departure was the solution to a stinking mess or merely a temporary reprieve was another matter altogether.

And Alec was still puzzled as to why Stephen was here. He'd said he had business here—unexpected business. But...with a sweet-faced whore who refused his money almost in disgust?

Alec paused at a branching of the stairs, his brow dark with thought. When, exactly, had Stephen started hating him? Probably the day Alec was born, unfortunately.

'You. Always you,' Stephen had hissed just now.

Long ago, on his fifth birthday, Alec had been tearing round the estate on a lively pony—his birthday gift—when it stumbled over a fallen branch on a woodland path. Alec had been thrown, breaking his leg.

He'd imagined he saw Stephen, a little ahead of him between the trees, watching him. And days later, lying bed-bound and drowsy with medicines for the pain, he'd heard their father say to their mother, in Alec's bedroom, 'To think that Stephen was capable of such mischief. God help me, but, young though they are, I find myself wishing more and more that Alec were the heir...'

His parents had not seen, as Alec had, his brother lurking outside the half-open door, his eyes venomous with the beginnings of the hatred Alec had noticed just now.

Yes, it was Stephen who'd laid that branch across Alec's path and their father knew it. So did the groom, who warned Alec, grim-faced, when he was getting used to riding again after his leg healed, *You watch out for that brother of yours, Master Alec, sir.*

As he grew up, Alec had never cared that Stephen was the heir rather than himself. But he knew that Stephen would never forgive him for what their father had said—ever.

He'd barely reached the first-floor landing of the Temple of Beauty when he heard heavy footsteps on the stairs above him. He glanced around. Two of Dr Barnard's footmen, burly brutes both, were heading downwards also and he stepped aside to let them pass.

They didn't.

They came directly towards him. Their faces were twisted with an emotion Alec recognised all too easily. The hunger for a fight. *Damn it.*

The bigger one, a beefy wretch with some missing teeth, went for Alec with his fist, clearly intending a blow straight to the gut. But Alec caught the man a swinging punch to the jaw that made his victim stagger and fall with his hand to his mouth. *More of his teeth gone, hopefully.* In virtually the same moment Alec whipped back his elbow into the stomach of the other brute, driving the wind from his lungs so that he bent double and had to gasp for air.

If they wanted a mill, they'd got it. But Alec knew this would be Stephen's doing. And now—hell, now was going to be difficult, because three more of Dr Barnard's henchmen were coming from the other direction, speeding up as they saw their two felled comrades struggling to their feet...

Not playing fair, Stephen. But then, you never did. With a bit of luck Alec knew he could fling a couple of his opponents down the nearby staircase. But even so, the odds were not good. They were coming for him purposefully, with evil leers on their faces.

'Oh, my brave, brave boys,' said Alec Stewart gently, 'five against one—but even so I'd bet money on me. Do you know why? Because you're a bunch of thick-skulled bastards who would just turn and run at the prospect of any *real* fighting...'

They charged him like enraged bulls, which was Alec's intention. Anger slowed both brains and fists, especially when Alec, moving with light ease, tripped two of them up as they blundered forwards, then sliced another across the throat with the edge of his hand and brought his fist up beneath the fourth one's jaw so the ruffian bit on his own tongue and let out a bloody cry of pain. But Alec knew the odds were against him; it was only a matter of time before he went down.

Suddenly he glimpsed someone else sidling down those damned stairs. A girl looking as if she didn't want to be seen, glancing behind her all the time as if fearing pursuit. But on hearing the noise of the fight, she turned to look down and Alec saw her gasp with shock.

Hell. He flung another punch as one of the brutes ventured too close. It was Athena, in her diaphanous gown. Another enemy. Would the blonde-haired whore stand and gloat at his plight? Or actually join in? The latter at present seemed most likely, because as more of the brutes closed in on him she hurried down the last few steps to the landing where the action was and picked up a small pedestal table that stood in a corner.

Dear God, thought Alec a little faintly, *I'm in for it now.* There was an expression on her face of utter and relentless determination. Alec mentally prepared himself for a final, nasty blow from that small but heavy table.

Shifting her grip to hold it by its base, she swung the table hard against the thighs of his biggest opponent. The man let out a howl of outrage and toppled to his knees. Another man reached out to grab her with an oath—'Come here, you blasted—' but she dropped the table, slipped neatly from his grasp and kneed him in the groin.

Alec blinked. *Ouch.* Dirty tactics. But he could hear more footsteps, running *up* the stairs this time; then a familiar voice accosted his ears.

'Captain! What ho, Captain Stewart, is that you?'

Not more of Dr Barnard's men, but curly-haired Lord Harry Nugent. Swiftly Harry took in the scene, then gestured his friends forwards with a whoop of delight. 'Come on, lads!' Harry cried. 'Don't like the odds here, against a hero of Waterloo! Let's show 'em a bit of the home-brewed!' Instantly the crowd of young men launched themselves at the footmen, cheering.

The footmen, aghast, tried to flee up the stairs, to the room where the dancing was. But Harry's friends followed and within seconds, Dr Barnard's Inner Temple was more like a rowdy backstreet tavern than a gentlemen's club. As more footmen joined the battle, Harry fought at Alec's side; Alec watched with widening eyes as each of Harry's vigorous punches found its mark—perhaps Harry should take up boxing rather than the foil.

But then Alec began to realise that the girl had disappeared.

Harry caught his eye as the number of assailants dwindled. 'A more exciting night than you thought, Captain!' he called. 'Did you see me draw the stout one's cork?'

Alec shrugged his wide shoulders, laughing. 'Indeed. I underestimated the Temple of Beauty. But do you know what happened to the girl who was here a few moments ago, Harry? The blonde girl who played Athena?'

'She ran past us, on her way down the stairs.' Harry paused to enthusiastically thump a footman who was trying to sneak away. 'Apparently she's in trouble with Dr Barnard's men, too.'

'Is she, by God?' breathed Alec Stewart. 'Is she, now? Look out behind you, Harry!'

Wham. Harry planted a first-class facer. Alec grinned, then turned his back on the battle. He was off, to find Athena.

Chapter Five

Rosalie's heart was sinking fast. Where was she in this labyrinth of passages and stairs? How on earth was she going to find her way to Dr Barnard's office? She needed to see his precious private register, *now*. Because after tonight, returning to the Temple of Beauty just wasn't an option.

Coming to the aid of the Captain had been so stupid! She should have just quietly slipped past all those brawling men while she had the chance! But seeing him there, fighting all those ruffians by himself, had struck her as so unfair...

You fool. He believes you to be a whore. And you're out of your mind to waste precious moments even thinking *about him, when Dr Barnard knows you write for* The Scribbler, *and has sent his men to scour the place for you!*

She stole along yet another dimly lit corridor. The sounds of fighting reverberated round the entire building. What an evening. What a place. And she wasn't out of it yet, because someone else was coming towards her. Someone who reached her before she'd even had a chance to run.

'So here you are, Athena,' said the Captain softly. 'I've a few questions for you.'

Damn. She whipped round and went tearing back the way she'd come, but she heard him striding after her. Swinging past a corner, she pushed at a half-open door into a shadowy room where only a single candle spluttered in a sconce. Charging inside, she flattened herself against the wall, closed her eyes and uttered a fervent prayer that he'd go straight past.

He didn't. He came in. Rosalie dived past him for the still-open door, but he caught her easily by the wrist; when she opened her mouth to utter a scream, she found his other hand clamped firmly across it. She struggled. Yet at the touch of his palm, strong and warm against her lips, a strange tingling sensation started up in all her nerve endings.

'Keep still,' he hissed, kicking the door shut with one booted foot.

She tried to bite his hand. He cursed. Then she froze. More heavy footsteps were coming down the corridor outside. Her chest was so tight she could scarcely breathe. Were they after the Captain? Or—her?

The footsteps went past. She sagged, tension leaving her weak.

The Captain was no longer holding her. But there was no chance of escape, because his broad-shouldered figure completely barred the way.

Something else was just starting to dawn on her. This room was one of *those* rooms that gentlemen paid for. Heavy curtains shrouded the windows and a rather large and obvious velvet couch draped with a shabby silk counterpane filled one corner. The mingled odours of patchouli and tobacco filled the air, and the paintings on the walls—*oh, Lord, those paintings*...

'I understand, Athena,' he said softly, 'that you're in trouble.'

'Trouble?' Rosalie tried to laugh. 'What nonsense. I simply work here, as you've seen…'

He was watching her with inscrutable eyes. 'Then why were you running? Why has Dr Barnard set his men at the main exits to stop you escaping?'

As Sal had said. She sagged again.

'Exactly,' he went on tersely. 'And just for the moment, you're better off—believe it or not—in here. With me.' He tilted his head to indicate the riotous noise of brawling on every floor of this tall house.

The candles flickered, warningly. And oh, how their shadows highlighted the hard slant of his cheekbones, the wicked curl of his sensual mouth. Rosalie swallowed on the dryness in her throat. His dark eyes—she saw now they were velvet-brown, almost black—glowed with golden flecks as he gazed down at her. For a reason she couldn't explain, a sudden lick of heat uncoiled from deep within and suffused every part of her body.

In trouble. Oh, yes.

Suddenly, like an eel—*my God*, thought Alec, *this one's used to fighting her own corner*—she twisted from his grasp and ran for another door she'd spied at the far end of this whore's boudoir. He lunged after her and caught her easily, this time trapping her by planting his hands firmly against the wall on either side of her shoulders. Her small breasts rose and fell in agitation; her amazing turquoise-blue eyes were wide with defiance.

'Steady. Steady, Athena,' warned Alec. 'You know, I'd really like you to explain why you came to my aid in that brawl back there.'

She hadn't the faintest idea. She jerked her head up.

'How about *you* explaining why you're reduced to paying for your pleasure in a place like this?'

And her lips spouted insults. Surprisingly eloquent insults, registered Alec. And the scent of her gleaming blonde hair was quite bewitching. She tried again to wriggle away, knocking a small painting off its hook on the wall so that it crashed to the floor. He stepped back, involuntarily; she swooped to the ground and picked it up.

'Oh!' she cried. 'Look what you made me do, you fool! Luckily it's not damaged...'

Alec looked on, incredulous as she turned her back on him and very carefully replaced the painting on the wall. He said at last, 'You know, you're in all sorts of trouble, Athena. And you're worried about—a *painting*?'

She looked at him furiously. 'It's not just a painting, like the other cheap nonsense in here!' The colour tinged her cheeks as she glanced round at the other works of art, whose content, Alec had noted, was decidedly bawdy. 'Any fool can see that this painting is by Boucher and he's famous for his watercolours! His paintings are masterpieces, though what one of them is doing in *this* dreadful place I cannot imagine!'

Dreadful place. Alec noted that. 'How, Athena, do you know about art?'

Her hands were on her hips again; she tossed back her hair defiantly. 'Why shouldn't I know about art? Anyway, I'm not the only one in trouble—what did *you* do, to make those men attack you?'

'I rather think,' he said, 'that I offended someone here tonight.'

'If you go around speaking to people as you did to that man you called Stephen, then I'm not in the least surprised!' she said tartly. 'Why were you so rude to him?'

He shrugged. 'I don't like him very much,' he said. 'And

judging by the way you threw his money back in his face, you didn't take to him either.'

Rosalie caught her breath. Something she'd never experienced before surged warmly through her. She, normally so resistant to men and their various wiles, could not even look this one in the eyes—those dark, glinting eyes—without her stomach turning peculiarly upside down.

Alone in a whore's boudoir. With him.

Outside beyond this room the mayhem continued, with the sounds of men brawling and furniture breaking, followed by the crashing jangle of Mrs Barnard's piano as it went over on its side. Rosalie forced herself to meet his dark eyes. 'Do you have this effect wherever you go?'

'Not my fault. I told you, someone paid those louts to attack me. Though it's true that I attract attention,' he said. His sleepy eyes gazed, unblinking, into hers. 'Yours, for example, Athena. Earlier I saw you watching me. From the stage.'

Her heart juddered. 'Watching you! Ridiculous! I'm short-sighted, I couldn't possibly see that far!'

'Strange, I gained the distinct impression you were watching me quite carefully.'

His hand, unbelievably, was curling round her slender waist. Drawing her close. Even more unbelievably, she was letting him do it. His fingertips were warm and firm through the filmy fabric of this stupid gown… She jerked herself away, the blood racing through her veins. 'Oh, no! You can *stop* this, right now!'

'Stop? But isn't this why you're here?' His expression was innocent, but there was a hint of dark irony in his voice. 'To—make yourself available?'

Damn the man. 'Yes,' she lied, her heart racing, 'yes, of course, but at a time like this—it's absurd—it's like…'

'Fiddling while Rome burns?' he murmured, eyes glinting. 'Deuce—I forgot—we're supposed to be in Grecian mythology tonight, aren't we? Athena, I appeal to your sense of justice. My God, I've had to pay *a lot* for tonight's entertainment!'

She let her eyes rove scornfully over his shabby coat, which had certainly seen better days. 'Too expensive for you?' she said sweetly.

'It's a matter of principle.' He smiled pleasantly back. 'You see, I normally never have to pay for female company.'

Unbelievable arrogance! She gasped and tried to slap him; a mistake, because he caught hold of her raised wrist, and of course once more she was in his power. She fought hard to free herself. 'Let me go. You *know* that I'm in danger here and need to get out!'

Just then a couple of men tangled in drunken combat blundered through the doorway, grunting and swearing. Releasing her, he moved swiftly to push them back into the hall and kicked the door shut again, hard, before locking it.

And he came slowly back towards her. Dear Lord, this man was dangerous. Hadn't she registered it from the moment she saw him? That velvet couch seemed to fill the blasted room. Even the single candle flickered as if in warning. A coil of something dark, something forbidden, snaked down to her stomach even as she clamped down desperately on the effect this man was having on her pulse rate. Her breathing. Her *existence*.

'A bargain, Athena,' he said quietly. 'I'll get you safely out of here, if you'll tell me why that man Stephen claimed to have business with you.'

She shrugged and moistened her dry lips. 'How should I know? He just said—he was eager to get to know me better. As they all do,' she supposed.

His dark eyes flashed with incredulity. 'Yet you threw away his money?'

Rosalie glanced towards the locked door. 'Let me go now. Please.'

Still his lithe figure blocked her way. His strong hands were warm on her shoulders again. 'Not before you promise me that you won't throw yourself away, in a place like this. To a brute like Lord Stephen Maybury.'

She breathed in sharply. The touch of his fingers was nothing less than a caress. Gathering her wits to protest, she couldn't help but notice that on one of his hard cheekbones a livid bruise was appearing. And there must be other injuries, all over that lithe and supple body...

'Perhaps you should stay away from here yourself,' she said, tossing her head. 'Those men were trying very hard to kill you.'

He arched one eyebrow. 'And that's why you launched yourself into the fray—*on my side*? Surely you're not telling me that you actually care?'

'No! I mean, you're just another client of Dr Barnard's, your private affairs are no business of mine whatsoever!'

'A true professional,' he was murmuring, in that husky voice that made her blood pound. 'How much does it cost for a kiss, Athena? And don't try telling me again that you're not for sale.'

He was drawing her closer. She could feel the heat of his body now. See the texture of his skin, his lightly stubbled jaw that her fingers ached to touch...

'Let me tell you,' he was saying softly, 'that on closer inspection I'd have paid twice the usual rate—for *this*.' His eyes never leaving hers, he lowered his head and brushed her lips with his.

It was a fleeting caress, but even so Rosalie had never experienced anything like it. A sweet, melting sensation was pouring through her nerve ends. A moment later his strong arms were cradling her even more securely and he was kissing her properly, his mouth possessing hers, his tongue stroking her soft inner moistness in a sensual dance that stirred the blood in her veins to white heat.

He was masterful. Dangerous. Exquisitely provocative. The worst of it was that she wanted more and he knew it. She felt one of his strong hands slide up to cup the back of her head so his tongue could continue its rhythmic thrust, the slight roughness of his stubbled jaw providing a sensuous counterpoint to the silken sweetness of his mouth. His other hand slid tighter round her waist, pulling her closer against the hardness of his powerful body, his chest, his thighs. The urge to succumb to this dark magic and open herself to his potent masculinity was irresistible. Her hands crept upwards of their own volition to cling to his shoulders, feeling and savouring the vital force of his body.

This should not be happening. She'd sworn to let no man touch her again, yet her body was melting to his every caress.

He let out some sort of sigh and pulled her still closer. Now his right hand was sliding over the thin muslin that covered her breasts and, as her nipples peaked beneath his touch, she shuddered. The liquid warmth in her lower abdomen was like a burning ache of need; her mouth opened wider to his relentless plundering, and for Rosalie, for that space of time, nothing else existed. The fighting, the clattering of furniture up above, the bursts of raucous shouting, all receded into a meaningless background noise. There was no one else in the whole wide world but her and him.

Until he let her go. She felt bereft. Her legs were so weak that she could almost have sunk on to that blasted sofa in the corner.

Alec stepped back. *Damn.* He knew he'd come to his senses a little too late. It was a long time since he'd been so tempted by a woman. *Too* long, if he was feeling like this about one of Dr Barnard's wenches. And he certainly wasn't prepared for what this one's melting pink lips did to him.

Shy. Delicate. God, it was almost as if she'd never experienced a man's kiss! Yet at the same time she was so sweetly, wonderingly responsive that sheer lust had for a moment gripped his loins...

Damn it. She was a bewitching little hoyden, feigning innocence when the rouge was still fresh on her face—hoping, perhaps, to lure him into making some sort of offer for her, because she sure as hell wasn't going to be working *here* again. Gazing down at her, he held up his five-shilling ticket for the dancing that he'd drawn from his pocket and, tearing it into tiny pieces, let it flutter to the floor.

'Well worth it, for that kiss,' he said flatly. 'You're surprisingly good at what you do.'

Rosalie felt, suddenly, as if her heated blood had turned to ice in her veins. Of course. He thought her a whore.

'Do you know,' she said steadily, 'I was a fool to come to your rescue earlier. Doubtless you thoroughly deserved the beating you were about to get. Will you let me past, please?'

'Feel free to go.' He shrugged. 'And I hope you find a new job soon. You'll certainly need to. Remember what I told you. They're watching for you down at the main exits.'

He saw the colour leave her face beneath that rouge. 'The main exits...'

He jerked a finger towards the far door, the one she'd already tried to make a run for. 'One of the first rules of warfare, blue-eyed Athena: always plan your escape before the battle begins. If this house runs true to form, through there is a flight of stairs that leads down to the back of the house, where you should find an unguarded door.'

'And—and you?' *Curse the man*, thought Rosalie. Why did she ask that?

He lifted his eyebrows as if the same thought had struck him. 'You still care? I'll go and check that Harry and his friends aren't doing too much damage. Then I'll leave, too.'

He held the door open to show her the stairwell. Head high, she marched past him.

'Remember,' he called out softly, 'watch out for Maybury.'

She made no acknowledgement. But halfway down, where the staircase turned so he could see her no more, she leaned her back against the wall. Oh—*fiddlesticks*. The man called Lord Stephen Maybury posed no threat whatsoever as far as she was concerned. But dear God, the Captain was another matter altogether.

She felt dazed. She'd been out of her mind, to let him caress her like that. She had been pressed so close to his body that the potent force of his manhood had been all too evident in the heat of their embrace—and *he* had been the one to move away first!

She felt shattered. She felt bereft.

And his kiss had been the most magical moment of her life.

She hurried on down the stairs, ashamed because her legs were shaking. *If those brutes caught her...* But he was right. None of Dr Barnard's men were to be seen in the back room she emerged into.

The dressing room first. No time to get changed, so she thrust the clothes she'd arrived in into a bag, rammed on her cloak and bonnet, and stole into Dr Barnard's silent office. *Back to business, you fool*. Reaching up, she heaved down that heavy tome—*The Myths of Apollodorus*—then laid it on the desk and opened it.

As Helen had said, the pages had been carved away to form a cavity. Inside was a book bound in green morocco, where the names of Dr Barnard's many customers were listed by the dates of their visits, together with their addresses.

But the name her dying sister had whispered was not here. She flicked to and fro, her agitation increasing. She checked all through the spring and early summer of 1813, but there was no sign of it at all. All this effort, all this risk, and she was no nearer in her search. For a few moments the disappointment crushed her.

But towards the back of the book, she found a list of the girls who'd been employed here. *June 1813. Linette Lavalle*. She caught her breath. That was the name Linette had used at Marchmont's theatre. Their mother's maiden name. She read on hurriedly. *From the country... The girl has fancy ideas above her station. Refused to do anything except the stage show—then one day just didn't turn up. Found herself a rich protector, I suspect...*

Her throat aching with sadness, Rosalie carefully replaced the book in its hiding place, then stole from the house, using the door the Captain had told her was unguarded. Outside it was starting to rain, heavily. Rosalie hailed a hackney cab—her one concession to Helen's concern for her safety—and the driver gave her a look indicating what he thought of young women out on their own at this time of night. She tossed her head defiantly as she gave him directions.

But all the way back to Clerkenwell the usual questions tormented her. When had Linette realised that she was pregnant? Was that when her—*protector* discarded her? Had her poor sister lived for a while in the agonised hope that her seducer might marry her?

Oh, Linette.

Alec Stewart rode back to Two Crows Castle as the rain poured down on London's dark streets. Those damned footmen would have been paid to attack him by his brother, as Stephen's cowardly revenge for Alec's ultimatum to-night.

As revenge on Alec for *existing*.

When Stephen went away to boarding school, distance had temporarily eased their relationship. But Alec's arrival at the same school two years later had sparked off the old jealousy, especially since Alec, as ever, had excelled at sports and had a light-hearted manner that made him friends far more easily than Stephen did.

A crisis came when Stephen, aged fifteen, had set up a secret gambling clique and, when discovery threatened, had slipped the evidence—cards, dice and money—under Alec's dormitory bed.

Alec had silently taken the blame and the beating for it. But since then Alec had not troubled to show his contempt for Stephen on the rare occasions on which they met. A year ago Alec had been utterly disowned by their father—told he was no longer part of the family, in effect—and Alec had thought Stephen would be satisfied. No danger now of Alec supplanting Stephen in the Earl's affections.

Yet still his brother diced with fate.

Why had Stephen come here, to idle away his time in a place like the Temple of Beauty, picking up girls like blonde Athena?

Alec felt his insides clenching again. That girl. The girl who knew about French watercolours, with her exquisite face and her clouds of silver-gold hair and that meltingly slender body... He remembered how, as he drew her close, her warm breath had feathered his cheek and the delicate scent of lavender had risen sweetly from her skin. Remembered how her fingers had almost shyly stolen up to his shoulders, how her lips had parted for his kiss.

But then had come the moment of pure shock. For as he took the kiss deeper, as he prised her lips further apart, she'd registered almost utter innocence. Her exquisite, thick-lashed blue eyes had flown wide open in surprise as he tasted the soft flesh of her mouth and, when he'd cupped her tender breast and felt it peak, he would swear she'd shuddered in his arms and clung to him as if she'd never experienced a man's caress before.

He'd only pursued her because he wanted to know what Stephen's business was with her. That kiss had been part of his strategy to wrongfoot her. Yet he, Alec, had been the one to leave that place with all his convictions shaken.

Be sensible, you fool. The rouge was still fresh on her face. Innocent? Impossible. Yet his body still raged for her.

His mouth set in a hard line. Just a clever act on her part, down to the detail of denying any interest in his rich brother's attentions. And she was in trouble with Dr Barnard—probably for arranging appointments with clients on the side and keeping all the profits for herself, a common trick.

His mind flew on in conjecture. Yes, she had an air of innocence that would draw men to her like moths to a candle flame. But she worked at the Temple of Beauty where she was attracting the likes of Stephen, damned Stephen, who, having spent years of debauchery with professionals like *her*, was now, whenever he could, secretly pleasuring the woman who just happened to be their father the Earl's beautiful young wife.

Chapter Six

By the time that Rosalie let herself into Helen's house in Clerkenwell, it was almost midnight. Lighting the lamp in the kitchen, she made a pot of tea quietly so as not to wake anyone. Then she sat down by the embers of the fire, still huddled in her cloak. Tonight had been a disaster—not least her encounter with the Captain, who'd managed to disturb her peace of mind in a manner that she guessed would cause her more than one sleepless night.

Why was he there?

Be honest with yourself, Rosalie. Why did any men go there? They went, of course, be they lords or tradesmen, to ogle the girls and pick out one for an hour of lechery upstairs. And at a place like that, her sister's seducer would have found it easy to spot Linette, with her head full of fanciful dreams.

She drew some blank paper from a nearby table towards her and by the light of the lamp started writing, assuming the easy-going tones of her *alter ego*, Ro Rowland. Since childhood, she'd found that it helped to write. Her earliest stories had been fantasies, a way of escaping into a place where happy endings existed. Later she'd found that wit was an even more effective weapon against the cruelty of strangers and this was now Ro Rowland's world—a world not one of heartbreak, but of wry, almost cynical humour.

Tonight your fellow about town Ro Rowland took himself to the well-known Temple of Beauty. And there he observed... The Captain. Damn him, damn him. She stared into the distance, her thoughts unravelling once more. A fencing master, Sal had said.

It had been a long time since Rosalie allowed herself to think of any man with anything other than suspicion. Yet the thought of an hour alone with that dark-haired rogue, using the private room in Dr Barnard's house for the purpose it was intended, set off a disturbing wobble somewhere at the pit of her stomach. She could not forget the rough silk of his lips and tongue; the warm, muscle-packed strength of his body—his *aroused* body—moving against hers... Oh, Lord. *You stupid fool.*

Suddenly she heard footsteps out in the hallway and Helen padded in, her long nightshirt covered by a large India shawl. Rosalie jumped to her feet. 'I'm so sorry, Helen. I didn't mean to wake you!'

'I was awake anyway. I heard the hackney and I'm just so glad you're back safely... Rosalie, why are you still wearing your cloak?'

Because I'm wearing next to nothing underneath it! Airily Rosalie replied, 'Oh, I'm a little cold, that's all. Would you like some tea?'

'Yes, please.' Helen pushed her loose brown hair back from her face, adjusted her spectacles and flopped down in a chair. 'How did you get on at the Temple of Beauty? Was it full of fat old *roués*?'

'They weren't all old!'

'But they're all despicable, the men who patronise such entertainments! Oh, I knew that you shouldn't go.'

Rosalie decided there and then that it just wasn't safe to

tell her friend any more. 'I was perfectly all right.' *What a terrible lie.* 'It was actually quite boring.' *An even worse lie.* Rosalie quickly poured Helen's tea and curled up on the small settee opposite her. 'Helen, did you manage to get *The Scribbler* out everywhere today?'

Helen immediately looked happier. 'I did. That piece you wrote about the swells in Hyde Park is going down an absolute treat.'

'Good! Though I hope none of the men I described recognises himself; I'd really hate to get you into trouble. Did you take Toby with you to deliver them?'

Helen sipped her tea. 'Yes, but I left Katy with Biddy; she's happy with her.'

Biddy O'Brien was a warm-hearted young Irish neighbour who kept house for her brothers, all in the building trade. She came in every day to clean Helen's home and the children adored her.

'Thank goodness for Biddy,' said Rosalie fervently. 'But, Helen, you really should allow me to pay you for letting Katy and me stay here.' She had offered before, but had always been refused.

Helen chuckled. 'Your Ro Rowland articles are payment enough, believe me. I've never sold so many copies of *The Scribbler*, and people are always asking me who the real Ro Rowland is!' Her face suddenly became more serious. 'We're two sides of the same coin, you and I. You expose the wealthy by making fun of them, whereas I hope to *shame* them by pointing out the truth. Just as in my report the other day about that haughty woman—the wife of an earl, no less!—who had a young maidservant whipped and dismissed, simply because she accidentally dropped a vase. A paltry vase, Rosalie!'

'I know. The poor, poor girl...' Rosalie hesitated.

'Helen, I did just wonder. If this earl or his wife should hear of your article...'

'I mentioned no names. And even if they guess, they'll not dare to take action. That would be as good as admitting their own guilt!' replied Helen crisply. 'You know, it's as if the so-called lower classes aren't *human* to these people! Though it's one thing for me to be as outspoken as I am, but quite another for you, you're so much younger. Sometimes I even wonder if you should be writing your articles for me.'

'What, me stop being Ro Rowland? Dear Helen, I adore writing; if you didn't print my pieces in *The Scribbler*, I'd find someone else to publish them, I assure you! I am twenty-one, after all! I *love* exploring London, and all the fascinating people I meet on its streets...' Her smile faded. 'Well, nearly all of them.'

'Be careful. That's all,' said Helen crisply. 'And, Rosalie dear—' Helen was already delving into a pile of notes on the table '—if you're determined to keep writing as Ro Rowland—'

'Try to stop me!'

'In that case, I thought that *this* might be just up your street, because I know that you were, only the other day, starting to write an article about the rapacious landlords of London who let out hovels for high rents to desperate people!'

Rosalie nodded. The practice known as rackrenting was a subject close to her heart, not least because of that dreadful room off the Ratcliffe Highway where her sister had died.

Helen was adjusting her spectacles and running her finger down a sheet of her own notes. 'As chance would have it, I heard today about a place in—yes, Spitalfields—that takes disgraceful advantage of poor soldiers. It's called

Two Crows Castle, and it's not a real castle at all, but a rundown barracks of a place, owned by some ne'er-do-well—I haven't got his name—who lets out rooms at exorbitant rents to unemployed soldiers. I thought you might investigate.'

'Of course! Spitalfields, you said? Where, exactly?'

'The house is in Crispin Street. It's an unsavoury area even by daylight, so I trust you're not even thinking of actually going there, my dear! But what I did hope was that tomorrow you might deliver a bundle of *Scribblers* to the news vendor in Bishopsgate, which is close by. You could take one of Biddy's brothers with you and just ask some of the shopkeepers there—carefully, mind!—about this Two Crows place.'

Building work was slack this time of year and Rosalie knew that one or other of Biddy's burly brothers could usually be relied upon to take on extra jobs for Helen—repair work to Helen's house, errands, or in this case, thought Rosalie wryly, a spot of personal protection.

Rosalie patted Helen's hand. 'It sounds just my sort of story. I'll get your *Scribblers* delivered, and I'll make sure I've got an O'Brien brother with me before I start asking any questions about crooked rackrenters.' She was just getting up to tidy away the tea things when the door opened and two sleepy little figures stood there hand in hand.

'Toby!' cried Helen. 'Katy! What are you doing, out of your beds?'

Toby clung to Katy's hand protectively. 'She was crying,' he explained. 'I thought one of you would hear her, but you didn't. She's upset.'

'Oh, Katy darling.' Rosalie picked up and hugged the tear-stained infant, who was clutching her battered rag doll. 'Poor Katy, what's the matter?'

'Mama,' whispered the child. 'I want Mama.'

Rosalie kissed her, at the same time fighting down the sudden ache in her throat. Taking Katy upstairs to the cot in the corner of the bedroom they shared, she gently sang her to sleep. Tenderness and love she could give in abundance; she would also fight, with all her strength, to make sure Katy was not pointed at, whispered at, as she and her sister used to be as children.

Taking off her cloak at last, she smoothed down her filmy muslin gown and stared into the darkness beyond the candlelight as another memory wrenched her: of her mother dressing both her children carefully for the Christmas service at the nearby church. It had been their second winter in England and snow lay thickly. 'Mama,' Rosalie had said, 'do we *have* to go? I don't think they like us there…'

'Christmas is different, *ma chère*,' had said her mother, wrapping Rosalie's scarf tightly against the winter chill. 'It is the season of goodwill to all.'

But not to the Frenchwoman and her family. The vicar had turned them away. And her mother's stricken face, as they trudged home through the snow, would stay with Rosalie for ever.

That same night Rosalie had written a story for Linette, about a party at a magical castle. Linette's face had lit up as she read it. 'Will I ever go inside a *real* castle?'

'Some day, why not? There'll be food, and dancing, and—oh, we shall wear such pretty dresses, Linette!'

'There might be a prince!' Linette's eyes shone. 'And he will dance with me, and I will be a princess… Won't I, Rosalie? Won't I?'

Now Linette was dead, along with all her dreams. As Helen bustled around downstairs putting out the lamps, and Katy slept, Rosalie vowed anew that she would never rest, until she'd found the man who'd destroyed her sister's life.

* * *

Lord Stephen Maybury was sitting alone in the candlelit library of his fine house in Brook Street. And the more he pondered on the events of the evening, the darker grew his thoughts. *The girl.* The girl with impossibly fair hair and turquoise eyes, at the Temple of Beauty tonight... Who in hell was she?

When Markin, his serving man, had informed him earlier about the new one who'd joined Dr Barnard's troupe of so-called actresses, and how she resembled the other, Stephen had put it down to Markin's imagination.

But Markin, whose visage was made sinister by a pale scar, had been, in his way, adamant. Markin had spies everywhere; that was what Stephen paid him for. Markin had seen her himself, he'd told his master, entering the building early this evening to get ready for her first night on stage with the other women. Looking nervous.

'This new one, my lord,' he told Stephen, 'no one could say she's the exact image. She's older, for a start. But I could see something...'

Could she be family? God forbid. The other one had been gently born, a virgin, a mistake in other words, and Stephen wanted no past scandal rearing its ugly head. So he'd gone to look for himself. And the new girl was not at all what he'd expected. There was a physical similarity, yes. But this one was spirited. Defiant. His lip curled. My God, he'd have enjoyed breaking that spirit.

But if there *was* a connection, it could mean danger. And his questioning of the girl tonight had been wrecked by damned Alec, who even after Stephen had paid those footmen to give him a beating, had friends running to defend him from all corners of the building!

More than ever Stephen wanted his younger brother destroyed. Alec had been a torment to him since childhood—taking Stephen's place in their father's affections, parading himself in his army uniform all around town. Then last year Alec had fortuitously sealed his own fate and got himself disinherited.

But his brother could still be a threat. Best for now to do what he suggested and leave town for a while. Just in case Alec was tempted to do anything rash.

As he cursed his brother anew, Stephen's eye fell on a cheap news sheet he had picked up earlier. *The Scribbler*, it was called. Idly, he flicked through it. And he froze.

Why Lady A. feels she has the right to so viciously punish a poor young maid for a minor accident—to inflict such suffering over a mere broken vase!—is, dear reader, beyond the average citizen's comprehension...

Stephen's blood boiled. He called Markin, who was dressed in black as usual, and thrust the news sheet at him. 'Find out where this sordid scandal-sheet is published, will you? And check out the Temple of Beauty, for more about that fair-haired whore!'

There must be a way to find some weakness in his brother's armour. And bring Alec to his damned knees—for good.

Rosalie got up purposefully the next morning. Last night she had been a scantily-clad Greek goddess, publicly on display. This morning—well, plump Biddy O'Brien, Helen's cheerful housemaid, had put it best as she settled Katy in her chair and gave her warm milk and toast. 'Oh, Miss Ros,' Biddy cried, 'you look ready to convert the heathen!'

And Helen added drily, 'My dear. You appear not only dressed for church, but set to preach the sermon.'

Rosalie smiled and poured herself tea. 'Hardly. Are any of your brothers at home this morning, Biddy?'

'They are, Miss Rosalie. They've got a roofing job this afternoon, but they've got the morning free, so they'll probably just lie around waiting for me to feed them, the great lummocks!'

Helen was looking puzzled. Rosalie quickly drew her aside and whispered, 'You remember? This morning I'm going to investigate the place called Two Crows Castle.'

'Oh, dear.' Helen looked anxious. 'Perhaps I shouldn't have mentioned it…'

'Of course you should,' soothed Rosalie. 'You can see I'm dressed as a drab little widow…' she pointed to the cheap ring she wore '…and I'm going to take Biddy's brother Matt with me, just as you suggested. I'll deliver your *Scribblers* to Bishopsgate, as well. Don't look so worried, Helen. It's broad daylight, and with big Matt O'Brien at my side no one will come near me!'

But Rosalie's plans went awry almost immediately, because Matt and his older brother had been called at short notice to another job that morning, according to little Joe, the youngest of the family, who at only ten was not much use as a protector.

Rosalie hesitated for only a moment. Then, heaving up her canvas bag of news sheets, she walked down to Clerkenwell Green to hire a hackney cab.

At busy Bishopsgate, the driver softly grumbled as he lifted her heavy bag out of the cab for her. 'You deliverin' the Bible or some such round 'ere, missy? Best make sure you're well away before the alehouses get crowded at noon. And don't say I didn't warn yer!'

Rosalie took charge of her bagful of *Scribblers*. 'Consider me warned,' she said lightly.

A slight breeze lifted the concealing veil of her severe bonnet. The driver looked at her curiously, then his eyes fastened on the plain wedding band on her finger. 'Why, yer only young. Quite a fetching little thing…' She snatched her veil down again. 'Well, well,' he sighed. 'You take care now, missy.'

Bishopsgate was busy. First she delivered the copies of *The Scribbler* to the news vendor, who took them eagerly. 'These should go like hot cakes, miss!' he said. ''Specially if there's a piece in by that fellow Ro Rowland—my gents are fond of them!'

Rosalie smiled. 'I do believe there is.' And, her bag now much lighter, she walked on towards Crispin Street.

Thank goodness Helen and Biddy didn't know she'd ventured here, alone.

Immediately she found herself in a different world. The ancient buildings leaned in over the street, three, sometimes four storeys high; they were unkempt, with broken windows, and in the roughly paved lane dogs nosed amongst heaps of rubbish. Ragged children gathered by doorways, even their attempts at play half-hearted in this oppressive neighbourhood.

As she hesitated, an urchin came up boldly to stare at her and Rosalie asked the grubby child, 'Can you tell me which house is Two Crows Castle?'

'It's the big 'un, see.' The child pointed. 'Can't miss it. All the soldiers live there.'

Rosalie swallowed and nodded. It was a huge old house set back from the road, with a bunch of men slouching outside, defying the freezing February drizzle that had just started to fall. It must once have been a grand mansion, but grand was no longer the word that applied to it. The broken crenellations resembled nothing more than gapped teeth; the stuccoed façade was cracked and stained. Clearly, as the district had sunk into poverty during the last fifty years, so had this place. And the man who charged the homeless ex-soldiers to live in such squalor was once an army officer. Shameful.

She became conscious of rough-looking people assessing her from open doors, of the smells of greasy cooking and ale from the various taverns. Her heart missed a beat. Time, most definitely, to go. She turned to head back to Bishopsgate, where the street would be busy with shoppers and the atmosphere less menacing. Suddenly, she heard footsteps coming up behind her. And a hand grabbed her arm.

'Now, what may you be wantin'?' a rough male voice demanded. 'Some kind of charity lady, are yer?'

She spun round to see a small but fierce-looking individual in a tattered soldier's uniform, his whole demeanour made even more sinister by the black eyepatch he wore. A big golden dog hovered close to him, growling softly. And soon there were more men looking her suspiciously up and down, men who'd been loitering outside the ominous building known as Two Crows Castle.

Despite her apprehension, she couldn't help but gasp, 'How many of you are there in that place?'

'None of your damned business, pardon my French,' Eyepatch said tersely. 'I'll let you off with a piece of advice—don't go stickin' yer ladylike little nose into other folks' affairs. Now, be off with you!' The dog barked in agreement.

In the circumstances, it seemed sensible to do precisely what he said, but at least a dozen ragged men had come to crowd round her in a distinctly menacing sort of manner. They were big. They were blocking her path. Rosalie's heart was thumping hard. *You idiot, coming here alone...*

'I'll be on my way just as soon as you let me pass!' she said, rather faintly.

She felt acute relief as the men slowly stepped aside.

Then Eyepatch said, 'Wait. What've you got in that bag of yours?'

Rosalie swallowed. 'It's empty. I've just been delivering something, and now I really must go.'

'Empty, eh? Let's just have a little look-see.'

Eyepatch was drawing closer. Rosalie looked round desperately for help that clearly wasn't going to arrive. She'd remembered that her bag wasn't quite empty, after all. Grasping it tightly, she turned to run. But her long cloak hampered her and suddenly Crispin Street was alive with scowling ruffians, appearing from every doorway, every alley, from the walls themselves, it seemed. Could things get any worse?

They could, and they did. She dropped her bag and saw it fall open. Oh, *fiddlesticks*. Yet more men gathered, and Rosalie whirled round, her heart pounding painfully. The lethal piece of paper that had fluttered from her bag was drifting towards the gutter; one of the men snatched at it and gave it to Eyepatch.

Rosalie, feeling a little faint, saw Eyepatch scowling at it. Not *The Scribbler*, but a few notes she'd been jotting down in the cab—ideas for her next article. Something not intended for public scrutiny *anywhere*, let alone here. What a tumble, as Ro Rowland would say.

'Please give that to me,' she said rather weakly. She was fervently hoping the ruffian wouldn't be able to read.

'No, hold on,' said Eyepatch, 'this looks interesting.' And slowly he began to decipher her scrawled notes, while his companions gathered round.

'*Your fellow about town wants today to draw your attention to the scandalous practice of rackrenting.* Rackrenting?' He lifted his head to glare at her. 'Who wrote this?'

'Just somebody—well, it's me! I—I amuse myself, during carriage rides, by writing things down, silly things—' She tried to grab the sheet back, to no avail.

He hung on to it grimly. Started again. *'Scandalous practice of rackrenting. What is truly—truly—'* Eyepatch broke off. 'Can't read the rest of this flummery.'

Thank God for that.

But there was no reprieve. For someone else—a big, redheaded man—was announcing, in a broad Scottish accent, 'Awa' with ye, Garrett, I can read the rest. It says, *"What is truly shameful is that many of those who are thus exploited are former soldiers, forced to live in squalor at a place called Two Crows Castle..."'*

The dog barked. They were all pressing around her again. Eyepatch looked at her with his one eye. 'Exploited? By God, we ain't exploited here at Two Crows Castle. We don't like people who write filthy lies about our Captain, do you hear? As he'll tell you himself—'cos he's on his way right now!'

Her heart, she was sure, had stopped beating. The Captain?

Don't be a fool, Rosalie. There must be dozens of ex-army Captains in town. Nevertheless she pulled down her veil as far as it would go, until she felt like a blinkered horse with a fly-gauze over its face.

Just in time.

For at that very moment, the crowd was parting to let someone through. A man who was saying, 'What in the devil's name is going on, Garrett? And—what's that damned dog still doing here?'

At the sound of that husky male voice, her heart sank to the soles of her little laced boots. *No. No. It can't be...*

Eyepatch had for some reason shoved the dog out of sight. 'This woman, Captain,' he was saying importantly, 'she's come 'ere bold as brass, with a pack of filth about this place, and about you!'

The bruise on his cheek had darkened since last night. Otherwise he looked just the same, in that loose grey overcoat that hung carelessly open over his tight buck-skin breeches and dusty riding boots. And, hands on his lean hips, he was just watching her, with those hard eyes in which, today, there was no hint of the humour or kind-ness that he had allowed her to glimpse last night. He took the sheet Eyepatch thrust at him, absorbing her brief but lethal jottings swiftly; then he said levelly to Rosalie, 'Well, madam? Are you or are you not responsible for this pack of lies?'

She prayed fervently for the ground to open up and swallow her. *He* must be the rackrenter. The owner of Two Crows Castle. The man whom she'd allowed, to her eter-nal shame, to kiss her last night. All she could hope was that, in her spinsterly garb, he would continue not to rec-ognise her. And it was too late, now, for denial; she just had to brazen this out.

'Lies?' She lifted her veiled face to boldly meet his dark gaze. 'Perhaps you just cannot stomach *the truth*!'

Eyepatch gave a nasty leer. 'Oh, you're a brave 'un, to challenge the honour of Alec Stewart, the best swords-man in town!'

Oh, my God. This time she really did feel the blood freeze in her veins. 'Did you say—Alec Stewart?'

The Captain surveyed her, still clearly puzzled by her veiled visage. 'That's me all right,' he said narrowly.

And horror—*nausea*—shook her.

For the name Linette had breathed as she lay dying was—Alec Stewart.

Chapter Seven

Alec had been up and about early, for he'd had appointments to keep. But he'd arrived back at Two Crows Castle to find the place in utter uproar, because of some sanctimonious lady do-gooder. Alec read those scribbled notes Garrett had handed him with dawning disbelief. *'The scandalous practice of rackrenting...rapacious landlords...Two Crows Castle...'*

Hell and damnation!

Well, the charity lady who'd penned this heap of lies had made one mighty bad mistake. She hadn't run fast enough. Alec's men were holding her tight; as he tried to scan her face, which was all but hidden by a truly hideous bonnet and veil, Alec began to feel sheer shock coursing through his veins.

'Take off that bonnet,' he grated at her.

'No! I won't!' The slender captive was struggling again in Garrett and Ackroyd's strong grip.

Alec walked up to her and pulled the repulsive thing off himself. Swathes of long, silver-blonde hair fell around her face. His men gasped. One or two of them whistled softly and clicked their tongues in lewd sounds of appreciation.

'God's blood, Captain, she's a ripe little piece!' 'Take off her cloak, then we can all 'ave a good look...'

'Shut up,' Alec told his men. And he grimly readjusted to this new reality.

Yesterday this *do-gooder* had been parading her delectable wares on stage at the Temple of Beauty. Last night the taste of her softly parted pink lips had disturbed his dreams. All through the hours of darkness he'd been haunted by images of her long fair hair cascading around her breasts, her naked limbs entwined with his between silken sheets... Yet this morning, she was dressed like a church mouse—a very defiant church mouse—and was in possession of some hideously insulting notes about himself and his men. Who the hell was she? What was she playing at?

He rapped out to her, 'Who wrote this filth? And why is it in your possession?'

She tossed her lovely wild hair back from her face. 'Why should I tell you anything?'

He registered the swiftly concealed fear in those blue eyes, along with something else that was almost hatred. But then it was gone again, replaced by steadfast defiance. 'Take her inside,' he ordered Garrett. 'We'll keep her here until she changes her mind.'

'No!' She started struggling again. 'You cannot do this!'

'Try me,' was Alec Stewart's terse answer.

Two of his men led her down a stone staircase and locked her in the basement, where the only light came in through a high-up single window. Rosalie had fought them all the way, but now she simply stood and shivered with cold and fear as her faith in her own judgement came crashing down around her.

Alec Stewart. Last night, he'd seemed—different. He'd

assumed she was a whore and that hurt, but otherwise he'd seemed totally unlike the rest of the men at that hateful Temple of Beauty—so much so that she, Rosalie, whose defences against men she'd considered bullet-proof, had let him kiss her. And had felt her insides melt with a strange, sweet sensation she'd never experienced before.

Could he be Linette's seducer? Yet there must be many more men of that name! Wildly she clutched at straws. His name had not, after all, been listed in Dr Barnard's secret book as having visited the Temple that fateful June nearly three years ago!

Her heart sank again. He might have given a false name to the doorman. And it might have taken only one night for him to cast his spell on Linette and whisk her away. For heaven's sake, she, Rosalie, had submitted to his charms swiftly enough! Captain Alec Stewart. *He has a castle, Rosalie. A wonderful castle...*

Clearly he'd never brought her sister to this crumbling heap. Her stomach cramped in torment. If it *was* him, he probably didn't know or care that Linette was dead. Probably didn't even remember her.

Rosalie would never, ever have guessed. But then, neither had Linette. *You idiot, Rosalie. You thought Linette was so stupid, thought yourself so clever...* She paced the floor. She lacerated herself with reproach.

Suddenly she thought she heard low voices out in the passageway. She'd been in here how long? An hour? It felt like for ever. She heard a bolt being drawn back and, as the door opened, she sprang round to face it.

Alec Stewart walked slowly into the room, loosening his necktie with his right hand. There was an unreadable look in his hard dark eyes, and somehow the sheer physicality of him, the extremity of male power emanating from that rangy, muscular body, slammed the breath from her

lungs. She was reminded, in a surge of excruciating emotion, of the sweet knowingness of his kiss. The melting
ache of his fingers on her breasts.

Then she realised he was holding that piece of paper.

He kicked the door shut with his booted foot and just
looked at her. Rosalie hitched up her chin. 'Locking up
women now,' she declared with scorn. 'What right have
you to keep me here against my will—Captain Stewart?'

He ignored her question. 'I've been making enquiries,' he said. 'About who you are. You're versatile, aren't
you, Athena?' He stepped closer and pointed at the finger
on which she wore the cheap little wedding band. 'You
weren't wearing *that* last night. Does your husband know
you were playing the whore at the Temple of Beauty?'

Fiddlesticks. She should have taken the stupid thing off.
She jutted her chin. 'I'm a widow, as it happens!'

'My condolences.' His sympathy was short-lived. 'And
your *real* name is…?'

'R-Rosalie.'

'Rosalie,' he echoed thoughtfully. 'And do you by any
chance pen scurrilous articles for a rag called *The Scribbler*?'

Oh, Lord. 'I don't see why you should—'

He waved the sheet at her. '*Fellow about town*. That's
how the journalist Ro Rowland describes himself—or
should I say *herself*? I wasn't born yesterday; I am ac-
quainted with London's gutter press.'

The colour drained from her face. That meant Helen
was being dragged into this! This was just what Rosalie
had wanted to avoid; this was one reason why Rosalie
had never told Helen or *anybody* the name of Linette's seducer, even though she'd realised it might have hastened
her search… *Helen, I'm so sorry.*

She squared her slender shoulders. 'Sometimes, I've

written pieces for *The Scribbler*. But often I just make notes—like the ones your men stole from me!—for my own interest. And what I'm doing isn't against the law!'

'It is if you're intending to print lies. Defame my reputation.'

'*Reputation!* Oh, believe me, I could write so much more about you that you wouldn't like, Captain Stewart!'

She saw the gleam in his steely eyes and dragged air into her tight lungs. *Too far. Too dangerous, Rosalie. You cannot possibly tackle him right here in his stronghold.*

He was still staring thoughtfully down at her. 'Is that so? Might I suggest you can hardly afford to take the high moral ground, Mrs Rowland, since I could retaliate by asking—what the hell were you doing last night, parading on that stage half-naked?'

'I really don't think that's any of your business!'

'Unfortunately it is, since you've set yourself in judgement on *my* affairs. You were putting yourself up for sale at Dr Barnard's—why? To dig up filth for your news rag? Is that why Dr Barnard was after you?'

Rather too close to the truth, that. 'I was not for sale!'

'All right, I correct myself.' One dark eyebrow arched. 'You were, in my case at least, offering it for free.'

She gasped and struck out at him. But he caught her hand in an iron-hard grip.

Blue eyes, turquoise-blue eyes, whose bed did you sleep in last night? Yesterday Alec Stewart had found himself rather hoping that there was some reason—and not the obvious one—for this girl to be appearing on stage at the Temple of Beauty.

Well, perhaps he'd found that reason and he didn't like it one bit. She made money out of digging up prurient details of other people's lives. Hence her appearance at Dr

Barnard's, hunting, he guessed, for lurid gossip about the visitors to that seedy place. Hence her temerity in coming here, to cast her blue eyes boldly over Two Crows Castle, while carrying in that bag of hers some nasty notes about the crimes of a so-called rackrenter. Yet—how stunned she'd looked when she realised *he* was the owner of Two Crows Castle! And why was it that everything she did, or said, challenged all his preconceptions of her?

He remembered the way she'd reacted to his kiss last night. Even now he caught his breath at the way her silvery-blonde hair tumbled like a silken waterfall around her shoulders, at the way her drab cloak had fallen apart to allow him a distracting glimpse of the small but ripe breasts that were prominent beneath her shabby gown.

Very pretty, and very professional. Get a grip, man. Not only is she a courtesan, but she writes for a news rag. She's damned dangerous.

As if to confirm his every suspicion, she made a dart for the door. He grabbed her easily with one outstretched arm. Still she struggled, panting to get away. He pulled her closer and his physical desire reared inevitably at the sensation of her warm body agitating against his. 'Little fool,' he uttered. 'Little fool, stop that. Or I won't be held responsible for my actions, do you understand?'

That quietened her. Her turquoise eyes flew up to his in shock and she went very still. Then she tossed back her glorious hair. 'You need not think, Captain Stewart,' she shot up at him, 'that I'm afraid of you and men like you!'

'Then you damn well ought to be,' he said dispassionately. 'Though to be fair, you dealt with Dr Barnard's customers—myself included—most *professionally* last night.'

She gasped. 'Last night was a mistake! If I'd *known* everything about you...'

'Known what, exactly?' he drawled.

'Do you deny that you pack this—this hideous old ruin with impoverished ex-soldiers?'

Frowning, he let her go. But now his broad shoulders and back were planted solidly against the door and he made a formidable barrier indeed to any thought of escape. 'My friends know the truth.' His eyes blazed danger. 'Write what you like, Mrs Rowland, and be damned to you.'

'I will, if I choose! And I could also write about the way you expect young women to just *melt* at your feet! How you promise them—promise them...'

His eyes gleamed. 'Promise them what, exactly?'

'Nothing,' she muttered. *Oh, Lord.* She should not have *said* that.

He was drawing nearer. 'Promise them what, Mrs Rowland? I want to know.' Now a truly wicked smile was curving his lips. 'Money? Pleasure? Perhaps you're more tempted than you care to admit by what you think our encounter last night promised?'

She gazed up at him, speechless. It was impossible. It was incredible. Yet—desire, raw and primitive, flooded her veins. Her breasts ached traitorously for his knowing touch. Her eyes were locked with his as she wildly sought inspiration that didn't come. And he was drawing nearer, a wicked light in his gaze. 'Playing coy, are you, Mrs Rowland? Who knows—if you promise to be... *generous*, I might consider letting you go, with no more questions asked.'

'Generous?' Her heart shrivelled. 'Exactly what—?'

'You were only too happy,' he silkily prompted, 'to allow me a sample of your wares last night. Now, what's the price of your freedom, I wonder?' He'd reached out, to touch her cheek. *This woman*, thought Alec grimly, *was testing his self-control with her dangerous games*. Desire was licking hungrily at his loins; his manhood was thickening, and though he had no desire to lower himself to her level of trickery, he most certainly wanted to teach her a lesson.

The realisation of what he was suggesting hit Rosalie like a hammer blow. The brush of his hand across her delicate cheek scorched her. 'You wouldn't. You can't...'

'I really cannot think of a more enjoyable way of bargaining,' he said softly. 'Can you?'

Her world spun. All she could feel were his hands, splayed across her back, his fingertips firm and warm through her clothing. All she could see, when she jerked her head up, was his hard face, lit with an emotion she could not name as he drew her relentlessly into his arms.

His dark eyes raked her. 'I think the price of your freedom, Athena,' he breathed, 'should be—this.' He lowered his head and pressed his lips to hers.

She meant to resist. She had no intention of letting him *do* this. But as he clasped her close, heat uncoiled from deep within and flooded her veins, awakening each and every pleasure point in her body. This time there was no gentleness whatsoever in his touch, but his mouth was wildly sensual as he took hard possession, parting her lips with ruthlessness. His tongue was thrusting, at the same time caressing; she felt her legs giving way, felt herself longing to surrender to more, much more, as he hauled her against him and she felt the lean length of his muscular body, felt the hard intrusion of his arousal pressing against her abdomen.

Her breasts were peaking painfully, demanding his touch; between her thighs was liquid longing. His kiss was slow, erotic and powerful, tasting faintly of brandy and the very essence of male domination. She'd thought she hated men and their ways. Yet she was powerless to resist this one.

Linette. Her sister's name tore through her. With all her strength she thrust him away. 'You are—you are *vile* to treat me in this way!'

He stepped back, his hard face bleached of every emotion. 'I thought it was maybe what you wanted. You are, it strikes me, a deceptive and muddle-headed young woman, Mrs Rowland. This gossip sheet you write for—if anything at all should appear in it about Two Crows Castle, then I warn you, I'll take strong action. Because there are people who depend on me and I won't let them suffer for the sake of your cheap scandal-raking, do you understand?'

Just then there was a knock on the door, which opened to reveal Eyepatch. Rosalie found herself shuddering at the scornful look he cast her way. He said, 'A word, Captain?'

Alec joined him in the doorway, bending his dark head to the other's in a brief exchange. Eyepatch left and Alec Stewart came back in, slowly.

Alec had to admit that this woman—Rosalie—confounded him at every turn. What was she? *Who* was she? A whore at the Temple of Beauty, who knew rather a lot about art? A pretty little widow and a digger-up of scandals, who had no idea of the effect she had on men?

And now Garrett brought still more news about his treacherous captive. Alec folded his arms and gazed down at her. 'Well, Mrs Rowland, investigative reporter amongst other things, it seems you've got certain obligations that you've neglected in order to come on your little jaunt this morning.' He pointed to the open door. 'You'd better be on your way.'

Obligations? What...? She glared up at him. 'You mean I'm free to go?'

'We made a bargain, remember?' He shrugged. 'That kiss was payment for your freedom. I've no desire to hold you captive.'

'You already *have*!' she flared. 'I've been here against my will for at least an hour! I could press charges on you.'

'That's a novel idea.' His dark eyes gleamed. 'Though I would, of course, be forced to press charges in return. Of robbery, perhaps.'

'I—impossible!'

He raised his eyebrows. 'Think about it, Mrs Rowland. It would be more than easy for me to say there are valuables missing from this place. After all...' he looked at his pocket watch coolly '...you've been here for quite a while on your own.'

'But I've been *locked in a bare room*!'

Again he shrugged those wide, powerful shoulders. 'Your word against mine. And I could produce plenty of witnesses who'd remember you from the Temple of Beauty. Do you really think you'd be taken seriously at the magistrates' court?'

She tilted her stubborn chin. 'Would *you* be taken seriously, Captain Stewart?'

'I'm a war hero,' he responded tonelessly. 'Though it means little in financial terms, my word would carry more weight than that of a courtesan who writes for a gossip rag.'

He saw the colour stinging her creamy cheeks. Saw her fighting to find words of resistance and failing.

He was almost disappointed. Almost felt his heart softening for the defiant little widow. But he clamped down hard on any errant feeling like pity. His face as stone, he went to open the door and pointed the way. 'As I was saying, you've clearly been missed. There are three people outside, looking for you. Including—' his eyes narrowed '—your daughter.'

Chapter Eight

Katy was outside, clinging to Biddy. As soon as she saw Rosalie, she reached out to her. 'Mama? I want Mama...'

'Oh, darling...' Rosalie hurried to hold her tight in her arms. Alec Stewart was looking at them both, sharply, knowingly. Naturally, Rosalie thought with scorn, that *devil* of a man had assumed Katy was hers. Well, let him. She realised Matt was there, too, looking rather warily at Captain Stewart and his crew.

'Biddy. Matt,' she said quickly. 'What are you doing here?'

'Miss Helen sent me after you, miss, and told me to bring Matt, too. She was really cross when she realised you'd not taken him, like you'd said.' Biddy glanced wide-eyed at the formidable figure of Alec Stewart, who had gone to say something to one of his men. 'She told me,' went on Biddy, 'to say you must come home, because you ought not to be on these streets alone! I brought little Katy, too, 'cos she was missing you bad, weren't you, chick?'

Katy, in Rosalie's arms, seemed quite happy now, and in fact had wriggled round to stare at Alec, who was strolling back towards them. She was clearly intrigued by the gleaming gold curb-chain of his pocket watch and her little fingers reached out to it.

'Katy, *don't*!' Rosalie backed away with her quickly. She feared that he would use this as an opportunity to castigate her still further. Accuse her of rearing a future child-thief, perhaps.

But Alec had forestalled her. He pulled out his gold watch so Katy could see it. 'This is all it is, sweetheart,' he told the infant softly. 'Something to remind me that I'm a busy man and I should have been somewhere else half an hour ago at least.'

'Tick-tock.' Katy looked up at him with her wide, dark-lashed green eyes. 'Tick-tock man.' She reached out to touch it, then gurgled in merriment.

Rosalie saw Alec's mouth curl into a brief but devastating smile as he patted Katy's chubby fist and put his watch away. Her heart jumped. So handsome. So beguiling. *So false.* As if to prove her point, he turned to Rosalie and the smile was quite gone. 'It appears to me that your duties lie elsewhere, Mrs Rowland. I warn you—and I assure you I mean it—that there'll be no writing about me or Two Crows Castle. My men will escort you and your companions as far as the hackney stand on Bishopsgate.'

Matt O'Brien was still watching him almost with awe; much use *he* was in protecting her from Captain Stewart, Rosalie thought in despair. Her chin lifted an inch. 'We will make our own way, thank you!'

'You won't,' he broke in icily. 'I want you well clear of this place.' He swung round and raised his voice. 'Sergeant McGrath!' The villainous-looking Scotsman with red hair came up. 'Find Mrs Rowland and her companions a hackney cab, will you? And make damned sure they get into it.' Without a further glance at her, he turned and strode off while McGrath led the way along Crispin Street, with Matt O'Brien at his side, eagerly asking questions.

'I hear your Captain fought like the very devil against the French at Waterloo,' Matt was saying to McGrath.

You traitor, Matt. Rosalie, holding Katy tight, walked furiously behind, with Biddy chattering away beside her. And she herself was a fool. Today, as Ro Rowland, roving reporter, she'd blundered straight into that man's stronghold. Twice now she had let him kiss her. She'd twice melted in his strong arms, and, even worse, had wanted more. She shivered at the memory of that powerful body, moulded hard against hers; dear Lord, she had not even *tried* to resist him!

Her cheeks burned at the recollection of her astonishing stupidity. If Alec Stewart truly was Linette's seducer—how on earth was she going to tackle him now?

McGrath beckoned a hackney, spoke to the driver, then strolled off. Biddy's brother said he'd walk, since his next job of work was close by in Fenchurch Street. So just Biddy, Rosalie and Katy got into the cab.

'Where to, miss?' asked the cab driver.

'Clerkenwell. St John's Church,' she answered distractedly, fumbling for her purse.

'No need for that,' said the cabbie. 'Your fare's bin paid.'

'No! I won't allow it!' she exploded with renewed fury. Captain Stewart must have given the necessary coins to McGrath. How *dare* he…?

'Suit yerself,' shrugged the cabbie. 'Pay me twice over if you wants to throw your money away.'

Rosalie slumped inside the carriage. Biddy was excited by the novelty of the trip and pointed the sights out to Katy through the window. 'There's St Paul's, Katy, see? And there's the Smithfield market…'

But Rosalie could see nothing except Alec Stewart's

hard, mocking face. She remembered his mouth and how it had branded her with the kind of kiss she hadn't even known existed.

Katy had become fretful by the time they reached Clerkenwell. As they climbed out, the clock of the nearby church was chiming one, and Katy, in Rosalie's arms, was crooning softly to herself, 'Tick-tock man. Tick-tock man.'

Thus Rosalie would always remember the exact time that she realised what her enemy was capable of. Would always remember, as she held little Katy tight, the moment when Biddy cried out, 'Lord have mercy, what on earth's happened *here*?'

Rosalie swung round to thrust Katy into Biddy's arms. 'Look after her,' she breathed. She was already hurrying towards the house.

The door was wide open. Helen was standing on the steps surrounded by neighbours and little Toby was clinging tearfully to her.

'Helen.' Rosalie pushed her way through. 'Helen, what's happened?'

'Oh, *Rosalie*... Come and see.'

A horrible sick feeling tore at Rosalie's gut as she followed her friend inside. In the front room the little square-built printing press, Helen's pride and joy, had been viciously attacked with what could only have been a strong hammer or a pick-axe. Leaden type and pieces of wooden frame were scattered all over the floor.

'Someone broke in while I was out. They picked the lock. Then—my printing press...' Helen's voice broke. 'Look at this.'

She handed Rosalie a note scrawled in ink. *Gossip-raking bitch.*

Rosalie felt quite faint. 'Did no one see anything?'

Helen shook her head. 'Mrs Lucas over the road went for the constables when she heard the noise, but whoever it was had run off by the time they arrived. Oh, Rosalie, I—I knew I had enemies, but—*this*? Who could have done something so malicious? How am I going to start, all over again?'

Rosalie was reeling, because *she* knew somebody who was capable of such a ruthless revenge. Someone who had, quite possibly, kept her locked in his basement to give his men time to do this. Would such a person feel any regret whatsoever for seducing and abandoning an innocent girl? The answer, surely, was no.

She felt physically sick. *I'm afraid I've found him, Linette.*

And, oh, Lord, he was going to be a powerful adversary.

Some hours later Alec was pacing the landing outside the main bedchamber of his father's magnificent Belgrave Square house.

As soon as he'd seen his unwelcome visitor—Mrs Rowland—off his premises, he'd ridden to give a fencing lesson in Piccadilly, then he had an appointment down at the Limehouse docks with a warehouse owner who wanted to hire a dozen men. Alec always tried to find work for his ex-soldiers if they were fit for it.

He'd got back to Two Crows Castle to find a message for him, written by the Earl's steward, Jarvis. *Master Alec. I'm afraid that your father has been taken ill. The doctor is with him. Please come.*

A thousand thoughts had raced through Alec's brain as he'd urged his horse westwards through London's busy streets to Mayfair. A thousand regrets. How serious was this? Had his father's bout of illness been brought on, perhaps, by the shock of evil knowledge? Would his father even want to see the son he'd disowned a year ago?

Jarvis, a loyal old retainer, came out of the bedchamber now, bearing a tray laden with medicinal beakers. 'Your father will see you now, Master Alec, sir.'

That was something. 'Is the doctor still with him?'

'He's gone, but he'll call back within the hour. He said there are no physical signs of illness, but your father needs to rest.'

Alec felt a great release of tension throughout his body. But— *No wonder he needs to rest, with a young wife who pleads to be taken to every party of the Season. With a young wife who…*

No. You must forget that, for now.

Alec went swiftly up to the lavishly furnished chamber. His father lay against the pillows of the four-poster in the half-light, for the curtains of the big room were already drawn against the early February dusk and only the coals in the fire lightened the gloom.

'Alec.' Slowly his father turned towards him. His gaunt hands twisted the bedcovers fretfully. 'It's been so long, Alec. So long since I've seen you…'

When you told me you'd no desire to see me ever again.

'Sir. If there's anything I can do, you have only to say the word. How are you?'

'Oh, the doctor says I'll live.' His voice rasped. 'Your brother—he was here the moment he heard I was ill.'

I'll bet he was. Alec merely nodded. 'Jarvis told me what the doctor said. That your affliction is thankfully nothing serious.'

'Yes,' muttered his father. 'Damned quack poked and prodded everywhere. But he said it would do me good to get away from London.'

Away from London. *Yes.* But… 'What does Lady Aldchester think of that, sir?' Susanna adored London life. She'd once said that she would die in the country.

The Earl shuffled against his pillows and coughed. 'I don't know, I don't know; she's been out shopping with friends all afternoon, she won't even be aware that I've had this damned turn. But she'll come with me, she's devoted, Alec, despite what you said! And so is Stephen. Would you believe it, he's just told me he was setting off for Carrfields himself today, to see that everything was in good order!'

Alec's fists tightened at that. So his brother had taken heed of him then, last night.

'But now,' went on his father, 'he needn't go, of course. Because I'll travel there myself, with my dear Susanna.'

I would die in the country.

'And,' went on his father, 'no doubt Stephen will escort us there and visit us regularly.'

Alec exploded. 'The hell he will!' He dragged his hand through his hair, said in a quieter voice, 'I do beg your pardon, sir.'

His father was silent a moment, kneading the bedcover with his fingers. 'Do you remember the times we used to have, when you were home on leave? We used to sit up till late into the night, didn't we, and you'd tell me, oh, such tales, about the battles, and the sieges in Spain...'

'I've never forgotten it, sir.'

'But now...' and his father's voice was growing fretful '...now, all I hear about you is that you avoid civilised company, you avoid your brother, except to fight with him. And my wife has told me, reluctantly mind, that it's you, always you, stirring things up...'

'I suppose she would,' said Alec bitterly.

'What? What did you say? Do you take heed of me, Alec? Your mother died so long ago—am I never to be allowed happiness again? Will you make your peace with your brother and your stepmother?'

Alec stood ramrod straight. 'You ask the impossible, sir.'

The Earl stared at him. Then he waved a tired hand. 'Go back to your soldiers' drinking dens. Go on, go. And once I'm at Carrfields, I want you to clear out everything of yours that's left in this house. Your old army journals, your maps of Spain—all the paraphernalia that clutters up your room and my study. It hurts me to see them all, to remember... Take them away, do you hear?'

'Everything will be removed. Though I hope you know that if you ever need me, I'm here for you—'

'Leave. Just *leave*.'

And Alec turned, with a heavy heart, to go.

He found Stephen in the first-floor drawing room, gazing with narrowed eyes at the paintings on the walls—some of them inherited, some acquired from auction houses—and worth, like everything in this palatial house, a small fortune.

'So, little brother.' Stephen, on observing Alec's entry, turned from staring at a French landscape to sink on to a sofa, where he tapped his fingers rather nervously on its satin upholstery. 'Come in hopes of taking advantage of the family drama, have you? Planning, perhaps, to weasel your way back into our father's affections?'

Alec gazed at him calmly. 'You've had a respite, Stephen. Last night I suggested you leave London. Now there's no need. Because our father's going to Carrfields with his wife.'

'No! Has he just told you that?' Stephen was on his feet again, his face flushed. 'Susanna will die of boredom there!'

'Perhaps. But if you do anything other than tell her she must accompany our father, then your game is at an end.'

'You wouldn't…'

'Oh, I would. Believe me, I would.'

'She's young, Alec! Younger than me, younger than you. And Carrfields—it's like a prison for her!'

'She should have thought of that before she married him,' rapped back Alec. 'Obviously his wealth distracted her from the practical realities of playing wife to a much older man.'

Stephen drew in a hissed breath. 'Now, look. As far as London society is concerned, I'm merely being the dutiful stepson by escorting her to her various engagements…'

His voice faltered, because of the way Alec was gazing at him. 'You won't be escorting her *anywhere* in the foreseeable future—' Alec pointed a finger at him, casually '—because she's going to Hampshire with our father.'

Stephen opened his mouth, then shut it again.

'Oh, and there's one more thing,' went on Alec. 'Why were you talking last night to the blonde whore who played Athena?'

'Why? The usual reasons.' Stephen's lip curled. 'So *you* noticed her, too, did you? Are you going back there tonight to tup the wench? I'd be interested to know what bedroom tricks she employs—'

Stephen broke off, because his brother's bunched fist was suddenly in front of his face. 'Oh, Stephen,' Alec said softly, 'I've no intention of paying for anyone's services. But I've another question. You paid those men to attack me last night at the Temple of Beauty, didn't you? Why?'

'I really don't know what the hell you're—'

'Don't waste your breath trying to deny it. Because I'm just longing for an excuse to give you the beating you deserve.'

Stephen cowered away. 'Not here. Not in our father's house!'

Then the door opened. And Susanna was there.

Lady Aldchester, the former Contessa di Ascoli, was exquisite, everyone was agreed on that. Her origins were obscure—she had been born in England to an Italian mother and had married a Milanese count, considerably older than she.

When he died in Italy two years ago his widow had decided to come to live in London, where she had made her entrance in considerable style. She had rented a fine house where she held glittering soirées with her mother, and soon half of London's gentry were in love with her.

Including his father.

Now she looked from one to the other, lovely as ever, with her clouds of raven curls and her sultry dark-blue eyes. She was younger than both of them. Then she said, in her silken voice that bore the allure of her Italian heritage, 'Stephen. Alec. I've just been told that your father is ill.'

'It's nothing serious,' said Stephen. 'Rest assured.'

'I will go up, then, to see him…'

Stephen strode forwards. 'I will come with you.'

'No. Best if I see him by myself.'

Alec had already turned to go. But he became aware that she was following him out on to the palatial landing above the staircase, where they were, momentarily, alone. The faint scent of gardenias clung to her skin and hair.

'Alec,' she said, 'my dear, please will you speak with me one moment before I go up to your father?' Her delicate gloved fingers were touching his arm. 'It's been so long since we spoke. I'm sad, because you used to be at every society gathering. You are missed,' she added softly.

'Do you know,' he said in a curt voice, 'I find that London society doesn't appeal to me very much at the moment. Susanna, my father wants to go to Carrfields.'

The colour left her cheeks. 'Carrfields! But he promised me—'

'I take it,' Alec cut in, 'that you'll go with him? Stephen, by the way, is staying in London.'

She hesitated. Then, 'Of course I will go.'

With a tight bow, he turned to leave, but she caught again at his arm. 'My dear, I so wish we could be friends again! And I'm sorry about the Bedford Street house. I told your father that my mother wished for a residence in London. But I didn't realise you would be made homeless!'

'Didn't you?' This time he couldn't help the bitterness showing through. 'Believe me, that's the least of my worries.'

Her eyes were clouded. 'What can I do, to redeem myself?' she murmured. 'Alec, I am not happy, you must know that. I am not, if it's of any consolation to you, in the slightest bit proud of myself.'

'I think you know, Susanna, what you ought to do. Whether you do it or not is entirely up to you. You have a better side. Use it.' Alec gave a curt bow and left.

She watched him go down the vast staircase that swept to the entrance hall below. Stephen had come out of the drawing room and was looking at her.

'Carrfields,' he said. 'How will you bear it?'

'It seems,' she answered, 'as if I must.'

And she went upstairs, to visit her husband.

Shortly afterwards, Lord Stephen Maybury went back to his house in Brook Street and spoke to the man with the scarred forehead. 'Well, Markin? Did you do as I ordered?'

'Hire a couple of ruffians to wreck the printing press that produced that foul stuff about Lady Aldchester? Aye, my lord. And there's more. The fair-haired piece from the Temple of Beauty that you asked me to follow last night—turns out *she* lives there, as well! She's some kind of writer!'

And Stephen's narrow green eyes widened.

He had been absolutely enraged to see the way Susanna looked at Alec out there on the landing. The way she had agreed, in spite of all her earlier protestations about hating the country, to go with his father to Carrfields.

Was she tiring of her secret games with Stephen?

Now, though, the blonde girl from the Temple of Beauty drove everything from his mind. If there was a connection, with the other one from three years ago, he needed to shut the girl up. And fast.

Chapter Nine

The next two weeks were blighted by the blustery rain of late March and the leaden skies reflected Helen's mood of despair. 'I'll never feel safe again. Oh, Rosalie, who could have done such a thing?'

'The constables are hunting the culprits,' Rosalie soothed her as she brought her a cup of tea. 'Why not start writing again? You have a gift for it and for teaching. I'll never forget how you inspired us in the village school, about art and history. You opened up a new world to me, Helen.'

Helen gave a glimmer of a smile. 'You had a hunger for learning anyway. Every book I brought to you, you used to devour. When I took you all to that art gallery in Oxford, I could hardly tear you away!'

'My father was an artist, remember?' Rosalie sat down next to her on the little sofa. 'I think I hoped there might be some paintings there by him. Of course, there weren't. But I looked, and looked—so foolish of me!'

Helen gazed at her. 'Oh, I'd no *idea*... Rosalie, you must have missed him so!'

'Always,' said Rosalie quietly. 'I was so young when he died. But I never forgot him.' She tried to smile again.

'Do you remember how on the way back from Oxford, I wouldn't stop asking you questions about everything we'd seen? How you put up with me, I can't imagine. Seriously, Helen, I know you feel dreadful, but how about writing again? Stories, poetry, anything!'

Helen shook her head. 'I worry far too much to write. I still feel as though I'm being watched.'

Rosalie shivered, because sometimes she felt the same. But aloud she said resolutely, 'Nonsense! Biddy's brothers are close by, remember—and you have such loyal friends. Do please try to stop worrying.'

'Oh, Rosalie. You are being so good to me.'

'Not as good as you've been to me, Helen,' answered Rosalie quietly.

And she felt a liar and a hypocrite. *All of this is my fault. I drew down the wrath of Alec Stewart upon you.*

The constables, she privately thought, would be doing very little about Helen's wrecked press; you needed money and influence to stir the forces of law into action. Who else but Alec Stewart would have set his men to do this vile deed? He had left that note to warn Rosalie to be quiet about his exploitation of those poor soldiers. What would he do if he knew that Linette had whispered his name as she lay dying?

It was up to her to confront him. But how could she, secure as he was in his castle of rogues?

At least Rosalie had been right to assure Helen that she did indeed have friends, because Francis Wheeldon, the kind churchwarden who lived in nearby St John's Square, called round almost daily; one afternoon he asked Helen if she would write some articles about the history of Clerkenwell for the parish magazine.

Rosalie had seen Helen's face brighten with interest,

and tactfully she had left them alone, taking Katy and Toby to the Green to play in the spring sunshine. She liked Francis. Quite a few years older than Helen, he lived with his spinster sister and was a scholarly, gentle man.

Indeed, when Rosalie got back, Helen was looking almost happy and was already sitting at her writing desk.

'So you managed to get rid of Mr Wheeldon at last?' teased Rosalie gently.

Helen turned with a smile. 'Oh, yes. It's a little embarrassing really, the way he fusses over me.'

'He's sweet. And he thinks a lot of you, Helen.'

'Nonsense!' Helen was brisk again. 'But, well, writing these articles about Clerkenwell will be interesting. Francis is so *knowledgeable*. And that reminds me, Rosalie— I hadn't realised before, but Francis knows such a great deal about French history. So I mentioned your mother's family—they owned property south of Paris, didn't they?'

Rosalie swallowed the lump in her throat. 'They used to, but they lost everything in the Revolution and were scattered far and wide, my mother said.'

'That's what I told him. But Francis corresponds with a friend in Paris and he said he'd ask for any news. Isn't that kind of him?'

'Incredibly kind, yes.' Rosalie was anxious not to dampen Helen's enthusiasm. 'And it's so good to see you writing again!'

Helen clapped her hand to her forehead. 'Oh, Rosalie, that reminds me—will you do me a very big favour? I was asked to a poetry reading above Hatchard's bookshop in Piccadilly tonight—they wanted me to write a review. But now I'd much rather get on with this, for Mr Wheeldon. I wonder, will you go instead?'

Rosalie hesitated. Amateur poets did not always make for the jolliest of evenings.

'Please,' urged Helen. 'I'd be so grateful!'

'Of course I'll go,' Rosalie said swiftly. She owed Helen so very much.

But later, as she was upstairs preparing herself for a night of would-be versifiers communing effusively with nature, she was disturbed by a knock at the front door. She knew Biddy was in the kitchen giving the children their supper, and of Helen there was no sign; doubtless she was engrossed in her writing and deaf to the world. So Rosalie hurried downstairs to answer it—and found Sal, from the Temple of Beauty, wrapped in a hooded mantle against the cool March night. Rosalie flinched inwardly. The Temple of Beauty could only mean trouble. 'Sal,' she said. 'This is a surprise. How did you find me?'

'Caught sight of you earlier, gal, at the market in Cheapside!' grinned Sal, hands on hips. 'Then I simply asked around and tracked you down—a neighbourly visit, that's all!'

Rosalie nodded. 'How is the Temple of Beauty?'

'Put it this way, it's not been the same since the night *you* were there. Remember that fight? Dr B.'s still got a black eye from it and Mrs B.'s given Charlotte the push, 'cos she realised that same night what the pair of them was up to between the sheets! So the place has had a right old turning-over, though that wretched piano's busted to bits, so it's not *all* bad news.'

Rosalie shivered slightly. 'Dr Barnard's not still after me, is he?'

'For bein' some sort of writer? Lord, no, he forgot that in all the trouble over Charlotte.'

'And—you've not seen the Captain in there again?'

She tried to make her question casual, but Sal arched one painted eyebrow. 'Still hankering after him, gal? No, no sign of *him*. Forget his handsome face, that's my advice.' She peered inside the hallway. 'Nice-lookin' place. Stayin' with family, are you? I remember you mentioned a sister to me.'

Rosalie was puzzled. She didn't think she'd mentioned Linette to anyone there. 'I did have a sister, but she died.'

'I'm sorry, gal, real sorry. Your only sister, was she?'

'That's right.'

'Well…' Sal looked up and down the street and shrugged her shoulders '…just thought I'd call to see how you was and everything. You look mighty smart. All dressed up for something, or someone?'

Rosalie glanced down at her serviceable blue gown and managed a smile. 'Oh, it's a poetry reading in Piccadilly, though to be honest, I'd much prefer to be indoors on a night like this.'

Sal laughed. 'Poetry. La-di-dah! Walkin' there by yourself?'

'I'll take a hackney cab. But once I'm there I'm sure I'll be perfectly safe among the poets!'

'Well, I'm one of the Three Graces tonight at Dr B.'s, so I'll be dressing up, too, but I shan't be wearin' as much as you. Just thought I'd see how you are, you know?'

'Yes. Of course. My thanks for calling.'

Rosalie watched Sal hurrying away as the cold wind whipped some rubbish down the street. With a catch in her throat, she remembered seeing Alec Stewart for the first time, lounging at the back of Dr Barnard's hall. He'd quite simply taken her breath away. So stupid of her. She knew now that her judgement had been most terribly awry.

Alec Stewart would be unaware that Linette had whispered his name to Rosalie as she lay dying. But surely,

surely he realised she would guess instantly that he was the one behind the destruction of Helen's press?

No doubt he dismissed her as powerless, she thought bitterly. As he'd said, no magistrate would take seriously the word of a woman who'd appeared on stage at the Temple of Beauty. But she wouldn't, she *couldn't* let him get away with his crimes!

Meanwhile—oh, Lord, she was going to be late for the poets.

Sal pulled up her hood and hurried round the corner to where the man waited for her. She looked up at him defiantly. 'She *did* have a sister. But she's dead. That's what you wanted to know, ain't it?'

'Dead! Are you quite sure?'

'Sure as I'm standin' here—look, am I gettin' paid, or what?'

'When you've earned it, slut,' snarled the man. 'Did you find out if she has any plans for the next few days?'

Sal hesitated, then muttered, 'She'll be at some sort of poetry affair in Piccadilly tonight.'

'*Tonight...*'

'Remember, mister, you swore to me she'd come to no harm!'

The man with the scar on his forehead pushed some coins into her palm with contempt. 'Take your money, slut. And get out of here.'

Sal gave a shudder of revulsion and ran off into the dark night. She could only pray that the girl would come to no harm...

Rosalie smothered a yawn as she listened to yet another soulful poet describing in verse, to a hushed audience, the joys and agonies of the sensitive heart.

Deciding that Lord Byron—whose *Childe Harold* she adored—would have given the fellow a crushing set-down, she edged her way to another part of the big reception room above the Piccadilly bookshop where food was being served. Heaping a plate with several small but delicious savoury patties, she found herself a chair in a quiet corner, pulled out her notebook and pencil and began to write.

Tonight your fellow about town Ro Rowland took himself to a literary reception. Who, dear reader, would have guessed that so many London citizens long to express their innermost thoughts in verse? Who would dare to tell these would-be poets that their innermost thoughts are better kept precisely where they are?

She chewed the end of her pencil, frowning as her mood darkened once more. Even if Helen were miraculously to get hold of another printing press, there would be no more *Scribblers* until Alec Stewart was dealt with…

'I don't believe it! My dear girl, what on earth are you doing here?' The voice came from behind her and she jumped up, quickly slipping her book and pencil into her reticule.

It was Lord Stephen Maybury. Last time she'd seen him, at Dr Barnard's, he'd had a heated argument with Alec Stewart. And of course Lord Maybury must still think she was one of Dr Barnard's girls. *Fiddlesticks.* She swiftly composed herself. 'Poetry happens to be an interest of mine, my lord!' she answered lightly.

He drew a little closer. 'You don't write the stuff, do you?'

He was wearing a fine blue kerseymere tailcoat with a striped-silk waistcoat and a shirt with a high, starched collar. Rosalie stifled her instinctive dislike of fashionable men. 'No, no,' she said, 'I have no such talent.'

'Thank God for that. But—' she saw Lord Maybury was

taking in her plain gown with its long sleeves and high neck '—this is rather a different setting from the place where we last met.' He raised one questioning eyebrow.

She ventured a smile. 'I can see I must confess to you, my lord. In fact, I was only at Dr Barnard's for one night...'

'Ah.' He was pulling up a chair and beckoned her to sit again. 'Some kind of challenge?'

She seized on that. 'Yes. Yes, a challenge! We ladies like to wager occasionally, you know! Although—' she leaned a fraction closer '—some of my more timid friends would be just a little shocked were they to hear of it, so I do hope that it will remain our secret!'

His eyes had fastened on her wedding ring. 'What about your husband? Would he be shocked, too?'

She'd got into the habit of wearing the ring. So many people assumed Katy was hers that her story of widowhood protected them both. She pretended to dab at her eyes. 'My husband sadly died some time ago, my lord.'

'My dear,' he said sympathetically, 'you look scarcely old enough to be married, let alone bereaved. Tragic. Well, my lips are sealed about your little adventure at Dr Barnard's. Indeed, I would not normally visit such a place myself, but certain—circumstances demanded it.' He looked around. 'I was, to be honest, about to leave here. Can't stand much more of this drivel. However—if *you* were to keep me company for a while, it might be just tolerable. Would you care for a drink? Lemonade is your preference, I believe?'

Before she could reply, he was snapping his fingers for a waiter and murmuring his order.

Then he shifted his chair closer. 'Do you know,' he confided, 'I shall always think of you as Athena, goddess of wisdom. But I would be truly honoured to know your real name.'

'It's Rosalie,' she said.

'Charming. And here are our drinks.' He was putting money on the waiter's tray and passing her a chilled glass. 'Now, I am so glad,' he went on with fervour, 'to learn that you were only at that place for one night! Indeed, my own visit was, as you no doubt noticed, sadly curtailed.'

In the background, the chatter of all the guests rose and fell; her pulse was racing because here, perhaps, was a heaven-sent chance. 'I noticed you seemed dismayed, my lord, to meet Captain Stewart there. May I ask why you dislike him so very much?'

She saw a shadow cross his features. 'Do we really have to talk about that dissipated wretch? Couldn't I just advise you to keep as far away from him as possible? The man is a disgrace.'

Her pulse thudded. *A disgrace...* 'I'm aware, of course,' she said steadily, 'that he extorts money from former soldiers.'

He'd been sipping his wine, but now he spluttered a little. 'What?'

'I know he's a rackrenter,' Rosalie explained. 'Letting out squalid accommodation.'

'*Ah.* You've heard all about that.' He ordered fresh drinks from the same waiter, then leaned closer, bringing with him the strong scent of his citrus cologne. 'You'll realise, then,' he went on, 'that it's no wonder I and other men of decency cannot tolerate the sight of him! There's also—no, I really mustn't talk of it.'

'Please.' Rosalie gulped too much lemonade in hope that it would ease the sudden dryness of her throat. 'Please tell me.'

He pursed his lips. 'Very well, since I see you have no illusions about the scoundrel. I'm afraid that Alec Stewart is an utter reprobate. Ex-soldiers, ladies of the night—he keeps company with the lowest of the low.'

Ladies of the night. *Oh, no.* If she'd had any doubts, they were banished in that instant. She put her hand to her forehead, which throbbed with the beginnings of a headache. *Linette...*

'I'm extremely sorry,' said Lord Maybury with concern. 'I do not mean to offend you, Rosalie, but you are a woman of intelligence and you saw him yourself, at the Temple of Beauty.'

'You were there also,' said Rosalie.

Something—some alertness—flickered across his smooth face. 'I had certain enquiries to make. That was all. I was *not* there to watch the show—you might have noticed. But I believe Captain Stewart was.'

Yes. Yes, he was. She was going to say so, but her throat was still horribly dry and now her head was starting to swim. 'I'm sorry,' she said, 'so stupid of me, but I really am beginning to feel rather unwell.'

Lord Maybury leaned over her, concerned. 'Indeed, you look quite pale. I hope I haven't upset you by speaking of that unpleasant man, Captain Stewart. You were most spirited to fulfil your wager by appearing there and now we will say no more of it. Finish that drink and I'll take you home.'

She got to her feet and was horrified at how unsteady she felt. 'I really will be quite all right, I assure you...'

'Do you have someone here who can take you home?'

'No, I will find a cab...'

She'd dropped her reticule under the table; he bent to retrieve it for her. 'Correction—*I* will fetch you a cab. No arguments, please, Rosalie.'

He escorted her down to the entrance hall, where he brought her cloak to her and left her while he went outside to find her a hackney. She saw a seat and rested there with her hands to her throbbing temples.

How could she even for one minute have been taken in that night at Dr Barnard's by Alec Stewart's façade of integrity? How ever was she going to deal with him? Why did she feel so ill? *This is ridiculous. I will be all right soon. I must simply be tired.*

Chapter Ten

Lord Maybury came frowning back into the hall. 'No sign of any hackneys at all and it's started to rain, so it could be some time before we find one. Now, I will brook no argument, my dear Rosalie; my own driver will take you home.'

'No, really.' Everything seemed to be getting worse and worse. She shook her head, but he was already adjusting her cloak around her shoulders as he led her outside.

'I absolutely insist,' he said firmly. It had begun to rain hard and Piccadilly was crowded with pedestrians and vehicles. 'My carriage should be just down the road. Stay here, will you, while I tell the driver to bring it round?'

She watched him stride off. Then she blinked. Of all people, there was Biddy, hurrying towards her along the wet, crowded street, with her brother Matt at her heels. *What on earth...?* And Biddy was holding Katy in her arms.

'Biddy! Matt! Oh, Katy darling!'

The small child, wrapped up in a cloak against the rain and clutching her rag doll, looked fretful. 'Want Mama. Want Mama.'

Quickly Rosalie gathered Katy close. 'Poor lamb, hush now... Biddy, what are you doing here with Katy, at this hour?'

Biddy looked breathless and terrified. 'There's been a fire! At Miss Helen's house!'

'A fire!'

'Yes,' said Matt grimly. 'Started deliberately, the constables reckon!'

Oh, no. 'Tell me everything.'

'Miss Helen and the children got out in time,' Biddy went on in a trembling voice. 'My brothers Matt and Dickon and little Joe did everything they could to put it out, but by the time the fire engine arrived, the place was a ruin! Mr Francis, he came straight away, and she and little Toby have gone to stay with him and his sister. But little Katy was crying so hard for you, Miss Rosalie, that Helen said to take her to you and to tell you to join her at Mr Francis's house in St John's Square, see.'

No. Rosalie's stomach clenched in anguish. Not possible—for this fire must be the work of Alec Stewart, continuing to wreak revenge for her allegations about his rackrenting. And if he started to guess that she knew about him and Linette, he would be even more dangerous. Rosalie could not abuse Helen's friendship still further by endangering her in her new-found place of safety with Mr Wheeldon.

Then Biddy was curtsying wide-eyed, because Lord Maybury was back, his gaze immediately fastening on Katy in Rosalie's arms. He didn't look pleased. 'What's this?' he said rather abruptly.

'Some bad news,' breathed Rosalie. 'There's been a fire at the house where I live.'

He stepped back in shock. 'I'm so sorry. How terrible.'

Rosalie said quickly to Biddy, 'Please tell Helen I'll be all right. Tell her to look after herself and Toby; I'll send word to her in the morning.'

Matt was stepping forwards, squaring his broad shoulders. 'Now, Miss Helen said we was to see you safe to Mr Francis's house, isn't that so, Biddy? Or you could stay with us.'

Rosalie summoned the last of her strength. 'Thank you, but my mind's quite made up. I'll find lodgings close by.' There were several small, respectable hotels round here and she and Katy would be safe enough, for one night at least. But what next? Her head was reeling.

'I'll be off, then, and tell Miss Helen you're fine.' But Biddy still looked worried. 'Oh…' and she reached inside her cloak '…Miss Helen sent this for you.' She handed over a folded note, which Rosalie pushed in her pocket; then, darting one last shy glance at Stephen, Biddy hurried away with Matt.

'Rosalie,' Stephen was saying, 'what dreadful news about this fire! For the sake of your child, you must allow me to take you straight to my house in Brook Street, where my staff will see that you have everything you need, both of you.' He reached out to touch Katy's hand, but Katy started crying.

Rosalie was shaking her head. 'No. I cannot accept. My intention is to find lodgings.' She was already reaching in her reticule for her purse. But cold fingers of dread, as well as nausea, were stealing down her spine. It had gone. Her purse, with all her money, had gone.

Just then, a fast-moving hackney cab splashed through a puddle close to the kerb and sent water flying up to soak Rosalie's cloak and boots. Katy was crying bitterly in her arms.

Stephen put his hand on Rosalie's shoulder. 'This is no time to go looking for lodgings with the child. Surely you realise she could catch a dangerous chill if she's out in this rain for much longer. Look, there's my coach.' He was already guiding her towards an elegant vehicle with a coat of arms emblazoned on its doors.

What he said was all too true; Katy was shivering and sobbing, 'Mama, Mama.' Rosalie was feeling dizzy now, as well as sick.

Stephen was calling curtly to his driver. 'Take us to Brook Street.'

And he climbed in after her, watching her from the corner of his eye as the carriage rolled away.

This was his chance. His chance to investigate this girl who looked like the other one. This girl who, even in her drab, damp-stained clothes, was a tempting little beauty. The gin he'd paid the waiter to slip in her drink had achieved its purpose swiftly in fuddling her wits. His man Markin had done well, too, in getting information from the slut Sal that the girl had a sister who was dead. Markin had also got the fire started at exactly the right time.

There was just one problem. No one, unfortunately, had made any mention of this woman Rosalie having a child—Stephen detested children. But that was a minor issue. He had her in his power, and now was his chance to find out exactly what mischief she might be about to stir up.

Alec Stewart had spent the afternoon at his father's house, gathering up the possessions the Earl had ordered him to remove.

The Earl had gone to Carrfields with his young wife and the big house was quiet as Alec sorted through his various maps and campaign diaries, his bound volumes of war sketches done by talented comrades and some books about eighteenth-century art that he'd inherited from his mother. She'd died in a hunting accident when Alec was ten and the whole house, for Alec, still bore the stamp of her loving devotion to her family. Many of the paintings around the house had been hers.

Jarvis, his father's loyal steward, had helped him to pack up some biographies of the commanders Alec had idolised in his youth. 'A pity we see you here so rarely nowadays, sir,' Jarvis had said gravely.

'My father's got a new wife, Jarvis. Things were bound to change.'

Jarvis's silence was telling.

'Have you heard from Carrfields yet?' Alec asked.

'Indeed, sir, they arrived safely. And the longer they stay there, the better.'

Another enigmatic remark. 'The country air will certainly do my father's health good,' agreed Alec. But he reckoned that wasn't what loyal old Jarvis meant.

He'd filled up three packing crates and Jarvis had promised to have them sent over to Two Crows Castle the next morning. 'My thanks.' Alec nodded. 'I'll be back for more in a day or so.' He was already on his way to the door, when something in the entrance hall caught his eye. He halted. 'Do you see that painting, Jarvis?'

'Which one, sir?'

'The oil, of the British troops at Blenheim.' Alec stepped closer. 'It looks different. Brighter. Or has it always been like that?'

'Lord Stephen's been telling your father he ought to get some of those old paintings cleaned, sir. In fact, Lord Stephen's been seeing to it himself over the last few months, taking them off to be restored. That one's just come back.'

Alec frowned. *Restored?* But his father had always declared that he liked the patina of the old oils…

'You'll realise, Master Alec, that I had no choice but to agree,' Jarvis was saying anxiously.

* * *

That evening Alec had had a fencing lesson and was tidying away his equipment when Garrett came in. 'One of the lads has got some news of a poetry reading in Piccadilly, Captain.'

Alec almost laughed. 'Poetry! God's teeth, why should that be any concern of mine? And confound it, Garrett, didn't I tell you to get rid of that dog weeks ago?' The big golden mongrel bounded happily up to Alec, wagging its tail.

'His name's Ajax, Captain. And I keep tellin' him to go, but he won't.'

'He'll eat us out of house and home!'

'I'm payin' for his food myself, Captain.'

'Anyone ever told you you're a fool, Garrett?'

'I know that, Captain.'

Sighing, Alec continued putting away his foils. 'This poetry reading you mentioned. I can only assume there was some purpose in your raising that unlikely subject?'

'Well, yes, Captain. The girl's there, you see—the one that was writin' those lies about you and this place, the other week.'

Alec went still. 'Mrs Rowland?'

'Aye, Mrs Rowland. You ordered us to keep an eye on her, since we told you about that printing press of her friend's bein' all busted.'

'Indeed,' muttered Alec. *Busted*, as you put it, by some enemy Mrs Rowland's made with her scurrilous writing, no doubt.'

For God's sake, she looked for trouble! She'd been blatantly on stage at the Temple of Beauty, half-clad, then she'd written some vile stuff directed at him and confronted him with a whole pack of lies in his own home. Yet she was so young, so vulnerable, despite her bold defiance… The dog came up to him, wagging its tail, and Alec absently stroked its head. 'So you've discovered she's at a poetry reading. Is that the sum of your information, Garrett?'

'Not quite, Captain. We've got an informer there— a cousin of McGrath's—who was hired as a waiter, 'cos there was refreshments, see. And he's told us that someone else you know is at this lit'rary faradiddle. *Your brother.* He and the girl seem pretty friendly.'

Alec's hand went very still on the rapier he held. Despite her defiant words to him, the little widow knew Stephen!

'What do you expect me to do, Garrett? My opinion of her is already pretty low,' he answered, sliding the rapier back into the wall rack. 'Finding out that she's a friend of Stephen's does nothing to alter that.'

Red-haired Sergeant McGrath had come in also. 'There was somethin' odd, Captain, if they're friends,' McGrath offered. 'My cousin told me your brother ordered some gin to be put in the girl's lemonade. And she was startin' to look a bit sick, apparently.'

Damn it. Alec gave up hope of a quiet evening. 'Saddle up my horse, Garrett. This place is in Piccadilly, you say?'

'You will remember she ain't no friend of yours, won't you, Captain?' Garrett warned. 'Remember that nasty stuff she wrote about you…'

'I'll not forget it, never fear,' Alec gritted, heading for the door. 'That's why I'm going to see what they're both up to. Oh, and saddle a horse for yourself, too.'

'Why's that, Captain?'

'You're coming with me.'

Pulling on his greatcoat, Alec left. And Garrett muttered to McGrath, 'I hope, I do hope, that our Captain's not laying himself open to the tricks of another sweet-faced whore.'

'Now you know and I know, my lad,' replied McGrath, 'that our Captain's no fool in dealing with the muslin company…unless you're talkin' about that society lassie with all the money who ditched him just before Waterloo?'

Garrett snorted. '*Her?* The bird-witted little Lady Emilia? He was well rid of *her* and he knew it. No. It was someone else I was thinkin' of. Someone who's a real bundle of wickedness and is out to make more, unless I'm very much mistaken.'

'Who—?'

But Garrett had hurried on after Alec, leaving Sergeant McGrath scratching his head in bewilderment.

'Wait,' Rosalie said urgently to Stephen as his carriage turned into Holborn. She clutched Katy tighter. 'Can we stop? *Please?* I—I don't feel well.' Thanks to the lurching of this heavy coach, she was actually feeling desperately sick.

'You're just cold, my dear,' Stephen said soothingly to Rosalie. Solicitously he placed a plaid rug across her knees. 'We'll soon be at my house, you and your little daughter.'

Katy hid her face from him. Rosalie tried to say, 'She's not my daughter.' But something choked in her throat and her head was swimming. 'I need fresh air *now*. I must get out…'

Suddenly she realised that the carriage had indeed come to a juddering halt, but not at Stephen's bidding. As Stephen exclaimed, 'What in God's name—?' Rosalie was already on her feet and heading unsteadily for the door with Katy in her arms. It was opened before she could reach it by a tall, rain-soaked man who looked blazingly angry.

Alec Stewart was here. Alec Stewart, from Two Crows Castle, had stopped the coach. She saw suddenly that his horse was close by, held by none other than Eyepatch, who looked at her balefully. Stephen's driver up on his box was swearing, but Alec rapped out a few choice words that silenced him utterly.

Rosalie's stomach was roiling. With Katy still in her arms, she stumbled down, swaying. Alec grabbed the child and held her very tight as Rosalie leaned her hand against the side of the carriage and vomited into the gutter.

The gin, thought Alec. He cursed under his breath. Garrett had warned him that Stephen had doctored her drink. But no one had warned Alec that she had the child with her. At a poetry reading? What the hell was going on? He held the infant close, protecting her from the distressing sight of her mother being sick. She reacted by reaching up her chubby fists to his cheek, instantly smiling through her fretful tears. 'Tick-tock man,' she said.

And now his damned brother was climbing out of the carriage, his face livid with rage and, yes, fear as he growled out, 'Alec. What the hell do you think you're doing here?'

'I've come to see what *you're* up to, Stephen.' Alec's voice was harsh. 'It's not your usual style to be conveying a sick woman and her infant in your carriage.'

'Do you know,' breathed Stephen, 'it's absolutely none of your business. Now, I know you fancied this little blonde slut that night at the Temple of Beauty...' he glanced swiftly at Rosalie, who, still leaning against the carriage with her head bowed, was beyond hearing anything '...but if you've come to try to blacken my name with her, don't expect her to believe a word you say!'

Alec didn't, especially as last time they had met, he'd locked Rosalie in the basement of Two Crows Castle.

She was an interferer. A troublemaker. But she didn't deserve *this*.

She was turning towards him, white but resolute. 'Give me the child, Captain Stewart!' she declared rather desperately.

Dark rings shadowed her eyes. Dear God, she was scarcely fit to stand, but still defiant! 'No!' he snapped back. 'Not until you can show you're fit to be in charge of her.'

She wasn't. She knew that and he knew it. Alec Stewart, her enemy. He looked vitally, frighteningly male, in his greatcoat and boots, his white shirt all crumpled, his neckcloth loose. His over-long hair, almost black in the rain, was all askew. His lean jaw was already dark with stubble, and his eyes were narrowed to angry slits.

The man Linette denounced on her death bed, thought Rosalie with a shudder. The man who was most likely responsible for the destruction of Helen's house. Why was he here, with Eyepatch? Somehow she summoned up the last of her strength and lifted her head to blaze resistance. 'How dare you *interfere* like this? Give me the child!'

Stephen smirked. 'Well, well, Alec. Think you've really overstepped the mark this time.'

Alec, ignoring him, said curtly to Rosalie, 'Did you let this man buy you a drink?'

'Yes! But it was only lemonade!'

'Only lemonade. You surely don't intend, considering the state you're in, to let him take you and your child to his house?' Alec knew Stephen's acquaintances. Their ways of passing the night-time hours made the Temple of Beauty look like a haven of respectability.

She was gazing fiercely up at him, but her face was white as a sheet. 'I—I had no alternative.'

'You could have made him take you to your home!'

'I couldn't!' She clenched her hands. 'The house where I stay has been burned to the ground!'

He was stunned. 'Burned to the ground... Deliberately?'

But she'd bent over to be sick again. Alec held Katy tight—'Mama?' the child was saying uncertainly. Dear God, this woman's home had just been burned down. And now she was going to Stephen's house, with her child—when Stephen had as good as poisoned her!

He couldn't stand seeing her there, so wretched. So damned foolish as to trust his brother. Alec swung round, Katy still in his arms, to fix Stephen with a steady, burning gaze of contempt. 'That's it, Stephen. Take your fancy carriage and leave—*now*.'

Stephen glanced angrily at Rosalie. 'You forget. Rosalie and her child are under my protection. Give me the infant—' He reached for Katy, who began to scream and clung to Alec even tighter.

'Your protection! That's a joke,' breathed Alec. 'Do you value your inheritance, Stephen? Do you value your *life*? If so, then you'd best get the devil out of here!'

Stephen paled. Then he squared his shoulders and turned to a trembling Rosalie, murmuring, 'My dear, you'll observe that the matter is out of my hands. But I suggest you think carefully about believing anything this man says, especially if it relates to me. I'll see you again soon, I hope. And as for you, Alec—I hope to see *you* in hell.'

With that Stephen barked orders to his driver, climbed back into his carriage and it rattled away down the street.

Chapter Eleven

Rosalie moved quickly. Snatching Katy from Alec, she began to march off in the rain, her mudsoaked clothes clinging coldly to her legs. She didn't know where she was or where she was heading. She felt sick and desperate. Katy was crying again.

Alec charged after her while Eyepatch, face set, held the two horses. '*Stop*, Rosalie. Where are you going?'

'I don't care! Anywhere!' she cried. The rain was pouring down; they were all wet through.

'*Rosalie.*' Urgently he caught her by the shoulder and swung her round. 'You surely didn't believe that Lord Maybury intended to *help* you!'

'I think he'd have found us better accommodation than his basement!' She tilted her chin defiantly. 'Why do you hate him so? What *is* he to you?'

It was a timely reminder for Alec that she didn't even know Stephen was his brother. And now was perhaps not the moment to tell her. 'Sorry,' he grated, 'sorry, there was I forgetting that you had an appointment with him, back in Piccadilly.'

'I did *not* have an appointment with him!'

'So you believe he was at the same place as you by chance, do you?'

'Of course! Why else?'

'He bought your drinks. And now you're sick as a dog... Yet you were going back with him, in his *carriage*?'

She clutched Katy tighter, her face blazing defiance again. 'I had nowhere else to go! And you, of all people, should know why, since you are responsible!'

Alec drew a deep breath. Light was just beginning to dawn. 'I take it you're talking about that fire again.'

'Yes, and don't insult me by pretending you don't know! My friend Helen's home was burnt to the ground tonight, because you took exception to my comments about your way of life, that day at Two Crows Castle! And I know you also set your men two weeks ago to destroy my friend's printing press—her *livelihood*!'

Oh, devil take it. The smashed press, the fire. She thought it was *him*. He clenched his jaw. 'Certainly I did not like the garbage you spouted that day you came to my home, chiefly because it in no way resembled the truth. But to think I would take such squalid and petty revenge...' Alec took a deep breath. 'Listen to me. I was *not* responsible for the damage done to your friend's printing press. I did not set fire to your friend's home tonight.'

She lifted her chin, in defiance and disbelief. 'You have plenty of men to do your dirty work, though, haven't you?'

'You are insulting them,' he snapped. 'I thought you as Ro Rowland pretended to be on the side of former soldiers. Now you're assuming, as so many others do, that they're all common criminals. Well, *don't*. And your friend with her printing press has no doubt made countless enemies if she regularly publishes vitriol-filled, inaccurate pieces like the one *you* were starting to write about Two Crows Castle that day you came to visit.'

She swallowed hard. Either he was an extremely good liar, or he was telling the truth. *Impossible.* But…

He was reaching into his pocket, pulling out a folded sheet of paper. 'Here,' he said tiredly. 'You dropped this.'

It was the letter Biddy had brought to her, from Helen. She had forgotten all about it. Still clutching Katy, she unwrapped it with fingers that were numb with cold.

Dear Rosalie, we are all safe, though the house is a burned-out shell. I am sending Katy to you with Biddy, because the child was inconsolable and wanted you badly. As Biddy will tell you, you must make haste, both of you, to Mr Wheeldon's house.

I have more idea now, Rosalie, who our enemy is. Because shortly before the fire another note was delivered, just like the first—on the same notepaper, in the same handwriting—saying, 'If you write one more word about Lady A., then you and those close to you will be the target next, not just the house.' *I fear I have made a vicious enemy, Rosalie. But Mr Wheeldon and his sister and their servants here make me feel most secure…*

Rosalie felt the world tilt around her. An enemy Helen had made, then, not her. So the finger of blame was no longer pointing at Alec Stewart… Oh, Lord. She tried to shove the letter back into her pocket, impeded because Katy, upset, was fighting to get free.

'Hush, sweetheart,' Alec was saying softly to the little girl. He'd picked up the tattered rag doll she'd dropped and gave it to her.

Katy gazed up at him, her crying hiccuping to a stop. 'Polly-doll,' she said.

Decisively Alec took her in his arms. 'News?' He nodded curtly towards Helen's letter.

The colour crept hotly up Rosalie's throat to her cheeks. 'It seems I might have been mistaken. In the matter of what happened to my friend, and the fire at her house. I—apologise.'

His expression remained iron hard. 'You make rather a lot of mistakes, don't you, Mrs Rowland?'

'I've said I'm sorry!' she flashed. 'Let me have Katy back.'

'You're not fit to look after yourself, let alone a child!'

Katy stared up at Alec, wide-eyed, interested. 'It's all right,' he said soothingly to her. 'It's all right, sweetheart.' He gazed narrowly at Rosalie. 'You've nowhere to go, you're not well and you have the child to think of. You're what I'd call in trouble.'

'Lord Maybury would have helped me!'

His lips thinned. 'If you believe that, you're even more foolish than I'd thought. And as Lord Maybury's gone on his sweet way, I'd say you've actually no choice but to let me take you both to my house for the night.'

Fear jolted through Rosalie. She'd always intended to tackle this man. To enter his lair somehow, and find out all she could about Linette's enemy. But, oh, Lord, not like this. Not with her legs shaking, and her stomach heaving, and her brain a woolly mess. And with—Katy.

Yet what else could she do? She had no money. No means now of even getting safely to Mr Wheeldon's house. 'Wonderful,' she said bitterly. She pushed back her hair. 'So it's your basement again, is it?'

Her legs wobbled and he saw it. 'Take hold of my arm,' he ordered. 'I've got the child safe. And this time, we'll try to do better than my basement. Garrett!' He was turning to call out to Eyepatch.

'Captain?'

'I want you to take the horses home. But first find me a hackney, quickly. I'm bringing Mrs Rowland and her child to Two Crows Castle.'

Garrett's face was a picture of dismay. 'My God, Captain, have you lost your wits?'

'Button it, Garrett. Just do as I say, will you?' Glancing down, Alec saw that Rosalie looked white as death.

The child looked anxious. 'Mama?'

'She's all right,' Alec said gently. 'Your mother will be all right, Katy.'

Alec realised he was getting himself into a fine pickle. No wonder Garrett had looked aghast. But when Alec had seen her struggling to get out of Stephen's carriage, he'd wanted to punch his brother into the gutter. She looked so defenceless in her drab wet cloak, with her rain-soaked hair clinging to her face. Yet not only had she paraded her wares at the Temple of Beauty, but she'd been with Stephen tonight. *She's no innocent, you fool. Young though she is, she's a widow and has a child. What's more, she's a gossip-raking troublemaker who's wrongly accused you of all sorts of rubbish...*

The hackney summoned by Garrett rumbled to a halt close by. He thought he could see tears misting her eyes as she turned to him and whispered, 'You promise me the child will be safe?'

'I promise,' he said, tight-lipped. *God, she could barely stand.* Grimly he climbed after her into the dingy hackney with Katy still secure in his arms and cursed himself for a fool all the way back to Two Crows Castle. His men would be far from delighted to see her after her last visit. But he couldn't leave her out on the street. *'Why not?'* loyal Garrett would say. *'She deserves no better.'*

Alec sighed. The trouble was that even now, bedraggled and sick and hostile as she was, she was still so eminently desirable that his loins ached. Dear God, she was prey to *anyone* like this, let alone his evil brother. She was clearly of gentle birth and educated. So what the hell was she doing, getting involved not only with the gutter press, but with Dr Barnard's place and with Stephen? She could be big trouble. Could? She already *was*, damn it. Nowhere to go, apparently. No one to turn to except him.

The child slept in his arms. If he'd not tried to warn his father off his new wife, and if he himself had married that heiress as he was supposed to, he might have had a child of his own by now…

A hell of a lot of *ifs*. The coach was pulling up. They were there.

Rosalie's heart plummeted as they pulled up outside Two Crows Castle. The smoky lanterns that hung on either side of the big front door did little to relieve the gloom. She insisted on holding Katy herself as soon as she was out of the cab. *For one night. One night only.*

'What've you got there, Captain Alec?' That big red-haired Scotsman—oh, she remembered *him*—was drawing closer, frowning suspiciously. 'Och, now, you're not forgettin' she's the one that accused you of all those bad things the other week?'

'That was a misunderstanding,' said Alec curtly, guiding Rosalie towards the door. 'And she's here to stay, Sergeant McGrath, just for a day or two.'

More men were gathering round. Rosalie clutched Katy tighter. 'A child,' they were muttering. 'He's brought in a child and that woman.' Eyepatch was there, too; he must have stabled the horses, and his frown was equally dour.

Panic-stricken, Rosalie swung round to Alec. 'Look. I've changed my mind. Katy and I will find somewhere else.' *Anywhere else.*

'We've been through this,' Alec answered tightly.

'Where else, exactly, would you find shelter at this time of night?'

Nowhere. She shrank back from all their cold stares.

'Don't worry, Mrs Rowland.' Alec sighed. 'You and the child will have a room of your own, with a key on your side of the door—not that you'll need it. This place is far from luxurious, but at least we're all honest.'

Suddenly Katy opened her eyes and reached out to Alec, who touched her chubby hand very lightly. And when just the smallest of smiles crinkled his sombre eyes, the result was so devastating that Rosalie felt her insides lurch again. He said to her, more gently, 'Garrett will show you to your room. We'll discuss what's to be done in the morning.'

Already McGrath was trying to draw Alec to one side. 'Captain, there's more fellows needin' rooms tonight. They're waiting in the Rising Sun for you…'

She watched Alec's tall, rangy figure disappearing from view, with red-haired McGrath at his side. And she felt as if her one pillar of safety was abandoning her.

Safety? Was she insane? Was this how Linette had felt? Still feeling sick, she held Katy close and struggled to gather her disarrayed thoughts as Eyepatch—oh, Lord, she must remember his name was Garrett—led her surlily up the stairs.

The accommodation she and Katy were to share consisted in fact of one small room. Garrett had lit a lamp before he left; as she looked around, she felt a tiny but welcome sense of relief. There was just enough space for two narrow beds; the blankets, though threadbare, looked clean and the floor was swept, with a closet for clothes and even a small mirror nailed to the wall over a washstand.

A middle-aged woman knocked on the door a few minutes later. 'My name's Mary, ma'am, and I've brought you both clothes, 'cos the Captain said yours were soaked and here's some milk and bread for your little one. You'll be sure to let me know, won't you, if there's anything else you want? Bless her, isn't she sweet! My little granddaughters, now—'

'Thank you, that will be all,' Rosalie cut in. Unable to find the promised key, she jammed the door shut with a chair after the woman had gone. On the one hand, she rebuked herself for being abominably rude. On the other hand—she was in the domain of her enemy.

And she was so tired, all she wanted to do was sleep. But first she changed Katy into those dry clothes, then took the plate of bread and, after hesitating—*they wouldn't stoop to poisoning an infant, don't be a fool*—she sat Katy on her lap and fed her.

That was when she heard the noise of men talking somewhere outside. Going over to the window with Katy still in her arms, she pulled back the faded curtain to gaze out.

'Tick-tock man. There,' Katy announced with satisfaction.

The window overlooked a large, overgrown garden at the back of the house. A flagged terrace was lit by the glow of a brazier, and gathered around it, with tankards of ale in their hands, were a dozen or so rough-looking men—and two young women, with whom the men were clearly on familiar terms. In their midst was Alec, laughing and joking with them. One of the women, who had dyed black hair and upthrust breasts on full display, had her hand possessively on his arm.

What had Lord Maybury said? *I'm afraid that Alec Stewart keeps company with the lowest of the low...*

Shivering with dismay, Rosalie turned away from the window, freshly appalled at the situation in which she'd landed herself. Katy was nodding off in her arms; Rosalie

wiped her face and fingers clean and put her in the spare
bed with her rag doll next to her. She remembered, with
a wrench at her insides, how in the cab Katy had slum-
bered in Alec Stewart's arms, her thumb in her mouth, her
dark curls tousled around her angelic face. *I envied her,
in those strong arms... Don't be stupid! Don't be so utterly idiotic!* She blinked away her own hot tears of weariness and despair.

No matter how much she tried to tell herself that this
was her heaven-sent opportunity to find out more about
the dangerous master of Two Crows Castle, she was in a
mess, she acknowledged bitterly, an almighty mess. She
changed into the nightdress Mary had provided and settled herself awkwardly on the bed, preparing herself for a
sleepless night. Why did Alec Stewart and Lord Maybury
hate each other so? There was so much that she couldn't
make sense of...

But suddenly something that should have been obvious struck her with a dreadful jolt. *No wonder Katy was
so happy in Alec Stewart's arms. She had, after all, most
likely found her father.*

Alec didn't reach his bed until late. Tonight he knew
he'd vastly added to his problems by taking in Rosalie—
Mrs Rowland—and her child.

Why had he done it, when she so clearly hated him?
When she was preparing to go off for the night with Stephen?

It was because Rosalie still struck him as Stephen's
victim, rather than his whore. And—though he despised
himself for this—because he found her irresistible. He'd
been fool enough to kiss her twice and both those kisses
had been delicious. She was sweet, tenderly responsive,
yet almost innocent... Impossible! For God's sake, she'd

been selling herself at the Temple of Beauty! Displaying herself, on stage, looking for the highest bidder!

His raging doubts were succinctly echoed by Garrett, as the two of them went as usual round the big place one last time, to check all was well before locking up for the night.

'You've let yourself in for a whole heap of trouble, taking that one in, Captain, if you don't mind my saying,' warned Garrett softly. 'A whole heap.'

Alec was awake early the next morning as ever and went down to breakfast, brushing aside that damned great dog, who'd jumped up to greet him from a warm spot by Mary's cooking range. Quite a few men were already at the big table, eating. The newcomers were especially hungry and shovelled down the food as if they couldn't believe their luck, while the two new women Garrett had hired to help out were cheerfully dishing out the plain but hearty food.

They all greeted him warmly. 'Mornin', Captain!' He nodded in reply. The dark-haired wench who'd tried her luck with him last night lifted her face for a kiss, but he'd already made it plain she was hired to work and nothing else. He couldn't see Mary, though he knew she couldn't be far away, because only she could have got so many pans full of sizzling fried bread and bacon on the big cooking range.

He went to pour himself some coffee, then saw Mary coming through from the breakfast room—with Katy in her arms.

'Where's the child's mother, Mary? Isn't she down yet?'

Kind Mary, a mother and grandmother herself, looked anxious. 'She's still a-bed, Captain. The little one was heard cryin', so I went up to fetch her. Took her clothes to freshen up, as well. The mother, she didn't wake!'

Garrett entered just then. 'Doubtless she's not used to keeping early hours, Captain,' he said pointedly.

Alec whipped round on him. 'She has a *child*. No mother normally sleeps when her child's crying!'

'This one does.'

Alec said grimly, 'In that case, I'm going up to her. She cannot be well.'

But first, Garrett handed him the note.

Hell's teeth.

Chapter Twelve

Rosalie was in an old dark castle, where every room was full of sneering soldiers and gaudily dressed whores. She was running along endless passageways in search of Linette, for ever glimpsing her, but unable to reach her; then she was faced with a door which turned out to be not a door, but a mirror. In it she saw herself wearing nothing but a silken underslip, through which her hips and her breasts were outlined. Her hair was tangled, her cheeks flushed, and Alec Stewart was coming up behind her, lithe and dangerous, pulling her to him, kissing her, plundering her mouth with his lips and tongue…

Linette's destroyer. A rackrenter, who sought out the company of loose women.

Darkness enveloped her again. Flames were burning her. She could hear Katy crying, *Mama, Mama,* and Rosalie was struggling to get to her, but was powerless to save her. *There is no hope,* someone was saying, *there is no hope.*

Tears were streaming down her cheeks. Weakly she hauled herself up against the pillows, still light-headed, still nauseous. Daylight poured into the room. And she saw that Katy's bed was empty.

She began to scream.

The door opened and Alec Stewart was there. Instantly he strode to her bedside. 'Rosalie. You're having nightmares—my God, you look as though you're burning up!'

'Katy.' The tears were still rolling down her cheeks. 'What have you done with Katy?'

'She's safe. Do you hear me?'

'I must go to her. I must…'

He sat quickly on the chair by her bed and gripped her hands. 'She's downstairs, having breakfast. Mary is looking after her; she's quite safe. *You're* safe.' He touched her forehead. 'But you have a fever. You're not fit to go anywhere.'

She was trying to pull away. 'I must get up, I must get out of here.'

'And go where precisely, damn it?'

She sank back, pulse thudding. She had no money. Helen's house had been destroyed. And she was clad only in a loose nightgown—*where were her clothes*?

Alec had gone over to the dressing table and was pouring something from a jug into a cup. 'Here,' he said, coming back to her, his face strangely shadowed. 'Drink this. It's Mary's barley water.' He sat on a chair next to the bed, supporting her shoulders with one hand and holding the cup for her with the other hand. She felt as weak as a kitten. Her throat was parched, and the barley water was cold and pure. His hand was unnervingly comforting against her back. But—

'You will be *all right* here,' he emphasised softly. 'Katy will be all right. Mary has her two young grandchildren here nearly every day while her daughter works at a bakery in Bishopsgate. The little girls are playing with Katy now and Katy is perfectly happy. I'm going to send for the doctor.'

'*No.*'

'I know that you hate this place, and me,' he said quietly. 'But unless you can tell me of somewhere else you can go—somewhere *safe*—you really have no option.'

She hesitated, her stomach pitching. 'I will find *somewhere*...'

He shrugged his wide shoulders. 'If you insist. But I take it you're going with a bodyguard to accompany you?'

The blood pounded through her veins. 'What—what nonsense is this?'

'Not nonsense, unfortunately. *This* was delivered at the house this morning.' He passed the crudely written note to her. She took it with trembling fingers.

Stop asking questions, whore. Your friend has already suffered the consequences, and you're next.

The writing. The notepaper... Her stomach lurched.

He said, 'Do you know who it's from?'

'I think—I think it could be from the same person who has been threatening my friend Helen. The same writing. The same notepaper.'

He drew in a sharp breath. She went on, in a voice that shook despite all her efforts to control it, 'This is ridiculous! I cannot be threatened like this; I will go to the constables, or a magistrate—they will help me!'

'Save yourself the trouble,' he said.

He didn't need to explain. He'd told her before that no magistrate would take the trouble to listen to her. *A courtesan who writes for a gossip rag.* That was how he'd described her. 'Then I am even more determined that we will leave here!' she cried. 'Katy and I, we will find somewhere...' She was trying to push back the bedclothes.

'No!' he rasped, flinging out his arm to stop her. 'Whoever it is, they'll follow you—you and the child!' Then, a little gentler, 'I don't make a habit of throwing women and children out on the street. Stay here.'

He must have seen the downright fear shoot through her. 'I realise the idea doesn't immediately appeal,' he said. His eyes darkened. 'But believe me, as soon as word goes around that you're under my protection, you'll be far safer than anywhere else in London. And rest assured I will require nothing of you at all. Except, perhaps, obedience.'

She swallowed, hard. 'Then—you truly think I'm in danger?'

He pointed at the note. 'Don't *you*?'

She sank back against the pillows. Oh, Lord. Where else could she go? But how could she possibly think herself safe *here*, of all places?

Alec was mentally cursing himself. If he hadn't gone to Dr Barnard's to tackle Stephen, he would never have seen her. She'd have been left to deal with her own problems, which she'd surely brought upon herself. But—was she really used to earning her living on her back, as well as with her vitriolic pen?

She was trouble. Even in that voluminous nightgown, she was treacherously alluring. He remembered her slender waist, the sweet curve of her hips, the warm scent of her skin as he'd hauled her against him in that kiss, the last time she'd paid a visit to Two Crows Castle. The memory sent a nagging ache of need throbbing through his veins.

You fool, Stewart.

'Have you decided?' he asked curtly.

Her eyes looked bruised with distress. 'Will you truly promise me Katy is safe here?'

'Of course she is,' he said. *Safer than she was with you last night, since you were dragging her around the town.* No. He wouldn't rebuke her—yet—for her idiotic trust in his brother.

She drew herself up and said, with that air of defiant dignity that so confounded all his preconceptions of her, 'Very well. For as long as the danger stands, I will—accept your protection.'

He nodded, as if it were a matter of as little importance to him as the hiring of a hackney cab. 'I am overwhelmed by your gratitude,' he said.

'Some day you must let me pay you!'

He shrugged. 'Why? Nobody else does.'

Her eyes flashed. 'Only those poor soldiers!'

'My soldiers?' He looked coldly angry now. 'I'd like to make it quite clear that none of them pays me a penny.'

Oh, God. She bit her lip. For some reason she believed him. 'I'm sorry. Oh, I'm sorry. I thought you were a—a...'

'A rackrenter,' he said tightly. 'Indeed. As you implied in those scribblings of yours—wait! Where in hell are you *going*?'

She'd suddenly slid to the side of the bed away from him. Was trying to heave herself out, but was instead doubled up and starting to retch helplessly.

In a couple of strides Alec had pushed the porcelain bowl from the washstand on to the floor beside her. 'I'll send Mary up. I'm going for the doctor.'

'No—'

'This time,' he said, 'I'm giving you no choice.'

Exhausted with sickness and with Mary quietly tidying up around her, Rosalie sagged back against the pillows in despair. *Oh, no.* She'd made so many dreadful mistakes. She'd been wrong about Helen's printing press, and the fire, and about his rackrenting. In return he despised her as a cheap little widow, a courtesan. And even though Alec Stewart might be a despicable seducer—*my own sister denounced him to me!*—just now she'd found comfort and something even more disturbing in his calm voice, his very presence...

You are mad. You are ill, Rosalie.

Ill indeed, because during the course of that morning the fever took her more firmly in its grip. Bed rest, the doctor ordered.

The next few days for Rosalie passed in a haze. She was sometimes aware of Mary serving her with the powders the doctor had prescribed, or bringing her a fresh cotton nightgown. Of Katy being brought up to see her, her little thumb in her mouth, sometimes with Mary, sometimes in Alec's strong arms, which Rosalie found almost unbearable.

Sometimes, she would hear the physician's grave voice. 'The fever lingers... She must have caught a chill on the night you found her.'

Then Alec's low tones. 'Mrs Rowland was drenched that night, in the rain. And I've reason to believe she was served drinks that had been tampered with.'

'That would not have helped. Rest is what she needs; a little light food, plenty of liquids...'

That threat, that note Alec had shown her, hung over her all the time. *Stop asking questions, whore. Your friend has already suffered the consequences, and you're next.*

Who could it be from?

One morning—Rosalie guessed her fourth day here—Alec knocked and came in after the doctor's daily visit. She had tried getting up earlier, but her legs were as shaky as a newborn colt's.

'I've brought you a letter,' he said. Her pulse began to race. 'It's from your friend Helen.'

Helen. Oh, poor Helen would have been so worried, so angry... 'How did she know I was here?'

'I told her,' Alec said quietly. 'I went to see her at Mr Wheeldon's house two days ago to explain that you were ill and had taken shelter at my home. She—expressed her disapproval quite strongly.'

Rosalie could imagine. She opened the letter quickly. *Rosalie, my dear. What can you be thinking of, staying at that place? You know you are welcome here, with Francis and his sister! I have news. But first please write, to let me know you and Katy are safe.*

'She wanted to visit you,' Alec said. 'More than that, I think she wanted to drag you and your child away from here and tear me limb from limb. Her friend Mr Wheeldon was more reasonable. Do you wish her to visit?'

'No, I don't. Because that threat was directed to her, too, wasn't it, Captain Stewart?' Rosalie managed to sound calm. 'So at the moment I imagine it's best if she has as little as possible to do with me.'

'Then I'll tell her that the doctor still advises you to rest. And if you wish to write to her, I'll see that your letter's delivered.'

So Rosalie wrote to her.

A reply came the next day from Helen. Alec waited while she read it. *Rosalie. I am disappointed that you have chosen to place any trust in that man. Since you don't wish me to visit, I am obliged to write with my news. Francis has asked Toby and me to travel to Oxford with him for two weeks, because he has been approached to set up a church school in a village there and wants me to help. Just think, it's not far—ten miles or less—from where you used to live, and I used to teach! I am considering making a permanent move— I don't think I can be happy in Lon-*

don again. I hope you know, Rosalie, that I will be there whenever you want me. Yours, Helen.

Alec was watching her. 'Are you all right, Mrs Rowland?'

She pushed some loose strands of hair back from her cheeks. 'Helen is leaving London for a little while. I—I think she feels I've rejected her.'

'You did so for very good reasons,' he reminded her quietly. 'Unselfish reasons. Some day, you'll be able to tell her so.' He hesitated. 'I'll leave you to rest.'

She lay back against the pillows.

Now, she really was on her own.

Whenever she was by herself she would get up from her bed and try to walk a little further around the room, but Rosalie was frightened by how weak she was after these days of illness. Katy was brought up to her regularly, but was always happy to return to her new friends.

Time for Rosalie hung heavily, until she noticed some books on a shelf by the window. She was surprised by their quality. Several of them, she realised, were sketchbooks that must have belonged to someone in the army. Quickly she became captivated by the swiftly but skilfully drawn portraits of soldiers at rest, or marching, the deft water-colours of mountains and villages, in Spain, she guessed. There were also other, heavier volumes containing reproductions of the work of more famous artists.

Mary had brought her some spare clothes, and on her seventh morning there Rosalie took off her nightgown and pulled on a sleeveless cotton chemise, intending to wear the plain rose-pink cambric dress that lay over the foot of the bed. But it was warm in here with the sun pouring through the window, so she decided to continue reading the book on Boucher she had found while sitting curled on the bed. The doctor had been and there was no danger of any other visitors just yet.

She was fast learning the rhythms of the household. She'd heard from Mary, always willing to chatter, that the soldiers were usually up and about early. Some went off to local places of work, at building sites or timber yards. Others were organised by Sergeant McGrath into doing repair work around this ungainly great building. Alec was often out until his fencing lessons began in the early evening.

But now, as Rosalie sat cross-legged on the bed in that flimsy chemise, engrossed in her book, Alec Stewart walked in, carrying a tray laden with a steaming teapot, china cups and a plate of bread and butter. He almost dropped everything. He clutched the tray and steadied it with a clatter of crockery, but not before one of the cups had rolled off and smashed on the floor.

He said, 'My God.'

She dropped the book and jumped off the bed, putting it between herself and him. With his tousled dark hair, his rumpled white shirt, black boots and breeches that clung to every inch of his muscular thighs, he looked utterly devastating.

Her pulse was hammering. 'If you'd knocked first,' she declared, 'you might have saved yourself a broken cup! How dare you just march in?'

'It's my damned house,' he pointed out reasonably. 'And Mary asked me to bring your tea. Normally you're hiding under the sheets. I had no idea you'd be putting on such a display.' To be truthful, Alec was flummoxed. He knew he should leave. But—he was entranced. He felt lust stroking his loins. In that simple white chemise, she looked exquisite.

Already she was tugging on the rather faded rose-pink gown.

But that was hardly any better at concealing her charms either, thought Alec, cursing under his breath as he picked up pieces of the broken cup, because the soft fabric had moulded itself tightly to her small but rounded breasts. Earlier she must have tied back her hair, but now some blonde tendrils had escaped to cling enchantingly round her face. And as she gazed up at him with those defiant turquoise-blue eyes, he saw that they were shadowed with fear.

He sighed. He poured her some tea. 'Please sit down again. How are you feeling? I see you were looking at one of my books.'

The big book still lay outspread by her pillow. She struggled to fasten the last button and sat on the edge of the bed because her legs were suddenly unsteady again. 'I'm feeling a good deal better, thank you. I'm sorry, I shouldn't have looked at them without your permission...'

'Permission? Don't be ridiculous! What were you looking at?' He'd pulled up a stool by the bed and was reaching to examine the open pages. 'These paintings are French, aren't they? By François Boucher. You told me about Boucher at the Temple of Beauty, remember?'

Rosalie swallowed. *Be prim. Be polite.* But as she watched his lean brown hand gently lifting and turning the corners of the pages, some sort of inner turmoil set her blood racing.

'I remember,' she said as steadily as she could. Oh, Lord, how could she forget? *Just before that kiss.* 'And they're in Boucher's early style,' she went on, pointing. 'In fact, he served his apprenticeship as an engraver, but moved on to historical paintings and portraits—' She broke off. 'I'm sorry, I sound as if I'm giving a lecture.'

'You're knowledgeable.'

'Only because my father was an artist. He painted watercolours and studied the French artists of the seventeenth and eighteenth centuries.'

'Why French artists?'

'Because he lived for some years in Paris and married my mother there.'

'She was French?'

'Yes. My father died when I was seven.'

There is no hope. No hope at all, I'm afraid, madame…

Memories. The doctor, talking to her mother in Paris, at her father's sickbed. Her father, holding Rosalie close with what little strength he had. *'Be a brave, good girl, my Rosalie. Look after your mother and your little sister for me…'*

Alec said, 'Was that when you came to England?'

'Yes. My father had told my mother, often, about a cottage he owned in Oxfordshire.'

'And is your mother still there?'

She gazed up at him, her blue eyes wide with loss. 'She is dead, too.'

Alec tried not to look at the slenderness of her neck. The faint pulse beating there. *What had happened to her life next?* he wondered. An impulsive early marriage, he supposed, and pregnancy followed by her husband's early demise, leaving her penniless with a child to support. So she'd decided to come to London to seek her fortune— as a writer? As a courtesan? Whatever, somehow she'd made bad enemies.

Yet he found it so damned hard to believe she was capable of selling herself. She'd looked so innocent when he'd come in just now, wearing that pure white bit of nothingness and intently poring over that book…

He forced himself to remember how she'd been parading on stage at Dr Barnard's—for sale, or as good as. Unfortunately, the memory did nothing to quell the nagging of harsh desire between his thighs. *A French mother*—perhaps that explained her grace, her allure, her *beauty*, damn it all.

'Being left alone with a child to take care of can't be easy,' he said. 'But you must admit you've made some rash decisions.'

She closed the book rather abruptly. 'I have always paid my own way, I assure you, Captain Stewart. And I have never before been forced to stay in a place like this!'

He was angry now. 'No one is forcing you. And considering you were dragging a small child round London with nowhere to go except Lord Maybury's on the night I found you, you can hardly claim to be a model parent!'

She'd risen shakily to her feet, her colour high. 'I've done what I could for Katy. How *dare* you criticise, when you've no *idea*!'

He stood up, too, to make her sit down again. 'Hush. Hush, I'm sorry. Everyone can see that you adore her.'

'Everyone can…?' His warm hands on her shoulders made her fury melt into something far more disturbing. She was struggling for breath.

'Of course.' His eyes, she saw, were concerned, Almost—*tender*.

'I'm sorry,' she whispered, 'it's just…' she swallowed and rubbed her hand across her eyes '…it's just that sometimes I think I will go mad if I have to stay trapped in here another day!'

'You have been ill. Don't be so hard on yourself, Mrs Rowland.' He sat next to her and smiled quizzically down at her. 'Now, I'm going to tell you a secret. Actually, I used to rather enjoy your Ro Rowland articles.'

'You—*you did*?'

'Yes. You have talent and wit. You have—courage.'

'No. No. I've been stupid, I've made a mess of everything!' Bitterly she looked up at him. 'Oh, if only I had not been *ill*.'

'Poor Rosalie. Taking the whole world on your shoulders.'

'I can look after myself!' she flared. 'I—I am in temporary difficulties, that is all.'

He tilted her chin up with his fingers, frowning. Temporary difficulties? The sight of her struggling defiantly against the troubles that life had thrown her way had touched some part of him that he'd long buried. That belonged to a better part of him, perhaps.

But it wasn't the better part of him that made him ache to kiss her. To feel the softness of her tender body in his arms...

'Stop fighting the whole world,' he said quietly. 'Stop fighting *me*.'

And he kissed her. My God, he knew he'd regret it, but—he kissed her.

Rosalie went very still at the first brush of his lips against hers. But as his warm mouth cherished hers, her lips parted instinctively, her heart thudded and she felt that in the whole world there was only this man. Only the heady, floating sensation of his slow, deliberate kiss. Only the need to feel his hands, his lips, caressing her body, arousing, promising...

It was as if he *cared*. 'Forget it, gal,' Sal would warn bitterly, 'forget them all. Once a feller's got what he wants, he'll throw you away like rubbish.'

But Rosalie was beginning not to care what Sal had said. This was where she wanted to be, in his arms. It was so good to breathe in his clean male scent and all that mattered now was his mouth on hers, his tongue delicately probing, deliberately possessing her with a skill that was utterly devastating. Her heart was beating quite wildly.

Then she gasped, because he had unbuttoned her dress and slipped aside the shoulder of her chemise and was cupping one breast with his sword-calloused palm, caressing it deliberately, wickedly until the sensitive peak leapt to his touch. She felt an answering pulse at her very core, full of liquid warmth as she realised it would be so easy just to melt into his strong arms. So easy to let him bed her…

A sharp knock, at the door.

Garrett's voice. 'You've got a visitor, Captain.'

Alec drew slowly back from Rosalie and swore under his breath. 'Whoever it is, tell him it's not convenient.'

A pause. Then—'I think you'll want to see him. Captain. Sir.'

Alec turned to Rosalie, his jaw set. Once more he was tough Captain Stewart, master of a lowlife soldiers' hostel. 'I must go. Don't do anything stupid. Don't even *think* of leaving.'

He was gone. And she felt desolate. She clutched the bedpost, white-faced. Once more she'd succumbed to this dangerous man—she was surely losing her wits. She pushed herself up from the bed. Despite what he said, she had to get out of here! But—that threat. *Stop asking questions, whore…*

Talk about being trapped between the devil and the deep blue sea. She tried again to get up and walk around the room, but within a few moments she had to sink back on the bed, because her legs felt like cotton wool.

She closed her eyes and surrendered briefly to despair. And the worst thing was—she was just starting to realise how very much she *wanted* to be wrong about Alec Stewart and Linette.

* * *

Garrett was waiting for Alec out on the landing. 'Listening at keyholes, Garrett?' queried Alec caustically.

'No!' Garrett looked hurt. 'No, God's truth... Captain, Lord Conistone's waitin' in the fencing hall for you!'

Lucas. Indeed, this was the first good news Alec had had for a long time. And his friend had called at the right moment, because a few more minutes with Mrs Rosalie Rowland and he'd have been hard put to stop himself seducing her there and then. My God, whether she intended it or not, everything about her was an erotic enticement: the defiant flash of her eyes; the way she tossed her hair to face up to him; the stubborn pout of her full, rosy lips.

Alec was no stranger to female enticements and he'd enjoyed many a willing bed companion. Yet something about her was so damned *vulnerable*. If she was playing games, she excelled at them, because she was driving him wild.

He'd longed, how he'd longed just then to caress her into submission with his lips and hands. He was possessed by an image of her naked, her slender legs wrapping around his as he sheathed himself in her again and again...

God, Alec, don't. She's dangerous. A whore and a scandalmonger. A dousing of cold water for you, man.

That threatening note had been nasty. Someone vicious was after her—the same person doubtless who'd made her homeless through the fire. She would make enemies easily, with the mixed messages she sent out. One minute all erotic allure, the next, prim as a young school miss...

You can't take her as your mistress. You mustn't.

Physical pleasure for a man of Alec's station was easy to come by, but intimacy of any other sort he'd sworn to avoid for good. His mind wandered back to the painful memories of a spell of home leave when he'd become betrothed to a pretty young heiress who thought herself in love with him. She'd been an innocent, of course, well chaperoned because of all that money. She'd kept asking about the battlefields of the Peninsula, but she'd not wanted to know the harsh reality, so he kept it from her. Kept *himself* from her, until in a fit of petulance she'd broken their betrothal last spring. Which was as well, considering the dark secrets already unfolding at the heart of his family.

Now Alec's thoughts ran riot as he made his way to the fencing hall. What the hell was he to do with Rosalie Rowland? He cursed anew when he saw that some of the plaster-and-lath ceiling had fallen in overnight thanks to a spell of heavy rain; cursed again when he had to push aside that great mutt of a dog who leapt up eagerly to greet him. 'Garrett, I thought I said—'

'Aye, Captain. I'll find a new home for him soon enough.'

Alec sighed and went to greet his oldest, his truest friend.

Lucas Conistone, Earl of Stancliffe, looked just the same as ever: effortlessly elegant, his clothes exquisite. Alec clasped his hand. 'Lucas, by God! I thought you'd become a rustic, never to grace the city again. When did you arrive in town?'

'Late yesterday.' Lucas smiled. 'Even Verena felt it was time to catch up on the gossip of the *ton*.'

Alec noted how his friend's handsome features lit up as he spoke his wife's name. 'How are Verena and the children?'

'Well, all well; the children cannot wait to see Hyde Park, and the Tower, and so on. Verena—oh, she pretends, you know, to take an interest in clothes and balls and such, but really...'

'Really, she's just happy wherever you are, Lucas, admit it!'

'Indeed.' Lucas's elegant drawl softened. 'I'm a lucky man, Alec.'

Garrett came in, grinning all over his face because he thought the world of Lucas Conistone. He carried freshly polished glasses and a bottle of burgundy. Alec glanced at the label and whistled.

'Brought by his lordship, Captain,' explained Garrett, expertly wielding the corkscrew.

'Are we celebrating something?'

Lucas nodded. 'Remind him, Garrett. And pour yourself a drink also, man. You were there, too.'

Garrett lifted his head proudly. 'Two years ago to the day, the garrison at Bordeaux surrendered to Lord Wellington! There was still Toulouse and Waterloo to come, of course. But Bordeaux was the beginning of the end for Mister Nap!'

'Indeed,' affirmed Lucas, lifting his glass. 'Here's to victory.'

'And here's to those who didn't make it back,' added Alec softly. Suddenly serious, all three raised their glasses, thinking of the dead and wounded. Then Garrett, a broad smile once more splitting his face to see these old friends together again, left them with the wine.

They talked for a while about the war and mutual acquaintances. Then Alec wryly indicated Lucas's fine clothes. 'You said you were a lucky man, Lucas. You're also a damned expensively dressed one—now, let me guess—boots by Hoby, coat tailored by Weston? I wonder what it's worth to keep quiet about the filthy clothes you wore to play the spy in Portugal? My God, you used to go unwashed for days on end!'

Lucas pointed at him, laughing. 'You, too, Alec—you were with me on some of my most dangerous adventures, remember? We were ragamuffins, both of us! But that's all behind us. And your father's not well, I hear.'

'My father's not well and I've got a brother I wouldn't wish on my worst enemy.' Alec finished off his wine. 'My father's gone to Carrfields, though that's not the solution. Lucas, I'd do anything for him—you know how close we used to be. But he won't have me near!'

'Then he's his own worst enemy,' said Lucas levelly. 'Look, Alec, you need a change of scene. We're opening up our Mayfair house and we want you to visit us—in fact, we'll be offended if you *don't*. Though you seem to have your hands pretty full here, from what I've seen...'

They talked on, about Two Crows Castle and a parliamentary bill that was going forwards to secure better rights for the injured soldiers. Then it was time for Lucas to leave, but out in the hallway he paused.

'Alec, tell me if this is none of my business, but I was in Rundell's yesterday—you know, the art dealers on Ludgate Hill? And I noticed two rather fine oil paintings there that I'd swear I'd last seen in your father's drawing room. Were you aware that he was putting some of his collection on the market?'

'No,' breathed Alec, suddenly tensing. 'No, by God, I wasn't. And I wonder if my father is!'

As soon as Lucas had gone, Alec clenched his fists. That painting, of Blenheim. Sent to specialists, to be cleaned? His suspicions ran riot. But how to go about this? How to tackle this new, damnable problem without letting the whole world—especially his father—know?

His mind flew to Rosalie Rowland.

He'd been a fool to kiss her again; that had helped

nothing. If he'd been hoping to breach her defences, he'd learned not a fragment more about the enigmatic little widow from the Temple of Beauty—except that she knew rather a lot about art.

Then Garrett came in. 'You know you told the lads to ask round careful-like about Mrs Rowland, Captain? Well, they've found out that when she arrived in London last autumn, she stayed with that printer friend of hers, in Clerkenwell.'

Alec nodded tiredly. Helen Fazackerley.

'And she spent most of her time,' went on Garrett, 'goin' round theatres.'

'Going round *theatres*! With her infant?'

'She didn't have the infant with her then, see?' said Garrett patiently. 'The little 'un—Katy—seemed to turn up some time in December. Mrs Rowland left 'er then for an hour or two at a time with her printer friend, or a neighbour of theirs. And she carried on traipsing each day from one playhouse to another. Askin' about someone called—Linette.'

With that, Garrett nodded and left.

Alec frowned, rubbing the tension from the back of his neck.

Who the deuce was Linette?

He'd gone easy on the questions so far, because of Rosalie's sickness. But now, perhaps, the time for soft-footing it was over.

She'd just told him that she was going mad, confined to her room, hadn't she? Well, he'd thought of rather an interesting outing for her—*and* a way to put her secretly to the test.

Chapter Thirteen

By the time Alec got back upstairs, Rosalie was sitting by the window, with a drab shawl over her gown and her hair pinned up, and—

'What exactly are you doing, Mrs Rowland?'

She stiffened. 'Mending some shirts. Mary came up after you'd gone and I asked her if there was anything I could do.'

'Mary had no business giving you servants' work!'

Her blue eyes flashed. 'Captain Stewart, I'm aware that I've been taking up a room, and your time and your servants' time. That you've been feeding both myself and Katy for *days* now—'

'And neither of you eats enough to keep a bird alive,' he retorted, glancing at her slender frame, which was a big mistake, because he remembered with a jolt just how it had felt, spanning that tiny waist with his hands, feeling the feminine swell of her hips, the sweet warmth of those lips...

Damnation. He clamped down hard on the sudden surge of desire.

He went on, in a voice he strove to make less abrasive, 'I take it you're feeling considerably better. Would you care to come out for a while with me?'

'Out…?'

'Yes. To look at some paintings. They're at a private house, to the west of the city. It will take us perhaps half an hour to get there.'

She hesitated. 'You think I'll be safe?'

'I don't think the coward who sent that note would dare to do anything in broad daylight, not while you're with me.'

She nodded tightly. 'But Katy…'

'Your daughter has already been in Mary's care for days, with my men watching the house—and her—constantly. I thought you might like a change of scene, since earlier you told me you feared you would go mad, trapped in here.'

Rosalie bit her lip. *And then she'd let him kiss her.* What a fool he must think her. For all her protests and defiance, she'd surrendered to him yet again, so very easily! No wonder he didn't question her role as a whore at the Temple of Beauty—she played the part so well. Heat unfurled in her insides just at the thought of his lips once more caressing hers.

It was time, finally, to confront him, but not here. Not in this place where he was master. 'An outing to look at some paintings?' she said pleasantly. 'That sounds—*delightful*, Captain Stewart!'

He gave her twenty minutes to get ready, then came to lead her downstairs. 'Why not go and see your daughter first?' he suggested. 'She's out in the garden. I'll let you know when we're ready to leave.'

He'd pointed to an open door and she blinked to find herself in the bright sunlight. The garden was larger than she'd thought, a walled quarter of an acre or so of trees and tangled shrubs that ran quite wild. The sound of children's laughter drew her around the corner to a flagged terrace, where Mary sat sewing in the sun and watching over the children.

Mary beamed a welcome. 'It's so good that you're up and about, my dear! You'll see for yourself how happy your little girl is with my granddaughters—there's Jenny, she's three, and Amy with the pink dress, she's four...'

Indeed, Katy seemed engrossed in the game she was playing with two merry girls. And nearby at another table were two old soldiers, playing cards idly; but Rosalie remembered what Alec had said—that his men were watching the house and Katy constantly. Again, a pang of warning clamped her ribs.

Who to trust? Who to believe?

'I need to thank you,' said Rosalie quietly, 'for taking such good care of her while I've been ill.'

'Bless you, she's no trouble at all.'

Just then Katy saw her and ran up to her; Rosalie hugged her tightly. 'I'm going out for just a little while, Katy, sweetheart!'

Katy gave her a kiss, then ran off to her game again. She was happy here, as Mary said. Had settled as quickly as she'd settled into Helen's house, with Rosalie.

She realised Alec had come out and was watching. 'She makes friends easily,' he commented.

Rosalie nodded. 'She's always been adaptable.'

'How old was she when her father died?'

The question made her catch her breath, sharply. 'She was—only a baby.' She stumbled over the words. 'Really, she never knew him.'

Was there doubt in his dark eyes? If so, he let it go. 'I've just got to attend to the horses. I'll see you in the entrance hall.'

* * *

She went back to the house, her apprehension rising again. But then a great big golden dog with woebegone eyes ambled up to her and seemed to be leading her into the kitchen, where a tray of freshly baked biscuits sat on a high shelf.

He was wagging his tail so eagerly that Rosalie just had to reach for two of them, which he wolfed down as if he hadn't eaten for days. As she petted and fussed him, she didn't notice that Garrett had come in.

'Like dogs, do yer, ma'am?'

His voice made her jump out of her skin. 'Oh! Not always, to be honest. But this one—he's gorgeous! What's his name?'

'Ajax. He's a good lad, Ajax is.' Garrett was actually looking at her with something approaching friendliness. 'Been giving him some of my wife's biscuits, have you? That's good, she'd have my hide if she caught me doing it, but 'cos it's you, it's all right, see?'

Rosalie struggled with the logic of all this, but Garrett was already pointing to the door. 'The Captain says he's ready for you outside now, ma'am.'

Indeed, Alec had obtained a curricle from somewhere, harnessed to two passable greys, and Garrett rode at the back like a rich man's tiger, so private conversation was impossible.

But—she enjoyed it. She enjoyed sitting at Alec's side, wrapped up against the fresh spring breeze, looking round at London's crowds, at the shops and other carriages. She enjoyed Alec's steady presence beside her, his skilful hands so sure on the reins. The admiring glances he got from passing women, their looks of envy at her...

Pretending. That was what she was doing. Just pretending, she reminded herself. And she found talking to him easier than she'd thought, for she had a neutral topic of conversation: that garden. 'Such a beautiful place,' she said warmly. 'Or at least it must have been, once!'

He nodded. 'I'm afraid my priority is in keeping the actual house in one piece. But you're right, it was once beautiful. Don't tell me—you know something about gardens also, Mrs Rowland?'

She hesitated. 'We had a garden with the cottage in Oxfordshire. My—my mother loved it.'

Her voice faded away. Her mother had planted it with such care, to remind her of the man she'd loved. It bloomed with the English flowers: roses, hollyhocks, heart's-ease. When Linette had gone, their mother used to sit out there day after day, hoping that her lost daughter might return....

'Mrs Rowland, are you all right?'

Rosalie quickly dabbed her handkerchief to her eyes, pretending that a little dust had blown in them. 'Yes. Yes, thank you—perfectly.'

Impossible that he could have guessed at her grief— and yet it was as though he did, because Alec went on to distract her, as he drove the curricle expertly through London's streets, with descriptions of the wonderful gardens—many of them sadly ruined by war—that he'd seen in Spain and Portugal. Then he became silent, concentrating on the busy traffic, and she felt her spine tingle in renewed warning. *You have to ask him about Linette.*

But then what? If he was guilty, what did she expect him to do? What did she *want* him to do?

She wanted him to say he was sorry, perhaps. But most of all—she wanted to be wrong.

When he told her they'd arrived, she was bewildered. She'd taken little notice of their surroundings for the last ten minutes or so, being too absorbed in her own thoughts. Now, she was speechless.

They'd stopped in a street where huge mansions with white-stuccoed façades gazed benevolently down on a square filled with trees and well-tended shrubs. Liveried carriages with bewigged footmen put Alec's equipage to shame. This was Mayfair, she realised with a jolt of alarm. About as different from Two Crows Castle as a palace from a pauper's hovel. Yet Garrett was marching up to the big front door and lifting the glittering brass doorknocker as if he *knew* the place! Rosalie turned white-faced to Alec. 'Is this some kind of joke?'

'No, indeed.' Alec was watching her, with a strange expression on his face. 'We're here to look at some paintings, Mrs Rowland—remember?'

'Why, Master Alec!' cried Jarvis, brushing aside the footman who'd opened the door.

Alec returned the greeting. 'Just a quick visit, Jarvis. Is everything all right? Has my brother been?'

Jarvis frowned and lowered his voice. 'He has, sir. He came for more paintings. And he said it was all on your father's orders, Master Alec!'

'Did he, now?' Alec's voice was lethally soft.

'Most of them are back. But take a look round, do. And I see you have a companion.' Rosalie had followed Alec up the steps and stood frozen in the doorway.

'An acquaintance of mine, Jarvis,' said Alec. 'Perhaps you could find us something to eat, in an hour or so?'

'If you're hungry, Master Alec, there's plenty of food, all delivered by Berry Brothers an hour ago. A feast laid ready, in fact.'

'Food? But the house is closed up, surely!'

'Indeed, sir. And your father's cook has gone with him

to Carrfields.' The old steward's face had darkened and he lowered his voice. 'But you'll guess, I think, who ordered it—all in your father's name. Some kind of party's planned here tonight. And were we, the staff, informed in advance? No!' He shook his head. 'If you ask me, it would be justice indeed, if you and the young lady were to partake of just a little of it! And there's clothes, sir—' he pursed his lips '—clothes we were told to dispose of, because they're *no longer the fashion.*'

Alec nodded thoughtfully. Then he turned to Rosalie, who was still staring around, stunned. 'Come inside,' he said and she followed mutely as he led the way to the main hall, from which a vast double staircase rose in gilded splendour.

'This,' he said, 'at least gives you the chance to look around and see what a change of fortune has been mine.'

'Change of—?'

'All in good time. But first—I want you to tell me about some paintings.'

He saw her draw her hand across her forehead. 'Indeed, I promised to do so. But I don't understand…'

'It's quite simple. I'd like the benefit of your expertise. Take a look round here, for instance. My particular favourite was always that Poussin, by the stairs—'

'I noticed that one straight away,' she broke in, 'because it's not a Poussin!'

Well. Ro Rowland was continuing to surprise him. 'Pray continue,' Alec said softly.

'It's a good likeness,' she persisted, swiftly walking over to it, 'any art lover would know that. But of course the brushwork, let alone the balance of opaque and transparent colours, is not typical of Poussin in the least.'

He blinked. 'But of course.'

'As for that pair of portraits by Le Brun—' she swung round and pointed to another wall '—the varnish on them is quite wrong. It's too new.' She walked across to peer more closely; he tried not to notice the way her slender hips swayed as she moved. 'And the signature is,' she went on, swinging round and almost catching his too-appreciative stare, 'a forgery!'

That concentrated his wandering mind. *Those were his mother's, damn it.* 'You're quite certain?'

'I am indeed! But if you're doubting my knowledge, Captain Stewart…!'

'Not at all,' he breathed. 'Not at all, Mrs Rowland.' He bowed his head. 'I am—grateful.'

Grateful, and stunned. By her knowledge, by her damned allure—and by Stephen's damned treachery. He led her onwards.

Rosalie was bemused by this house. By the wonderful treasures within it where he was so clearly at home. But, oh, what game was he playing with her *this* time?

Her mind struggled for answers. Perhaps he was an impoverished cousin, who'd been occasionally allowed to stay. For goodness' sake, he certainly knew the vast place backwards! And he knew the paintings, too, which made up a fabulous collection. Indeed, in every salon, every chamber to which he so coolly led her, wonderful works of art adorned the walls.

But she was growing more and more concerned about them, because she considered that at least one in ten were careful forgeries. She pointed them out to him without emotion, and Alec nodded and wrote down the details in a notebook he carried.

But Rosalie failed to see what business it was of his.

In inner bewilderment, she followed him through all

the ground-floor rooms, then up to other grand chambers. 'You need not worry about us being interrupted,' he said as she hesitated outside one fine room. 'The owner is away, in the country.'

Well. If that was supposed to make her more comfortable about this intrusion into another's home, it had the opposite effect. But Alec, unfazed, led her onwards, this time to the bedrooms and dressing rooms, where the paintings were smaller, daintier. One by one she examined each work of art and reported her conclusion.

'This is the final room,' said Alec gravely, flinging open the door to a beautiful dressing chamber and adjoining bedroom. 'And by the way, I'm extremely grateful to you.'

She nodded tightly. 'As long as you or I don't end up in gaol.'

'Not us,' he said. 'Believe me, not us. What about those?'

She turned to examine one last set of exquisite French figure drawings in black-and-red chalk. 'These are not counterfeit, I'm sure. They're by Watteau. They must be very valuable.'

'Good,' he breathed. 'He always loved those pictures.'

'He?'

But Alec was already putting his notebook in his pocket. 'And that's the last of them, thank God. Rosalie, would you like some new clothes?'

Again he saw apprehension glitter in her eyes. 'Not at all. I already have those you gave me, at Two Crows Castle!'

She was pointing to the plain gown she wore, but Alec's lip curled in an ironic smile. 'All women *always* need more clothes, surely. Come and take a look in here.' He led her through to another large dressing room, and she caught her breath at the gowns, pelisses and walking dresses that were simply scattered on couches at either end of the room like jewels from a treasure trove.

'Help yourself,' he drawled.

She whipped round. 'I cannot *possibly*!'

'Let me assure you—*they will not be missed*. I'm grateful to you for examining the paintings. You can take whatever you want as your reward.' His eyes impassively assessed her figure in a way that made her skin tingle. 'Put one of these gowns on now, why not? They should all fit you.'

She was still utterly bewildered. She wanted to ask so many questions, but he was already turning to go. 'I'll see you downstairs when you've made your choice,' he said. 'Then we may as well eat. The dining room is just off the main hall. Ring the bell for a maid if you need anything.'

And he'd gone. She sat down rather suddenly on the edge of the bed. Who did these wonderful clothes belong to? Who did this mansion belong to? What was Alec Stewart doing to her brain, her existence?

He was her enemy. She'd only gone with him that dreadful night after the poetry reading because she'd had no choice; only stayed with him because she'd been so ill. He *had* to be her enemy. But why, then, did he offer to protect her against the writer of that abominable note?

I don't know. I don't know.

He thought her a whore and the knowledge seared her. He thought she'd be delighted with this treasure trove of clothes. Sick at heart, she lifted the extravagant garments one by one, until she found a modest muslin gown in midnight blue, with three-quarter-length sleeves and a fichu to cover her bosom. Then she tidied her hair, using the silver-backed brush that lay on the mirrored dressing table, and dragged it back into a ribbon.

There! Most women of the *ton* would require the assistance of two maids to adorn themselves, but not her. And if he hoped she might betray her vanity, or her—her *availability* by her choice of clothes—he'd be disappointed.

She rang the bell for a servant—she had no hope of finding her way round this palatial house by herself— and the maid, arriving, curtsied with a smile. 'You ready to go downstairs, ma'am? Master Alec said to show you the way!'

Master Alec. Another servant who knew the renegade Captain rather well. Rosalie seized a filmy cashmere shawl to drape across her arms and followed the maid downstairs, nervous again. The afternoon dusk was gathering, but wax candles had been lit throughout the house. Expense was clearly of no account here. The maid opened a door off the main hall. 'There you are, ma'am.'

Rosalie blinked in fresh amazement. This was the dining room—a room Alec hadn't yet shown her—and on a vast linen-draped table were laid out smoked hams, cold joints of beef, pies and whole cheeses, surrounded by a glittering array of porcelain and silverware. This table was set for twenty people. Bottles of wine adorned the sideboard. *'We may as well eat,'* Alec had casually said—but this was a feast!

She suddenly became aware of Alec as he entered the room behind her. 'What's this?' she breathed, turning to face him. 'Is the owner giving a party tonight?'

'It certainly looks like it. Doesn't it? And I see you found yourself something to wear.'

His dark eyes were fastened on her, in a way that somehow made her lungs ache with the need for air. The colour flared in her cheeks. 'I chose the simplest gown I could find!'

'Indeed. And it suits you.'

Rather too well, thought Alec, *damn it all*. Indeed, his pulse rate had started hammering away the minute he saw her standing there, looking so lost and so alone. She'd picked a garment that was downright plain, perhaps hoping to deter him, perhaps not.

For the clinging fabric hugged her sweet curves like blue gossamer, moving whenever she moved, clinging to her gently swelling bosom and hips, her slim thighs... As for her hair, again she had confounded him. As far as Alec was aware women spent hours over their hair, crimping it, styling it. But hers was done so artlessly—pulled up into a ribbon, yet with those few trailing locks that looked delicious enough to run through in his fingers. Devil take it, did she truly not realise how beautiful she looked? And didn't she realise—he noted it and gritted his teeth—how the fichu of her gown, too loose for her slender form, hung away from her bosom whenever she moved, so that if he gazed down at her he could see...

Don't go there. She is cleverer than you think. Alec dragged his eyes away and wished the rest of his body could be as effectively controlled.

Rosalie, too, was in turmoil, because Alec looked different. Stunningly different. He'd changed into formal attire—a black tailcoat that fitted his broad shoulders to perfection, cream skintight kerseymere breeches that clung rather too well to his strong thighs, and highly-polished Hessian boots. Sudden heat surged through her insides. Although his jaw was starting to look darkly unshaven and his thick black hair was rumpled and ungroomed, he looked quite heartbreakingly handsome.

A ripple of warning, of danger, was squeezing at her chest.

She gazed round, rather wildly looking for something to fill her thoughts other than *him*. 'Alec,' she said, 'this is not right. These clothes. The food. We are *stealing*.'

Alec regarded her with speculative dark eyes. 'Hardly,' he said. 'The food was an oversight; we have every right to help ourselves. And my clothes are my own.'

'Your—'

'Indeed. After all, this is the house I grew up in.'

Her heart had juddered completely to a halt.

'I was trying to tell you earlier,' he went on. 'But you didn't believe me, did you?'

'I thought, perhaps...'

'You thought, perhaps, that I was some impoverished relative, kept hidden below stairs when the *ton* came to call?'

She flushed. Alec could tell those were her exact suspicions.

And yet in all other ways this woman was again confounding all his expectations. Damn it all, most females would exclaim avidly over this wonderful house and any hint of a connection to such wealth. Would cry out in delight over the clothes and dress themselves, if offered the chance, in the most showy, the most expensive. *Especially* a woman who'd worked at the Temple of Beauty.

Instead, she'd chosen the simplest gown there was, which showed off her slender yet gorgeous figure to absolute perfection. She was either utterly naïve or she was playing him at his own game very cleverly.

This whole visit was intended to test her—yet it was *he* who was being wrong-footed at every turn.

Sighing inwardly at the mystery that was Rosalie Rowland, he drew out a chair for her. 'Yes, I grew up here,' he said softly. 'My father—who is away at present—is a peer of the realm—an earl, no less. And as for me—I, Mrs Rowland, am his younger son.'

Chapter Fourteen

Oh, no. Why hadn't she guessed? The way he carried himself. The way he spoke. His natural air of authority. *His father—an earl...* She dragged in a ragged breath. 'I see. And for what reason, Captain Stewart, did you decide it wasn't worth telling me this earlier?'

'I suppose I never considered it important.' Alec pulled out a chair for her, his steady eyes never leaving her face. 'And anyway, I thought we were both being selective about the truth.'

Yes. She made a tiny gesture of despair and sat down slowly. Yes, indeed. 'But how can you turn your back on all this, to live in—?'

'A wreck like Two Crows Castle?' He pulled up a chair for himself at the table, next to her. 'Simple—my father and I are not on the best of terms.' His tone was dismissive. 'And before your eyes widen at the thought of my incredible wealth, let me just point out that I'm due to inherit not one penny.'

'Do you really think I'm interested in your *wealth*? I simply don't understand why you had to deceive me, and—and...'

She stopped. He leaned across the table to put just the

tip of his forefinger on her lips. And her words dried in her throat.

'Deception? Now, I thought *you* were the master of that, Mrs Rowland,' he said quietly.

At just one touch of his fingers, she found herself racked with stomach-clenching uncertainty. He was handsome. He was formidable. He was utterly dangerous. *And soon she must ask him why her dying sister had breathed his name.*

She forced herself to appear calm. 'Where is your father?'

'He's at his estate in the country, with his wife—my stepmother.' He was unfolding his napkin. 'The clothes from which you had your choice up there are about to become my stepmother's cast-offs. She feels that all fashions are sadly outmoded after three months.'

'So your mother…'

'Died long ago, in a hunting accident.'

Rosalie's cheeks flushed. 'I'm so sorry, I didn't realise.' She hesitated. 'But this…this place, this food! Who…?'

'I told you, my father is away. The food is an error.' He was watching her quizzically as he began to carve a slice of ham for her. 'And do you know, I think I've had enough of your questions for the time being, Ro Rowland. You're not an investigative reporter now.'

She shivered at the sting in his calm voice. But—Alec Stewart, the black sheep of an extremely wealthy family. In those clothes, she could believe it. So different from his usual attire, yet still so rawly masculine. She tossed her head. He'd put them on to impress on her, no doubt, that he was an earl's son! In case she started getting ideas above her station, perhaps.

'Why don't you eat?' he asked almost languidly. 'Take your pick. Chicken *gélatine*. Buttered lobster. Veal pie…'

'I—I can't. I'm worried about Katy.'

'I've told you—Katy is quite safe at Two Crows Castle with my men guarding her. Happy, too. And you're no use to her at all if you're half-dead from hunger. Eat. Drink. You've been ill— you need to build up your strength.' He'd already filled her glass with a fine white wine.

'You are rather taking my breath away with all these surprises,' she said as steadily as she could.

He was cutting some pie to put on her plate. 'Then get your revenge. Tell me more about your childhood. You've already informed me your mother was French and your father an English painter. But wasn't it a strange decision for your mother to move to England when he died?'

'My mother had no family left in Paris. And I think my parents had always planned to move back to England some day. So she decided to take us—'

'Us,' he broke in. 'Do you have brothers? Sisters?'

Oh, a blunder there. 'A sister. One sister.'

He drank his wine, still carefully watching her. 'And did your little family find a friendly welcome at this cottage in Oxfordshire?'

This time she met his brooding gaze steadily. 'Thanks to the war, my mother's nationality was regarded as little short of a crime. And the cottage turned out to be almost a ruin. Yet my mother would not leave—partly because she had nowhere else to go, but also because it had been my father's dying wish that she come to the place he'd loved...' She paused to fight back the ache rising in her throat.

'And now your mother is dead. Your husband, too.' His voice was soft.

Oh, Lord, her lies. 'Yes, indeed!' She drank some wine—she certainly needed it.

He met her eyes calmly. The light from the candles defined anew the sculpted planes and angles of his lean, square-jawed face. He continued, 'So you decided to come to London. As a writer of scandal-broth, or as a prostitute at the Temple of Beauty?'

She should have expected it. She should not have let it wound her so. But it did, oh, it did.

She tossed her head in defiance. 'Well, both, of course! I really do not see why I should not make extra money out of my experiences with the gentlemen of the town, by writing a piece or two!'

'I can see why not,' he broke in flatly. 'It could be damned dangerous. Men don't like their secret lives exposed.'

She gripped her wineglass. Was he warning her not to dig too deeply into *his* private life? 'Oh, I make sure everything I write is completely anonymous!'

She laughed, as if it were all very amusing, but she could see he wasn't amused in the slightest, because he cut in, '*Somebody* is worried about you saying too much, clearly.' His eyes were fixed, darkly, at some place below her throat, and she realised that her fichu had fallen to display a disgraceful amount of bosom. Colouring hotly, she snatched it back up.

'You're thinking of that threat,' she whispered.

'Naturally. And there's not only the threat, Mrs Rowland.' His features were sombre. 'My men have been offered money, to turn you and the child in.'

'They've—' The food she'd just taken stuck in her throat.

'That's right. There's an underworld reward out for you. The usual sort of thing, all done anonymously. The word has gone round the lowlife drinking dens that if you and your child are delivered up at a certain time and place, the money will be handed over, no questions asked.' He paused while the shock surged through her. 'I know, by the way,' he went on, 'that Katy is not yours.'

This time she had to grip the table for support. Her stomach knotted. 'What makes you think…?'

'How do I know you're lying? First: you seem to have no idea when her father died—indeed, you're not even certain of the child's age. Second: I've noticed that whenever Katy sees you she says, *'Mama?'*—but she's looking for someone else. Three: she was not with you when you first arrived in London.'

She stared at him, stricken.

'Enough, enough,' he said with a gesture of dismissal. 'I have no right to question you so, and I assume you are looking after Katy for the best of reasons. Now it's your turn—ah, how your writer's mind must be whirling with curiosity. "What was it like being born into a rich family, Alec? And how, for God's sake, did you manage to make such an almighty mess of it all?" Admit it, you're just longing to know!'

'I think perhaps you've already told me,' she said tightly. 'That you and your father are estranged.'

'Indeed. And of course it's the custom of the aristocracy anyway to leave everything to the oldest.' He drank more wine.

'But surely you could have married…'

'Married into wealth? Ah, yes, once I was betrothed to the granddaughter of a duke. But she was in love with a make-believe hero—and, by God, she must count herself lucky to have broken it off, now she sees that I run a damned seedy fencing school in Spitalfields packed to the rafters with destitute ex-soldiers—out of whom I make absolutely nothing.'

A reminder of yet another of her errors. She bit her lip.

'But surely,' she began, 'you would have had other choices! There can be no need for you to—to…'

'To live as I do? Mingle with men of the lower class?' His voice had become softly lethal. 'For a courtesan and a pedlar of news sheets, you're rather pompous, aren't you, Mrs Rowland? Perhaps it's your mother's French blood showing through—'

He broke off, because she'd put her knife and fork down suddenly. There were small spots of colour burning in her cheeks. 'Please do not insult my mother. You may say what you like about me—but not her!'

Alec looked at her, just for a moment. Curse it, this had been a stupid idea to bring her here. Doomed from the start. Furious with himself, he pushed back his chair and stood. 'Come,' he said. His dark eyes were shuttered. 'I'll take you back. Time we were leaving.'

She tilted her chin. 'Very well. But I will get changed first. I do not wish to wear this gown a moment longer.'

'As you wish.' Swiftly he came round to draw back her chair and help her to her feet.

But the sudden warmth of his hand on her slender arm unsettled her so badly that she tripped as she rose and stumbled against the table, and worse was to come, for she realised in horror that the cursed fichu had slipped down, almost baring her breasts. Even as she dragged it up again she saw the look of scorn in his eyes. *He thought she'd done it deliberately.*

'Well, Mrs Rowland,' he drawled, 'you're playing dangerous games today.'

She whirled on him. 'A gentleman, Captain Stewart, would have turned his eyes away!'

'Oh, did you want me to?' he asked softly. 'I rather thought all that was part of your plan.'

She tried to push past him, head held high. He stood

in her way. Her voice shook slightly. 'Please let me pass. I just want to go and get out of this—garment. And return to Katy.'

He captured her shoulders, his long fingers warm and sensuous through the fabric of her gown. 'Playing games,' he repeated softly.

'I think,' she said steadily, 'that *you* are the one playing games. And aren't you enjoying them?'

'Very much. Aren't you?'

The air around them changed. Tightened.

'Alec,' she began, her insides suddenly lurching, but she had no idea what she meant to say. All she knew was that his arms were around her, his chest like a wall against her soft breasts. All she could see when she looked up was his hard face, burning with an emotion she did not dare to name.

Fight him. You have to fight him.

Yet his lips were wicked temptation. His hard-muscled body was a challenge and an enticement. Sal had told her it was easy to deal with men—*Remember, they're all ruled by one rather vital part of their anatomy*—but Sal hadn't told her how very difficult it would be to resist her own primal urges.

He fitted his mouth to hers and her world spun.

There was nothing gentle about his kiss. And Alec didn't mean it to be gentle. His hands had snaked round her waist, pulling her close; her face was lifted to his, her eyes wide and flaring, her lips full—with doubt?—with desire? He claimed her mouth with the savage hunger he'd been feeling for hours. For days, damn it.

So had she, to judge by the way her hands had stolen up to cling round the nape of his neck, the way her slender body was moulding itself to his, as she surrendered to the fierce hunger of his lips and tongue. Heat consumed him as her hands swept his shoulders and he in turn let his own palms sweep down over the flimsy muslin to caress the curve of her hips, to splay his fingers and haul her against his hardening desire...

Dear God, swore Alec. She was *inviting* his ravishment. His sure hand caressed the column of her throat, sliding down to rest for a moment on the swelling curve of her breast, then slipping beneath the filmy fabric to caress one soft nipple with the pad of his thumb.

Rosalie felt the coral peak tingle and harden, tightening a cord of desire that reached to her womb, while his sensual wide mouth coaxed her lips apart and his tongue stroked hers with relentless, exquisite pleasure. His hand closed round her breast—warm, hard, erotic. Then he had her in his arms again and his kiss possessed her utterly.

Lost in a delicious haze of wine and longing, she was only faintly aware that he'd moved towards a sturdy chair and was guiding her on to his lap, still kissing her, as her arms clasped him instinctively.

And now, somehow, he'd eased her breast from her bodice. She let out a low cry of loss as he abandoned her mouth, but it changed to a cry of delight as his lips claimed one nipple. She gasped with amazement as his tongue, swirling round the stiffened peak, sent waves of rapture rippling through her entire body.

She clung to him as if he were her pillar of safety, when he was anything but; she was throwing her head back and gasping as his teeth nipped lightly, aware now that his hand was sliding up her leg, caressing the silken skin above her stocking top, stealing up to the juncture of her thighs, then seeking—and finding—the moist warmth at her feminine core.

She was damp, shaking, enraptured. Her hands digging

into his hard-muscled back were her only anchor on reality. With devastating skill he swept his strong, knowing fingers across the swollen bud again and again, watching her with smouldering eyes as she arched herself against him, all restraint forgotten, and cried his name aloud as the sweet, unfurling spasms of her climax shook her body.

Her eyes had fluttered shut. Her lips were tingling and parted. Even when the last echo of rapture had died away, she kept her eyes closed. She had not known that she could feel like this. A savage pain clawed at her stomach. Perhaps she *was* a whore, to give herself so readily, so eagerly.

He was already lifting her from his lap and setting her on her feet. And he was—just watching her. She gathered herself up, feeling cold away from the shelter of his arms. Feeling—*terrified* at what she'd just let him do to her.

'I rather think it's yourself that you should not trust, Mrs Rowland,' he said softly at last. 'Do us both a favour by going and putting on a dress that at least covers you. Do you hear me?'

A feeling not just of anger, but of utter loss, was squeezing at her heart. 'You misunderstand and misjudge me at every turn, Captain Stewart,' she said in a low voice.

'No doubt.' He dragged his hand through his dark hair and stood up also; he was trembling with tension, she realised, as if every muscle in his powerful body was held on the tightest of leashes. His lip curled when he saw her eyes slide, horrified, away from his skintight breeches. 'Indeed, I'm rather a handy scapegoat for all your foolhardy experiments, aren't I? You can see it's time you and I were leaving. *Now.* Go and wrap yourself in your usual drab attire, then we'll get back to the child in your care. Or had you forgotten her—again?'

That hurt. Oh, that hurt. She clenched her fists. 'It was *you* who insisted I stay here to be impressed by this place that was once your home! You who implied I ought to repay you for your dubious protection by spending two hours examining paintings, when I only wanted to get back to Katy! You are overbearing and unjust and hateful! Damn you to hell, Alec Stewart!'

He gazed down at her, his eyes bleak. 'No need. I'm already there.'

She stumbled away.

Chapter Fifteen

Alec sat there with his head in his hands. His lust for her was raging. The hardness between his thighs still throbbed.

Rosalie Rowland. Writer, courtesan and all-round troublemaker. In her way she'd been absolutely right to accuse him of trying to impress her with this magnificent place that he'd once called home. Certainly, he'd hoped to trick her into making mistakes. Yet it was *he* who had handled everything so badly.

In fact, until she'd let her damned fichu slip like that, he'd begun to feel that he'd got everything wrong about her. He clenched his jaw. Damn it, she'd had a lucky escape. One more minute of her passionate response to his foolhardy kiss and he'd have been hard-pressed to stop himself ravishing her there and then.

Alec got to his feet and paced the room like a caged animal. Why had he let things go so far? Well, he had plenty of answers. Not least of his motivations—and certainly the worst—was his impulse to prove to himself that she was indeed any man's for the taking.

Yet once again he'd been baffled by Rosalie Rowland. Most women of experience would have realised that Alec was aroused virtually to the point of no return. Most women would have offered some sort of physical relief— but she had made no attempt whatsoever to assuage his rampant desire.

The enigmatic, tormenting Mrs Rowland. Everything about her stoked up the fire of his vital male urges—but ever since that first night at the Temple of Beauty, he'd not been able to make sense of her. He was utterly perplexed by the way she moved and spoke so gracefully, by the way she'd so solemnly examined those pictures for him and calmly delivered her judgement.

At Dr Barnard's tawdry show she'd stood out from the other jades like a pure-white wax candle burning amidst a mass of burned-down tallow ones. But how could she be unspoiled? Innocent? No. For God's sake, she'd been married, she'd been at the Temple of Beauty! She was still lying to him; he'd still be thinking Katy was hers, had it not been for Mary's suspicions— *'She doesn't even know the child's age for sure, Captain Stewart!'* And of course there was Garrett's news that last winter Rosalie had been visiting one London theatre after another, asking for someone called Linette.

Who was Linette? Alec drove one fist against the other. Who had sent that nasty threat? Who was trying to bribe Alec's men to betray her? What the hell had he let himself in for, by offering to protect her?

Upstairs, Rosalie gazed at herself in the cheval glass. She'd swiftly got changed back into the old, drab gown, but she had yet to summon up the courage to go downstairs and face him after betraying herself yet again, this time with so much more than a kiss.

Dear God. The pleasure, the molten ecstasy summoned by his mouth, his long lean fingers…

She saw in the mirror that her lips were rosy and swollen from the harshness of his mouth. *You must tell him that Katy is your dead sister's child. You must ask him why Linette named him as she lay dying.*

Not tomorrow. Not later. But now.

She pressed her palms to her hot cheeks. One thing was certain. She could not go on much longer in this hell of uncertainty.

She went downstairs slowly, wearing her old grey mantle. Alec was at the far side of the room and he barely glanced at her. Clearly, she realised with a lurching stomach, he regretted what had just happened every bit as much as she did. He said, 'A few more minutes and we'll be ready to leave. I told Garrett to pick us up at six.'

She nodded, realising he was going round extinguishing the candles. He'd taken off his fine coat and his shirt sleeves fell back to his elbows as he reached for the higher sconces, revealing strong brown forearms that rippled with muscle and sinew.

Rosalie was about to tear her eyes away, but suddenly, in the flickering half-light, she saw an ugly, jagged scar that snaked up from his wrist. 'Oh, my goodness.' The words burst out on impulse. 'Whatever happened to your arm?'

He glanced at it almost casually. 'That? A French bayonet at Vittoria.'

Her mind reeled. 'But...'

'It was the battle that finally drove the French out of Spain,' he said tersely. 'June 1813.'

'I know.' Her lips and tongue would hardly work. 'I know... Alec, were you *there*?'

He let out a sharp laugh. 'Don't make a hero out of me. Any soldier who could hold a weapon was at Vittoria. We were outnumbered and it was a desperate struggle, full of scenes I hope you can't begin to imagine.'

'Were you with Wellington's army all that summer?'

'All that year,' he answered shortly. 'No home leave for the officers.'

The full implications of it tore through her whole being. *Dear God.* He was in Spain with the army when Linette was seduced. He could not be Katy's father...

'Alec,' she whispered. What could she say? She knew what she should say. *Alec, I have been so determined to misjudge you. I have wronged you grievously...*

He turned to her and at that very moment she saw just a man, a brave man—a hero, whatever he said, for some reason in a state of utter self-loathing. *Alec, I'm so sorry.* She went deliberately towards his tense figure and placed her hand on that ugly scar.

He caught her hand and pushed it away. He was towering over her and she felt fear scudding through her again as he said roughly, 'You have a liking for playing with fire, Mrs Rowland.'

She stood firm. He thought that her gentle caress—really an acknowledgement of her own fallibility—was just another attempt to entrap him. But now she knew. Now was the time to speak.

She lifted her head. 'Alec, you told me that Katy and I would be safe with you. And I wish, how I wish, that I'd trusted you. I—I've been foolish, I've been *wrong*... But now I want to tell you that Katy was my sister's child.'

He'd gone very still. *'Linette,'* he breathed. 'Linette was your sister.'

Her gaze flew up to meet his. 'You knew already—how?'

He was rubbing his forehead as if some tight band enclosed it. 'Damn it, I've been making my own investigations. I know you were only at the Temple for one night, but before then you'd been trailing all round London's theatres, asking questions. Asking about someone called Linette.' He pulled out a chair. *'Explain.'*

And her words began to tumble out.

'Linette was two years younger than me, Alec.' Her voice was so low, he strained to catch her words. 'She left home three years ago. She became pregnant in the summer of 1813; Katy is her daughter, Alec, and Linette, poor Linette…' her voice broke just a little '…died in abject poverty. I came to London to look for the man who did this to her.'

'You should have told me,' his voice rasped.

'I could not,' she breathed, 'I could not, because at first I thought it was *you*.'

As she uttered those fateful words, Rosalie felt as if something within her had died. Every syllable condemned her more surely in this man's eyes. Oh, how he would despise her now.

Explain, he'd said, and it all poured out: how Linette had whispered his name as she lay dying, how Linette had said he had a castle.

He had pulled a chair up for himself, and sat in the half-shadow from the dying fire, watching her. At last he said, 'She was looking for a refuge, perhaps. Sometimes we take in homeless women as well as men at Two Crows Castle. You'll have noticed them—often they help Mary with the housework, until we can find them somewhere better.'

'Yes.' She nodded, her throat still tight. 'My sister whispered, "Take me to him, please". I thought—I thought perhaps she'd loved you, but now I see that she'd not even met you, Alec. You don't turn anyone away and Linette must have heard that. I realise everything now.'

Too late.

From first seeing him, Rosalie had been drawn to his—*integrity*, that was the word. Alec had maintained Two Crows Castle because he cared about those soldiers. He had rescued her from Lord Maybury because he was concerned about her and Katy. Katy had trusted him straight away. If only she'd done the same. He would never, ever forgive her for her stupidity.

'Anyone would have told you I was in Spain with the army all through the summer of 1813,' he said, only echoing her own bitter regrets. 'And you were taking a great risk, asking your questions all around London.'

'I thought I was being careful.' She was defensive now and growing tired.

'You've managed to alarm someone—badly. Don't forget about that threat and the bribes offered to my men.'

She lifted her gaze to him. 'Is Linette's seducer behind it all?'

'I would think so indeed,' he answered quietly.

Oh, God. No word of reproach for her vile insults to him, her foolish actions, her multiple mistakes. She dragged air into her lungs. 'Alec,' she said, 'I'm sorry, to have so wrongly suspected you. I've been so stupid. Why are you being kind to me?'

He sighed, then got up and walked over to the mantelpiece to douse another flickering candle. 'Perhaps because I don't like injustice. And don't be so hard on yourself. On the contrary, I think you've been rather brave, coming to London and undertaking the search on your own.'

'Linette was my sister,' she answered simply. 'Wouldn't anyone do the same for their family? Isn't family loyalty perhaps the most basic human instinct of all?'

He caught his breath. 'Your loyalty is indeed admirable,' was all he said. 'Do you have any more clues, apart from the fact that Linette wanted to be an actress and once worked at the Temple of Beauty?'

She told him about Marchmont's theatre, and Dr Barnard's register, hidden inside *The Myths of Apollodorus*. He listened intently.

'I'll make enquiries, as well,' he said.

She gasped. 'You *will*?'

'Put it this way—someone dangerous is after you and I'd rather like to find out who. No promises, but my men are useful at unearthing secrets.' He looked at his watch and gave her a smile that sent her spirits plummeting, because it was a sad smile, a regretful smile. 'Time to get back to Two Crows Castle, Rosalie. Though there is just one more thing. You've already understood, I think, that you must place yourself in my care, under my protection. In return, I'll make a promise to *you*. From now on, I'll ensure that you can trust me. In absolutely every way. Do I make myself clear?'

Oh, yes. She knew exactly what he meant. In other words, he wouldn't lay a finger on her again. She got to her feet slowly and an ache of sheer loss swept through her at the memory of those burning caresses to which she'd so rapturously surrendered. 'I don't think you should take any blame for what happened just now,' she whispered.

Something of her inner misery must have shown, because he touched her hand gently. 'Nor yourself, Rosalie. We'll find the man who seduced your sister, never fear—and I suspect we'll find he's the same man who is threatening you.' His hand was gone, leaving her cold. 'In the meantime,' he went on, 'my men deserve a pleasant surprise. Don't you think?' He'd carelessly pulled on his fine coat again, then picked up some empty sacks she'd not noticed before and began to load food from the table

into them. Hams, pies, whole cheeses, loaves of bread—
in they went, until the sacks were bulging.

She gasped. 'What are you doing?'

He grinned, white teeth flashing. 'Taking this lot back
to Two Crows Castle. Jarvis brought me these sacks while
you were upstairs. I rather think this food is needed there
more than here, don't you?'

She thought of the hungry, ragged soldiers. 'Oh, indeed!
But—won't it be missed?'

'I told you my father's gone to the country and won't
be wanting any of this. So I'm helping myself. How does
that rate on your journalist's scale of crimes?'

'I think it's an excellent idea! But, Alec...'

'Hmm?' He was still packing the things, but he swung
round to look at her.

'Alec,' she said impulsively, 'there's always a cluster of
beggars at the corner of Lothbury. We passed them on our
way. There's so much food here—will you give a little of
it to them, on our way back?'

'Willingly. If you'll also take a sack and put in some of
those pies that are on the sideboard, I'll tell Jarvis we're
leaving. And I've got something for him.' He flourished
the list he'd made of the counterfeit paintings.

'The paintings! I'd almost forgotten. Oh, what are you
going to do about them?'

'Make sure the originals all mysteriously find their
way back here,' he assured her. 'Now, if you look outside,
I think you'll find Garrett's arrived with transport.' He
strode to the door. 'Jarvis!'

The elderly steward quickly appeared. 'Sir?' Alec gave
him his list and had a quiet word before heading for the
door. Indeed, out in the street were Garrett and big red-
bearded Sergeant McGrath with a shabby old carriage.

'Some supplies, lads, for Two Crows Castle,' Alec announced cheerfully, pointing towards the sacks of food assembled in the hall.

'Yes, sir!' Eagerly the men began to load the carriage. Alec helped, too, and when they were finished he guided Rosalie out to the vehicle.

'That's about it,' Alec said to Garrett. He looked around. 'Oh, and by the way—we're going to drop a sack of food off at the corner of Lothbury.'

'Right you are, Captain.' Garrett nodded. He turned with an awkward smile to Rosalie. 'All right, ma'am? Your little 'un, she's fine, but she'll be glad to see you back!' Then he scrambled up on to the driver's box next to Mc-Grath, who was already holding the reins.

Alec shot Rosalie a look of complete astonishment. 'My God. Garrett *smiled* at you. What magic have you worked on him?'

'I don't know really. Perhaps it's because I was kind to his dog?'

Alec lifted his eyebrows. 'You're a witch, Mrs Rowland,' he said softly, 'and in another few days you'll have us all eating out of the palm of your hand.'

Rosalie froze again. *Mrs Rowland*—oh, God. She'd told him about Linette, but she hadn't confessed to the rest of her lies—for example, her fictitious widowhood. But if she told him she was *not* married, he would perhaps start to doubt every single thing she'd ever said and might refuse to let her stay at Two Crows Castle. Might refuse flatly to help her any further.

He was watching her quizzically. 'Something wrong?'

'No!' She shook her head, forcing a smile. 'And, Alec—thank you. For offering me your help.'

'Think nothing of it.' He was about to hand her up into the carriage, but then he hesitated. 'Although one thing worries me. Even though we know—you and I—that you are quite safe with me, staying at Two Crows Castle, your reputation will be shot to pieces, to put it politely.'

She almost laughed. That was the least of her problems. 'Oh, goodness! And there was I, hoping for a top-lofty proposal or two at the start of the next Season! I'm afraid, Captain Stewart, that my hopes for a respectable future are already pretty low. And appearing at the Temple of Beauty most definitely did nothing to improve my chances!'

'You had no dreams of getting married again?' he asked quietly.

'Lord, no.'

'You feel that no one could replace your husband?'

She shrugged. 'If you wish to put it like that, yes.'

He was watching her carefully. 'Mrs Rowland—Rosalie—I hope we can at least be friends.'

She nodded mutely as he handed her in and followed behind. Out on the driver's box, Garrett and Sergeant McGrath were singing heartily as the horses pulled the laden coach briskly eastwards into darker, narrower streets. Alec joined in, his voice a melodious baritone that she instantly adored.

'Some talk of Alexander, and some of Hercules,
Of Hector and Lysander, and such great names as these.
But of all the world's great heroes, there's none that can compare
With a tow, row, row, row, row, row
To the British Grenadiers...'

He smiled at her. She smiled back, even joining in the chorus. But her heart was heavy. She had mistrusted him and lied to him. Yes, she now had him on her side in her struggle to find Linette's seducer. But he had also promised her that he would never touch her again and she was just realising how devastating those simple words could be.

'Horse,' said Katy, happily waving her new little wooden toy. 'Horse.'

Katy was in the parlour off the kitchen when they returned, sitting in Mary's comfortable lap. All around was evidence of a pleasant family shopping trip: gingerbread men, a penny whistle, ribbons and other toys. 'We took the children up Bishopsgate,' Mary explained. 'With some of the Captain's men, of course. I do hope you don't mind, ma'am?'

'Not at all.' Rosalie smiled down at Katy. 'Your little horse is beautiful, darling.'

'For Polly-doll.' Katy perched her little rag doll on the new horse. Alec had entered the room behind Rosalie and came over to gently ruffle the child's dark hair. When Rosalie saw the look of tenderness in his eyes for Katy, it lanced her.

'Bedtime, Katy,' she said lightly. She picked the little girl up, breathing in the sweet infant scent of her skin, and started for the stairs, but turned back. 'Thank you,' she said fervently to Mary and Garrett and all the others, 'for looking after her so well today. For looking after *both* of us so well.'

Mary beamed. 'It's a pleasure, ma'am.'

Rosalie put Katy carefully in her little bed and sang her sister's child to sleep. Alec had offered her his help and protection; therefore she had to endure living under the roof of a man who affected her as no man ever had done before. And Lord, it was going to be difficult.

Alec went to his room and cursed softly under his breath. Ever since he'd seen Rosalie Rowland at the Temple of Beauty, he couldn't get her out of his mind. And today, at his father's house, how he'd managed to control himself, he'd never know.

He could have taken her so easily. But he'd restrained himself with an iron will, because he still had not been sure of her motives. And—because, strangely, she seemed to trust him. She wouldn't if she knew *his* secrets.

He raked his hand through his hair. Earlier today, a note had been delivered for him. He'd cracked open the seal with a bitter heart, not needing to look at the signature to know who it was from, because he was already alerted by the faint scent of gardenias that imbued the expensive notepaper.

Alec. I am back in London before your father, who is following in a few days. I'm staying in Bedford Street, because the Belgrave Square house needs to be prepared. I know there are risks, my dear, but might I see you at Lord Fanton's ball? There are things I need to tell you.

It was from his stepmother. His beautiful stepmother. And Lord Fanton's ball was tomorrow night.

There was a knock and Garrett came in. 'Captain. You asked us to find out who started the fire at the place where the girl lived—and who smashed up the printing press there, too.'

'I take it you've found out?'

And Garrett told him.

After Garrett left, Alec paced the room. *Stephen's men.* In God's name, why?

He rather feared he was beginning to know the answer.

That night Stephen was at his father's house and in a raging temper. This evening's gathering was to have been a fine one for his friends: a delectable supper followed by drinking and gaming, with a few high-class whores performing their tricks at midnight.

But—there had been no food. No wine. Devil take it, Stephen's failure of a party would be sniggered over around the clubs of London for weeks to come, thanks to his damned brother!

And then Jarvis, the old fool, had directed Stephen specifically to the drawing room, where he was immediately confronted with—the paintings. The labels that had been tied to one frame after another. *Counterfeit*, those labels had screamed out in large letters. Stephen had roamed the house, his agitation increasing. *Counterfeit*. And every identification, without fail, was correct.

It must be Alec! But how had his damned brother detected it, when the whole business had been conducted with such care? Sending them for cleaning, having them copied and selling off the originals had seemed an inspiration.

Hell's teeth, would Alec tell their father?

Finally there was the fact—which he'd forced out of old Jarvis—that Alec still had the girl, Rosalie, from the Temple of Beauty, under his protection. And Stephen was beginning to guess that the child she kept with her might not be Rosalie's at all.

His threats had achieved nothing. He'd hoped to bribe some of Alec's ruffians into betraying her, but the opposite seemed to have happened. Damn it all, this could be lethal. Especially if Alec was starting to guess the truth!

Chapter Sixteen

When Rosalie came downstairs the next day, the place seemed altogether quiet. Most of the soldiers were at their various places of work and Captain Stewart was also out on business, she was told.

For a while she read stories to Katy and Mary's grand-daughters, then helped with their lunch. But when it became clear that Alec would be absent all day, she grew restless.

'Please let me do something to help you,' Rosalie asked Mary, who as usual was busy in the kitchen with her baking and her laundry. 'Are there any more shirts to mend?'

'Lord bless you, I've got my two women, Janey and Bess, to help with that. But the sun's shining, it's a lovely afternoon. Why don't you take the little ones into the garden to play?'

So Rosalie did. And looking round, while the girls busied themselves setting out their toys for a tea party, she could see how beautiful this place must once have been. Ajax had joined them, sprawling hopefully in the sun while Katy and her friends feasted on milk and fresh-baked scones. Rosalie smiled at the big golden dog. 'Ajax. You are a good, good boy. Aren't you?' She slipped him a buttered scone and the dog snuggled closer to her side.

The children were absorbed in their make-believe party and the usual soldiers were around to watch them, so Rosalie, with Ajax at her heels, began to explore the overgrown thickets of shrubs that lay beyond the paved terrace. Under the ivy and sprawling wild clematis she found old stone urns, intricate paths and trellised arbours. Everywhere were vivid pockets of flowers and unpruned shrubs— blackthorns, primroses, buttercups and half-wild blue hyacinths that filled the air with their sweet scent. Flowers her mother had loved so.

As she returned to the terrace she became aware of Garrett leaning against the back door, watching her. 'I was wonderin' where that dog had got to,' he said. 'So you've been explorin' our garden, ma'am, have you?'

She seized her chance. 'Yes, and it's beautiful! I don't suppose, Mr Garrett—are there any tools I could borrow to clear it? A trowel, perhaps, and a pair of shears?'

He blinked. 'You want to clear this 'ere garden?'

'Well, yes, just a little. Nobody would mind, would they?'

Eyepatch wasn't Alec Stewart's lieutenant for nothing. Within ten minutes he'd unearthed a store of ancient gardening implements from an old outhouse and recruited four ex-soldiers who couldn't wait to take on their new role as gardeners.

Under Rosalie's supervision, her team—three of them elderly, one a young lad, Mikey—began to turn the derelict old wilderness into something rather magical. Rosalie worked as well as keeping an eye on the children, who were making daisy chains to rope round the docile Ajax's neck.

But every time she heard a man's voice in the distance, she wondered if Alec was back yet.

* * *

In the evening she bathed Katy and put her to bed as usual. And as she headed down the stairs, she saw Alec standing in the hallway talking to Garrett.

Emotion jolted her. He must have come back a while ago and changed, because he was dressed formally, in the black tailcoat and cream breeches he'd worn at his father's house yesterday. He had shaved. And brushed back his thick hair. He looked relaxed, and devastating.

Dressed for supper, at Two Crows Castle? She thought not. 'I've got your horse ready, Captain,' Garrett was saying.

Then Alec spotted Rosalie. 'Mrs Rowland. I trust you've had a pleasant day?'

Rosalie came on down the stairs, forcing herself to sound calm. 'Very pleasant, thank you, Captain. You're going out this evening?'

'To a party,' he answered, absently fingering his starched neckcloth. 'A long-standing invitation, I'm afraid.'

A cold fist was squeezing the air from her lungs. He was going to a place that was part of his world, and of course she wasn't in it… *For heaven's sake, you little fool, once he was betrothed to the granddaughter of a duke!*

'You sound regretful,' she said mildly. 'But I hope you enjoy yourself—and I like your Gordian Knot.'

His hand flew to his cravat. 'You're knowledgeable.'

'Oh, I once wrote an article about men's neckwear for *The Scribbler*—' She broke off. *Idiot. He hates your writing.*

But his handsome face relaxed into a smile that made her insides turn over. 'Then I'm flattered that you approve of my choice.'

Mentally she was flaying herself. Yesterday at his father's house she'd dared to wonder if he'd put on those clothes to impress *her*. How stupid could she be?

He was smoothing his coat sleeves, glancing down to check his gleaming topboots. 'How is Katy?'

'Oh, she's sleeping now, but she was happy, very happy, with the toys you allowed Mary to buy for her yesterday, thank you. That little horse nearly went in the bath with her!'

Another flicker of a smile. 'I'm sorry I have to go out. We must find time to speak in the morning, Mrs Rowland.' He looked, for a moment, as if he was about to say something else. Then he quickly bowed his head and left.

She went to sit down in the little parlour off the hall. She'd wanted to talk to him, oh, about the garden, and about Linette, and—just *talk* to him. She felt hollow inside with his departure. She caught a sharp breath, surprised at how she could physically *hurt* so.

And then, through the open door, she heard Garrett saying in a low voice to McGrath, 'So *she's* back in town. That's why he's goin' to this fancy ball, our Captain. Dear God, she's beautiful, but she's wrecked his life, and you'd think he'd have more sense than to get within a hundred miles of her...' They wandered on towards the kitchen where the soldiers gathered in the evening.

And Rosalie had no doubt at all that they were speaking of his lost heiress. She could almost hear Alec's voice— *'She was in love with a make-believe hero and must count herself lucky to have broken it off.'* He was too proud, far too proud, to admit to anyone, let alone Rosalie, that he still had longings for what could never be.

'I hope we can at least be friends,' Alec had said to her earlier.

She felt like writing his words on her tormented heart.

Friends, Mrs Rowland, you idiot. And with that, you will be content. Do you understand?

A small string orchestra played discreetly in a corner of the grand salon of Lord Fanton's house in exclusive Sackville Street and the chink of glasses punctuated the murmur of polite conversation. It had been a long time since Alec had been anywhere like this.

Lord Lucas Conistone, laconic and immaculate, was at his side—in fact, they'd arrived together—and Lucas was murmuring, 'Brace yourself, dear fellow. Can't be worse than when you and I dressed up as Spanish peasants to sneak inside French-held Badajoz!'

'How we got away with it,' breathed Alec, 'God knows. Both of us are too damned tall.'

'And your Spanish was execrable,' accused Lucas with a grin.

'At least I didn't let myself be waylaid by every Spanish señorita who gave me a pretty smile!'

'They weren't just after me!' retorted Lucas merrily. 'Good Lord, those females were baiting their traps for you, too, just as they are now!'

Indeed, people were watching them and murmuring behind raised hands. The presence of Lord Conistone was always noteworthy at any social event, and though Alec was known to be estranged for some reason from his father, society's foremost hostesses were always eager to have a handsome war hero who was also the son of an earl to adorn their gatherings.

Soon the two men were in the midst of a babble of old army colleagues, though after a while Lucas was swept away to talk politics, since some of his Whig associates were hoping to persuade him into a government post. But before he went, he was at Alec's side, saying quietly, 'All right if I move on, old friend?'

'Certainly. I'll see you later, Lucas.'

Because the conversation Alec had come here for had to be held in private.

Alec had called at his father's house on his way, to be regaled by Jarvis with the tale of Stephen's reaction last night to the missing food. 'Was my brother angry, Jarvis?'

'You could say that, sir.' Jarvis's cheeks creased in a smile. 'His guests left almost as soon as they arrived, once Lord Stephen told them there was no food or drink.'

Alec pictured the scene. 'I hope he didn't take it out on you?'

'I pointed out, Master Alec, that the tradesmen's bills were in the Earl's name and that, since the Earl was away, I'd no clear idea for whom the goods were intended. As far as I was aware, you, sir, had as much right to the food and wine as Lord Stephen!'

'You're a good man, Jarvis.' Alec looked around the big hall. 'What about the paintings?'

'Lord Stephen said nothing about them whatsoever, sir. But he noticed those labels you'd asked me to fasten on. And only an hour ago, he was back here bringing in some new ones—or should I say, the *originals*, sir—and telling me some story about mistakes having been made at the restorer's shop!'

Alec had smiled grimly at the thought of Stephen's angry confusion. And now, at Lord Fanton's, he continued to mingle with the top-lofty guests and even allowed himself to be pressed into introductions by the determined mamas of marriageable daughters. 'He's the younger son of the Earl of Aldchester, you know,' he heard the old tabbies whispering avidly. 'There's some sort of family problem, and sweet Lady Emilia found him just a little difficult. But even so, he's a catch, my dears, a catch!'

Alec talked and smiled politely, but he never stopped watching as the guests arrived; he didn't have to wait long. He felt all his muscles tensing as she came in. She was so breathtakingly beautiful. No wonder everyone in the room turned to stare. No wonder his father had fallen in love with her so irrevocably.

Though the dancing had begun, Alec resisted suggestions that he might lead some fair maiden on to the floor. Likewise he refused invitations to a game as his friends moved through to the card room. Really he was just waiting for the moment he'd come here for.

He heard, at last, her silken voice at his shoulder. 'Alec, my dear. You got my note.'

The feline purr was all too familiar. Alec turned slowly to see Susanna, with her gleaming dark curls, her porcelain skin and sultry, dark-blue eyes.

'I got your note, yes, Susanna,' he said. 'You wanted to see me.'

She put her hand on his arm. 'And so you came. But they tell me you have not been to any affairs of the *ton* for, oh, many months! I remember you when I first set eyes on you, Alec. Dancing, laughing, surrounded by beautiful women, always—'

He drew his arm away abruptly. 'Susanna. I didn't actually come to enjoy the party.'

'Ah,' she sighed, 'the *ennui* of the times. You military men weary quickly, I think, of London's frivolities after the adventure of war.' The candlelight was glittering on her pale-pink satin gown, on the stupendous jewels—Aldchester heirlooms—that she wore to emphasise her allure. She toyed with her pearl-encrusted fan. 'Or perhaps you simply avoid society wherever you think I might be.'

His eyes grew harder. 'Perhaps I've come tonight because I heard rumours. And perhaps I wanted to know if they were true.'

She shrugged her gleaming bare shoulders. 'Ah—rumours, maybe, that you have brought my better nature to the fore, Alec! But you know, my dear, you *always* do that.'

'I wish I didn't know that was a lie,' he said quietly.

Her eyes glittered. 'If you are not careful, I vow I shall look for someone else to dally with!'

He put his hand swiftly on her arm. 'Don't, Susanna,' he said tersely. 'Don't for God's sake lower yourself with light and stupid jests, especially when you were perhaps starting to raise yourself in my estimation.'

She went still. 'So you've heard, then? That I have put an end to my—*dalliance* with your brother? It is indeed true. Alas—' she wafted her fan '—Stephen was becoming tedious. He visited us at Carrfields and I told him it was over.'

'Searching for fresh entertainment, Susanna?'

Her exotic eyes narrowed. Then she said, 'Can we move somewhere a little quieter?'

He guided her to the back of the room, away from the musicians and the dancing. And she began to tell him. 'Your brother came to us at Carrfields, for two days. But of course that man of his, Markin—' she shuddered '—was with him and my maid overheard them whispering. Something about a child, a little girl, that Stephen is desperate to get hold of.'

Alec froze.

'And do you know, Alec,' she went on, 'that changed my mind about everything.' She gazed up at him, her beautiful eyes for once clear and transparent. 'Men like you, women like me, we can look after ourselves. But I am worried about this child—I believe Stephen really intends her some harm—and I thought that you, of all people, might have the resources to do something…' She shivered suddenly. 'There. That is all. Take me into the dancing, will you? People used to say what a handsome couple we made.'

'No,' he said. 'I'm afraid I must go.'

He was already turning when she laid her gloved wrist on his arm. 'Alec. Can't you forgive me? It's how I was brought up, you know, to take what I wanted, and believe me…' she touched his cheek '…often I heartily wish it were not so! I only took up with Stephen to make *you* jealous. But I didn't succeed, did I? You are a good man, Alec, perhaps the best I've known.'

'I am a damned fool,' he broke in bitterly. He was suddenly finding the odours of perfume and pomade almost overbearing. His jaw clenched, he made his bow to Susanna and went to find Lucas in the card room. His friend was standing watching a game, but came quickly over to join him.

'News, Alec?'

'Yes, and not good. Lucas, the woman and child that I told you about, that I'm sheltering at Two Crows Castle—they could be in danger. And some day soon I may have to bring them to you and Verena. It seems the peril is greater than I thought.'

Chapter Seventeen

Alec was back at Two Crows Castle less than an hour later. Deuce take it, he thought, but he almost found the ruination of this old place a relief after the glitter of the *ton*.

Garrett came up to him as Alec heaved off his coat. 'We tracked down that oily cove Marchmont at his theatre today, Captain, like you asked us to,' Garrett announced. 'He told us—after a bit of persuasion—that he gave the girl Linette the push because she wouldn't—*oblige* him like he wanted.'

'Yet he suggested,' grated Alec, 'that she find work at the Temple of Beauty?'

'It was Mr Marchmont's *opinion*—' and Garrett's voice, too, was full of contempt '—that the experience would stand her in good stead.'

Alec ground out some words beneath his breath.

'Then we got into the Temple of Beauty, Captain—we bribed a footman who made sure the way was clear. And in the office we found that little green book what you told us about, hidden inside a heavy great thing called *The Myths of Ap— The Myths of Aplo—*'

'Apollodorus.'

'That's it, Captain. It said that your brother, Lord Stephen, had indeed been there three years ago. The summer of Vittoria. In fact, he visited several nights in a row—it was in Dr Barnard's notes. Here you are, McGrath wrote it down: *Paid particular attention to the young blonde innocent from the country. Reckon his lordship took her away for his own purposes...*'

Alec was breathing hard. That must be it. His brother, Stephen, had seduced Rosalie's sister. Was quite possibly Katy's father. That was why Stephen had been after Rosalie that night at Dr Barnard's; why he had hunted Rosalie down at the poetry reading, after setting fire to her home; why Stephen had sent that threat and offered the underworld reward for her. His damnably craven brother wanted to stop her search. Perhaps more.

How in hell was he going to tell Rosalie?

His next question—*should* he tell Rosalie?

Rosalie didn't even know that Stephen was Alec's brother. Hell's teeth, she would fly at Stephen, she would go for him hammer and tongs; she wouldn't *care* that Stephen, as well as being despicable, could also be damnably dangerous, with his money and his powerful friends.

Alec would have to deal with Stephen himself. He fisted his hands. The question was—*how*? Not, unfortunately, by telling her the truth.

Garrett was still watching him. 'She's out in the garden, Captain,' Garrett said quietly. 'And we're keeping an eye on her, never fear.'

It was a little after ten and the darkness outside was illuminated by the pale moon's glow. The lingering scents of rosemary and lavender filled the air, because Rosalie had been working earlier to uncover an old herb garden. But now she was just sitting on a bench and watching the stars come out, with Ajax lying by her feet. *Why are you waiting up for him, you fool?* He could be hours. *If* he came back tonight…

The thought stabbed her. *So she's back in town.*

Time and time again she'd told herself she was mad to allow this man whom fate had hurled in her path to hurt her so, but apparently there was no end to her stupidity. Indeed, she was just getting up to go inside when she heard the back door opening into the yard; as Ajax barked eagerly, her stomach did a painful flip-flop.

Alec came around the corner and stopped when he saw her there. The silvery moonlight outlined the stark masculinity of his features. *Be calm. Be controlled.*

He came closer. He'd taken off his coat on this warm night, so only his white shirt covered his powerful upper torso. Ajax jumped up to greet him, pawing at his tight cream kerseymere breeches and polished boots; Alec simply stroked the dog's shaggy head. 'Mrs Rowland. I thought you would be in your room by now.'

His dark, brooding gaze caused her pulse rate to race. Somehow she smiled back and gave a little shrug. 'It's such a lovely night.'

'You've been looking at the stars?'

'Looking at the stars.' She nodded.

'Tell me what you see.'

'There's Vega—the brilliant blue-white star in the constellation of the Lyre. My mother used to say it was the sign of summer returning when Vega climbed overhead—' She broke off. *Stop babbling, you fool.* 'I hope you enjoyed yourself at your party, Captain Stewart?'

He had tugged loose his cravat—the Gordian knot—and unwittingly rumpled his hair. Already, dark beard-growth was shadowing his lean jaw. He was looking like Captain Stewart of Two Crows Castle again. And, oh, she had to resist the physical onslaught on her beleaguered senses.

He shrugged his broad shoulders. 'It was tedious. These affairs always are. So I left early.' He was looking around the garden with an air of mystification. 'You've done something to it all. It looks different.'

'To be truthful, I was glad to find something here that I *could* do,' she said quickly. 'And Garrett recruited some men to help. I hope you don't mind?'

'Twisting us all round your little finger, Mrs Rowland? No. Why should I?'

'There are so many wonderful plants out here.' She was pointing. 'My mother used to have this one—it's called *anemone pavonina*. Isn't it beautiful?'

He was looking at her, not at the scarlet flowers. She just kept on surprising him with her knowledge. With her own damned beauty. 'You told me your mother loved her garden in Oxfordshire. But surely it was only small?'

'Yes, but her home in France used to be famous for its gardens; people would travel from far and near to admire them—' She broke off, seeing his expression.

'Would travel... Where did your mother *live*?'

She had frozen. 'I thought I told you. She was born in a fine house—a château...'

'You didn't tell me *that*.' He was watching her with a slight frown. 'It strikes me you've seen even more changes of fortune than me.'

Around the lantern that hung by the back door, the moths fluttered in a distracting dance. She felt as if she were being drawn to a flame also, helpless as those poor creatures. *Alec.* She remembered his kiss. His hands caressing her. Heat flooded her at his nearness.

She eased her dry mouth and tried to smile. 'I've only really known our rather penny-pinched existence in Ox-

fordshire. My mother's family's fortunes vanished during
the Revolution and she always told us that all her relatives
fled from Paris.'

'You have lost a great deal in your life, Mrs Rowland.'

She lifted her gaze to him steadily. 'So many have lost
more. You know that.'

'You're thinking about my soldiers?'

'Indeed. I know nothing about war, but I hate to hear
it glorified. I know that Lord Byron visited the field of
Waterloo and detested all the pointless spilling of blood.
The red rain, he called it, that made the harvest grow, but
achieved so little else…' Her voice faded away.

For one brief moment Alec recalled the horrors of the
battlefield. The screams of the dying. The heaps of dead…
He turned to gaze at her, unable to help himself. Such tenderness. Such—*awareness* of all the sadness in the world.
So very different to those harridans who'd surrounded him
at Lord Fanton's tonight, with their simpering daughters
who adored a war hero in uniform, but knew nothing of
the reality of war. Damn it all, he wanted to kiss her again.
He wanted to take her in his arms, carry her up to his bed
and soothe away the sadness in her eyes by making passionate love to her.

You fool. He clamped down hard on the arousal that
was pounding through his veins. 'Rosalie. I think I might
have picked up some more news about your sister tonight.'

'Oh, is that why you went out?' Immediately she could
have bitten her tongue off. 'I—I'm sorry,' she stammered.
'Ridiculous of me to expect you to become as obsessive
about my sister's story as me.'

'Obsessive is hardly a fair word,' he said, 'for a search
after justice like yours. But will you tell me exactly what
you remember about the threats that were delivered to
your friend Helen?'

Her brow puckered slightly. 'When her press was wrecked? And the fire started? Let me see. The first note said, *Gossip-raking bitch.* That was all. But the second one said, *Write one more word about Lady A., and you and those close to you will be the target next, not just the house.*'

Alec was very still. 'Do you know who this Lady A. is?'

'No. But I do know that she had a maidservant whipped and dismissed for dropping a vase. Helen wrote a piece about it.' She was looking up at him anxiously. 'Does that help?'

Alec had heard that story, too. About his stepmother, Lady Aldchester. Somehow he forced a smile. 'Possibly. Look, it's getting cold, you're shivering. Don't you think it's time to go inside?'

Ajax nudged at her hand and she fondled him abstractedly. She picked up her shawl. 'Alec—'

'Hmmm?'

'Alec, I've been thinking. Up till now, my one aim has been to find this man and confront him. But now I'm starting to think that perhaps I don't *want* Katy's father to know about Katy.' She looked up at him anxiously. 'Do I sound very foolish? You see, I don't want him to have anything at all to do with her.'

His hard-boned face was grave. 'Then what do you want, Rosalie?'

'Oh, I was thinking that I'd find him and get an apology from him, perhaps. Above all I wanted to make him realise just what he'd *done* to Linette. But now?' She gave a little sigh. 'Sometimes, I wish I'd never even begun this.'

Then she realised that his hand was over hers, his strong, long-fingered hand that had wrought such wicked magic on her at his father's house. He meant it as a gesture of friendship, she knew, of reassurance, but it felt so wonderful that she hardly dared to breathe. Suddenly all she wanted was to lean into him, and lift her face to his, and perhaps he would kiss her again…

No. He is not for you. The moths were still fluttering helplessly round the lantern, scorching themselves. It was time to pull herself away from a similar fate.

Alec was saying, steadily, 'You know the story of Pandora's box, don't you, Rosalie? I'm afraid you've opened it and there's no going back. The threat is still there—my men hear the word on the streets. You still need guarding, as does Katy.'

'Yes. Yes, I'm sorry; you're more patient with me than I deserve.' She dragged herself away from him and pulled her old shawl around her with resolution. 'You're right, I really must go in now, it's getting chilly. Tomorrow, I thought perhaps we could find out if anyone remembered Linette from that place off the Ratcliffe Highway, where she died. Your men might be able to help.'

'What a good idea,' he said, heartily despising himself for his duplicity. 'I'll speak to Garrett in the morning and get him to send someone out there.'

She hesitated. 'Alec, I don't know why you're helping me like this, but I just want you to know that I'm truly grateful to you for offering us shelter here. I don't know why you became estranged from your father, but I think it is his loss, not yours!'

'Please don't make me out to be anything that I'm not.' His eyes, she saw, looked bleak. 'I must warn you again that I have nothing, I *am* nothing beyond the man you see before you. I've been living a hard life, with hard men, for years, which *alters* a person and not necessarily for the better.'

She lifted her head, her eyes bright with—what? Defiance? Obstinacy? 'I don't believe you have nothing, Alec

Stewart!' she said steadily. 'I don't believe this—this façade you put up, of being of no worth to society! You have this house, for a start.'

'A wreck,' he said, shrugging bitterly as he looked around. 'A ruin.'

'No!' she persisted. 'It's of enormous value to many poor ex-soldiers! And you have your reputation as a hero of the war. Your superlative skill as a fencer. You have friends like Lord Conistone, Mary told me.'

His face softened at last. 'Lucas is one in a million.'

'And some might say that you are also,' she breathed, so quietly that she wasn't sure he heard her at all.

But unless her whole world was totally awry, Alec Stewart was good and brave and true. And she'd discovered it too late. 'Now, I really must go in,' she went on lightly. 'I've already taken too much of your time. But, Captain Stewart, I'm so *very* glad to have your help. Goodnight.' She turned to walk steadily into the house, leaving a faint trail of the scent of her skin and hair.

Alec watched her go. A flower—honeysuckle—lay close to where she'd been sitting. He picked it up, then let it drop again as the stars twinkled in the dark sky overhead. Her sweet face had brightened with such hope just now when he'd told her he might have found more news of her sister.

The dog had come to nudge sympathetically at his hand. 'Well, Ajax,' Alec said softly, 'I've landed myself in one hell of a mess, haven't I, boy?'

How was he going to tell her that the villain they were looking for was his own damned brother?

Family loyalty. Oh, God.

Chapter Eighteen

Whenever Alec came across Rosalie over the next few days, she was busy organising her small but eager band of soldiers in the garden, or helping Mary with the sewing, or playing with the children. Always she was cheerful and kind to his men, who were coming perilously close to adoring her.

Yet always now she kept her distance from him and jumped if he so much as touched her hand by accident. As well, thought Alec bleakly. He couldn't forget how she'd melted to his shockingly intimate caresses at his father's house. And he'd resolved that such a thing must never happen again.

She'd entrusted him utterly with her quest and with the safety of her tragic sister's child, and Alec was determined not to break that trust.

There were no more direct threats, though his men reported that the underworld reward was still out for her and the child. Alec didn't tell her this. He just doubled the guard on the house by night as well as day and made his men swear never to let her know that her little team of gardeners had actually been hand-chosen, by him, to protect her.

Nor did he tell her that next on his agenda was a meeting with his brother.

* * *

Stephen rose abruptly from his seat when he saw Alec entering the Pall Mall club. Though he hadn't seen his younger brother since the night of the poetry reading, he still fumed every time he remembered the way Alec had taken the girl from him. Then there was the humiliation of the party he'd planned at his father's house. And the business of the paintings.

He'd received the message this morning, to meet Alec here tonight. Alec, as he came in, looked tall. Imposing. Well dressed, for once. The doorman bowed as he let him in.

'Good day to you, Stephen,' said Alec softly. 'I thought it was time that you and I got together.'

Stephen had deliberately chosen a quiet corner; now he gestured Alec tensely to a seat. 'Indeed.' His voice was already shaky with suppressed anger. 'But first—damn you, Alec, last week I had a party arranged!'

Alec ordered brandy from a hovering waiter. 'Ah, you're talking about my visit to our father's house. I realised that our father, being absent, must have forgotten to cancel a rather large order for party food. So I took it away.' His hard eyes fastened on Stephen. 'To a place where it wouldn't be wasted.'

Stephen's face was tense with rage. 'You interfering ruffian—'

'And as for those paintings,' continued Alec as if his brother hadn't spoken, 'it was exceedingly kind of you to arrange substitutes, while the real ones were away for cleaning. I take it you've got the originals back in time? Our father will be returning any day, I believe.'

Stephen was pale. *Yes, and it had cost him a fortune to buy back those paintings.*

'Are they all back?' repeated Alec softly.

'Yes. Damn it, yes, they are!'

'Good. Then I'll get on to my real business of the night.' Alec leaned forwards. His voice was knife-edged. 'Listen, brother mine. Those who stay at Two Crows Castle—*all* of them—are under my protection. Including the young woman you were trying to take home after the poetry reading.'

'That slut? I'd forgotten her.'

'Really? But you took an interest in that same woman a couple of weeks earlier at the Temple of Beauty, didn't you? She had a sister—is that why you were interested in her, Stephen? A sister who had a child.'

'What the hell has that to do with me?'

'I'm hoping you'll tell me. A threat has been made, on Rosalie Rowland and the child. There's even an underworld reward out for them.' Alec leaned back in his seat, but his eyes never, for one second, left Stephen's face. 'I do hope it's nothing to do with you.'

Stephen laughed shakily. 'You've got a wild imagination, brother.'

'I'm not the imaginative kind,' said Alec flatly.

'I could retaliate by asking—why is this Rosalie Rowland of such interest to *you*? Though she's a spirited jade, isn't she, if a little outspoken for a whore.'

Alec's fist stopped just short of Stephen's jaw. 'You'll never call her such names again. *Ever.*'

Stephen flinched, then began to sneer. 'Really? Why not?'

'Because,' said Alec softly, 'I'll take retaliation if she and that child are in any way harmed.'

'Is that what you've come here to tell me?'

'I think it is, yes.'

'Falling for Athena, are you?' Stephen's lip curled. 'Has she submitted to your rugged charms yet? My God, and you've still got Susanna hankering after you, too—she's had enough of me, that's for sure. Thanks to you.' His voice was bitter.

Alec caught his breath. 'Our stepmother pleases no one but herself. I don't imagine for one minute that *I* can influence her decisions.'

'But I heard you were with her at Lord Fanton's ball.' Stephen's voice was rising. 'And I know that you spoke to her when our father was taken ill, before he went with her to the country. You must have said something, to make her spurn me!'

'Perhaps it took very little. And keep your voice down, brother. You're beginning to sound hysterical.'

'Hysterical! My God!' Stephen was on his feet. People were looking. He sat heavily back in his chair. 'I think it would be suitable revenge,' he ground out, 'to tell your Rosalie *everything* about you and Susanna.'

So. The blow Alec had long expected had at last been struck. *Family loyalty.* Aloud he said nonchalantly, 'You'll not win on that one, Stephen. I don't think for one moment that Mrs Rowland would care.'

'No? Should I tell her, then?'

'By all means, if you wish,' said Alec shortly. 'It would mean exposing your own sordid secrets, remember.' He got up to leave. 'I repeat—Mrs Rowland and the child are under my protection. My warnings, as you'll know, are not to be taken lightly. You see, unlike you, Stephen, I've nothing whatsoever to lose.'

He turned to go. Stephen said, in a voice tinged with venom, 'So sure of yourself! So confident, damn you! Have you considered, Alec, what would happen if the father of this bastard child actually decided, quite legally, to claim his brat?'

Alec swung round to face him, jaw clenched. 'Let him just try it, brother mine,' he breathed. 'Let him try it.'

After Alec had gone, Stephen ordered another brandy and sat alone. He most definitely could not afford to have any more dirt raked up over his past; he'd been flying too close to the wind anyway because of Susanna and he'd always half-suspected that she only used him to get closer again to damned Alec!

But now this widow, Mrs Rowland, had emerged and things were looking more dangerous by the minute.

Most of the gentry paid for their pleasure from time to time, or kept discreet mistresses. But Linette had been a mighty big mistake, because she had been gently born and a virgin.

The stupid girl had thought Stephen would marry her. Kept pestering him, until he'd paid her off—generously, he'd thought—and by God, he'd taught her a few skills she'd find useful in earning her living keeping other men happy! But he'd not known she'd been pregnant and had gone to her grave lamenting him. If word got around that he'd abandoned her, that she'd died in deep poverty…

He could deny it! But hell's teeth, there was a child. Damned Alec had clearly worked it all out. And now, Alec had taken both the child and Rosalie Rowland under his wing.

Alec was, unfortunately, pretty unassailable in his fortress-like house that was, not without reason, called a castle. Alec was considered a hero amongst his band of ex-soldier ruffians and didn't give a damn what society thought of him. But if the child really was Stephen's, which seemed all too likely—what should he, Stephen, do?

What would a true gentleman do?

Stephen's lip curled in an unpleasant smile. He would

do just what he'd hinted at to his brother. He'd admit, sorrowfully, that he'd sadly lost contact with the mother whom he'd adored, but announce that he was willing to provide for the child. To claim her as his own, in fact.

Oh, how Alec and his pretty little widow from the Temple of Beauty would hate that.

Francis has news, my dear, such surprising news, of your family...

That night while Alec was out, Rosalie received a letter. It had been delivered earlier to Two Crows Castle—Sergeant McGrath had taken it from the post boy, grumbling at the charge—but then McGrath had been called out and forgotten it; it was past nine in the evening when Mary spotted it lying on the kitchen table amongst a heap of bills and brought it to Rosalie.

The letter was from Helen. As Rosalie opened it, another folded-up missive slipped out; she put it aside and started on the first one.

Helen's letter began with the usual expressions of concern for herself and Katy *in that place*. Rosalie could almost hear Helen's disdain. There was news of Toby, who was well, and good news, too, of the church school that Francis had been asked to set up. There were also fervent wishes that Rosalie and Katy would join them in Oxfordshire—in time for Helen and Francis's marriage!

Rosalie was glad because she felt that Francis was ideal for her old friend. Helen went on to tell her that the first banns had already been read.

But then came the real bombshell.

You know, of course, Rosalie, that Francis has contacts in Paris and lately he received interesting news about the Lavalle family.

Rosalie's hand tightened on the letter as she remembered how her sister, alone in London, had called herself Linette Lavalle—their mother's name, before she married.

Francis asked me to enclose another letter for you, Rosalie, from an attorney in Paris... Swiftly Rosalie unfolded the second missive. And felt her world changing, for ever, around her.

When Alec got back to Two Crows Castle half an hour later his men melted away rather hastily at the sight of his brooding expression. Only Ajax came up to nudge sympathetically at his hand.

Garrett pulled the dog away quickly. 'Think I've found 'im a new home, Captain!'

'What?' Alec was looking abstracted.

'A new home. For Ajax.'

'You're getting *rid* of him?'

'Thought that was what you wanted, sir.'

Alec shook his head. 'Oh, no. He might as well stay. After all, he's doing no harm.'

He didn't see Garrett's secret smile of satisfaction, but went straight up to his own room and tugged off his coat. Running his hand through his hair, he went back down the stairs to the kitchen, where Mary was tidying up for the night.

'Where is Rosalie?'

'She's just in the parlour, Captain.'

He went through. Somehow she'd made this little parlour into a different place, tidying it in the indefinable way that women had. Evidence of her quiet feminine touch was everywhere.

But there was also danger everywhere.

She was arranging a bowl of flowers on the window sill, and at first she didn't see him. He thought that she looked—*different* somehow. As if she was hiding something, and whether it was good or bad, he could not tell. She was so self-contained, so strikingly lovely, even though she refused to believe it...

And you are no damned good to her, Alec Stewart.

Faint colour tinted her cheeks as she spun round. 'Captain Stewart...'

'Mrs Rowland. Have you had a quiet day?' he enquired.

She nodded. 'Indeed, but I've had a letter, from Helen and Francis. Such good news—they are going to be married, Alec, and the school Francis has set up is going well...' She hesitated.

'And they want you to go and join them, I imagine. Is it close to where you used to live?'

'A few miles or so. I would like to see it all again. My mother is buried there.'

'Of course.' His voice was calm. 'So what will your answer be?'

She met his eyes directly. 'Some day it would make sense for us to go there, I feel. But—' she looked up at him '—you warned me, Alec, that the person who threatened me might trace us there. Might trace us *anywhere*.'

He looked around. 'Do you mind if I sit down? Were you in a hurry to retire?'

She put the flowers aside and sat down herself. 'No. Not at all.'

He sat opposite her, on the sofa. 'Rosalie,' he said, his face shadowed in the candlelight, 'have you ever considered that the man who seduced your sister might have a legal claim on Katy, as her father?'

She looked absolutely stunned. 'Oh, no. But—why would he *want* to make such a claim, when he abandoned both mother and child so cruelly?'

'He could say that the mother left him of her own will and he didn't know the child existed.'

'Yes. Yes, I see...'

Pity for her twisted rawly in Alec's gut. She took a moment to calm herself before going on, 'Alec, could this man—would he be allowed to take Katy away from me?'

'If he's her father, it's possible, yes.'

Her hands were clasped tightly in her lap. 'Would money help?'

'What money?' he answered grimly. 'That's one commodity neither of us has and for once I'm sorry.' *Stephen, damn him, has enough money to buy up lawyers by the score.*

Rosalie nodded, biting her lip. 'What do you think I should do?'

Alec regarded her steadily. 'I know you will hate this. But there is one solution. Agree to a betrothal.'

'A—' She looked even more stunned.

'A betrothal. With me.'

Dear God. She looked—horrified. He raked his hand through his hair and tried again. 'Look. It need only be a temporary arrangement. You and I would always be aware of that. But if this man should try to claim Katy, you do need to assume respectability. I may not be rich, but I am an Earl's son—and a betrothal to me would strengthen your reputation, Mrs Rowland, in the eyes of the world.'

Rosalie sat very still. *Do you really think that you—a courtesan who writes for a gossip rag—would be taken seriously at the magistrates' court?* Those caustic words of Alec's still seared her. 'So—you would pretend that you'd asked me to marry you...'

'Exactly. It's not going to be so very surprising to anyone, is it? You have, after all, been married before. And people already know that you're living here.'

Rosalie lifted her head at last. The scent of the flowers on the window sill seemed almost overpowering now. 'They already assume I'm your mistress?'

'I'm afraid it's inevitable.' He saw the tinge of colour under her fine skin.

'Is there nothing else I can do?' she asked quietly. 'No alternative?'

How she hated the idea. 'It's the best way, I fear. We would need to make a formal announcement, of course, in the papers and so on, but I'll give you the night to think about my proposition. I can see you hate it, so let me remind you that once the danger is over, you can break it off any time you want.'

And he went, not even glancing at her as he left the room. Dimly she heard him in the hallway talking to Garrett, his mind already on other things, no doubt.

She gathered up those letters from Helen that she'd thought of showing him and clutched them to her, feeling quite sick.

She remembered overhearing Garrett saying sourly, *'So she's back in town. Dear God, she's beautiful, but she's wrecked his life...'*

Alec had offered her this betrothal even though clearly he detested the notion. And she *must* agree to it, for Katy's sake. But, oh, it was going to be difficult.

She looked again at the letter from France.

It reminded her that her mother was part of the Lavalle family, who'd owned land, châteaux and great vineyards in the Loire region of France, but lost them in the tumult of the Revolution so long ago. Rosalie had always assumed that the wealth of the Lavalles had gone for ever.

But six years ago, this letter told her, her family's fortune had been restored by the Emperor Napoleon in a deliberate ploy to gain the political backing of France's foremost aristocratic families. And the letter told her that a portion of that fortune—not vast, but large enough to make a difference to her life—might be hers.

She folded the letter in her fingers and gazed into the dying embers of the fire.

Even if this was true—how could it help her, now? For she had lost her heart to a man who was scarred for ever by a past commitment and who felt nothing but pity for her.

And if he knew all her lies—he wouldn't be able to bear to have her near him.

Chapter Nineteen

That night Katy lost her much-loved rag doll. Rosalie had realised Polly was missing at Katy's bed time and was apprehensive, because she clutched the battered toy in her sleep every night. But Katy had fallen asleep so very quickly that it had slipped from Rosalie's mind.

Until, a little after midnight, Rosalie was woken by Katy's woeful cry. 'Polly-doll. Gone.'

Rosalie scrambled out of bed in her nightgown and hurried to comfort the little girl. 'I'll look for her, darling. Don't fret—I'll be back very soon.'

Her fault for not doing it earlier, she reproached herself. Quickly pulling a shawl over her nightdress, she took a candlestick and tiptoed barefoot downstairs. She was aware that a rota of Alec's men kept watch both inside and out, night and day—a relic of their old army routine, she assumed. But the sleeping house was quiet as she hurried down the staircase and along the unlit passageway to the parlour off the kitchen where she guessed the doll was most likely to be.

Indeed, the rag doll was lying half under a chair. Retrieving it with a sigh of relief, she set off back up to Katy, and a watery smile was her reward.

'There, darling.' Rosalie stroked Katy's cheek. 'Everything's all right now. Sweet dreams, my love.'

As soon as Katy was asleep again Rosalie tiptoed back to her own room. So stupid of her to go without shoes, for she'd somehow caught her left foot on a splinter of wood—on the rough staircase, perhaps—and now it was bleeding slightly. She wrung out a cotton handkerchief in cold water and knotted it tightly around her foot to cover the small wound. Then she remembered she'd left the candlestick burning on the landing and limped out to fetch it.

And nearly collided with a tall male figure. Alec.

Shock quivered through her veins at the raw masculinity of his body, so close to hers.

'I thought I heard someone,' he was saying. 'Is anything wrong?' He was assessing her sharply, taking in her shawl flung over her nightgown, her pale face, her loose hair.

'Katy woke up just now and realised she hadn't got her rag doll.' Somehow she kept her voice calm. 'Major crisis, of course. So I've just been down to find the doll, then I remembered I left this candle out here…'

Her voice trailed away. She hadn't realised, and she should have done, that he wasn't all that fully dressed himself. His lean, hard-boned face was shadowed with beard growth. His white shirt had been hastily thrust into his tight buckskin breeches, but was unfastened almost all the way down his chest, and… Oh, Lord, she could see, as his shirt gaped, that astounding musculature. His sculpted shoulders and chest, the bronzed gleam of smooth male torso, that line of silky dark hair that ran down towards his abdomen and…

Don't look as though you're about to faint at the sight of a half-naked male body, you silly fool. He thinks you a widow and a whore.

'So Katy's all right?' he asked.

'Oh, yes, indeed—she's fast asleep, now, and quite happy, thank you!' She gave a brief nod and turned to go.

His hand was on her shoulder. 'And what about you, Mrs Rowland? Perhaps you'd like to tell me why your nightgown is spattered with water and there's a handkerchief tied around your foot?'

'I caught it on the stairs just now. So stupid of me. It's only a scratch. I'm sorry I've disturbed you—'

His voice was softer. 'You must stop blaming yourself, you know, for everything.'

Something tight caught in her throat. 'Who else *should* I blame?' she whispered.

His hands were warm and strong on her shoulders. 'Listen to me. *No one* could have done more than you for your sister. You've searched high and low for her, you've taken extraordinary care of her child...'

'But I had to. *I had to.*' She gazed up at him in despair. 'Because it was my fault, Alec!'

'For God's sake! What was?'

'It was my fault that my little sister ran away from home!'

His gaze was steady. 'I really find that very difficult to believe,' he said.

'Then you must,' she told him bleakly. She dragged herself away from him. 'Why do you think I care so desperately for poor Katy? Because it's the only way I can make amends!' She was trembling. 'You've been so kind to me, you and your men, but I've drawn you into all this on a lie, because I should have told you everything from the very beginning, I've *deceived* you... Excuse me, I've disturbed your sleep. I'll go back to my room now.'

But she couldn't go anywhere, because he'd caught her again by her arm.

'Rosalie. This is an order. You're not going anywhere until I've looked at your foot.'

She stared down at it blindly. 'No, really, it's just a splinter…'

'Then it needs removing. You'd better come to my room. And at the same time you're going to tell me—*everything.*'

After it happened, Alec reviled himself bitterly. But what else could he have done? He couldn't leave her so obviously in pain, though she tried so hard to hide it. Couldn't leave her so full of *contempt* for herself.

And he couldn't take her downstairs, where any of his men, as they made their nightly rounds, might see them. But he was playing with fire. And he damned well knew it.

She followed him to his room. He could tell by her uneven tread that she couldn't put her weight properly on her left foot. He saw her glance at his bed and catch her breath before perching on the edge of a chair with her nightgown buttoned up to her throat. But her lovely pale hair was loose, as it never was by day, and—*damn*, he thought. Damn, didn't she realise, with that lamp glowing away behind her, that despite that garment being long and all-enveloping, he could see almost *everything* through that sheer material? She looked exquisite, with her slender legs outlined beneath the filmy fabric, her pert breasts jutting…

Dear God, you're no good for her. Remember it, you fool.

He fetched a low stool on which she could rest her foot and bent to swiftly examine the damage. Yes, there was a splinter—tiny, but if it wasn't removed it could turn nasty. Her foot was small and soft. Clenching his teeth, he fetched water. Then, bringing a lamp very close, he said, 'This will hurt, just a little.'

Rosalie nodded, biting her lip. His strong, warm hand cupping her foot was such sweet torment that it sent a surge of longing through her veins. With swift skill he eased out the splinter and she suppressed the low cry that forced its way to her lips.

He glanced up at her, concern and reassurance in his dark eyes. 'That's it,' he said. He bathed away the slight trickle of blood, knowing it would cleanse the wound, then tied one of his laundered neckcloths around her foot and stood up. 'Better?'

She lifted her chin staunchly. 'Thank you. Much, much better. I'll go back to my room—'

'Not just yet,' he said quietly. 'You were going to tell me—remember?—about your sister.'

And so she began. He reminded himself, as he watched her, how young she was, how vulnerable still. Twenty-one and a widow, with her life in tatters around her. He stood with his back to the window, hoping that the distance across the room might help to quell the physical arousal of which he was all too aware.

She clasped her hands together. She raised her face to him and said quietly, 'Alec, I loved Linette, so very much. But I've already told you that everyone was unkind to my mother for being foreign—even for being *pretty*. And Linette was just like our mother—so sweet and lovely, wanting everyone to adore her, and not understanding why they didn't.'

'And so you took it upon yourself to defend your little family?'

'My father asked me to.'

'Your father? But—how old were you when he died? Seven, I thought you said?'

'My age did not matter—I'd promised!' She gazed at him almost defiantly, her blue eyes dark with emotion.

'And as I grew older I did what I could to protect my poor mother from those who—wished to hurt her. Helen was my one good friend; she was the village schoolteacher. I loved my lessons, I loved learning about—oh, about *everything*. And I used to write stories. They were my way of escaping a rather cruel world, I suppose—Linette used to love hearing them.'

She took a deep breath. 'But Linette didn't enjoy school at all. And as she grew older, she grew very pretty, not like me.'

Alec found himself about to say something, but stopped.

'Then Linette realised that a lot of the local boys and men were starting to notice her,' she went on. 'I couldn't blame her for enjoying their flattery, but I just asked her to be careful...' Rosalie shook her head and blew her nose with the big, clean handkerchief Alec had silently offered her. 'I'm sorry, Alec, you must find this tedious!'

'No,' he said. 'What happened? To make her run away?'

He saw the pulse fluttering in her throat, the faint colour that tinged her exquisite cheekbones. She moistened her lips. 'There was someone in the village...'

'Go on.'

'And he used to lend me his books. His name was Thomas—he was the local squire's son. He often came riding past our cottage, and when he saw me, he would stop and talk. I thought he was—a friend. I was eighteen, nearly nineteen—he told me he would protect us, against the troublemakers.'

Alec listened. 'And he didn't?'

She shook her head quickly. 'I was a fool. I'd gone to tell him that some men were persecuting my mother again— oh, in little ways, harassing her for being a foreigner as she walked to the village shop and so on. He told me to meet him that evening, in the churchyard, and he...he tried to seduce me.'

Alec had gone very still.

'I *told* him that I'd only agreed to meet him because he'd promised to help us. But he said—' she clenched her hands '—he said I was deluding myself if I thought that anyone would trouble to defend a French trollop and her brats without—some sort of reward.' She shuddered. 'And he told me I was too thin for him anyway.'

Too scrawny to give a man a comfortable ride had been his exact words. She could still remember the horrible wet thickness of his lips as he'd tried to thrust his tongue into her mouth, the hateful grabbing at her breasts. She'd kicked him away, panting with nausea. 'And then,' she went on rather desperately, 'he said I had been deliberately leading him on. Which I hadn't! I'd no *intention*—'

Alec had hardly moved. 'He sounds a pleasant specimen. Was that the last you saw of him?'

She was struggling to be calm, but he saw her chest rising and falling rapidly beneath her nightgown. 'Unfortunately, no. A few months later, I discovered that he had been meeting my sister and giving her gifts.' She lifted her blue eyes to Alec's; he saw how they burned with distress. 'I don't know what, if anything, occurred. But we argued, terribly. She told me I was jealous and had wanted Thomas myself; I told Linette she was being very foolish.'

'Couldn't your mother have said anything to your sister?'

She shook her head. 'Our mother was by then not at all well. When I warned Linette that his intentions could *not* be honourable, she said I was making life unbearable for her. And a few days later she'd gone. Packed some things and taken the carrier's cart to Oxford.' She caught her breath. Despair etched her features. 'I knew that she wanted to be an actress, so I guessed she'd gone to London, and I went there again and again to look for her, but it seemed hopeless. And then I had to go back to my mother, for she was very ill, and bed-bound; she passed away last summer. But last October, I got a note from Linette to say that she was in trouble. I found my sister, with Katy, just before she died. And it was *my fault*...'

Rosalie was standing up, running her hands through her long hair. 'So now you see why I'm not worthy of your kindness, Alec—you who are so generous to waifs and strays. I drove my sister away. I'll understand completely if you no longer wish to help me.'

She was already limping towards the door, her head held high.

Something in him—some iron band of self-control—snapped in that instant. Something was wrong. Something was *very* wrong in the story she'd just told him. Yet all that mattered now was that she was in distress. In utter despair.

He blocked her way. He put his hands on her shoulders. Feeling her start to tremble, he tilted up her small chin with one warm finger. 'Rosalie. Listen to me. You were just trying to guide her in the right direction, as a caring parent does with a wayward child. And—forgive me—your sister left home without a word, which must have caused untold distress to your unwell mother. Not an act of consideration on her part, surely? You did everything that you could. Do you hear me?'

'You are being kind.' She shivered. 'But you must still hate me, for failing my sister. Perhaps Thomas was right—I *was* jealous of Linette, because she was so pretty, and I am not.'

'Not pretty?' Alec stared at her. Her low opinion of herself was beyond belief. 'Why in God's name do you *persist* in believing that?'

She shrugged, meeting his gaze defiantly. 'I'm too thin.

My face is all bony. My nose doesn't turn up prettily like Linette's did, my eyes are too big, my hair is too straight.'

'You list those things as if they're *faults*,' breathed Alec. 'Listen to me. Your bone structure is exquisite. Your high cheekbones, your perfect nose, your figure...'

Alec was stunned to find himself having to say all this. If there was one thing the females who had been his mistresses in the past were aware of, it was their own allure. They were always fishing for compliments and Alec would oblige—or not. But this time—this time he found, to his astonishment, that he really *meant* it.

'Rosalie,' he said. 'Many women are pretty—but you are beautiful.'

His hands were still on her shoulders—*dangerous*. The tightness pulling at his loins was a heavy, throbbing ache.

'You must despise me, then,' she said almost defiantly.

It was no good. Her lips, tremulous, were barely inches from his own. Her lovely, turquoise-blue eyes that were so wide with despair melted all his carefully built defences.

He bent down to kiss her. It was meant to be a gesture of reassurance. Of tenderness.

Damn. It was anything but.

Something else that was entirely wrong. She was supposed to be a *widow*. All that had been just slightly askew, slightly off kilter about her accounts of her past, now fell into place.

Never once had she told him about...her husband!

Too late. Too damned late. She was opening to Alec's kisses like a tender flower yearning for the sun.

There was no way in the whole of this world that he could pull back from the inevitable now.

Rosalie felt the caress of his warm lips through every fibre of her sensitised being. Every nerve she possessed was sparked by that one instant. Licking flames of desire surged through her veins, burning her up. Alec's hands pulled her closer, sliding down her back to span her tiny waist, hauling her against him. Then he reclaimed her mouth with a low growl of male hunger and Rosalie found herself responding, parting her lips to accept the thrust of his tongue.

The warm male scent of him all but overwhelmed her. The hard ridge of arousal pressing at her abdomen tormented her with sweet desires. His tongue was plundering her mouth strongly, sweetly. She wanted to nestle into his big, muscled arms and melt into him, to be one with him...

At one point she realised that Alec was, with a great effort, pushing her away. Was trying to say, through clenched teeth, 'This should not be happening.'

Her cheeks were burning hot, but inside she felt so cold. *French whore's daughter.* Perhaps what she'd told him about Thomas repelled him. Her eyes were wide and haunted as she stared up at him. 'Of course. I'm so sorry. You were only being kind to me and I'm behaving like a fool—'

'*Kind* to you!' grated Alec thickly. He cupped her sweet face and tilted it up so his eyes blazed forcefully down into hers. 'You think this is kindness?'

Her heart fractured. 'Just—don't send me away,' she whispered. 'Not now.'

'Rosalie, I'm trying to *warn* you.'

'Alec, I feel safe with you. As safe as I've ever felt in my life.'

Her hands had stretched up round the nape of his neck, daring to feel the dark hair that grew so closely there, sliding down a little to caress his strong muscled shoulders beneath his shirt. With a low groan he'd pulled her to him again to hold her close against his aroused body, while his other hand unfastened the buttons of her nightgown until he could push the cool linen aside and cup the aching fullness of each rounded breast.

Rosalie clung to his shoulders as her nipples peaked and her whole body sang with longing. Alec swept her up in his arms and carried her tenderly to his bed, where he laid her down as if she was something precious. Then he lowered himself to her side, still kissing her. Instinctively she arched her whole body towards him, her head falling back in rapture as she pressed her own flat palms against his strong, naked chest, feeling the smooth skin stretched over swelling muscles, feeling his heartbeat.

This was like coming home. Like something she'd dreamed of, all her life. This might be all she could have of this incredible man. But she would remember it, for ever.

She shivered with exquisite sensation as he tenderly eased her nightgown away; gasped with delight as she felt her breasts pressed against the hard wall of his chest. And all the while she was aware of his lips on her hair, her forehead, her cheeks…

Quickly he pulled down his breeches, then drew her now-naked body close again. His strong, hair-roughened thighs were against hers, while he kissed her throat and murmured her name. She felt his aroused manhood and shock thudded through her. But with an achingly tender touch, he caught her gasp with his kiss and continued to caress her breasts with his hands, sending wave after wave of pleasure through her. Then he dipped his dark head to catch one stiffening bud in his mouth and drew it in, laving it with his tongue.

She cried out as sensation pulsed through her. She raked her fingers across his wide shoulders and, as his tongue worked at her nipple, she wanted more, *needed* more. The hunger spiralled from deep within her, surging through her blood like a fever. *'Alec...'* Then her breath stopped in her throat as he trailed his hand beguilingly down her abdomen and began, using gentle fingertips, to explore the very heart of her femininity.

Dear God. She arched against him, eyes squeezed shut, her legs opening instinctively to his hard lithe body as he shifted to take his own weight on his arms and eased himself between her slender thighs.

She glimpsed it, in the candlelight, the proud essence of his masculinity, the dark, lengthy shaft, its silken head positioned just at the secret heart of her. Then he was lowering his head to kiss her again, his lips and tongue taking hot, needy possession of her mouth. At the same time he was gliding into her, inch by powerful inch. At first she was afraid, but then she was awash with pure sensation, pure need, as he gentled her, stroking her hair, her breasts, kissing her face and eyelids, murmuring, *'Rosalie. Sweetheart...'*

For just that one moment in time, it was almost possible for Rosalie to pretend that he loved her.

Then something happened. Then Alec encountered— resistance. He froze. His suspicions clenched at his insides. 'Rosalie. What—?'

'Don't stop,' she pleaded, pulling him to her, arching herself to meet him in raw hunger, revelling in the sensation of his hard length at her core. 'Alec, please don't stop now!'

And indeed, how could he? He surged in deep. She uttered one sharp cry, which he cherished with his kiss, then he pulled her to him, coaxing her into his rhythm. And Alec made love to her, being as gentle as a man of such power could be, caressing her, soothing her with his mouth on her lips and breasts, his fingers working skilfully at the core of her being as she was caught up in a surge of incredible pleasure she thought could rise no higher, until there began a soaring, glorious, impossible ecstasy as he took her over the edge.

Alec reached his own powerful release moments later. Hard reality began to creep in. He pulled himself up, breathing thickly. He'd been right. *She had not known any other lover.*

Hell. How could he have made such a blunder?

Easy. Because he had believed her when she'd told him she was a widow. The alarm bells had only begun to sound tonight, with her anguished tale of the young brute who'd tried to seduce her.

Which he himself had now done, most effectively.

He got up and started heaving on his clothes. 'Oh, Rosalie.' His voice was harsher than he'd meant it to be, because this was his fault, his stupid mistake with which to lash himself mentally. 'Rosalie, why, in God's name, didn't you *tell* me? How was I to perform some miracle of mind-reading and to know that you were, in spite of your much-vaunted widowhood, in spite of everything—a *virgin*?'

Her face was so white that it was as if he'd taken to her with a whip. She sat up on the edge of his bed, pulling on her crumpled nightgown, fastening it with frantic fingers. She tossed her head in that defiant way of hers that smote him utterly. 'I—I pretended to be a widow for Katy's sake. For her safety, Alec, and for mine! And somehow the time never seemed quite right to tell you...'

'Not even in my damned bed?'

'I'm sorry,' she said quietly.

He dragged his hand through his hair. Deceit all round, then. For wasn't he deceiving *her*, by keeping the truth from her about his despicable brother? 'What about practicalities?' he said tiredly. 'When was your last monthly flow?'

The blush of utter mortification flooded her cheeks. 'It ended three days ago,' she whispered.

'Little chance of pregnancy, then,' he said. 'That's something.' He sighed and drew her near. 'We will talk properly tomorrow. Shall we? Hmmm?' Gently he tilted her face towards his and saw there were shadows of sheer exhaustion under her lovely eyes.

'Tomorrow,' she echoed. She looked—frozen.

Something twisted in Alec's gut. He kept his arms around her. 'This isn't the end of the world,' he said. His eyes were grave, but his voice was gentle. 'We'll find some way forwards, trust me. But in the meantime—we'll speak of this to absolutely no one, do you understand? Now, I'll just check that the way is clear before I see you back to your room.'

He left her there, while he went to look out on the corridor.

Oh, God, thought Rosalie, sinking to the edge of his disarrayed bed. What had she done *now*? He'd offered to stop, after that first kiss. But she'd lied to him. She'd encouraged him. She'd longed for him, even though she *knew* he could never love her.

And she had dared to criticise Linette for her behaviour all that time ago! Alec had been so kind. But he would be thinking now, *She is a slut, like her sister.* She drew in a deep, shuddering breath.

Then she saw the letter, lying open on his desk. It was written on fine paper, in a beautiful script, and from it drifted the faint scent of gardenias. Something fateful dragged her towards it. *I know there are risks, my dear,* she read, *but might I see you at Lord Fanton's ball? There are things I need to tell you...*

She tore her eyes away. Remembered Garrett muttering,

when she wasn't supposed to hear, *'So she's back in town. Dear God, she's beautiful, but she's wrecked his life...'*

The letter must be from the woman he was once going to marry. The woman he'd loved and lost—only, perhaps he *hadn't* lost her.

Alec was coming back into the room. 'All's clear,' he said. 'And I've been thinking. I'm going to send you and Katy to some friends of mine in Mayfair, where you will be safer.'

'Safer...'

'Yes.' He gazed at her steadily. 'In all possible ways. I've been considering it for a few days.'

She could hardly speak. 'I see. Do I take it you also wish to end the pretence of our betrothal?'

'No!' he answered sharply. 'More than ever I'm afraid we must make our betrothal public, to safeguard your reputation, and in case it comes to a legal action for custody of the child. I'll send you to my friend Lucas's house tomorrow.'

Oh, God, she thought. He hated all this. She met his gaze steadily. 'You are high-handed, Captain Stewart.' Her voice broke, just a little. 'I take it your friend Lucas has been consulted?'

'I have spoken to Lord Conistone about it, yes.'

'Lord Conistone...' Mary had told her he was one of Alec's friends. He was also head of one of the most prestigious families in England and a member of the Prince Regent's set.

'Indeed,' went on Alec, 'Lucas understands the situation, though I've not burdened him with all the details. His wife, Verena, is extremely kind and discreet; they have two children, a boy and a girl, who are just a little older than Katy, so she will fit easily into the nursery there.'

'Lord Conistone is generous.'

'He is my friend.' Alec escorted her back to her room then, his face set. Just as she was turning to go in, he said, 'Rosalie. I can see that you are flaying yourself over the secrets you've kept from me. I should even the score by telling you that I've lied to you also.'

Her eyes flew up to his. *He was going to tell her about that letter.*

But it wasn't what she thought. 'I have a brother,' he went on. 'An older brother. I've told you that. What I *haven't* told you is that he is—Lord Stephen Maybury.'

She just stood there, frozen. At last her lips moved. 'Why didn't you—?'

'Tell you before?' His voice was heavy. 'There were reasons. But what you need to know, *now*, is that my brother is not to be trusted in any way at all.'

She said quietly, 'So you hate him and he hates you. Am I—was *tonight*—part of your campaign against your brother?'

He ground out some words under his breath. 'For God's sake, Rosalie! You must not believe that, ever!'

'Then what am I to believe?'

He said, between clenched teeth, 'That I count the welfare of you and the child as one of my chief responsibilities!'

Rosalie dragged in a deep breath. 'And if I could relieve you of that responsibility, I would. Oh, believe me, I would.'

What could he say? He ushered her to her room. Then he went back to his own chamber, feeling sick with himself. Haunted, by her words.

If I could relieve you of that responsibility, I would.

So there it was. She had deceived him and he had deceived her. A recipe for utter disaster.

But he would never forget how she had given herself to

him. The way that her whole being splintered into rapture at the crisis of her pleasure…

Never again. *That* was why he was sending her to Lucas's. Because it must never happen again.

For Rosalie, sleep would not come.

It seemed she wasn't the only one to keep secrets. Alec, and Stephen Maybury—brothers! Yet it all made sickening sense. Their bitter familiarity. Their deep-rooted enmity. Alec's warning: *Promise me you won't throw yourself away on a brute like Maybury.*

She suddenly remembered how she'd even thought they'd resembled one another, ever so slightly, when she first saw Lord Maybury at the Temple of Beauty… Oh, why hadn't Alec *told* her? Then again, why should he tell her, when she'd clothed herself in such lies?

Tonight, just for a fleeting and magical hour, her dreams had seemed within her reach. *Never again.* The clock struck down in the hall. His words tolled in her ears. He'd blamed himself—but she was the one truly to blame, for so stupidly giving away her heart to a man who could never return her love.

Never again. The bleakness of utter despair tore at every fibre of Rosalie's being.

Chapter Twenty

If Rosalie had thought that she would never see again the kind of love that existed between her mother and father, she was proved wrong at Lucas and Verena's house. For their utter devotion to one another was evident in every word, every gesture.

It made her sad, for what her parents had lost. It made her happy, that such love could indeed be found. Perhaps, if she and Alec had met in another place, another time...

No. Best not to think of that.

But it was cruel indeed that everyone thought she was betrothed to him.

Rosalie had been terrified on arriving at this palatial place in Mayfair. Lucas had at first looked so haughty, so aristocratic, and Verena, too, seemed dauntingly refined. But they had welcomed her so very warmly. Katy was fussed over by Verena and the servants and had quickly grown used to sharing the nursery with Verena's little girl, Isobel. If her hosts knew that Rosalie was not a widow, they were far too polite to mention it.

The notice of betrothal between Captain Alec Stewart and Mrs Rosalie Rowland had appeared now in the papers and Alec visited every day. He was unfailingly kind to her, but was careful never to be alone with her for long. She burned to ask how his men were progressing in their hunt for Linette's seducer, but she sensed that the quest was a heavy burden to him now.

Watching him in Lord Conistone's company made her realise just how highly Alec was regarded in society. Sometimes she would catch snatches of conversation between Alec and Lucas's top-lofty visitors, often government ministers and senior army officers. She heard them talking politics, discussing the new European boundaries that had been drawn up at the ending of the war. Though more often, during those bright spring afternoons, she found herself in the garden of Lord Conistone's lovely house, with Verena and her children, Isobel, who was three, and four-year-old Adam. Adam looked after Katy with the kind of tender gravity that reminded Rosalie of her father. The garden here was an exquisite place, its shrubberies and flowerbeds kept pristine by a team of skilled staff. But she would rather be in the overgrown, scented garden of Two Crows Castle any time.

'We'll take care of all your plants, don't you worry, miss,' the soldiers had assured her when she bade them goodbye. 'You'll come back and see us, now, won't you?'

'I'll certainly do my best.' She smiled. The youngest of them, Mikey, shyly gave her a posy of flowers that sat, fading, in her bedroom here.

She doubted that she would ever set foot in that garden again.

So many mistakes. Too many mistakes.

One evening Alec had stayed on for dinner, because Lord Conistone had some important guests who were interested in Alec's opinions about the unjust fate of the many unemployed soldiers. Alec was sitting some way down the vast table, so she had no chance to talk to him, but she could see him. He looked so darkly handsome, so charismatic as he talked to Lucas and his guests. Once he glanced her way and caught her looking at him; he smiled and her heart was wrenched.

He would not even touch her hand now. There was a look of strain in his dark eyes when they spoke, and lines of tension bracketed his mouth. To be so near to him still, to have to present herself as his betrothed and know that he could never love her, was apt punishment indeed for her mistakes.

After dinner, she and Verena left the men to their port. 'They are sure to join us later,' Verena said, misunderstanding Rosalie's low spirits. 'Perhaps then you will get a chance to speak to Alec alone, my dear.'

'Perhaps, but I'm afraid I feel rather tired tonight. I think I have a headache coming on. Will you tell Alec so, please, if he should ask?'

'A headache? Would some powders help? Our housekeeper has various tisanes, or sometimes a lavender cologne can be soothing!'

'Really, no, thank you. But you've been so very kind.'

'Any friend of Alec's is a friend of ours,' said Verena earnestly. 'You must be very happy, to be marrying him.'

'Indeed.' Rosalie managed to smile.

She had almost reached the broad landing that led to her bedroom when Alec caught up with her. 'Rosalie?'

Why was it that just the sound of his husky voice so weakened her usual stubborn resolve? She turned to face him, her heart pounding as his dark eyes scoured her. 'Rosalie,' he went on, 'Verena told me just now that you were not well.'

She shook her head slightly. 'It's a headache, that is all.'

'I hope you're not worrying too much. You know that

Katy and you are perfectly safe here. I'm sorry that we've had so little opportunity to talk.'

She lifted her head so her eyes locked with his. 'Then here's our chance. I told you before,' she went on, her voice ragged because of the pain that gripped her, 'I don't think I should continue this search. I don't *want* to know who Katy's father is!'

He broke in then, his voice harsh. 'And I've told *you*, it's not a matter now of mere curiosity. This man could claim Katy as his child. That's why it's so important that our betrothal stands, that we appear in public together, that you have the public approval of figures in society like Lord Conistone and his wife. I thought you understood all this!'

She put her hand to her forehead. 'For how long must this pretence go on?' *This torment?* she added silently to herself.

'The end might just come sooner than we think.' His voice was abrupt. 'In the meantime, we must keep up appearances. That's what I've come to tell you. We have been invited to a ball at Lord Stokesay's in three days' time, along with Lucas and Verena.'

'Do I have to endure it?'

His jaw clenched. 'We must make this betrothal convincing. We must proclaim to the world that you are under my protection. For I have sworn to keep you and Katy safe, and I've no intention of breaking my word.'

Hateful though it was to him, thought Rosalie in despair. He might as well have said that. His eyes said it, his curt nod. His back as he turned to leave her. And after he'd gone Rosalie felt as alone, as full of despair as she'd ever been in her life.

Alec rode back to Two Crows Castle that night, the blood thundering in his ears. *You fool. You colossal fool.* Wouldn't it be better to tell her *everything*?

No. Because then Alec would have to tell her about—
Susanna. And the crisis was at hand, anyway, for Alec had
learned today, from his loyal men of Two Crows Castle,
that Stephen was preparing his own desperate attempt to
get his revenge on Alec. An attempt in which the child
would be the innocent pawn.

'Try on this one, dear Rosalie! Yes, the lilac silk. Oh,
you look adorable in that colour!'

'Do you really think so?' Rosalie touched the exquisite
gown with trepidation. Verena's dressmaker had arrived
earlier at the Mayfair mansion with a range of gowns for
her to choose from and Rosalie was overwhelmed. She
had never worn anything as fine as this, ever.

'It looks *wonderful* on you!' declared Verena, laughing. 'I grew up with three sisters and a vain mama forever fretting about fashion, so believe me, I know what
I'm talking about!'

It was four in the afternoon, on the day of Lord Stokesay's ball. The children had gone on an excursion to St
James's Park to feed the ducks; Rosalie had demurred a
little, hating to let Katy outside the safe haven of Lord
Conistone's house.

But Lucas Conistone had strolled in then and said, in his
elegant drawl, 'You don't think I'd be lax about the safety
of my own children, do you, Mrs Rowland?'

'No. Of course not, my lord.' Rosalie hung her head.

'Your anxiety is understandable, my dear,' Lucas said
more gently. 'But Alec has everything in hand, believe
me. You must trust him.' Then he added, quietly, 'I always have.'

Perhaps *she* was the one who was untrustworthy, because earlier that morning she'd lied again, or at least
omitted a rather crucial truth, by asking Verena if she

could borrow one of the footmen to accompany her into the city. 'I have a small business affair to attend to,' she'd explained.

A letter had arrived for her while she was breakfasting with Verena. It was from Hathersleighs' bank in Seething Lane, requesting that she visit them at her earliest convenience. Verena had insisted that she make her journey in Lord Conistone's coach, with three of his men in attendance.

When Rosalie had returned, she'd found Verena arranging flowers in the drawing room. 'Is everything all right, my dear?'

'Indeed.' Rosalie had forced a smile. 'Thank you.'

But everything had changed. At the bank they'd told her the exact size of her inheritance. Once all the details were settled, and suitable investments made, she would be able to lead an independent life, with Katy. Without Alec.

But an iron fist squeezed at the core of her being at the thought of never seeing him again.

Meanwhile, Lord Stokesay's ball loomed large. 'You can borrow my cream pelisse to wear over that gown tonight, my dear Rosalie,' Verena was chattering on happily. 'The lilac suits your colouring so well, I declare you will set a new fashion!'

'No one will notice me, surely!'

'You underestimate yourself,' said Verena softly. 'You look beautiful. Do you know, you're about the same size and height as my youngest sister, Izzy,' she went on, smoothing down the ruffles on Rosalie's dress, 'who drove all her suitors mad during her first Season, since she fell in love with someone new once a week at least!'

Rosalie tried to pull herself together and return Verena's warmth. 'Did you meet Lucas during your first Season?' she asked shyly.

'Oh, Lucas's estate bordered ours, in Hampshire.' Verena's eyes softened with what was almost adoration. 'I never needed a Season. I think I always knew he was the one for me.'

Rosalie felt her heart constrict. *It had been the same with Alec.* The minute she saw him, standing at the back of the hall in Dr Barnard's stupid show, she'd known.

But since then everything had gone so terribly wrong.

'Of course,' Verena went on, putting the muslin pelisse aside and adjusting a trailing cream ribbon on Rosalie's sleeve, 'my sisters and I knew Alec, as well, because he was Lucas's best friend. We all adored him; in fact, my youngest sister, Izzy, suffered several months of being utterly in love with him, until he kindly made it plain she was not the one for him. Dear Alec! You know, he could have made a good career for himself in the War Office, but instead he chooses to champion the cause of the poor soldiers.'

Verena continued to sing Alec's praises, talking about his heroism in battle and how respected he was by officers and men alike. She meant well. The lilac gown, Verena enthused, was the one and Rosalie agreed just to please her kind hostess, for her heart had gone out of the topic of ballgowns altogether. The dressmaker was called upstairs to take in the waistline. 'Madame has such an exquisite figure!' she exclaimed over Rosalie as she got out her tape measure.

There was then much fussing over the gauze overgown and the elbow-length kid gloves. Rosalie was glad when it was all over. She wanted to go back to her room, to gather up her courage to appear in public as Alec's betrothed, when she knew he was doing this out of a sense of duty. When she knew that he would never love her.

And then she heard the noise out in the cobbled courtyard that adjoined Lucas's stables.

Horsemen must be riding up, a dozen of them at least; as she ran to the window she saw they surrounded the open barouche just drawing in from the roadway, in which sat Katy and Verena's children, with their nursemaids. She saw that Alec was amongst the riders and was already dismounting from his horse, while talking rapidly to Garrett. Alec held a cloth to his right temple, from which a scarlet stain was spreading.

Something had happened. Her heart stopped. What had Alec said to her? *'The end might just come sooner than we think...'*

Rosalie had already gathered up her lilac-silk skirts and was running, running downstairs, with Verena hurrying after her.

Katy.

Chapter Twenty-One

Alec had lifted Katy from the carriage and was holding her tight in his arms. Garrett and the rest of the men—some of them Alec's, some Lucas's—were talking in muttered voices as they saw to the horses.

A quiet trip to the Park?

She didn't think so.

Rosalie hurried across to Alec. 'What has happened?' she breathed.

She reached for Katy, but Alec shook his head. 'Let Katy go with Verena and the children,' he mouthed to Rosalie over Katy's head. 'You're frightening her. She doesn't even realise anything's wrong.'

By now Rosalie was terrified. Verena had come up and reluctantly Rosalie saw Alec pass Katy to her. Rosalie turned back to Alec, her heart thudding. He'd put his handkerchief to his temple again; it was still bleeding. 'Are you going to explain, Captain Stewart?'

'An attempt was made to kidnap Katy.'

A sharp pain clamped her ribs. 'You promised me she would be safe!'

'And so she was.' His tone was curt. 'We were expecting the attempt, you see. We let it be known that the children were going to the Park, with just two nursemaids.'

'You—*encouraged* this?'

He looked around. By now the courtyard was empty except for them. 'We set up a trap,' he said. 'It's not as crude as it sounds. As well as myself and Lucas, at least a dozen of Lucas's and my men were within fifty yards of the children all the time in the Park—posing as passers-by, horsemen, whatever was necessary. The minute that Katy's would-be kidnappers started moving towards her, our men were on to them. The children were not even aware of it.'

'Who were they?'

'There were four of them and they're being questioned at the Queen Street police office right now. But I already know whose pay they were in.' He tensed his muscles. Looked at her steadily. 'It was news I was prepared for, I'm afraid. The would-be kidnapper was my brother, Lord Stephen Maybury.'

Her first emotion was incredulity. For a moment the world seemed to stop. But already she was starting to realise what she should have realised a long time ago. And now the truth of it all—the terrible truth—punched the air from her lungs like an iron fist. 'Oh, *no*,' she breathed. 'You mean—Lord Maybury and—*Linette*...'

He'd clenched his hands. 'I know what you're going to say—I should have told you. But if I had, you'd have tackled him head on, wouldn't you? And he's dangerous, believe me.' Already he was helping her towards a bench, where she sat down, her brain reeling. Yet it was all becoming dreadfully clear.

'So Stephen found me deliberately at the Temple of Beauty, and at the poetry reading.' She looked up at Alec. 'Oh, I walked straight into his *hands*.'

'Yes. And once he knew that *I* knew, Stephen became

extremely frightened that I would expose his brutality to your sister. But I just wanted Katy—and you—to be safe. When Stephen heard that you and I were betrothed, I think he resolved—in sheer desperation—to try to kidnap Katy. As a hostage? For revenge on me?' His face was grim. 'Fortunately, someone...' he hesitated a fraction '...let me know that he intended to use Katy in his plans. So I decided there was only one way to put an end to his dangerous mischief. To lay a trap.'

Sickness pooled coldly in her stomach. 'The poetry recital—I was so *stupid*. I should have guessed...'

'How could you? My brother's good at deception—thanks to years of practice,' said Alec curtly. 'So far he's got away with his iniquities. But not for much longer. Rosalie, if you can bear it, I think it best if we continue as though nothing has happened, because I want to know how Stephen will react to the arrest of his men.'

'Will he be charged?'

'I imagine he'll have done everything through a third party, just as he did with the threats, and the reward for you. But he'll know that I know.' He turned to her. 'If you're sure you can face it, we'll still go together to Lord Stokesay's tonight as planned. Being with me is your best defence, much as you may hate it.'

She heaved in a tight breath. Alec had done all this, regardless of the gulf it would doubtless widen between him and his already estranged family. For Katy. For *her*. Why? Simply because of his overpowering sense of justice. His integrity. How she'd misjudged him. A leaden weight seemed to be crushing her shoulders.

Be sensible. Be practical. 'Alec,' she asked calmly, 'how, when the time comes, will we break off this—betrothal?'

Some impenetrable emotion flickered across Alec's

face. 'It will be up to you, of course. You can think of what's appropriate—for example, that we've decided we're ill suited. I believe that's a common enough reason.'

Ill suited. Dear God, she hadn't thought so when she was in his arms. When he was making passionate love to her. But that had been a wild stupid dream.

Somehow Rosalie swallowed down the ache that squeezed her throat. 'Of course. Oh, Alec, that cut to your forehead, it's still bleeding, here, have my clean handkerchief…' She pushed it towards him, hoping he wouldn't notice how her hand shook. 'Your poor face, what happened?'

'That?' He dabbed with the handkerchief. 'I had one of Stephen's brutes cornered. He managed a punch before I felled him.'

She tried to joke. 'Clearly you needed me there. I came to your aid at the Temple of Beauty, didn't I?'

'Swinging that little table at them.' He smiled back and her heart shook. She hurried to rinse her handkerchief at the nearby pump and came back to bathe the cut, fussing over him. *This was probably the closest she would ever get to him again.* Tenderly she pushed back his dark hair from his forehead, aware of the warmth of his skin beneath her fingers, the strength of him, so close to her, yet so impossibly distant.

'You must keep my handkerchief until you can get a proper bandage on it.' She was blinking the stupid tears back from her eyes even as she placed it tenderly across his temple. 'There!' she said brightly. 'You look fit for anything now, even a ball, Captain Stewart!'

He stood up and gazed down at her. 'Is that the gown you'll be wearing tonight?'

'I—yes, it is.' She faltered. 'Is it all right, Alec?'

'More than that,' he said. His face was suddenly grave. 'You look exquisite.'

She stared at him, her heart pounding as she searched for words that wouldn't come. 'Ridiculous man,' she uttered lightly. But inside something was breaking.

'I must go and change my clothes,' Alec said, then hesitated. Touched her cheek, with fingers that lingered. 'Rosalie. Oh, Rosalie. I don't think you'll ever know how much I wish that things could have been different.'

Then he was gone.

It took her a little while to realise that Verena had come to lead her back into the house.

'I don't think I've ruined the gown,' Rosalie said somehow. 'But it was a close thing…' She fought the sudden sting of tears.

Verena took her hand. 'I told you that you should trust Alec,' she said, squeezing it warmly. 'Lucas and I do.'

Rosalie nodded blindly. But she hadn't. She hadn't, and that had been her utter downfall.

It was early evening and Rosalie was alone in her room. She'd had her bath and the servants had gone. She was wearing a cream silk wrap Verena had lent her; the lilac gown lay ready for her on the bed.

She hated it now. It seemed a symbol of all she had lost.

At seven Verena knocked and came in, her bright smile somehow making Rosalie's world even darker. 'The children will be going to bed soon,' Verena announced, 'then it will be time to set off.' She hesitated. 'You'll still be upset, I know, by what happened this afternoon. But Katy and you couldn't be in safer hands than Alec's—I've heard Lucas saying it often!'

His hands. Oh, God. Rosalie remembered his exquisitely tender lovemaking and fresh pain surged through her. She tried her hardest to smile. 'To be honest, I'm slightly daunted by the thought of tonight's ball. Though you've been so very kind.'

'No kindness is too much for a friend of Alec's!' declared Verena, sitting cosily on the bed beside her. 'Once Alec actually saved Lucas's life, did he tell you? In the Pyrenees. Lucas had injured his leg and was likely to freeze to death in the snow, so Alec got his men to build a rough stretcher and between them they carried him miles across the mountains in winter, to safety! I somehow *knew* Lucas was in trouble. But I also knew that with friends like Alec, Lucas would come home to me.' Verena patted Rosalie's hand. 'Now, I'm going to send my maid to you again, to help you to put on your gown. And I have an amethyst necklace and ear-drops you may like to borrow. They will match the lilac of your gown quite beautifully—I'm sure Alec will think so...' She hesitated again, then went on, 'Alec might sometimes seem a little distant, a little cold. But life has treated him harshly, you know. His family— well, his family quite frankly do not deserve him. What are your plans, my dear?'

Rosalie tensed. 'Plans?'

'I mean—when will the two of you be married?'

Rosalie forced out each word as if it drew the lifeblood from her. 'I am not sure now that the marriage will take place.'

Verena's face said it all. 'But we thought—Lucas and I thought you were made for one another! Oh, I know Alec seems distracted often. He worries about the funding of his soldiers' hostel—the hostel was his father's idea, you know, but his father abandoned it, so Alec had to take it all on. And unfortunately he refuses all offers of help from friends like Lucas. He is too proud!' She shook her head. 'Now, I know it's really none of my business, but

Alec thinks the world of you. Didn't you *see* the look in his eyes, when he saw you in that gown?'

'He was betrothed once before, I know. I think he is so wary of another commitment...'

Verena's brow creased in perplexity. Then—'You aren't thinking of Lady Emilia?' Verena raised her hands in amusement. 'She was a silly little thing; he never had a shred of anything except *pity* for her. You didn't really imagine... Oh, my goodness, I can tell by your face that I've said quite enough. I'll go and fetch that jewellery.'

When she'd gone, Verena's maid came to help Rosalie put on her lilac ballgown, then dressed her hair. '*Madame* looks beautiful!' she enthused. 'I will just pin up your hair—*so*—and leave a little of it trailing down your neck, like this—*madame*? Are you listening, *madame*?'

Rosalie was miles away, gazing at herself in the mirror. 'You look exquisite,' he had told her just now. And Verena: *Didn't you see the look in his eyes, when he saw you in that gown?*

Rosalie sat very still. The beginning of an unfamiliar emotion—hope—was just beginning to tingle through her veins.

For months afterwards, Lord Stokesay's ball was talked about as one of the most splendid events of the Season. 'The food! The guests! The gowns!' everyone was fond of exclaiming as they reminisced over it. 'Do you remember how the garden was lit up like a Venetian carnival? And there must have been over five hundred people in the ballroom! Of course, the Prince Regent was there, with the elegant Lord Conistone and all the other members of the royal set. And even Prinny looked dazzled by it all!'

Rosalie, sitting inside the Oxford mail coach the next day with Katy in her arms, gazed unseeing out of the window as London's western suburbs turned into rolling green countryside. Katy, who'd been sleeping, was looking around at the other passengers with a frown. 'Tick-tock man?' she asked Rosalie.

'We won't see tick-tock man for a little while, darling,' she said with an ache in her throat. *For ever* would be more like it.

She had so much to thank him for. It wasn't his fault that Rosalie's heart had been broken into little pieces. That her whole being *hurt* so, every time she remembered his smile, the touch of his fingers, his kiss…

All over, now. She blew her nose hard on a handkerchief—it was Alec's, she'd laundered it and kept it from that night when… Oh, Lord, those stupid tears were coming again. People were looking at her.

She sat up straight and pointed out of the window. 'Look, Katy. There are some sheep. And some calves, do you see them?' *What a fool she'd been.*

Last night Rosalie, Verena, Alec and Lucas had travelled to Lord Stokesay's ball together. Lucas was as charming as ever, paying compliments to Rosalie on her gown, though his eyes burned with passion when he turned back to his much-loved Verena. Alec was courteous, but distant. Their only chance to speak privately came as they lined up to be presented to Lord and Lady Stokesay, when Alec said quietly, 'I'm so sorry you had to find out, in such an abrupt and unpleasant way, about my brother's wickedness to your sister.'

Her hand was on his arm—so warm, so strong—and the painful thudding of her heart made her realise just how much she was starting to *hope*. 'I understand,' she said quickly. 'And Alec, I understand how hateful all this has been for you, as well as dangerous. Oh, your poor face!'

Her eyes had flown up to the bandage almost, but not entirely, hidden by his wavy dark hair. 'You patched me up beautifully,' he said. He reached to touch a stray curl that brushed her cheek and the intimacy of his touch jolted through her. 'The main thing is,' he went on steadily, 'that you can now be quite sure Stephen will never dare to threaten you again. He knows that I hold all the cards now.'

'Because you could expose his attempt to seize Katy?'

'Indeed. The kidnapping of a young child—whatever the motive, whatever the relationship—is unforgivable, whatever one's rank.'

Vividly across Rosalie's mind flashed the imaginary scene of a terrified Katy, delivered to a man—Stephen—who told her he was her father. Unforgivable. *Unbearable*. Her hand tightened just a little on Alec's arm; he looked down at her with concern etched across his features. 'Are you all right?'

'Thank you, yes. I'm fine.'

'One thing,' went on Alec in a level voice as the queue moved slowly forwards. 'I've just heard that my father and his wife might be here. Had I realised it, I would have declined the invitation. I hope you are not embarrassed by it.'

All she knew about Alec's father was that he had withdrawn his support for Two Crows Castle and cut Alec off, both financially and socially. An older version of Stephen, she'd assumed with scorn. She lifted her chin stubbornly. 'Your friends are not embarrassed to be with you. Far from it. So why should I be? It's your father's loss.'

'Thank you,' he said quietly.

At first Rosalie was terrified of being introduced to all these grand people, but she curtsied and spoke clearly, aware always of Alec's firm hand on her arm. And to her surprise, she found she was beginning to attract admiring glances.

She'd always considered herself too thin. Straight fair hair like hers was not fashionable, she'd thought. Men preferred lively, curvaceous women with curling locks and flirtatious conversation—didn't they? People came up to speak to Alec, of course, not her. But his friends' eyes would slide to her and widen. 'Congratulations, Captain Stewart!' she heard one of them say. 'You're a sly dog—glad you've brought your intended out in public at last!'

Verena spoke to Rosalie as she passed by on her way to the dancing. 'I told you that you looked beautiful!' she beamed.

'Ah—flattery.' Rosalie smiled back, waving her hand lightly in self-deprecation.

But Alec's eyes were warm whenever he looked at her and he seemed relaxed, almost happy. Until his father and stepmother arrived.

Alec and Rosalie were sitting down to supper with Lucas and Verena and all their friends when the late arrivals were announced. 'The Earl and Countess of Aldchester.'

Rosalie saw that Alec went very still. Verena said worriedly, 'I had not thought they would be here tonight...' The conversation was restarted by Lucas talking lightly to Alec across the table. But Rosalie watched as Alec's father and his wife came in.

He was a distinguished figure, in height and profile more like Alec than the hateful Lord Maybury. Yet he and Alec were estranged. Why?

Then she saw the beautiful woman at the Earl's side. Could she *really* be the Earl's wife, Lady Aldchester? But she was so young, only a little older, surely, than Rosalie! She had curling dark hair and a pale, exquisite face. Her gown, a precious thing of pink silk covered with layers of gauze and embroidered with pearls, revealed satiny bare shoulders and the curve of a perfect bosom.

An inexplicable cold warning tingled down Rosalie's spine.

But it appeared that father and son were happy to avoid one another's company; after supper Alec took her into the room where the dancing was, to lead her into a cotillion. There was just a moment, with his hand holding hers as he smiled gravely down at her, that she felt like confiding in him about her plan. But then he'd said, as the music stopped, 'Will you be all right with Verena and her friends for a short while? There are some people I need to speak to, you see.'

He led her to the edge of the dance floor, where Verena's friends crowded round Rosalie as she watched Alec's tall figure disappear. 'You are fortunate,' some of them sighed. 'We've all of us had our eye on Captain Stewart, at one time or another.' They chattered on and she tried to concentrate on what they said. But it was very warm in here, too warm; she didn't like the noise and the heat, and she missed Alec. She moved nearer to an open doorway, fanning herself.

Out there was a veranda and the night air suddenly tempted her. She walked slowly along it, gazing at the lit-up garden, the sparkling fountains. *Linette would have loved all this.* She would have loved the dancing, the beautiful house, the people strolling along the paths just below her...

And she saw them there. Alec and—his stepmother.

They were talking in low voices, intent only on each other. Rosalie was frozen to the spot. His stepmother— *so beautiful*—had her palms pressed to Alec's chest and looked as though she was pleading with him; while Alec, his expression grave, was shaking his head. His stepmother spoke a little more, then reached up on tiptoe to kiss him lingeringly on the lips. After that she turned and walked swiftly along a path that led back into the house—and Alec stood very still, as though he might never move again.

Half-remembered words were tumbling in chaotic confusion through Rosalie's brain. *'So she's back in town! Dear God, she's beautiful, but she's wrecked his life.'*

And that letter. *I know there are risks, my dear, but might I see you?*

Desperately she tried to make sense of it all. Perhaps Alec had loved this woman years ago, before she was married. And then she chose his father, for his title and money, thus embittering Alec for good. Yet still she toyed with him, summoning him with a scented note, a silken look…

Lady Aldchester was so very lovely. Rosalie felt her stomach pitching with nausea as she somehow got back into the house to find Verena. Her lips seemed to be refusing to form the right words as she said, 'I'm not feeling very well. I'm really sorry to be such a nuisance, but I wonder, would your carriage take me back now?'

After that, it was easy. The next morning she got her things together, then found Verena and told her, 'I received an invitation a few days ago, from an old friend who's moved to the country. I've decided to go and stay with her for a while.'

Verena was bewildered. 'But Alec… Is your betrothal at an end? Aren't you going to speak to him before you go?'

Rosalie couldn't bear to. Her heart would surely break. 'I think he will understand.'

Verena looked grave. Disappointed in her. 'I hope you'll leave a note to tell Alec where you will be?'

Rosalie hesitated 'Of course.' Not that he would need it. He would realise, surely, that she knew his secret at last. *I don't think you'll ever know how much I wish that things could have been different...*

Quickly she wrote down Helen's address; Verena took it, tight-lipped.

So here she was, on the mail coach to Oxford, with a new life ahead of her. And she knew she would never stop missing Alec Stewart for as long as she lived, but now she understood. Why his betrothal to Lady Emilia had been so brief. How he'd tried to stay away from his lovely step-mother. Why he'd deliberately excluded himself from polite society, to live an austere life with his soldiers.

But that woman clearly still held his heart in her smooth white hands.

Katy was sleeping again as the coach rocked on its way and Rosalie held her close. With her portion of the Lavalle fortune, she was free to do as she wanted. To live where she wanted.

And she wished, she wished she was back at shabby old Two Crows Castle, with Alec. In Alec's arms. In Alec's bed.

Chapter Twenty-Two

Two days later Alec was striding up the front steps of the house in Belgrave Square. A footman opened the big door, then Jarvis was hurrying towards him. 'So *very* glad you could come, Master Alec! Such news, such dreadful news...'

'My father said very little in his message. What's wrong, Jarvis?'

'I think your father would prefer to tell you himself, sir. Would you mind waiting a little, until I can inform him you're here? His man of business arrived a while ago and they are still closeted in the library.'

'Shall I wait in the parlour?'

'Very good, sir. I'll let you know the moment his lordship is free.'

And so Alec had time to remember the conversation between himself and Susanna at Lord Stokesay's the other night.

She had looked so self-conscious, so artificial in that over-elaborate gown of pink silk and gauze. She'd also looked tense. She'd begged him to come with her into the garden, for privacy, and once there she'd murmured, 'I realise you find it difficult to trust me. But I helped you last time, did I not, with my news about Stephen's intentions towards the child?'

'You did,' he answered curtly, trying to keep his senses clear of that over-strong scent she used.

'That little girl. Is she safe, Alec?'

'Most certainly.'

She let out a breath of relief. 'At least, then, I can feel I've done something of use, before I leave.' She sighed.

'You're leaving the ball already?' Alec asked sharply.

'Not here—London, I mean! Oh, Alec, I have decided that your father does not deserve my wickedness. You are the one honest member of this family and I want to tell you that I am leaving England for good. I'm going back to Italy. Please tell your father I am sorry. And I know, my dear, that I do not deserve your good wishes, but I hope you believe me when I say that I truly wish you well.'

One lingering touch of her silken mouth upon his lips that left him cold and she was gone, leaving behind only her scent and the rekindled memories of the night he'd so bitterly regretted ever since.

In the winter of 1814, Napoleon was a prisoner on Elba, and London had become a city of parties and frivolity. By then Alec's father was besotted with Susanna, the Contessa di Ascoli. Alec had been forced to acknowledge she was enticing indeed, with her soft raven curls, her ripe mouth and her sultry, dark-blue eyes. But he was wary, too, because he read lechery in the sidelong glances she cast his way.

That Christmas his father was at Carrfields, holding a house party that was to continue into the New Year. Alec, whose engagement to Lady Emilia was already faltering, had promised to come from London, but would stay for just two nights. He was due back with his regiment in early January, because Lord Wellington did not expect the peace to last.

By the time he arrived at Carrfields he was dog-tired, and dismayed by his father's news that he and the Contessa—who was there as a guest—were engaged to be married. Last time Alec had met her he'd heard her saying that she would die if she had to stay in the country. But here she was at Carrfields, his father's betrothed.

Alec had forced himself into his usual light-heartedness, drinking toasts in champagne to the happy couple with the rest. But thanks to his fatigue the drink had gone to his head and he was glad to make his excuses at midnight and retire to his room, where he'd fallen asleep the moment his head hit the pillow.

He thought he heard his door open two hours later, but imagined it, in his alcohol-induced languor, to be a dream. He stirred and muttered something, but the dream persisted; he imagined that someone was there in his room, a sinuous creature with long dark hair, who was starting to ease off her satin nightgown, then lowered herself to bed beside him, her silken hands stroking his powerful naked shoulders, her scent enveloping him.

'Alec. Oh, Alec. How I desire you,' she breathed.

Alec was aware of trying to fight his way through the confusion of heavy sleep, his mind still hazed by champagne and exhaustion; but in his dream the dark-haired nymph was pushing back the sheets to reach for his thickening member and twisting her lithe body to slip astride him. Uttering little cries of delight, she coaxed him and passionately caressed him into the act of love, then lay curled in his arms.

He'd woken before dawn to memories of that shadowy, erotic dream. His manhood was pulsing again, troubling him…

Then he realised. Someone was pressing herself against him, fondling him with languorous fingers, her tongue sliding between her lips and her dark-lashed blue eyes hot with invitation—

His soon-to-be stepmother. His naked, soon-to-be stepmother. He'd jumped from the bed. Hell. This nightmare had been only too real.

She watched his naked body as he started reaching for his clothes, her eyes lingering on his erection. 'It's early. Come back to bed,' she'd murmured.

He was already struggling to pull on his breeches. Self-disgust fractured his being. 'My God,' he'd said through gritted teeth, 'I hope you're not still seriously considering getting married to my father.'

'Why not?' she'd queried softly. 'Surely you are not going to tell him about this?' She'd slid out of the bed and swayed towards him; he continued pulling on his clothes. She put her hands up to his chest, toying with the buttons of his coat. 'We can do this again, whenever it's convenient, can't we? Your father need never know.'

'You're joking.' Alec had pushed her away.

He'd set off back to London before the rest of the house was astir, filled with self-disgust. Surely his father could not marry this woman?

He'd tried to warn his father, before he was sent abroad again on his last spell of active service. The result was total estrangement between father and son. And the young Lady Emilia, already peevish at Alec's devotion to his army duties, and bewildered by his increasingly sombre moods, hastily broke off their betrothal.

The Earl and Susanna had married in the summer of 1815, the summer of Waterloo. When Alec returned from the war he went to live at Two Crows Castle, effectively cutting himself off from his family.

That autumn he'd gone to a house party in a grand Kensington mansion, hosted by an officer of his regiment—Grenville—whom Alec hadn't seen for some time. Alec had been under the impression it was to be a kind of army reunion, but clearly the event had grown in size. And Grenville hadn't told Alec until he arrived that night that he'd also invited Alec's father and his wife.

As it turned out, the Earl, unwell, had been unable to attend.

'A shame about your father,' Grenville had said to Alec. He was either unaware of father and son's estrangement, or was bent on causing mischief. 'But your stepmother's turned up. Your brother offered to bring her, you see.'

Alec was deciding he liked Grenville less and less. And—Stephen, with Susanna? It wasn't unknown, of course, for a male relative to escort a married woman to a social event. So Alec, trapped in a situation he had not foreseen, was curt to Stephen and coldly civil to Susanna. He stayed for barely two hours, then made his excuses to leave.

Like the other guests, the intention had been that he stayed overnight, so he first had to go upstairs and get his things from the chamber he'd been allotted on arrival. It was a little past eleven; his mind was already on his journey home.

But he'd pulled up with a jolt of utter disbelief when he came upon Stephen and Susanna, stealing out of a nearby bedroom.

To Alec it couldn't have been plainer that they were fresh from intimacy. 'My God,' he'd breathed.

Stephen, straightening his neckcloth, had drawled, 'Say one word about this, little brother, and you're finished. I know from Susanna that you have no reason whatever to preach virtue at me.'

'At least she wasn't my stepmother at the time!'

Stephen said, 'Do you think that would matter if our father were to find out?'

So Stephen had been able to hold that knife to Alec's throat ever since.

Jarvis came into the parlour where Alec waited. 'His lordship is ready to see you, Captain Stewart.'

'My thanks, Jarvis.'

The Earl was still in his library, pacing the floor. When Alec entered, his father came almost hesitantly towards him.

'Alec,' he said. 'You were so right, my son, to warn me about—about...' He suddenly gripped Alec's hand. 'God help me,' he whispered, 'I've been such a fool.'

'No, sir,' said Alec quickly. 'Never that. Please. Sit down.'

'A fool is what I am,' repeated the Earl bitterly. He sank into the chair to which Alec guided him and ran his fingers through his greying hair. 'She's gone back to Italy. She as good as told me it was tedious, living with an old man like me. And she's taken all the family jewels!' He began to laugh, a hollow sound. 'Well, there's no fool like an old fool, they say. And do you know? Stephen has set off after her. He says it's to get the jewellery back. Says he feels huge concern for me and all the rest of it...'

Alec had gone very still. *Stephen*, gone after her. To get the jewels? To get Susanna? Or was it because he realised that, thanks to his attempt to kidnap Katy, Alec could now expose Stephen for the blackguard he was?

Alec said, 'It's good of Stephen to try to get the jewels back for you, sir.'

His father looked up at him in utter despair. 'There's no need to gammon me any longer, Alec. Stephen and she were rutting together whenever my back was turned. Weren't they? Weren't they, damn it?'

Alec braced himself. 'For how long have you known this?' he asked quietly.

'There were signs I'd ignored, for months.' His father clenched his hands. 'But I knew for certain when Stephen came to visit me in the country. They thought I was in my bedchamber. I came downstairs and saw the two of them whispering together. *Touching* each other. God damn it, I tried to pretend I didn't realise what it meant...' The Earl shook his head. 'Of course she probably cares for him even less than she did for me—he'll just be an idle diversion for her. You, Alec, realised what she was from the start—that was why you tried to warn me off her, before our wedding—' He broke off, coughing.

Now. Now was the time. 'Sir, there is something I must tell you.'

And Alec told him the story of that one despicable night. He made no excuses for his own behaviour. 'It was unforgivable of me,' he said quietly.

After a long silence his father turned to Alec and said, 'You did try to tell me, didn't you?'

'I did, sir, but not strongly enough.'

His father waved his hand dismissively. 'Ah, I was an old besotted fool, I wouldn't have listened to a word anyway.' He got up and went to the window, his shoulders rigid. Then at last he turned round and said, 'Did you take all your war diaries away, my son?'

'Almost all, sir. But there were just a few left, which of course I intend to remove as soon as possible.'

'You know, Alec...' his father's voice was hesitant '...you never did tell me about Waterloo. I wonder, are you free for an hour or so?'

'For as long as you wish, sir,' said Alec quietly.

'Perhaps,' his father said, 'you would spare a little time to go through the battle with me? I find myself rather in need of company. And, you know, I never did understand why Wellington said that the whole outcome of Waterloo turned on the Coldstream Guards holding some damned gate at a place called Hougoumont…'

Alec went over to the bookcase for his father's maps, spread them out on a nearby table, then pulled up chairs for himself and his father and started pointing out the battle lines. 'Here's Hougoumont, below the escarpment. It was a farm with gated grounds that Wellington had fortified, a crucial position—the French attacked it all day.'

'And is that the north gate?'

'Yes. There the enemy might have broken through were it not for Macdonnell and his Coldstream Guards defending it hand to hand. Then Halkett's Hanoverian Brigade reinforced Macdonnell's men and they somehow held on, despite heavy losses.'

'Ah, Halkett's men.' The Earl nodded.

'Indeed, sir. Lord Wellington always said that between them they won the battle for him there…'

Alec was in no hurry. He had all the time in the world spreading out empty before him, now that Rosalie had gone. For he had realised what he should have acknowledged weeks ago: that he simply could not bear to live his life without her.

Yet clearly—she couldn't have made it plainer—she wanted nothing at all to do with him. Had removed herself entirely from his life. *Why had she left so suddenly?*

Alec knew that the attempt to kidnap Katy, and the news that Alec's brother was the villain, had shaken her badly. Perhaps she'd been right and he should have told her earlier about Stephen. But surely she'd forgiven him, when she realised how thorough had been Alec's preparations to safeguard the little girl? Hadn't Rosalie tended Alec's slight injury herself, her eyes full of something like tenderness?

But she'd gone, and there was no message for him, only an address—Helen's address—that he gathered she'd been reluctant to give. Perhaps Rosalie had decided she could no longer bear to be in the company of someone who would always remind her of Linette's evil seducer. Remind her of Katy's father, God damn it.

It was as well she'd never know how he'd betrayed his father with Susanna. Or—perhaps she did. His stomach pitched as he realised—*that could be it*. At Lord Stokesay's ball—somehow she'd realised. She'd somehow found out—and that was why she'd left.

Oh, God. Who could blame her?

Meanwhile, he'd neglected his fencing lessons lately for the other matters, and day after day more soldiers came to Two Crows Castle begging for shelter. Alec knew it was possible now that his father might offer to restore his aid. But in the meantime drastic action was called for, if they were not to close down within weeks.

After leaving his father, Alec rode to his bank in the Temple, to ask for more time to pay his bills. As he was ushered into a private office, he braced himself.

Then a senior clerk hurried in, smiling. 'Captain Stewart. This is indeed a lucky chance! I was about to contact you...'

And Alec listened, almost in disbelief, as the clerk told him that a large sum of money had been given into the bank's care—for the benefit of the soldiers at Two Crows Castle. And the donor wished to remain completely anonymous.

His father? His father would have told him, surely! The

clerk refused to say any more. But Alec, on his way out past the rows of junior clerks at their desks, was stopped by a scrawny lad in black, sweeping the floor.

'Captain Stewart?' the boy whispered eagerly. 'You remember me, don't you, Captain Stewart? I got a job here now, Captain, running errands and the like!'

'Mikey! You stayed at Two Crows Castle for a couple of weeks, didn't you?'

'I did, and it was thanks to that place I got this job. And funnily enough, I saw someone else here from Two Crows Castle only the other day, Captain!'

'You did? Who was he?'

'Not a he, Captain,' said Mikey importantly. 'But a *she*.'

As Mikey explained who, Alec began to understand. And—to hope.

Chapter Twenty-Three

It was a warm May afternoon and Rosalie was in the orchard at the back of Helen and Francis's pretty house, sitting on a rug in the shade of a blossom-laden apple tree while she read stories to Katy and Toby.

She had been here for a few weeks now, renting a cottage close to the village of Heythrop. The banns had been read three times in Heythrop's pretty church; Helen and Francis were married now and Helen had welcomed Rosalie like a lamb returned to the fold.

'Oh, my dear Rosalie, I knew you'd see sense in the end!' she had cried.

'Captain Stewart proved to be a true and honourable friend,' Rosalie had replied quietly. 'And he helped me to find Katy's father.'

'So—is the villain going to be made to pay for his wickedness to poor Linette?'

'I think he *has* paid, Helen.' Rosalie could still hardly bear to think of the kidnap attempt on Katy. 'Though the fewer people who know of it, the better. And Katy and I are quite safe from him, thanks to Captain Stewart.'

Helen had kept hugging them both, and laughing and crying, and trying to ask more. But sensible Francis had drawn his wife aside gently. 'Give Miss Rowland time to get her breath, Helen! You'll be tired, my dear,' he added to Rosalie, 'after your journey.'

'I'm fine.' But Rosalie had smiled at him, in gratitude. 'Mr Wheeldon, I cannot thank you enough, for putting me in touch with my mother's family. And I want to tell you and Helen that I would like to give some money towards your school—no, I will not allow any arguments! There will still be more than enough for me and Katy, I assure you!'

And for Two Crows Castle. She hugged that thought to herself over the next few days, remembering her visit to the bank. It was so strange that she'd bumped into Mikey there, who told her how much he'd enjoyed working in the garden. She'd had to hurry away, because of the stupid tears brimming in her eyes.

She and Katy had settled quickly into their little cottage. The fact that it was less than ten miles from the place where she grew up gave her a sense of peace, of redemption even, to be here again with Katy. To visit her mother's grave, and their old home, which was inhabited now by a pleasant young family. To watch Katy, so happy in the places like the riverside where she and Linette had played.

Helen had offered to send over their daily maidservant to help her in her new abode, but Rosalie preferred to do everything herself, brushing and sweeping from dawn till dusk. Action was a necessity, for a great ache of loneliness—of sheer *loss*—filled her almost unbearably whenever she thought of Alec Stewart.

Once the cottage was neat as a new pin, she helped Helen in the school, teaching the small ones to read. But now school had finished for the day, which was why she was in the orchard with Katy and Toby, equipped with buttered scones and a pitcher of lemonade for when the storytelling was over. Helen and Francis had taken a trip into Chipping Norton in their dog cart to visit the shops there, so she was surprised to hear the sound of steady hoofbeats approaching.

Katy heard it, too, and wandered off towards the low hedge that separated the orchard from the lane. She turned back to Rosalie, her little face alight.

'Tick-tock man!' she cried in joy.

Rosalie felt her heart do a topsy-turvy somersault. *No. It could not be...* She got slowly to her feet.

But it was. It was Alec. Lithely dismounting, he looped his horse's reins over the gatepost and was striding towards her, his hair rumpled, his boots dusty from the road, but still so handsome that her breath caught thickly in her throat.

Katy was the first to reach him; he swung her up in his arms and kissed her cheek. 'How's my girl?' He smiled.

But his eyes—his dark, burning eyes—were on Rosalie. 'I've come to thank you,' he said to her. 'For what you did for Two Crows Castle.'

She'd scrambled to her feet, knowing her straw hat was askew. 'But you weren't supposed to *know*...'

'And no one deliberately betrayed your trust,' he assured her. 'But...' And he explained about Mikey.

'Of course,' she said wonderingly. 'I saw him there.'

'He misses the garden. And you,' he told her. There was something in his eyes, in his voice, that made her dizzy with an emotion she didn't dare to name.

Then Katy was tugging at his hand, and Alec sat with them all in the orchard, sharing their lemonade and scones. Afterwards he showed the children how to roll pennies along the smoothed-out rug, making Toby laugh with delight at his success and guiding little Katy.

Rosalie watched his long, lithe figure as he sprawled in

the grass in his shirt sleeves, the sun hot on his brown fore-arms, one of them marked by the jagged scar she remembered so well. Though a tight ache of longing squeezed at her chest, she tried her hardest just to be content that he was here, that he turned to her every so often with a look of such warmth in his dark eyes that her foolish heart leapt.

He has only come to thank me for the money, she warned herself. *Nothing else has changed. His heart is not free. Soon he will be leaving again.*

When Helen and Francis got back they were surprised to see him here. But Francis warmly invited Alec to eat with them and Katy was put to bed in the room next to Toby's so the adults could dine together that evening. Francis was aware of Alec Stewart's work with homeless soldiers; now he openly showed his interest. As for Helen—well, Helen was melting, slowly but surely.

'He is rather charming,' she confided reluctantly when she and Rosalie were alone together in the parlour after the meal, while the men took a glass of port. 'And so *very* handsome... Obviously I'd got hold of the wrong end of the stick about him. An earl's son, you say? And he dealt with the villain who wronged poor Linette. Hmmm.'

Rosalie didn't even want to think about Stephen now. All that filled her mind was Alec. Alec was here. *It means nothing. You know it means nothing...*

The men joined them very soon afterwards, and Helen began to say, 'You may stay here, of course, Captain Stewart, we have a bed made up!'

Alec looked at his watch. 'I actually planned on staying at the Heythrop Inn tonight. But on my way back, perhaps I could escort Miss Rowland home.'

'Oh, Francis will do that, won't you, Fra—?'

But Rosalie would swear that Francis had, most definitely, given his wife's arm a warning pinch.

Tomorrow, Alec would be leaving her life again. He'd only come to thank her for the money, hadn't he?

It was less than a quarter of a mile back to her cottage, and a beautiful, moonlit evening. He led his horse, and as they walked she told him lightly about the school and how well Katy had settled in here. He waited while she unlocked the door, then she turned to him.

He was going to leave her again now. She gazed up one last time at that proud, handsome profile that had stunned her at the Temple of Beauty. 'Thank you for seeing me home,' she began. 'Now you will want to ride on to the inn.'

Something blazed in his dark eyes. Some emotion that caught at her quivering heart, pounded through her veins, melting her very bones.

'Rosalie,' he said, 'why did you leave London so suddenly?'

Her throat seemed to have closed up. 'I really think you must guess why…'

'No,' he said. 'I can't. May I come in? Just for a brief while? We really must talk.'

She couldn't answer.

'Go inside,' he urged gently. 'I'll see to my horse. Is there a stable?'

'Round the back. A neighbour uses it sometimes, everything's there.'

She went inside. Her throat felt as though it could hardly drag air into her lungs. Tension made her sick. She'd just lit the fire that was ready laid in the grate when he came back in, bowing his dark head a fraction to enter the low-beamed door.

'Please tell me everything,' he said simply.

What had she to lose?

He joined her on the sofa, not too near, not too far. He was very quiet as she told him how she'd seen him with his stepmother at Lord Stokesay's ball. She began to shiver again. 'I saw how beautiful she was, Alec,' she said. 'And I'd heard your men talk about someone who had hurt you badly in the past. I'd assumed it was your fiancée...' Her clear voice, so steady till now, faltered at last. 'But that night I realised that you must have loved *her* and were devastated when she married your father...'

He said, 'That is not true. You must believe me. I never loved my stepmother, ever.'

And she began, at last, to hope.

A slow tide of exhilaration was surging through Alec's veins. He remembered Mikey's words. *'She went dashing out, Captain Stewart, with tears in her eyes when I talked about you and Two Crows Castle!'*

Those tears were precious. The money—her gift—had given him the excuse to make this journey. Rosalie's tears had given him hope.

He must not press her. He mustn't overwhelm her. Hadn't she endured enough, in her usual calm, courageous way? But she did, at the very least, deserve the truth.

Steadily Alec told her the whole sorry tale. How Susanna had come to him that one wretched night, when she was already promised to his father, and seduced him when he was befuddled with drink and fatigue. How he had tried to warn his father away from her, but had only alienated the Earl, badly. How he'd discovered that Stephen, too—Rosalie let out a low cry at this—had shared that woman's bed, often.

She listened to him intently and he saw the colour tinting her cheeks as his story unfolded. She clasped her hands in her lap throughout; only at the end did she say, 'But when I saw her with you at Lord Stokesay's, she—she looked as though she still *loved* you...'

His face became hard briefly. 'Perhaps she does care for me in her own way. But she was saying goodbye to me, Rosalie.'

'Goodbye?'

Again he saw the emotions fluttering across her delicate face like shadows. The anguish in her eyes as she absorbed all this. *Gently*, he told himself. Gently. She is not sure she can trust you, for God's sake.

Alec wanted to enfold her in his arms and soothe away her suffering, and tell her she was safe. But this wasn't over yet. Instead he took her hand in his and said, 'She left my father the day afterwards to return to Italy, taking the family's jewels with her. Stephen went after her.'

'To get them back? To get *her* back?' she whispered.

He held her hand fast and said, 'Ostensibly to get the jewels back. But who knows—perhaps Stephen felt some kind of affection for her? However, I think he probably seized on it all as a convenient reason to leave London for a while. He would have been afraid, you see, that I would spread the news about his attempt to kidnap Katy. That I might make known the whole, shameful business of his seduction of Linette and his efforts to silence *you*, Rosalie.'

'But if you'd told Linette's story, your family's reputation might have suffered. You would have sacrificed that?'

'Without hesitation,' he said steadily.

A jolt shook her heart. Was it possible that she meant so much to him? Or was it his sense of honour, of justice, that prevailed? Her hand still lay in his and the warmth, the strength of his grip, tingled through her veins, setting off that familiar, so-painful longing that tugged at every fibre of her being. Fighting it with all her strength she lifted her face to his to ask calmly, 'What will happen, Alec, when Stephen comes back?'

His hard-boned face was grim now. His voice devoid of emotion. 'He won't come back. He drowned when the ship on which he was sailing foundered in a storm off Brest. I'd have come so much sooner, but you'll understand my father needed me.'

'Oh...' The shock of it travelled through her. 'Oh, Alec. Stephen was Katy's father and your brother...' She was silent, wondering. 'Yet—yet everything about him was the very *opposite* of what you stand for.'

He'd gone very still. 'What do you think I stand for, Rosalie?'

'You stand for courage,' she said steadily. 'Honesty. Duty.'

Her words resonated through his body, bringing light somehow to the darkest recesses of his soul. He heaved a deep breath. 'Stephen's story is sad indeed,' he acknowledged quietly. 'He could have been so much more.'

'Your poor father—he will be grief-stricken!' Her blue eyes lifted suddenly to his face. 'Unless—he *knows*?'

'He's gone to his country home at Carrfields in Hampshire for a period of mourning. But, yes, he knows. I didn't have to tell him about Stephen and Susanna, for which I thank God. My father knows also about me and that one hateful night with her.' He shook his head, as though banishing dark dreams. 'We are reconciled again, my father and I. And he wants me to bring *you* to Carrfields, Rosalie.'

'Me?' A pulse was beating very faintly in her throat.

'Indeed. You,' he said softly. 'And Katy, too, of course. We are betrothed, remember?'

Again Rosalie felt an agonising surge of hope. Hope

that she'd crushed remorselessly, again and again, until her body felt battered with emotion.

She tried to smile dismissively. 'Alec, I know you only made your offer of betrothal out of duty! It was to keep Katy and me safe from your brother—but there is no longer any need. Besides, now that Stephen is dead, you are the heir to an earldom and marriage to someone like me is out of the question!'

That decided him. If he'd had any doubts at all about the complete *rightness* of this, they were gone. Vanished. Yes—his brother's death made him one of the most eligible matches in England. And only Rosalie—his enchanting, courageous Rosalie—would turn him down for that very reason.

He drew her into his arms, as he'd been longing to do since seeing her in the sunshine of the orchard that afternoon. 'Rosalie. Listen to me. I want you. I need you. I would have told you long ago, but I knew that you believed so very much in loyalty to one's family and I thought that my past—my shameful past—would repel you for ever!'

She'd lifted her hands to his cheeks now, outlining his dear, familiar features with her fingertips, feeling ripples of desire surging through her every nerve end as she traced his hard cheekbones, the stubble-roughened skin of his jaw, the soft sensuality of his lips. 'Alec, I did a dreadful thing in driving Linette away from home, remember?'

'You were trying to *save* her. You searched all of London for her. You risked so much for her daughter's sake. No one could be as loyal or as brave as you.' He drew a deep breath. 'When I realised that you'd left Lucas's house, I was terrified that you'd found out about my stepmother and hated me. And I couldn't endure it. I want to know—I *need* to know—if you feel that you could, some day, come to love me, Rosalie.'

Her heart was almost too full to speak. '*Love* you! Alec, I think I've loved you since that night that I saw you at Dr Barnard's!'

'Really?' He was speaking huskily now, his desire for her pounding through his veins, heating his loins. 'You're telling me that Ro Rowland, fellow about town, writer of scathing pieces about London's gentry, lost her heart to a patron of the Temple of Beauty?'

'Ro Rowland, fellow about town, was—quite frankly—captivated by a handsome soldier simply known as the Captain,' she breathed, running her hands across his shoulders.

'And I by you. Oh, God, *Rosalie*...'

In that same instant he gathered her in his arms. His big hands spanned her ribs, encompassing the slenderness of her waist beneath that old gown, feeling her tremble at his touch; then her arms were round his neck and she was breathing his name. He let one palm cup her breast, his thumb stroking the right nipple until it tensed and hardened beneath his touch.

She was lifting her face to him like a flower, her lips already opening for his kiss. Their mouths brushed once, twice, then were joined in a gliding of lips and tongues that had his body burning for more. Her kiss was delectable—shy, yet passionate. He roved deeply within the silk of her inner lips while he pulled her harder against his own body, until her breasts were crushed against the wall of his chest. The old sofa groaned and creaked. Alec broke off the kiss, swearing under his breath. 'This is *not* a good idea.'

He saw the desperate disappointment in her wide, desire-hazed eyes. Saw the way she drew herself back, her arms clasped across her bosom. 'Of course. I'm sorry. What you must think of me...'

'I meant,' he said softly, his dark eyes burning with need for her, 'that I think a bed would be far more comfortable.'

'You were going to the inn…'

'They're not going to lose sleep over my absence.'

Her sweet face lit up again. Her eyes danced with laughter. 'Oh, Alec. Let me just lock the door and put up the fire guard…'

'We'll do that together,' he said, his thumb still deliciously circling the sensitive skin of her palm. 'When you've explained one more mystery to me, Rosalie Rowland.'

'A mystery?'

'I've already thanked you for your donation to Two Crows Castle. But—forgive me—I thought you were penniless.'

And so she told him all about Francis Wheeldon's enquiries and her Lavalle legacy.

'Oh, Rosalie Rowland,' he breathed, 'fellow about town, I am fascinated. I can't wait to begin finding out the rest of your secrets… Oh, hell and damnation!'

'What?'

'I don't suppose I should touch you, let alone kiss you. Devil take it, now I've learnt you're a French aristocrat, I suppose I should ask permission from *someone* to court you!' His eyes danced with laughter and something darker that thrilled her soul—burning, all-male desire.

'My dearest Alec,' she whispered, pulling his head down to hers, 'you'd have to travel a long way to find anyone who'd trouble himself to fight for my honour. And I've told you—you are an earl's son and should be looking amongst England's aristocracy for a suitable wife!'

'God damn it all—' he frowned '—I will *not* face the

Marriage Mart at Almack's! Please, Miss Rowland, don't put me through that!'

She put her head on one side. 'On second thoughts,' she murmured, her eyes dancing, 'I *might* take pity on you. And if you do not kiss me this very minute, I swear I will most definitely have to seduce you!'

'Are you sure?' He was still holding back. 'This isn't all too—sudden for you?'

She ran, light-footed, to lock the door, then came back to wrap her arms around his neck. 'I'm fine,' she murmured, 'apart from the fact that I have missed you, my darling Captain Stewart, so very, very badly.'

He swung her up in his arms and carried her up the twisting stairs to her bedroom. 'Mind the beams.' She was laughing. 'Alec, I don't think anyone of your height was ever meant to live in a cottage like this—be careful of the doorway, and that old cupboard there—oh!'

'I was *made* to be in a cottage like this. With you,' he said. He deposited her on her bed and began to kiss her.

Rosalie had told herself all evening that all she wanted now was his touch and one kiss, no more, but it felt so wonderful to be held by him again. Inevitably her hunger deepened, burned like a flame as she pressed her lips to his warm skin and ran the flat of her palm over his dear, familiar face, his muscled shoulders.

He pulled off his shirt, then his breeches; already his desire was evident. He helped her to unbutton her gown, because sudden shyness made her fingers clumsy, but he reassured her with the kisses he traced from her throat up to her earlobes and lips.

She breathed, 'I want you, Alec. Come to me, now. *Please.*'

His dark eyes intent, he joined her, seeking her mouth

with his in gentle cajoling, giving her pleasure and reassurance with every touch of his hand, every caress of his lips. Sweetly he suckled at the tightened crest of her breast, while letting his fingers trail downwards to the heated core of her. Letting out a low moan of need, she wrapped her slender legs round his muscular, hair-roughened ones, urgently seeking him.

Whispering her name, he drove himself into her, sheathing himself in her warmness; she clutched him and moved with passion and love, until her whole being was shattered by a delirious extremity of pleasure in which he exulted even as his own climax convulsed him.

For a long time afterwards they lay breathing as one, hearts beating as one.

And still Alec's blood pounded with the urge to kiss her, caress her. By God, he'd fought his love for her. He'd been so reluctant to lay himself open, make himself vulnerable. But Ro Rowland had stolen her way into his heart and he had no intention of losing her, ever again.

She was stirring dreamily in his arms, her lissom body curled half-naked against his own hard-muscled form.

'Tired?' He kissed her throat tenderly.

'I shall not sleep all night,' she whispered. 'I shall always remember lying here like this, with you, Alec.'

He raised himself on one elbow, gazing down at her as the moonlight filtered into the low-ceilinged cottage bedroom. 'I've told you,' he said steadily, 'I love you, Rosalie. I want to spend the rest of my life with you.' He cupped her face with his hand and gazed into her eyes with a kind of raw and aching tenderness that set all her nerve ends tingling again with the need for his possession. 'Are you, or are you not, going to marry me?'

So much. He meant so very much to her. 'I really need

to remind you,' she said huskily, 'that I've appeared on stage, at the Temple of Beauty, which is truly outrageous!'

He gave a shout of laughter and gathered her close. 'So you did,' he breathed, 'and that's when I realised what was missing from my life. The goddess Athena, in the form of the adorable Miss Rosalie Rowland!'

She was beginning to laugh, too, tenderly. She was shifting beneath him, eager for his embrace again. Eager to feel the delicious weight of him, feel his virility pleasuring her, joining with her in a completeness she'd scarcely dreamed of.

'Try getting me to leave your life, Captain Stewart,' she whispered, pulling his face to hers to kiss him sweetly.

And Alec felt, after years of travelling through an uncharted wilderness, as if he'd come home at last.

Epilogue

Their wedding was in November and the reception was held at the Earl's Mayfair home. The six-month delay was inevitable, for the Earl and Alec were in mourning for Stephen, and an unspoken grief was felt by both, for the man he might have been. No one ever spoke Susanna's name again.

Prior to the wedding Alec moved back into the Bedford Street house that was originally his home, for Susanna's mother had followed her daughter to Italy. Alec left Garrett to manage Two Crows Castle for him, which he did most efficiently. The Earl had offered to fund the hostel fully and Alec had wanted to return Rosalie's money, but she refused.

'I'll think of it as my memorial to Linette,' she told him and he understood.

At the party after the wedding all the guests agreed that Rosalie looked radiant in her gown of white tulle, while Alec was splendidly, darkly handsome in his black tail-coat. But it was also agreed that little Katy stole the show, for she refused to be parted from Alec's side, and had to be cajoled away from the party and to her bed with the promise that she would see him again the next morning.

* * *

After an idyllic week spent in the countryside at Carr-fields, Rosalie, Katy and Alec returned to Bedford Street. Katy had been invited to Lucas and Verena's house for the afternoon to play with their children, so Alec showed Rosalie around. On the first floor she espied a sun-filled room with a bay window that was furnished with some as-yet-empty mahogany bookcases and a beautiful old writing desk. Rosalie turned to Alec with questioning eyes.

'For you,' he smiled. 'A study, for Ro Rowland. I know you'll never want to give up your writing.'

'Alec, it's a beautiful room. But you know I'll stop writing if you want me to!'

'Perhaps you could try something safer, like poetry?' he teased. 'My love, I don't want you to ever stop writing. You'll have some spare moments to fill, after all. We won't be at parties and balls *every* night, and when we are old and grey we'll have perhaps got over spending most of our days in bed together.'

She nestled against him. 'Mmm. Most of our days. Oh, good. And I'll be careful,' she promised, 'with my writing. I'll be *especially* careful not to tackle down-at-heel soldiers about rackrenting!'

'Wise of you,' he murmured. His strong hands, which had been caressing her breasts, were already starting to deftly unbutton the bodice of her pretty sprig-muslin day gown. 'Because one of these days, Ro Rowland, intrepid adventurer, exposer of wrongs, you might find that you've taken on more than you bargained for.'

She touched his wide, sensually curving lips. 'And so, indeed, might you—Alec! The servants!'

'Are well trained,' he grinned, undoing another button.

She sighed with happiness and ran her fingers over his shoulders, deliciously conscious of that powerfully masculine body beneath the formal shirt, of the way his breeches moulded his lean hips and powerfully muscled thighs. She could see that he wanted her. Was aroused for her, as she was for him.

She said softly, 'Here's an order, Captain Stewart.' She moistened her own full lips. 'I want those clothes off.'

'Wanton,' he said, shaking his head a little, 'utterly wanton...'

'Do I detect insubordination?' she retorted, a wicked gleam in her eye.

The look of mischief in her sparkling turquoise eyes made his throat go dry, his skin tingle. For answer he swung her up in his powerful arms and carried her to the bedroom, while she clasped her hands tightly around his neck and pressed her cheek to his chest, where she could hear his heart beating.

For her.

Tenderly, powerfully, he made love to her. And she indeed matched him in his ardour as he took her to the pinnacle of pleasure and beyond, until she felt herself shattering into a million shards of starlight.

Wrapped in his strong arms, she recalled the perilous, often sad journey that had brought her here. Alec was watching her, stroking her cheek with one finger.

'Not tears, sweetheart?' he whispered.

'No. Oh, no! At least—not tears of *sadness*. I love you, Alec, so very much. I just hope I will be worthy of you.'

'You've proved that and more, a thousand times,' he told her gravely, stroking a curl away from her temple. 'When I realised you'd left me, after that ball, I faced an abyss. And I knew then that I could face anything—anything at all, Rosalie—except the loss of your love.'

She nestled tighter into his arms. 'You have that for ever,' she breathed.

He kissed her tenderly, his lips warm on her cheek. 'For ever and always,' he echoed.

Rosalie twined her arms around his neck with a little sigh and her heart overflowed with pure happiness. For ever, with her darling Captain Stewart, was all that she could want, or need.

* * * * *

The Outrageous
Belle Marchmain

Chapter One

Sawle Down, Somerset—March 1819

It was the kind of spring afternoon that touched these green Somerset hills with magic—or so the locals, whose heads were filled with old folk tales, would say. Adam, a hard-headed businessman, had no time for superstitious nonsense, but he found himself doing exactly what an old quarryman would do. He let his long, lean fingers rest on the great slab of honey-coloured stone that had just been hewn from the ground—then he tapped it, once, twice, thrice.

For luck.

May there be three hundred, three thousand times this wealth in the earth below me.

His big roan Goliath was tethered nearby, unconcerned by the noise of the quarry workers and their equipment as they toiled at the excavations in the heat. Adam turned to the man at his side with just the hint of a smile curving his strong mouth.

'So it's going well, Jacob?' he asked softly.

Old Jacob, in his dusty quarryman's garb, clearly couldn't wait to tell him just *how* well. 'Like a dream,

Master Adam! Me and the lads, we were resigned to this quarry being worked out for good. Some of them never thought to get a job like this again.' The old quarryman could scarcely conceal his glee. 'But then *you* came last month and told us there was fancy folks in London interested in our stone.'

'More than interested, Jacob. Believe me, builders are clamouring for it.'

'And so they should be!' Jacob gestured towards the fresh-hewn blocks and rapped one with his callused knuckles, just as Adam had done. 'Rings true as porcelain, do you hear, sir? No faults inside her!'

Jacob followed as Adam headed across the uneven ground to speak to a group of bare-chested workers who'd been vigorously plying their pickaxes at the rock face. Clouds of dust rose and clung to their sweating backs, but they put their picks aside and grinned when they saw who was there.

Adam had slung his dark riding coat over one shoulder and moved easily amongst them asking questions, offering words of quiet praise. He was owner of this quarry and much else besides, but the rumour ran that the master had been known to wield a pickaxe himself when the going got tough and had vowed he'd never be too grand to stand shoulder to shoulder with his men.

Jacob Mallin kept close to his side, beaming with pride. 'You promised the lads you'd get this quarry workin' again, sir, and you've kept your word.'

Adam turned to him, the sun glinting on his cropped dark hair and hard cheekbones. 'I always do,' he said softly. 'Tell the men they'll be handsomely paid for their work. If there's anything else you need by way of equipment or supplies, just let my manager Shipley know.'

Jacob nodded approvingly. His men would whisper between themselves, *He's a good 'un, is the master. None works harder than him or treats us better.* Yes, Master Adam had his grandfather's instinct for making money. But he was also a fair man, a man who kept his promises, and the reopening of the old quarry had brought fresh hope to many lives round here.

'Aye, I'll tell the lads,' Jacob promised. 'Will you be sendin' the stone up to Bristol, sir, when it's ready?'

Adam gazed at the rolling green countryside which surrounded them, then turned back with a new light burning in his dark eyes. 'No. I'm going to build a railway to the Avon canal, and from there this stone—this *new* stone—can be taken by boat to the Thames and to London itself.'

'But it's not your land between here and the Avon canal, Master Adam—leastways, not all of it!'

Adam had moved towards his big roan and was already securing his rolled-up coat to the back of his saddle—far too warm for the garment on a day like this. 'My grandfather never let a simple obstacle like that hold him up. And neither will I,' said Adam in a voice edged with steel.

Jacob shook his grizzled head in wonder as he watched him ride off. 'There's no stopping him,' he murmured, eyes shining with delight. 'No stopping him, that's for sure.'

Goliath was ready to gallop and Adam let him. *There's nothing like the feel of the land under your horse's hooves being yours, my lad. Especially when that land but recently belonged to men who'd cross to the other side of the street rather than acknowledge you.*

Those were the words of his grandfather, who with his work-roughened hands and west country vowels had laboured night and day to remove the shame of the name the upper classes scornfully gave him—Miner Tom. But they'd all come to Miner Tom's funeral, oh, yes. All the gentry of Bath and London had hurried eagerly to the lavish ceremony—because they'd realised by then how much the man they'd despised was damned well worth.

Adam's grandfather had wanted nothing more desperately than for his grandson to be accepted by the society that had spurned him. That wish had come true. But now Adam often thought that he was happiest on days like this, riding Goliath across Somerset's lush green hills and knowing that the chief wealth of those hills, the fine stone beneath them, was his to be harvested.

They'd said the Sawle Down quarry was finished. It had last been profitable fifty years ago; then the expense of extracting the stone had deterred any prospect of new investment. But Adam had anticipated the surge in demand and hence in price for good building materials; he'd made his calculations and investments and proved the doomsayers wrong.

Now his detractors would say there was no way he could get the valuable stone to the canal, that vital water link to the Thames and London. Well, he would prove them wrong again.

Suddenly a distant movement caught his eye. Another rider was enjoying the afternoon sun—and blatantly trespassing on private land. A woman. Eyes narrowed, Adam urged Goliath into a canter towards her.

He swore aloud when he saw her turn her pretty

dappled mare's head and set off away from him at a reckless pace. A stupid pace, that was taking her towards the edge of another old quarry.

Adam swung Goliath into a broad circle to head her off. The ground here was treacherous. Yes, the grassy slopes of Sawle Down looked inviting, but—disused quarries aside—decades of quarry debris lurked beneath the sheep-cropped turf, waiting to catch the unwary. And indeed it was only a matter of moments before the dappled mare suddenly stumbled and sent its foolish rider crashing to the ground. Adam was there in moments, swinging himself out of the saddle to kneel beside that prone body.

She was clad in a riding habit of crumpled crimson velvet. Her abundant black curls fell in loose array; her little crimson hat, set with ridiculously jaunty red feathers, lay nearby. He saw that her face was a perfect oval, with a tip-tilted nose, a rosebud mouth and thick lashes dark against creamy skin.

The faint scent of lavender drifted up to him. Who was she? What the hell was she doing, riding up here on her own? She was a lady of quality, that was clear. Apart from her fine clothes he registered that her complexion was dewy, her figure lissom. Then Adam realised that her eyes were fluttering open. He noted the tremor of fear that surged through her as she saw him towering over her. Adam was suddenly aware that his boots and breeches—his open-necked shirt, too, quite likely—were covered with dust from the quarry.

She was struggling now to stand up. He fought the impulse to offer her his dirty hand. 'Are you hurt?' he said. 'Perhaps I—'

'Stay away from me!'

Adam's lip curled. As he'd thought. Quality. And

her age? Twenty-six, twenty-seven, perhaps, and that disdain just had to have been with her from birth. 'You took quite a fall just then, ma'am,' he said. 'I only came over to see if you needed my help.'

She looked so pale, yet there was such determination in that small pointed chin; something rebellious in those startlingly green eyes that were assessing him. Dismissing him, God damn it.

On her feet now, she brushed down her brightly coloured habit, pushed her luxurious curls back from her face and started hobbling after her horse. 'Poppy!' she called. 'Poppy! Here, girl!'

But the mare just whinnied and trotted off to join Goliath, calmly grazing nearby. The woman bit her lip, hesitating, uncertain.

'That's horses for you,' Adam said. 'Your mare's had a fright. It was perhaps a little unwise of you to ride up here. Don't you know there are quarry workings nearby?'

'How can one *ignore* the hateful things?' she shuddered. 'Always so busy. So noisy.'

'Particularly at the moment, yes. But they provide work and wages for many men, and food for their families.'

She stared up at him as if he talked a foreign language, then said, 'Excuse me. You're in my way.'

He did not budge. 'Quarries are no place for sightseers,' he pointed out. 'I'm trying, incidentally, to find out exactly what you're doing up here.'

He saw her tip-tilted nose wrinkle a little at his open-necked shirt and the dust on his boots. The old, familiar bitterness surged in his veins. So. Some lordling's wife, to judge by her mount and her attire, and the wedding band on her finger. She was the kind of woman who would look down on him—until someone enlightened her as to who he was.

He was damned if *he* was going to be the one to tell her.

She darted sideways to pick up her crimson hat then went marching off towards her horse again, clearly wanting no more conversation with a man she'd dismissed as a labourer. Something clenched warningly in Adam's gut as he absorbed the way she carried herself. Noted the way her pert little behind swayed under that luxurious fabric.

He called after her, 'Didn't you come up here with a companion or a groom?'

She swung round, her face still pale. 'I like riding alone. I like *being* alone.' She carried on stubbornly towards her mare, holding her hat with one hand and the red velvet skirt of her habit in the other. He couldn't help but notice small, neatly turned ankles in little leather half-boots.

Her dappled mare had trotted off again, away from her. Goliath watched, interested, and Adam called his big horse over. 'Here! Goliath!'

Goliath came and the little mare did, too; Adam caught the mare's reins and stroked its dappled silken neck. The woman walked back to him reluctantly.

'I'll help you up if you like,' Adam offered. 'Then I suggest you get off this private land before dusk falls. You could break your neck riding home once the light starts fading.'

'Private!' she breathed. 'Why, Mr Davenant has no more right to this land than—' she swept her ungloved hand expressively '—than those *black crows* circling above the trees!'

A sudden cool breeze chilled the perspiration on his

back. He said, 'I believe Mr Davenant bought this land a year ago, quite legally.'

She tossed her head. 'Money will buy anything, and anybody. And—legally? Some would think otherwise.'

Hell! This time Adam felt the heat surging through his blood. If she'd been a man he'd have floored her for that!

But she was a woman all right. Her face was piquant even in defiance, her body all slender curves…

Damn it. This was no time to be distracted. Adam said, 'Are you querying his right to this land?'

She faced him coolly. 'I assume you probably work for him, so I'll limit my words. I've not met Mr Davenant, but I've heard enough to know that he was not born to wealth and it shows.'

Adam hissed out a breath. 'Tell me. As a matter of interest, if you *did* chance to meet Mr Davenant, would you use those words to his face?'

She shrugged her shoulders, but he noticed she'd gone a little paler. 'Why not?' she said. 'He is no friend to my family. What else have I to lose?'

The sun passed behind a cloud; the moorland grasses shivered. 'You've clearly not lost your pride, ma'am,' Adam said at last. 'May I escort you on your way?'

'I know my way very well, I assure you!'

He clenched his teeth and said with icy politeness, 'Then will you—*condescend* to let me help you mount your horse? Or are we going to stand here till the sun goes down?'

She hesitated. 'My thanks.'

His mouth pressed in a thin line, he put his big hands round her waist and lifted her easily into her saddle. Then he went to check her mare's bridle—and give himself time to cool down.

She was feather-light. She was *icy* with damned arrogance. She'd set his pulse racing with rage—and a flicker of something else even more dangerous.

He looked up at her and patted her dappled mare's neck. 'All set,' he said flatly. 'You'd best be off.'

She nodded her head in curt thanks, then without a backward glance she rode swiftly and competently down the path.

Adam Davenant shrugged on his coat and watched her go, his gaze narrowed.

How her pretty green eyes had glittered with contempt when she spoke his name. *Mr Davenant has no more right to this land than those black crows circling above the trees.*

She hadn't recognised him. But one thing was very clear—she hated Adam Davenant like poison. He'd already guessed who she was. If his guess was correct, she had a brother who was heading for big, big trouble. With *him*.

Chapter Two

London—two months later

Belle Marchmain rather distractedly picked up a length of pink ribbon from the display on the counter, then put it down again in the wrong place. Apprehension shadowed her dark-lashed green eyes as she said at last, 'I'm sincerely hoping this is some foolish jest of yours, Edward.'

Outside in the Strand the May dusk was starting to fall and lamplighters with clanking ladders were hurrying about their business. Normally Belle relished this time of quiet after a busy day. Once her shop's doors were locked she would wander possessively amongst the bright lengths of silk and taffeta, herself resplendent in one of the boldly extravagant costumes that were fast making her one of the most talked-about *modistes* in London.

But just now, her current attire—a striped jacket of black and green over a matching taffeta skirt, with green satin ribbons adorning her luxuriant black curls—seemed ridiculously flippant. Futile, in fact, in the face of approaching disaster.

Belle was twenty-seven years old and had learnt to cope with much in her life. The humiliation in slow, steady steps of her once-proud family. The death of her husband five years ago. But now sheer, blind panic threatened to close in.

It had been no surprise to see her brother, of course, at her glass-paned door, ringing the bell impatiently. She'd known he was in London for two weeks, staying at Grillon's Hotel in Albemarle Street—'catching up on business and old friends,' Edward had told her blithely when he called on her a few days ago.

He'd certainly been spending money. Grillon's was expensive and so were the new clothes he was sporting: new boots, a new silk waistcoat, a new coat of blue superfine and smart yellow pantaloons. And now he perched on the end of her counter, full of casual confidence in his older sister's ability to sort out his latest mess.

'You can help me, can't you, Belle?' he cajoled. 'This little shop of yours is doing mighty well, I hear!'

Just then a young woman with curly brown hair burst in from the back room. '*Madame*, should I tell the girls—excuse me, I had no idea you had company!'

Gabby—Belle's French assistant—bobbed a curtsy to Edward, whose eyes, Belle noted with exasperation, lit up at the sight of her. Belle replied, more curtly than she meant to, 'I'll be with you shortly, Gabby. Yes, send Jenny and Susan home by all means, and thank them for all their hard work today, will you?'

'Of course, *madame*! But there is something else—'

Belle interrupted, 'Tell me later, would you?'

Edward watched Gabby go, then started talking again. 'I just need a *little* more money, Belle.'

'To pay your hotel bill? To pay for yet more new

clothes? Edward, I am *not* doing well enough to repay your debts as well as my own.' Belle had sat rather suddenly in one of the dainty gilt chairs her customers used.

'But your business is thriving. You *must* be plump in the pocket!' Edward, who was two years younger than she was, eagerly pulled up a chair to sit opposite her—admiring, she noticed, his own reflection in a nearby mirror. He was slenderly built and with the same shade of green eyes as she, the same raven black hair. But there was a hint of wilfulness, of weakness about his mouth. 'You have clients galore,' he went on, 'you have servants! And dash it, Belle, you're being as ratty as when you came back from Sawle Down that day in March, all of a stew about *something*.'

If Edward had been in any way perceptive, he'd have seen how his sister's cheeks became a little paler. 'I was saying goodbye to the land that was once ours,' she said quietly. 'As for my servants, Edward, as you call them, I have Gabby, two assistants and a manservant—Matt—who works for me a few hours a week. That's all.'

Edward shrugged. 'Yes, but you live the high life, sister mine—you're always being invited to routs and parties. And when you stayed with me and Charlotte you said you were even thinking of setting up another shop in Bath!'

'It came to naught,' she answered rather tightly.

'Hmm.' Bored already, Edward was picking up a little silk fan. 'Nice trinket, this.'

Belle snatched at it and put it down with something of a snap. *'Edward—'* she was gazing directly at her younger brother '—Edward, I think you'd better tell me *everything*.'

So he did. And Belle's heart sank almost as low as she'd known it, while Edward recounted the entire sorry tale. In which everyone in the world was at fault, except, of course, himself.

At twenty-one Edward had inherited the Hathersleigh family's estate near Bath—or what remained of it—and within the year he'd married his sweetheart, Charlotte. By the time of their wedding Belle was living in London. And whenever she saw Edward he was forever telling her how the estate was thriving, and, of course, how clever he was.

Just over a year ago he'd announced to her that he'd sold a large portion of the estate's land to a neighbour—Adam Davenant. Belle had felt apprehension and more. She'd never met the man. He owned, she was aware, estates all over the country and wasn't often in Somerset. But she knew her father had loathed Davenant—called him a money-grubbing upstart.

'Did you *have* to sell to him, Edward?' Belle had asked at the time.

'Yes,' Edward said flatly, 'and Davenant was desperate to buy. You know what all these new-money families are like, Belle. They want as many acres as possible in hopes of making themselves respectable.'

Belle had grieved the loss of the land at Sawle Down, but had hoped that Edward would concentrate on making a success of what remained of their ancestral estate near Bath. Hoped that marriage and family responsibilities might perhaps be the making of him.

Some hope. The amount Davenant offered for the land had, in fact, turned out to be derisory—though he was now set to make a fortune from his purchase, because the sudden surge in price of Bath stone had made the old quarry there workable once more.

He must have known. Must have deliberately set out to swindle them. And now, with the London dusk closing in around her and Edward staring at her with that half-defiant, half-scared look that she knew of old, Belle rubbed her temples with her fingertips as her brother told her anew—rather resentfully, as if it were her fault—that last summer's harvest had been a poor one, thanks to the rain that had ruined his wheat. 'And the taxes, Belle! Last year this blasted government brought in new taxes on barley, on farm horses—anything that grew or moved, basically!'

Then Edward proceeded to remind her that the roof of Hathersleigh Manor had needed replacing entirely. 'Uncle Philip neglected the place so badly,' Edward complained. 'The roof *had* to be fixed, or the thing would have caved in.'

Their father's brother, the dour Philip Hathersleigh, had overseen the estate from their father's death fourteen years ago until Edward reached his majority. Belle didn't feel particularly close to Uncle Philip—even less to his shrewish wife Mildred—but she'd formed the opinion that Philip was a sound, careful man whose advice Edward had rashly spurned, with the result that Uncle Philip and his wife had retreated back to their estate in the north with little love lost.

'Look after the paperwork, young man,' Uncle Philip had said grimly to Edward. 'And get yourself sound legal advice, if you want to stand any chance of holding your inheritance together.'

Edward had blithely ignored Uncle Philip's warnings; her brother's desk, Belle couldn't help but notice on her March visit, was overflowing with neglected files and unread correspondence. And, of course, with bills.

'So the new roof and taxes got you into debt,' she now said steadily. From the back of the shop she could hear the merry voices of her assistants making their departure. Could hear Gabby's laughter and Matt's deep voice as he began to lock up. 'Surely though, Edward,' went on Belle, trying to keep calm, 'the income from the estate could have kept your debts at bay?'

'I did get on top of my debts, Belle. Or at least, I thought I had. You see, back in February—it was just before you came to stay with us, actually—I sold some of the sheep from that land Davenant purchased from me last year.'

'You did—*what*?' breathed Belle. She felt suddenly cold.

Edward shrugged, but his cheeks were pink. 'I sold some of Davenant's stock. He's so rich I thought he wouldn't even notice.'

Belle said, 'You stole from him. Oh, Edward. You stole from that man.'

Edward jumped to his feet and walked around the candlelit shop with his hands thrust defiantly in the pockets of his new coat. 'Stealing? Hardly—his sheep had strayed because he'd not bothered maintaining his fences. And dash it all, Belle, you could say that Davenant was stealing from *me*, you know? He paid me a pitiful amount for that land I sold him and if *that* isn't stealing, I don't know what is! Belle—Belle, are you all right?'

A spring evening, on Sawle Down. A stranger, whose arrogance had made her cheeks burn. *Are you querying his right to this land?* he'd asked cuttingly. And he'd only been one of Davenant's labourers.

Something tightened painfully in her chest, as it did whenever she remembered that hateful day. She dragged herself back to the equally unpalatable present. 'You were telling me you'd stolen some of Mr Davenant's sheep.'

'I wouldn't exactly call it theft! But then Davenant found out about the sheep, curse it, and I got a lawyer's letter…'

Edward told her all this very rapidly, almost indignantly, as Belle sat there in her bright-striped jacket with the green ribbons trailing from her hair.

I have fought. I have fought so hard, to make this new life for myself.

'Davenant himself came to call on me two months ago,' Edward was continuing. 'In Somerset, just after you'd been to visit.'

Belle clenched her hands. 'What's he like?'

'Oh, positively detestable, you can imagine, risen from rags to riches in a generation. "Miner Tom", they called his grandfather—made the family fortunes from tin in Cornwall. As for Davenant—well, he's a big fellow dressed in black, a positive boor—what more can I say? I tell you, Belle, not a pleasant word passed his lips during our conversation. He told me I was nothing less than a sheep-stealer—as if a few sheep should matter to him!'

Belle was finding she could scarcely breathe. She twisted the slender wedding ring on her finger. 'Is this why you've come to London?'

'Well, yes. Davenant demanded another meeting— *demanded*, can you credit it? He said he'd travel to

Somerset again to see me if I preferred, but I—actually, I didn't prefer it, not with the baby due, you know?'

Belle *did* know. She knew that Edward's poor wife had already had two miscarriages within the past two years, and she dreaded to think what would happen if Charlotte lost this baby.

'Anyway,' went on Edward, 'we met the other day at my hotel, and Davenant had all the figures with him about his sheep—now, isn't it the sort of thing a normal fellow would leave to his man of business? But, no, I'd swear the creature had gone through all his stock lists with a toothcomb. Dash it, he must make thousands a week from his various interests!' He gesticulated angrily. 'Nevertheless, he told me that my debts regarding those dratted sheep could not be ignored.'

Outside in the Strand a crowd of merrymakers went by on their way to an evening in the clubs of St James's. Belle waited for the noise to fade and asked, 'Has Charlotte any idea of this?'

'No,' he said defiantly, squaring his shoulders. 'Poor Charlotte, not a thing, and I don't want her to. She's delicate, you know?'

And what if I were delicate? Belle bit back the retort, knowing it was ridiculous to expect Edward ever to see her as anything other than his capable, shrewd-headed older sister. But she had to think. This could be disastrous.

Adam Davenant was after Edward, not her. But her shop, her own small savings—would *they* be implicated? Would everything she had worked so hard for since her husband's death be lost?

For a moment sheer panic clawed at her chest. Somehow she fought it down and forced herself to say calmly, 'Is there any possibility that Mr Davenant will let you pay this sum back gradually, month by month?'

'Good God, I doubt it. He's a grasping wretch, Belle!' As Edward distractedly pushed his dark hair back from his forehead, he unintentionally laid bare the old, white scar that puckered the skin there. 'He's told me I've got to bring the money to his house in Mayfair within the week or he'll press charges. Damn it, if I had it, I'd hang it round the necks of a few sheep and get them herded up the steps of his fancy house.'

Belle briefly rested her forehead in her hand.

'You'll help me, won't you?' Edward pleaded. 'Charlotte. Our home. The new baby… I can't go to prison, Belle. I can't…'

Belle had always been aware that the once-renowned Somerset estate of the Hathersleigh family had, thanks to the profligacy of successive generations, dwindled to very little—unlike, unfortunately, the aspirations of its title-holders.

She'd also had to face up to the fact that her own prospects were bleak when her husband died five years ago in one of Wellington's final campaigns of the war. She'd had to make harsh choices: either to move in with Edward at Hathersleigh Manor, or to earn her own living. In fact, imposing herself on Edward never seriously crossed her mind and the idea of being a governess or companion horrified her. Certain offers she'd received from so-called gentlemen repelled her even more.

Then inspiration had come. She had always been a talented seamstress and was fascinated by the women's fashions that ebbed and flowed like the long Napoleonic wars, so—in the face of her brother's disapproval—she'd decided to open a dress shop in London.

Her designs were bold and eyecatching. *Outrageous*, some of the *ton*'s older matrons were heard to intone witheringly. Her shop, though small, was well situated in the Strand, and she and Gabby lived in the two rooms above it. Soon she'd begun to attract customers who were tired of soft pastels and wanted something different, but she was by no means making a fortune. She was lucky if her own rent and bills were paid every quarter day. How on earth could she deal with Edward's debts?

Now, as the candles flickered around the bright silks and satins in this little shop, which she felt sick at the thought of losing, she looked at her brother steadily and said, 'There's no point in my even asking the amount of your debt to Mr Davenant, Edward, for I know I won't be able to pay it. But I will go and see him for you.'

'Go and see him?' Her brother was astonished. 'And then what? I'm damned if you'll grovel on my behalf in front of that—that nouveau-riche upstart!'

A flash of anger darkened Belle's eyes. 'I have never grovelled in my life. I will simply explain that you realise you have made a grave error—'

Edward jumped up, about to protest, but something in Belle's steady gaze made him clamp his lips together and sit down again.

'That you've made a grave error,' she repeated, 'and would be grateful if Mr Davenant would accept your word of honour that your debts *will* be paid off steadily over—what? Three years, Edward?'

He looked sullen now, a little boy again. 'Three years! I suppose so. Times are hard, though Davenant's thriving, blast the fellow...'

'I shall go and see him,' said Belle quietly. 'And I'll let you know how I get on.'

He got up to pace to and fro, nodding. 'Very well. And put on some charm, eh? Come to think of it, Belle, a second marriage for you, to some rich fellow—not Davenant, of course, God forbid—could be the answer for both of us. You're really not at all bad-looking, if you'd just make an effort not to frighten the fellows off with those startling clothes and that sharp tongue of yours.'

This time, there was an edge of ice in her voice. 'Let me assure you I have absolutely no intention of getting married again. Ever.'

Her brother shrugged. 'Suit yourself. I'll stay on in town for a week or so at Grillon's, so you can let me know there when it's all sorted with Davenant, can't you?' He started putting on his hat, checking his reflection in the mirror.

'Edward,' Belle said suddenly. 'You're not going to visit any of the gambling dens, are you?'

He swung round. 'Gambling dens? Never. And thanks for this, Belle. Some day I'll return the favour.'

Breezily Edward let himself out. Belle sat with her hands frozen in her lap, immobile.

Gabby came in rather hesitantly. 'Are you free, *madame*? I wanted to tell you that there was a little trouble earlier.'

Belle's heart sank anew. 'What kind of trouble?'

'Jenny told me about it. It appears that when you and I were measuring Lady Tindall in the back workshop for her new gown, a customer came in and complained about a cuff that was loose on a pelisse she bought last week.'

'What did Jenny do?'

'She mended it there and then, and the customer left—but she was so unpleasant, Jenny said! And she declared she would *not* be using our shop in the future!'

'Well, it sounds as if we're better off without her,' Belle soothed and Gabby went off, looking happier, to tidy the workroom. Originally from Paris, the lively French girl had come to Belle's notice when she'd advertised for an assistant seamstress and Gabby had proved invaluable, good both with the customers and with the two girls Belle also employed.

In addition, it did no harm that Matt was smitten by Gabby—honest, stolid Matt Bellamy, who worked most of the time at his brother's stables just down the road, but was a joiner by trade. Belle had hired him to fit out her shop and he continued to do odd jobs for her. Though Gabby teased Matt outrageously, Belle could see that secretly Matt adored her.

Together against the world, Belle and her staff were a good team. But—*Edward*. Her brother had flushed with anger when she'd mentioned gambling dens, yet Belle couldn't help remembering that when he'd first come into his inheritance the lure of the gaming parlours had pulled him time and time again to London.

Marriage to Charlotte had at least cured her brother of that particular weakness. But trouble was still lurking, clearly. In fact, Belle felt that nothing had been quite right in her life since she'd clashed with the forbidding quarryman on Sawle Down. Just the thought of that encounter sent ripples of unease through her.

Stay away from me! she'd lashed out at him. Why had she been so rude, so hateful to him? Because he was clad so roughly? Because he was employed by Mr Davenant?

She'd never even met Davenant, but one thing was for sure. If he ever learned of the insults she'd uttered about him that day, then she and Edward were finished for good.

Chapter Three

London—four days later

Adam Davenant had issued the invitations to the meeting at his house in Clarges Street only yesterday, but despite the short notice every single person had come and he was under no illusions as to why. Quite a few of them had never visited his Mayfair mansion, and they would all be desperate to get inside and assess his wealth.

Greeting them, he'd cynically noted how their eyes leapt out on stalks as they registered the expensive if discreet furnishings. The number of liveried servants. The superb wine and food on offer. Everything was perfect; it damned well had to be when people were all too keen to rake up your lowly origins.

Though the plentiful wine was perhaps a mistake, Adam decided as the boasting grew louder amongst the rich and ruthless men who'd gathered to feed on the cold repast set out on the vast table in his first-floor dining room. When the boasting began to turn to bickering, Adam knew it was time to start the real business of the day. He rose to his feet at the head of the table and, as was his way, stated his case bluntly.

'In Somerset there's stone to be quarried that's as good for building, gentlemen, as any in the world. With London expanding so rapidly there's a never-ending market, and all of us—whether landholders or business investors—stand to gain. But the issue I wish to discuss today is—transport.'

Adam was dressed impeccably in black with a snow-white, plain cravat and he made an imposing figure. Though not yet thirty, he carried the authority of a man who was accustomed to power.

He carried the authority of money.

All eyes were on him as he turned to point to the large map hung on the wall behind him. 'Gentlemen,' he went on, in the polished voice in which there was no trace of his grandfather's west country vowels. 'What we need is a railway to convey this fine new stone from the Somerset quarries to the Avon canal and thence by water to London.'

'There are railways already, Davenant,' someone called out.

'You mean tramways for trucks, pulled by horses or powered by gravity,' replied Adam. 'I'm talking about a steam railway. All of us with goods to transport from Bath to London—not just stone, but farm produce and manufactured goods, too—would benefit. The carrying times would be halved and the profits doubled.'

Already several men were nodding and murmuring agreement. But Lord Rupert Jarvis—who had, Adam noted, been eating and drinking steadily since he arrived—was sneering openly. 'You mean *your* profits doubled, Davenant. Not mine.'

The blond-haired Jarvis, as well as possessing large

estates in Somerset, owned a big haulage business with networks of carriages and teams of horses all across the south of England. Known to be a cruel master of both men and beasts, Jarvis saw the emergence of the railways as the coming of Satan.

Adam countered him with icy calmness. 'There's still room for all forms of transport, Lord Jarvis. But we cannot ignore the chances that steam offers. Some of you will already know that the Yorkshire mine owner Charles Brandling has been using steam engines to carry his coal to the ports for years. I'm proposing that each of us become shareholders in this new Somerset railway. And apart from the profit motive, we'll all be aware, I'm sure, that a railway would spare our men and horses much hard labour.'

'Siding with the workers, Davenant? They're damned lucky to have jobs,' said the sleekly dressed, coldly handsome Jarvis crudely. 'If they aren't up to it, tell 'em to get their wives or brats to help out. That's what I do.' He looked challengingly round at the assembled company.

'I'm sure you do,' said Adam. His chiselled face was expressionless, but his grey eyes were hard as granite. A tense silence had fallen.

Jarvis leaned back in his chair. 'Show us your route, Davenant,' he said challengingly. 'Doubtless you've got it all worked out.'

Adam turned and pointed to his map. 'Here's the city of Bath, with the stone quarries to the south and the River Avon flowing close by. And *here*—' he pointed again '—is the canal that links the Avon to the Thames, offering seventy miles of navigable waterway. You'll see that the most practical route for a new railway would be from Monkton Sawle straight to the canal as it runs south, just before it swings east out of Somerset.'

There were murmurs and nods of assent. Then Jarvis, who'd been demolishing another portion of venison pie, cut in, 'I suppose you realise you'll need to cross my land for the last half-mile of your proposed railway?'

'In order to reach the canal at Limpley Stoke, yes, I would need to cross your land,' said Adam. 'Just as I'd need the consent of the other landholders gathered here today who would be affected. It's in all our interests, beyond doubt.'

'Like hell it is,' growled Jarvis, wiping pastry crumbs off his lips. 'And I've listened to enough of this. I'm off, to another more interesting appointment.'

Adam politely indicated the plate on which stood the remainder of the venison pie. 'Certainly. But I would hate you to leave hungry. Shall I ask one of the servants to wrap up the rest of that pie so you can take it with you?'

There was a stunned silence. Then someone chuckled and began to applaud; Jarvis's appetite for a free meal was well known.

Jarvis pushed back his chair angrily. 'Damn you, Davenant,' he muttered and hurried from the room, letting the door slam behind him.

Some of the others spoke up then. 'I'm with you, Adam,' said Tobias Bartlett firmly.

'And me.' 'Yes, you can count me in on your scheme, Davenant.' More pledges of support echoed round the room.

But there was still the problem of damned Jarvis; the big map made it all too clear that Jarvis's acres of land at Limpley Stoke barred the most direct route between Adam's quarry and the canal. Any other route would add miles to the journey.

'It's not as if Jarvis makes much use of that land anyway,' Adam's friend Bartlett was grumbling. 'And surely he realises he could expect a hefty share of your profits if he negotiated with you?'

'I don't think,' said Adam softly, 'that Jarvis's motive is based on thoughts of profit.'

Siding with the workers, Davenant? Jarvis had sneered.

Well, sometimes Adam wished he and Jarvis could resolve their differences like common workmen—with their fists. Then he would knock Jarvis's block off.

He looked thoughtfully down at his strong hands. As a boy at Eton, Adam had briefly been taunted with Miner Tom's name—until he'd pummelled the sneers from his rash tormentors' faces. On coming into his fortune he'd learnt to fend off his detractors in equally efficient ways. Both in his manners and attire he was unpretentious but faultless, never letting his cool façade slip. Being mighty rich he was happily accepted by most of society, especially by those who had daughters to marry off.

Jarvis, despite his oily good looks and title, was secretly despised by the *ton* for his coarse behaviour. If it wasn't for his damned land, Adam would have been happy to cut him dead—or thump him.

A young housemaid came in just then with more good wine from Adam's cellars. Adam didn't partake—he didn't enjoy fuddling his wits—but went instead to join the group who'd gone to pore again over the map of Somerset.

'If Jarvis won't give way, Adam,' a Somerset neighbour was suggesting, 'you could take the railway down the valley to Midford then head north—see?—to skirt his estates for the last mile. As I said, I would happily sell some land to you in return for some shares in the project.'

Adam was heartened that so many of these men were, like him, all for progress. 'We'll manage without Jarvis somehow,' he said. 'Though if we *do* head north, we'll have to blast some of the higher contours out of the way, here, and here...'

'It'll be worth it,' said another Somerset landowner eagerly. 'Davenant, you mentioned the coal mines in the north-east; I've heard rumours that Stephenson up in Stockton is planning to transport people as well as coal on his railways! Steam is the future, and this scheme of yours gets my backing, if only to take the sneer off Jarvis's face. The way he treats his men and his horses is despicable. Thank God he left early, is all I can say. We can make some progress now, Adam... Adam?'

'Hmm?'

It didn't happen often, but Adam, by the window, was temporarily distracted. In fact, he couldn't take his eyes off a remarkably shabby carriage that had just pulled up at the far end of Clarges Street, from which a woman was getting out; a woman wearing a big straw hat and dressed in a startling ensemble of turquoise and pink as striking on her pert figure as icing on a festive cake. She was probably an expensive courtesan, Adam decided, hired by one of his wealthy neighbours for an afternoon of bed sport. Shrugging, he turned back to his guests—then paused again.

Something about her looked familiar. The way she stepped proudly out of that ridiculous carriage. The slenderness of her waist, outlined by her short pink jacket; the swell of her deliciously trim *derrière* as she stood on tiptoe to say something to her coachman...

She reminded him of that woman on Sawle Down.

The memory made his breathing hitch. She'd insulted him to kingdom come—and he'd stood there and taken it from her! When what he should have done—the thought occurred to him time after time, usually at damnably inconvenient moments like now—was take her in his arms. Hold her close. Drown out those defiant protests of hers with a kiss...

Definitely time to get back to his guests, and his railway.

It *was* Belle, and she was standing on the pavement at the far end of Clarges Street, arguing with Matt. 'This will do, Matt!' she announced firmly after letting herself out. 'I can walk the rest of the way, I assure you.'

Matt Bellamy, up on his seat, frowned down at her. 'Here, Mrs Marchmain? But we're not quite there yet.'

I know, thought Belle tightly. *And no way on earth am I going to risk allowing Mr Davenant or his servants to see me arriving in this rickety old coach.*

She'd tried already to shut the carriage door, but failed; now she tried again. Blast, it was nearly falling off its hinges.

She'd hoped to make an impression arriving outside Mr Davenant's house and had asked Matt to borrow something suitable from his brother's stables. But when Matt had turned up outside her shop at half-past two with this, Belle had been secretly horrified.

And the door still wouldn't shut. She tried again; this time the handle came off in her hand. Somehow she rammed it back. Matt had jumped down now from the driver's seat to hold the horses and was simply gaping at the four-storeyed, cream-stuccoed dwellings that surrounded them.

Belle resisted the same impulse to let her own jaw drop. She'd known, of course, that Davenant dwelt in the most exclusive part of London. But the thought of confronting him in one of these magnificent mansions made her heart quail within her.

It was four days since Edward had called at her shop with his dire news. She'd written twice to Davenant requesting an appointment and heard precisely nothing, so she'd decided there was no alternative but to confront him in his lair. Sternly quelling her apprehension, she'd dressed appropriately and left her shop in Gabrielle's capable hands.

Of course, *appropriate* wouldn't be the word most people would use for her twill silk gown of turquoise and pink or her snug-fitting pink jacket. *Appropriate* didn't perhaps apply to her large straw hat adorned with turquoise satin ribbons. Oh, dear. When she'd put on the outfit she'd felt full of confidence. But now she was feeling rather sick.

Davenant's grandfather made the family fortunes from tin mining, she remembered Edward saying scornfully. But as she gazed down Clarges Street, she felt her breath catch in her throat because the miner's grandson had done rather well for himself.

Still standing by the rickety coach, she smoothed the sleeves of her jacket, adjusted her straw bonnet and emphasised to Matt a little too brightly, 'This will most definitely do, Matt. Return the vehicle, will you? I shan't be wanting you again.'

Big Matt set his face obstinately. 'Don't seem right,

Mrs Marchmain, leaving you here alone, callin' on an unknown gentleman.'

Belle very much wanted to say crisply to Matt and to anyone else within hearing, 'Believe me, Adam Davenant is no gentleman!' But that would simply make poor Matt even more anxious; so instead she retorted, 'Matt, I'm a twenty-seven-year-old widow and, as you see, I'm at no risk whatsoever in a neighbourhood like this. There is absolutely no need for you to stay. Besides,' she added in a moment of inspiration, 'Gabby will be expecting you. You promised her you'd fix that loose counter in the workshop today, remember?'

As she spoke she was horribly conscious that half-way down Clarges Street a couple of liveried footmen stood on the steps of the biggest house of them all, gossiping in the sun. She'd been aware for some time that the footmen were staring in her direction and felt newly embarrassed by the scruffy equipage and the presence of loyal Matt in his ancient greatcoat and battered hat.

'Won't you want escortin' home afterwards, ma'am?' frowned Matt.

'I shall walk,' Belle announced. 'I shall enjoy the fresh air.'

'But…'

Just then the door handle fell off again; she kicked it under the carriage. 'Matt!' she hissed. 'Please—just go!'

Matt, his burly visage expressive, heaved himself back on to the driving seat. Belle found herself urging his departure under her breath rather frantically. Then, lifting her head high, she set off down Clarges Street. The footmen watched her as she drew nearer.

She knew it. She knew, before she reached them. They were outside Adam Davenant's house. They were his footmen. *Oh, drat and botheration.* And they had seen everything; the ancient carriage, Matt, herself kicking the blasted door handle out of sight...

They had sprung to attention, stiff-faced, their arms straight at their sides, but Belle had seen a hint of malicious humour in their eyes.

'Is this Mr Davenant's house?' she asked crisply.

'This is Mr Davenant's residence—ma'am.'

'Then I wish to speak to him, if you please. And before you ask, I have not an appointment, though I have written to him twice informing him that—that it is in his *interests* to see me.'

The footman's lips pursed. 'Mr Davenant happens to have company.'

'Then I will wait.'

The impudent scoundrel almost sniffed. 'Very well, madam. I will take you to await Mr Davenant's convenience.'

'But...' Belle bit her lip. She didn't exactly have a choice, did she? He held the door open; she sailed inside.

Oh, my. This place was incredible. Her entire shop would fit inside this lofty hallway, with its huge chandeliers and sweeping staircase. *Money from mining and quarrying*, she reminded herself steadily. Money from other men's backbreaking toil.

The footman—who she reckoned might stop breathing soon if he lifted his nose any higher in disdain—ushered her along the vast hallway to a room that led off it, pointed her inside, then disappeared, closing the door rather firmly on her as he left.

She was too agitated to notice much, beyond the fact that she could hear the sounds of loud male talk and laughter from upstairs. Would the sneering footman trouble to deliver her message? Would the hateful Mr Davenant even bother to leave his rowdy companions and grant her a few minutes' audience? She paced to and fro. This had to be one of her stupidest ideas ever.

Suddenly she heard a man's bellow of rage from out in the hallway, then the pattering of feet and the sounds of a girl sobbing. Just as she turned towards the door it burst open and a young maidservant tottered in, clearly in a state of some distress. Tears were rolling down her cheeks.

The maid saw Belle. 'Oh! I beg pardon, miss, I'm sure!' Knuckling the tears from her eyes, the girl was already turning to hurry away, but Belle grabbed her by the shoulder. 'What is it, my dear?'

The girl, in her white cap and apron, was shaking. 'Nothin'. It's nothin', miss...' She hurried out again into the hall, Belle following. But the girl stopped with a low cry when she saw, from the other direction, an extravagantly dressed, fair-haired man prowling towards her with an unpleasant smile on his face. 'Now, what's all this, missy?' he said to the cowering maid. 'I thought we were having a pleasant conversation. Not trying to run from me, are you?'

This time it was Belle who let out a gasp of shock. She knew this smooth-tongued aristocrat whom some would call handsome. Her stomach clenched. Dear God, if this man was a friend of Davenant's, things were even worse than she'd thought.

Belle said to the young maid quickly, 'I will see to this. Go, now.' The maid scurried off, still sobbing. The man lurched closer—clearly he had been drinking, she could smell it. He was staring down at her. 'By God. Mrs Marchmain. Well, isn't this a happy coincidence?'

Belle held her chin high. *Loathsome, loathsome man.* 'Not for me, Lord Jarvis, I assure you.'

At first Jarvis scowled. 'I see your pride is still as damned lofty as ever...' Then he began to laugh—a bitter, ugly sound. His pale blue eyes were assessing her greedily. 'Hold a minute. Now, let me think. Here you are, in Davenant's house—can it be that my money wasn't enough to tempt you, but Davenant's *is*?'

He laid his hand on her shoulder and let it slide to her breast. Belle's stomach heaved as she knocked it away.

'You disgust me, my lord,' she breathed. 'You did when we last met and not a thing has changed—'

'What the deuce is going on?'

The man's voice came from the wide staircase above them. Jarvis jumped away from Belle and looked up angrily at the speaker. 'Davenant. Damn it, I'd no idea you were there...'

Belle looked up, too. And with this second shock she felt so dizzy that her ribs ached with the need for air. No. Impossible. *Please...*

The newcomer scarcely glanced at her. It was on Jarvis that his iron gaze rested as he came steadily down the stairs; he was tall and broad-shouldered; dressed in the sober perfection of black tailcoat and pristine white neckcloth.

He said to Jarvis, 'I thought you were on your way out a while ago.'

'And so I was,' declared Jarvis furiously. 'Until I was delayed, by an encounter with this woman here.'

'Not true,' breathed Belle.

'Oh, it *is* true. She insulted me, Davenant, damn it!'

Belle thought she'd been prepared for almost anything. But not for the fact that Adam Davenant, her brother's enemy, was the man on Sawle Down into whose ears she'd poured insult after insult.

Desperate hope rose in her breast. *He might not remember me. He might not recognise me...*

Lord Jarvis did though, all too well; Jarvis was still glaring at her, and to him she said as steadily as she could, 'You claim I insulted you, Lord Jarvis. All I did was tell you to stop pursuing that serving girl because you were frightening her out of her wits.' Belle met his glare squarely, though she truly wished the ground would open up and swallow her.

'I'll escort you to the door, Jarvis,' she heard Davenant saying.

The two men were moving away from her along the hall; she saw Jarvis pausing by the open doorway, still muttering angrily to Davenant, jabbing his finger in her direction. Dear God, she could just imagine what foul lies he'd be concocting.

'Good day to you, Jarvis,' Davenant was saying.

Jarvis gave a swift nod. 'Good day to *you*, Davenant. We'll speak soon, I've no doubt.' The footman closed the door after him and Adam Davenant was coming back towards her. The footman hadn't bothered to ask her name; there was a chance, just a chance she might still somehow be able to wriggle out of this...

'Well,' Mr Davenant said softly. 'So we meet again, Mrs Marchmain.'

Her last hope died.

Chapter Four

Adam Davenant was astounded and annoyed. As if Jarvis wasn't enough—the damned man caused trouble wherever he went—*she* was here.

A footman had warned Adam that a rather odd lady had come to call and within moments of first seeing her in the hall it had all fallen into place. She was the woman who'd emerged from that dreadful old carriage.

And who'd stirred memories of that sunlit March afternoon in Somerset.

Stirred more than memories, in fact. She was clad outrageously in a clinging outfit of turquoise and pink with a loud bonnet trailing ribbons everywhere. Her eyes were emerald, her raven-black curls set off the perfect creaminess of her skin, her lips were full and rosy.

And he steadily reminded himself that just a few weeks ago she'd heaped such insults on the name of Adam Davenant that they were etched like acid on his memory. Even more ominously—she knew Jarvis.

'You're very quiet, Mrs Marchmain,' he drawled. 'Surely you aren't trying to conjure up *more* insults to hurl at me? Or have you exhausted yourself being rude to Jarvis?'

Belle swallowed on the dryness in her throat and lifted her chin. 'He was treating that young serving maid *abominably*. You will perhaps remark, Mr Davenant, that I had no right to interfere, but I could not stand by!'

He was watching her with something unreadable in his eyes. 'You do tend to say what you think, don't you?' he said. 'You have a neat way with put-downs. You told me, for instance, that I wasn't born to wealth and it showed.'

Oh, Lord, thought Belle rather faintly. He hadn't forgotten or forgiven a single word. Something shook inside her, seeing him like this, no longer wearing the garb of a rough quarry worker, but dressed as the rich, powerful man he was, here in his mansion. And how well he fitted the part. To say he was handsome wasn't enough. His strong features and formidable stature implied power and dominance. Edward had described him as a boor. No one else in their right mind would.

But she was damned if she would grovel. 'How was I supposed to know who you were? How could I have guessed, when you were—you were—'

'Dressed like a labourer?' he cut in. 'That was because I'd been inspecting my quarry. I judge people by their words and actions, Mrs Marchmain, not their attire; a lesson you might try learning. Now it's my turn for questions, the most obvious being—why exactly are you here?' His voice licked somehow at her senses, soft and dangerous. Dear God, her errand was doomed before it had even begun.

But she had to try. 'I have business with you, Mr Davenant, which concerns my brother. I wrote to you, but you did not deign to reply!'

'I leave begging letters to my secretary, Lowell.'

Begging letters. 'How dare—?'

'Mrs Marchmain,' he interrupted, 'I'm an extremely busy man. And your brother—Hathersleigh—has taken up too much of my time already.'

Heat surged through her veins. 'You could at least give this matter your *attention*!'

'Why? Because you're members of the once-illustrious Hathersleigh family?'

She bit her lip. 'We are not without influence still.'

He sighed heavily. 'Please don't remind me that you have a great-uncle who is a duke, as your brother once did.' She visibly flinched. 'I really don't care,' he went on, 'if you can trace your ancestry all the way back to William the Conqueror. Why should I waste my time on you, when your family is reduced to sheep-stealing?'

Oh, Lord.

She remembered how at Sawle Down the dust had clung to this man's breeches and boots and perspiration had gleamed on his hard cheekbones. Today, he could have claimed to be a duke himself and no one would have doubted it. His clothes were exceedingly plain, yes, but that coat of his had clearly been cut by a master to fit those broad shoulders so perfectly. Sleek buckskins clung to his powerfully muscular thighs and his polished top boots were exquisite. His thick dark hair was cropped short, his pristine neckcloth was quite perfect.

He made no effort to clamour for attention. He didn't need to. And as his slate-grey eyes rested on hers, she felt a sharp jolt of awareness implode quietly yet devastatingly inside her. Awareness of what, precisely? Of his sheer maleness, that was what. It was impossible to look at him without thinking: here was a man of power, with a man's desires, and all that implied.

And he was her family's enemy. *Her* enemy.

She said, her head lifted high, but her pulse rate in tumult, 'I hope you will accept, Mr Davenant, that I spoke in the heat of the moment that afternoon on Sawle Down.'

'It gave you a wonderful opportunity to reveal your true thoughts, though, didn't it?' he observed caustically. 'So please don't lower yourself in my estimation by trying to take back what you said.'

The smouldering look she gave him said, *Don't worry. I won't.*

Inside Adam was rigid with tension. The witch. The insolent little green-eyed witch.

What Jarvis had said to him just before he left was still ringing in his ears.

I don't know why that woman's visiting you, Davenant, but you'd be a fool to believe a word she says. She's a greedy little widow angling for money—some time ago I made the mistake of not offering her enough.

She'd come here to plead with Adam for mercy for her brother, no doubt. And she must realise her mission was already doomed—because Adam knew exactly what she thought of him.

'I'm in the middle of a meeting,' he told her curtly. 'I'll be with you in fifteen minutes.' He was leading the way along a corridor. 'You can wait here, in my library.' One big hand pushed open a panelled door.

She swung round on him, head held high. 'You expect me to wait? *Again?*'

'You are uninvited,' he pointed out. 'Be glad that I see you at all, Mrs Marchmain.' He turned to go, clos-

ing the library door on her. She could cool down in
there. And so, damn it, could he.

Adam was a highly physical man and his lifestyle
usually accommodated a mistress, kept in enviable
style in return for companionship in bed and out of it.
He'd recently ended just such an arrangement with an
elegant widow, Lady Farnsworth—mainly because she
was starting to hint a little too often about marriage.

Marriage was one big mistake as far as Adam was
concerned. But it was also an error on his part, he now
decided grimly, to be without a mistress. It made him
think hungry thoughts about a raven-haired terma-
gant dressed in turquoise and pink who quite simply
detested him.

Belle just stood there when he'd gone, sunk before
she'd even begun. *I really don't care if you can trace
your ancestry all the way back to William the Conqueror*, he'd said. *Why should I waste my time on you,
when your family is reduced to sheep-stealing?*

She cringed anew. The ducal connection came
through their mother, who'd died shortly after giving birth to Edward when Belle was only two. It was
Belle's father who used to point out to his children that
their mother's uncle was the Duke of Sutherland, but as
far as Belle knew the Duke wasn't even aware of their
existence. Either that or he'd heard of their dwindling
fortunes and kept well away.

Belle's father had died when Belle was just thirteen,
and that was when the estate had to be put in the care
of stern Uncle Philip and his wife. Edward, at twenty-
one, had come into his inheritance with considerable
joy, hence the youthful gambling spree. But Belle had

already grasped the reality—that her family was in actuality impoverished.

Since Belle's widowhood her dressmaking business had given her independence; but it did not give her the deference or protection she might once have expected in society. She'd met Lord Jarvis two years ago, when he'd expressed an interest in investing in her shop and invited her to his big London house for a business meeting with his lawyer.

The lawyer never arrived. Lord Jarvis had locked the door to his study and had proceeded to make her an offer which had left her breathless and shaking.

'Let's *really* get down to business, shall we?' he'd smirked, sidling closer. 'How do you fancy a change of profession?'

He was, in effect, bluntly suggesting that she be his mistress. He'd silkily gone on to tell her that if he didn't appeal to her tastes, he had a choice of stalwart grooms from whom she could have her pick. 'As a young widow you must be quite desperate for male companionship. I'll enjoy watching.' He'd smiled. 'I'll pay handsomely, of course. One hundred pounds a month, Mrs Marchmain—I promise you won't be bored.'

She'd struck him hard on the cheek. His smile had vanished at the same time as the red mark appeared on his pale skin.

'So you want more money, do you?' he'd whispered. 'A greedy little slut, are you, Mrs Marchmain?'

'Let me out,' she'd breathed. She'd run to the door and was struggling frantically to open it. 'Damn you, let me out of here!'

He'd unlocked the door with an ugly look on his smooth features. 'Don't even *think* of telling anyone about what's passed between us today,' he'd rasped. 'Or I'll have you damned well ruined.'

Now she walked round this opulent book-lined room in utter agony of spirit. With a huge effort she tried to steady her racing pulse. She had dealt with Jarvis and she would deal with Davenant, though how, God only knew.

It was scarcely four, but outside the sky was growing overcast. On a nearby table some papers were scattered and, if only to distract herself from her dismaying thoughts, she went across to look. There were maps of Somerset, along with some geological sketches—to do with quarries, she guessed. Towards the back of the table was a tray of mineral samples together with a brass model of some kind of engine about a foot high, beautifully crafted.

Even though Adam Davenant's family fortune had been made in mining and quarrying, it was unusual for anyone to display such an obvious interest in the practicalities of money-grubbing. 'Showing his base blood,' Edward and his friends would sneer.

Yet in spite of herself Belle's attention was caught. She remembered how Davenant had defended the quarries to her that day on Sawle Down—*they provide work and wages for many men and food for their families.*

She remembered her inner acknowledgement that he was right. That sudden, instinctive feeling that he was a man of integrity...

A terrible mistake. An illusion.

She turned the model of the engine by its base, finding that the cold precision of it somehow soothed her roiling mind. A steam engine, she guessed; Uncle Philip Marchmain used to tell them both that steam was the future, and that the end of the world of the horse was in sight.

Well, the end of *her* world was in sight if she didn't find some way of extricating herself from this appalling mess.

She put the model down and sank into a chair. What would Davenant say—what would he do—if he knew that almost every night since that fateful encounter she'd been haunted by dreams of him?

When she'd fallen from her horse that afternoon and opened her eyes to see him towering above her—dust-covered, muscular, roughly clad—she'd felt something tight impeding her breathing. He'd offered to help her to her feet and she'd rejected him, so rudely.

But she'd never forgotten the strength of his hands on her waist as he'd lifted her on to her horse. Never forgotten the sense of sheer male power that emanated from his body, the gleam of the sun on his hard cheekbones; the glimpse of his naked chest revealed by that open-necked shirt…

Her pulse thudded at the memory. She was turning the ring on her finger in nervous agitation when suddenly the door opened. Adam Davenant—Lord Jarvis's friend and her enemy—was here again.

She jumped up from the chair as if it burned her. He pushed the door shut, folded his arms and studied her. Belle in turn acknowledged the spectacular lines of his tall, broad-shouldered figure with bitter eyes. *Handsome. So handsome.*

And trying so very hard to be a gentleman, she'd heard people say. But she didn't think anyone would dare to say that to his face. Whatever his origins, this man was formidable. And most women would simply—melt.

'Ah, Mrs Marchmain,' he said. 'Still here, I see.'

'I'm sorry to disappoint you, but, yes, I am.'

He looked at his watch. 'I can spare you ten minutes,' he said.

Outside the afternoon sun had vanished behind dark clouds. She thought she heard the ominous rumble of thunder in the distance—which was apt, since Thor the thunder god, in the person of Mr Adam Davenant, had her in his lair. *Oh, Lord...*

Belle took a deep breath and began. She explained how Edward had been heir to a much-diminished estate but was working so hard to hold his inheritance together. 'And then there were the new taxes on landowners,' she went on, 'and the weather was truly dreadful...'

She saw Davenant's dark eyebrows rise in faint contempt. 'Ah,' he said. 'So these iniquitous taxes and the unkind weather landed solely on your brother's portion of Somerset, did they?'

She coloured hotly. 'I see it pleases you to mock me, Mr Davenant. But I haven't *finished* yet! A year ago, as you well know, Edward sold some of his land to you because of pressing debts. And you paid him a truly pitiful amount for that land...'

Something happened then. The previously impassive features of his chiselled face had become hard as granite.

'I paid him two thousand guineas,' said Davenant.

Her hand flew to her mouth. 'Two *thousand*?'

'Yes.' His narrowed eyes never left her face. 'You see, I guessed that the old quarry there might benefit from reinvestment. I told him this and also offered him some shares. He turned down my offer and told me I was wrong. Nevertheless I paid him the two thousand—far more than he'd have got from anyone else.'

'Because you *knew* you could make that amount many times over from the stone!'

'Have you any idea,' he countered grimly, 'how much it costs to invest in equipment and labour for a re-opened quarry? It will be years before I start to see a profit; certainly no one else would have paid your brother so much. But fool that I was, I felt sorry for the young idiot.'

Outside thunder rumbled again. Davenant went to light the lamp on the table where the model engine was; his movements were lithe, almost graceful for such a powerfully built man...

Stop it. Stop it, you fool.

Two thousand guineas. Belle sank into the nearest chair. Now Davenant was saying with lethal politeness, 'I take it there's some discrepancy over figures. Am I right?'

Belle thrust aside a long bonnet ribbon that trailed down her cheek. 'I don't know—I might have misunderstood—'

'I doubt it,' he cut in crisply. 'Try asking your brother again. On this occasion you might find that he remembers the truth.' His expression was glacial. 'You could ask him, at the same time, why he stole my livestock.'

Belle was truly floundering now. 'It must appear to you as theft, I know. But that was all a mistake.'

'I suppose he told you that my sheep had strayed on to his lands,' he drawled icily. 'Told you that it was my fault, for not maintaining my fences.'

The hot blush rose to Belle's cheeks. That was *exactly* what Edward had said.

'I maintain my fences very carefully, Mrs Marchmain,' went on Davenant. 'In fact, every detail of my life is conducted with the utmost rigour. Now, I'm a busy man…' he glanced again at his watch '…it's gone four, and I'm sincerely hoping you've come here with some concise suggestions as to how your younger brother intends to pay back the not inconsiderable sum he owes me for selling off my sheep. Which is a criminal act, incidentally.'

Adam Davenant usually kept his emotions on a tight rein, but by now he was deeply angry. Somehow this woman had got under his guard and he shouldn't have let her. Turquoise and pink, for God's sake—he had to blink every time he looked at her! He should have abided by his first instinct and ordered her off his premises.

'Mr Davenant,' she was saying, that pointed chin still tilted defiantly, 'you must realise that it has been extremely difficult for my brother to see our heritage so diminished.'

She wasn't giving up yet, registered Adam. 'Ah,' he answered. 'The precious notion of blue blood and entitlement. Spare me, Mrs Marchmain. The Hathersleigh estate has been lurching towards ruin for generations, thanks to a fatal mixture of greed, complacency and sheer carelessness. Have you observed the way in which your brother conducts his business? Have you *seen* the great piles of unsorted paperwork that litter his so-called study?'

'He is busy,' Belle faltered. 'His wife is not well…'

'And so he sends his older sister to make his excuses for him. I repeat, I bought that land at an excessive price from your brother—not out of generosity, nor out of greed, but because I simply had no desire to have a bankrupt neighbour in Somerset. It's not good for appearances.'

Belle gazed at him whitely. This man was surely as cold and hard as the rock his men hewed from the ground. She rose to her feet. 'Exactly how much does my brother owe you for the sheep?'

'I don't see how you can hope to pay me off. You must have even less money to spare than he does.'

'I run a successful dressmaking business!'

'Not successful enough.'

She sat down again. Adam watched the turquoise ribbons, ridiculously flippant, fluttering from her straw bonnet and reflected that her brother was a goddamned weakling. Adam had rashly hoped to help young Hathersleigh by buying that land, but the fellow was a fool, and a liar, too—he'd not even equipped his rather pluckier older sister with the truth.

And the fact that she was still assuming her god-damned *superiority*, and laboured under the misapprehension that he, Adam, was somehow under obligation to show leniency, sent bitterness surging through Adam's blood.

He knew that people like her despised and feared men of Adam's mould, who were a symbol of things to come, of old values passing. She thoroughly deserved humiliation at his hands. Yet even while she glared up at him as if he was the devil incarnate, he felt something simmer, damn it, that was very like lust in his traitorous loins. Felt the longing to take her very firmly in his arms and plunder that sweet, rose-pink mouth with his lips and tongue...

Jarvis had clearly tried to make her his at some point in the past. Jarvis had failed.

Adam could see her hands trembling now. Yet still she faced him with that damned defiance, still she came up with fresh excuses for her sibling.

'My brother does not deserve prison, Mr Davenant.'

'Really?'

'Indeed. You see, he has a wife who is expecting their first baby very soon—'

'He'll have that in common with many of his fellow-prisoners in Newgate gaol, then.'

She tightened her fists. Then: 'You are despicable,' she said quietly. Her voice was steady, yet he noted how her small, high breasts heaved with distress beneath that tightly buttoned little pink jacket. 'Despicable,' she repeated. 'Both in your behaviour to me now, and your deliberately not telling me who you were that afternoon on Sawle Down. Your deception was truly dishonourable.'

Dishonourable? Damn it! *She's a greedy little widow, angling for money.* Adam went in with all guns blazing.

'Your kind talk always of honour and status,' he retorted harshly. 'Would you say your brother was showing *honour*, in sending his sister to me to plead his cause? There are names for that kind of behaviour.'

She recoiled as if he'd struck her. 'It was *my* decision to come here! If you think that Edward intended—'

'I think,' he cut in, 'that your cowardly brother told you about his plight in the hope that your feminine charms would soften my steely peasant heart. If that's an example of blue-blooded behaviour, you can keep it. In my world, we call it pimping.'

'Oh! I think—my brother did not mean—' She was stammering now, and backing away; somehow her dangling sleeve caught the little steam model and it went crashing to the floor.

She let out a cry of dismay and bent to start picking the pieces up.

'Leave it,' he commanded harshly. 'A footman will see to it.'

'*No!*' She was still flurrying around the floor. 'No, I will pick it *all* up and then I am going, you hateful, hateful man! Edward was right to say you are a boor and a tyrant. And—and I will see Edward and I in gaol *together* before I grovel any more to you!'

With that she bobbed down again, to pick up more pieces of the ill-fated model. As she did so she was presenting that very pert, very rounded *derrière* to Adam's narrowed eyes. Hell. He did try to look away. He despised himself for registering even the slightest flicker of interest. But a picture of her unclad appeared rather tantalisingly in his mind, and his body responded accordingly.

Adam had decided long ago that marriage was not for him. He had neither the time nor the inclination to play the games of courtship, flattery and lies that a permanent commitment would involve. God knew he was offered enough suitable brides; they were pushed before him at every opportunity, thanks to his wealth.

But the example of his parents' marriage had put him off for good. Miner Tom's only son, Charles, had been so rich he was able to choose a bride from the aristocracy, but his well-born wife—pushed into the marriage by her parents—had thoroughly despised her low-born husband and after producing two male heirs she'd embarked on a string of affairs.

Adam had spent a good deal of his childhood trying

to protect his young brother, Freddy, from their mother's promiscuity and their weak father's rages. Both parents had died years ago, and Adam felt not the slightest desire to emulate their unhappiness; hence his custom of keeping suitable mistresses to satisfy his own male desires.

He treated them generously, but always Adam made the terms quite clear: 'This ends when I say it ends. Afterwards, if we happen across each other in society, we will acknowledge each other civilly. No more and no less.'

Most of his former mistresses knew better than to cause him any trouble; Lady Farnsworth, his latest, had been an exception. Adam had quickly wearied of the elegant widow's clinging possessiveness and her withering contempt for any suspected rivals.

The trouble was, he hadn't yet chosen himself another woman for his bed. Usually they were either widows or amicably separated from their husbands and the choice was plentiful. But no one had tempted him to make an offer, since...

Since he collided with this little minx, who'd insulted his name to high heaven one March afternoon on Sawle Down.

The realisation struck him like a thunderbolt. *No.* He *couldn't* have held back from singling out a new *chère amie* because he was thinking of Belle Marchmain. It was damned impossible! But...

She'd come here to ask him a very big favour, but her plans—so far—had come crashing round her pretty ears. Now he looked at her again as she furiously picked up the last bits of his model from the floor.

Her straw bonnet had fallen off and her glossy raven curls were tumbling around the slender column of her neck. 'There! That's all of it!' she breathed, putting two more pieces defiantly on the table. Her face had become a little flushed. 'Whatever you call it,' she added rather darkly, her hands on her hips.

Mrs Belle Marchmain looked delectable. Her pink silk jacket had fallen apart, and the brightly patterned gown that fitted so snugly to her bosom and tiny waist almost made him smile.

What would she be like in bed? If she was, as Jarvis suggested, well practised in the erotic arts and open to offers, it might be interesting to find out...

'And—and you can stop *looking* at me like that!'

Her rebuke shocked him out of his reverie and Adam stopped smiling. 'You were asking about the model you almost destroyed,' he said. 'It's a miniature of a Newcomen steam engine. And that's not quite it, Mrs Marchmain. You came to me with a problem. And I think I might have the solution.' He'd propped his lean hips against the sideboard and watched her with cool, assessing eyes.

Belle suddenly felt that the room was too small. Either that or this formidable man was too close. Something tight was squeezing her lungs. 'Let me tell you now that Edward will never sell more of the estate to you and I wouldn't ask him to. It's his heritage!'

'But of course,' answered Adam imperturbably. 'And your brother shouldn't be expected to dirty his hands for a living as so many men—and women—do.' She swallowed. 'I also imagine,' he went on in the same calm voice, 'that most of the rest of his estate is entailed. You want me to drop charges against your brother for stealing my livestock, don't you? Well, I certainly require payment. And as to what that payment shall be, I have the perfect answer. I think you do as well.'

What? Belle paled. 'I—I thought perhaps we could come to some arrangement, for Edward to pay his debts off gradually...'

His lip curled. 'Impossible, I'm afraid. But I still see no reason, Mrs Marchmain, to dismiss the obvious solution.'

So frozen did she look that her lips could clearly scarcely frame the words. 'What exactly are you suggesting, Mr Davenant?'

'Let's be clear. You surely realise you have only one thing you can offer in payment of your brother's debts,' Adam said softly. 'Yourself. Be my mistress.'

Chapter Five

Belle felt, in that instant, as if all the breath had been squeezed from her lungs. Lord Jarvis's insults had made her feel sick. This man made her feel as if the safety of her world had been rocked to its foundations.

Be my mistress.

He was just watching her, leaning back against the sturdy oak sideboard with his arms folded across his broad chest. The candlelight fell on his cropped dark hair, on his sleepy grey eyes, on his hateful, sternly handsome face. And her pulse was skittering with the unsteadiness of a new-born colt.

The way he was looking at her. Assessing her, damn him. She felt his presence in the pit of her stomach and her dry mouth. She couldn't look at him without tingling anew at the sight of his powerful figure: those heavily muscled shoulders, his broad chest tapering down to slim hips and powerful thighs… Oh, just his being *near* her made the air difficult to breathe.

His mistress. How dare this man make such a proposition? How *dare* he? Yet—oh, goodness, she'd been an arrogant idiot to come here. Straight into the lion's den, armed only with her own stupid defiance—and her brother's lies. She bent to rather shakily pick up her fallen bonnet; how ridiculous its gaudiness seemed now.

She remembered how she'd felt when her husband died and the enormity of the debts she'd faced. Remembered how she'd stood her ground against Lord Jarvis—only, dear God, this man was far more dangerous than Jarvis.

When she eventually spoke her words were, to her, miraculously steady. 'To be perfectly honest, Mr Davenant,' she replied, 'I'm not quite sure whether your—*offer* is intended as a deliberate insult or a very poor joke.'

He shrugged. 'It's neither. There happens to be a vacancy.'

'But I thought you already had a mistress…' She clamped her mouth shut. *You stupid fool, Belle.* She shouldn't have shown the slightest interest. Yet she couldn't help but hear, in her shop, the gossip of the *ton*. Couldn't help but know that Adam Davenant attracted the attentions of the most beautiful women in London.

His dark eyebrows had already arched in amusement. 'So you take an interest in my *affaires*, do you? Then you should be aware that my latest companion and I have recently parted company.'

Belle returned his smile, sweetly. 'She has had a lucky reprieve.'

He laughed. He actually laughed. 'I wish you'd tell her so.' His voice was silky. 'I thought I was making you quite a reasonable offer. I would provide you, of course, with a London house and an income, so I do wish you'd stop acting like some virgin schoolgirl, Mrs Marchmain.'

She let out a sharp breath. 'I'm merely, as a woman

of the world, trying to assess what *you* would gain from such an arrangement. You'll understand I find it hard to believe you are suggesting this out of any kind of—of *liking*.'

He shrugged. 'I'm rather bored with women who think I'm the answer to all their prayers.'

'*So* tedious for you, I'm sure!'

He nodded. 'A little, yes.' Belle gritted her teeth. 'I think,' he went on blithely, 'that you, on the other hand, would enter the kind of relationship I'm suggesting with a refreshing honesty. And of course your weakling brother's error regarding the sheep would be forgiven—' He stopped. He suddenly noticed that she was trembling. 'Is something wrong, Mrs Marchmain?'

'You thought I came here to—to bargain with you.'

'And didn't you?'

'Yes! But *not in that way*.'

He was silent a moment. Then he said steadily, 'I see. Not now that you know exactly who I am, you mean. Tell me, does my low birth make me so much worse a prospect than Jarvis?'

She shuddered. 'Jarvis is *despicable*.' She spoke with such absolute disgust that Adam felt a bolt of uncertainty shoot through him.

'I was under the impression that you were holding out for considerably more money from him.'

'Holding out for… Oh, you are a friend of his,' she retorted bitterly, 'so it wouldn't matter what I said. But do you really think I would contemplate a proposal of any kind from Lord Jarvis?'

Adam shrugged. 'Jarvis would offer a solution to your problems. He's not as rich as I am, but he does have a title. And, oh, I believe his family goes back almost as far as yours, although there might not be a duke in the family...'

Belle had stepped shakily away from him. 'You are hateful,' she whispered. 'Mr Davenant, I will find some way to pay back the money my brother owes, I swear. But you'll understand, I hope, if I tell you that I can no longer bear to spend another moment in your presence.'

He shrugged. *The taint of Miner Tom.* Well—let her face the consequences of her and her brother's damned arrogance.

She was already making for the door when he saw something sparkling under her dark lashes. *Tears.*

'Stop,' he said.

She turned. She was almost broken, he suddenly realised; he saw it in the paleness of her cheeks, the trembling of her fingers as she crammed her straw bonnet over her dark curls.

Something dangerously like pity twisted at his throat.

'Jarvis is not my friend,' he said curtly. 'He was here on a matter of business and, believe me, that was almost more than I could tolerate. What exactly happened between the two of you?'

She lifted her eyes steadfastly to his. 'Two years ago Lord Jarvis invited me to his house on the pretext of investing in my business. He made me an offer that I found...obscene. Though—' *Oh, what was the use?* Belle was shivering. 'You don't believe me, do you? You still think I'm in the market for... That I visited you to... Oh, I've been so *stupid.* I should never have come here.'

Not now she knew who he was. Adam started towards the door. 'Unlike Jarvis,' he said, 'I don't—

ever—force myself on unwilling females. You came here of your own accord and you're equally free to leave.'

She started towards the door, then stopped. 'But—'

'As for those sheep,' he went on pitilessly, 'I'll get my secretary to send you a bill so you can pay me for them. You told me your shop was flourishing, didn't you?' He was holding the door open for her.

Belle froze. Her shop—flourishing? *Oh, Lord, this was bad.* What could she do? He'd offered her a solution and she'd discarded it.

Think again, Belle.

She heaved in a great breath. 'Mr Davenant,' she said.

Now, Adam wanted this woman and her insults out of here. But something was happening. Some new desperation in her voice riveted his attention. 'Yes?'

'Mr Davenant—what if I were to consent to becoming your mistress after all?'

What? What in hell...?

Suddenly she'd tugged off her straw bonnet and tossed it to the floor again. He closed the door. That hat would be lucky to survive the day, thought Adam rather dazedly. Then she was sidling across the room to him and lifting her sweet face with its tempting rosebud mouth to his and—

Hell. She'd raised her arms to run her fingertips along his broad shoulders.

'Mrs Marchmain,' he began.

His voice was thick in his throat as her small hands tugged him closer. That delicate scent tickled his nose again—lavender soap, he guessed. He could feel the warmth now, of her tender body; her nearness was turning his blood to fire and making his pulse throb.

He reached out his big hands to take hers and hold them away.

'I thought,' he grated at last, 'that you were going to repay me from your business.'

Her voice was husky. 'Perhaps I've had second thoughts.'

She was playing a mighty dangerous game. Adam swore under his breath; Jarvis had warned him she was a conniving minx, damn it, and Adam wasn't one to be toyed with. With a low growl—half of anger, half of lust—Adam pulled her to him and let his lips capture her soft mouth.

And Belle's world spun until she no longer knew if she was on her head or her heels. In this man's arms, she didn't much care either way.

Faced with that open door and his chilly dismissal, it had struck her most forcefully that—like a drowning seafarer—she couldn't afford to be choosy about her rescue options. Pay him back from her shop? Dear Lord, she'd no idea how much a flock of sheep cost; she *did* know that if this man wasn't going to show mercy she and her brother were sunk.

It wasn't as if she was a youthful, shrinking maiden. One by one the frantic thoughts raced through her brain. *Other women do this.* In fact, he assumed that was why she'd come to his hateful abode in the first place. *Other women use men of influence and wealth to get what they want—why shouldn't I?*

The trouble was that he didn't repel her as Jarvis did. Far from it. The instant his firm, demanding mouth started caressing hers, she forgot she was supposed to be in charge. She forgot he was her enemy. All she wanted was more.

The sweetness of his kiss pulsed through her veins.

As his strong hands caressed her she could feel the heat of his body against hers; then he coaxed her lips apart and deliberately set about ravishing her mouth with his tongue. She could taste the maleness of him. He was filling her senses, branding her with shocking demands.

She'd meant to fake her response but, dear heaven, this was no pretence. Her hands instinctively curled tighter around his heavily muscled shoulders; somehow she could not get close enough to him. When he grasped her waist and hauled her against him, she felt his rock-hard arousal pressing against her stomach and it stopped her breathing. Stopped her thinking.

Her response was primeval and passionate. She plied her tongue in his mouth, tasting him, shuddering as he thrust his own tongue between her lips in measured response. She yearned to press her aching bosom closer to the hard wall of his chest, then gasped aloud because his hand, warm and strong, was cupping one desperately sensitive breast, his thumb teasing her stiffened nipple through the silk of her gown, rubbing it gently to and fro until she was crying out for more…

Then he drew away.

Belle swayed where she stood. Needing the warmth of his arms around her. Missing the heat of his hard male body.

He said levelly, 'This is an absurd situation, Mrs Marchmain, and both of us know it.'

She gazed up at him, imagining she saw a glint of concern in his dark grey eyes, but if so it was quickly gone. She felt as wretched as she'd ever felt in her life. 'Absurd? But, Mr Davenant,' she said with a forced smile, 'I was merely indicating that I'd had second thoughts about the offer you'd made earlier—'

'I was damned wrong to make that offer,' he broke in harshly. He was making for the door again, straightening his coat. 'Mrs Marchmain, please forget my proposition. You were foolish to come here alone, foolish to make yourself so vulnerable.'

She gazed at him, white-faced. 'But what about my brother, and…?'

'You can tell the young idiot he owes me nothing for my livestock,' Adam rapped out. 'The matter's dealt with. Finished.'

Belle drew back as if he'd hit her with a sledgehammer. 'So you've got your revenge,' she said steadily.

'What?' His hand had been on the door; now he swung round to her, his jaw set, his eyes ominously dark.

She shrugged and lifted her chin. 'I was desperate and you realised it. You've achieved my humiliation— that was what you wanted all the time, wasn't it?'

Adam said through gritted teeth, 'You misunderstand me.'

'On the contrary—' Belle's voice shook now '—I think I understand you only too well.' Not even Jarvis had made her feel as wretched as she did now.

She saw him utter some low expletive under his breath. Then: 'I'll call my carriage for you,' said Adam curtly, turning to the door again.

She looked distraught. 'I would prefer to walk. In fact—I insist on walking!'

He threw her one last, withering look. 'There's a fine line between independence and sheer stupidity. I repeat: I'll summon my carriage.'

As the luxurious coach moved off Belle was aware that the thunderclouds had passed overhead and once more the sun shone brightly in the late afternoon sky. She was still able to move, she was able to breathe. Yet it seemed as if nothing was working any more. It reminded her of how she'd felt when they came five years ago to tell her that her husband had died. The world went on, but for her nothing could be the same.

Belle was crushed and humiliated by what had just occurred, yet it was her fault for breaking all the rules—not just of civilised behaviour, but of survival. Davenant was a cruel man with massive power; she'd insulted him badly in Somerset and he'd not forgotten. Men like him never did.

Today she'd stupidly attacked him again and he'd swiftly resolved upon the most devastating revenge possible. Without pity he'd provoked her into the ul-timate degradation of offering herself to him. In re-sponse he'd proved to her with lethal finality that it took only one touch of his firm lips for her to melt helplessly in his arms—then he told her he didn't want her after all.

It was done with utter and casual contempt, because all he really wanted was to be rid of her and her brother as swiftly as he could.

But—what would have happened if he *had* accepted her offer? If he'd carried on kissing her, and…

It simply didn't bear thinking about. She looked around at last, recoiling with a shudder from the rich velvet seats, the satin linings of this luxurious carriage. She'd rescued Edward from the threat of prison and her enemy had got his revenge in spectacular fashion. Her whole body still trembled from his wonderful caresses.

And she felt as wretched as she'd ever felt in her whole life.

* * *

Arriving back at her shop just before five, Belle slipped in through the back door, hoping to get upstairs and restore herself to some sort of calmness before joining Gabby in the shop.

But Edward was there, pacing the tiny office at the back with the door open. He sprang towards her as soon as he saw her.

'Well? How did it go with Davenant?' he said importantly. 'I have to set off back to Somerset tomorrow, to poor Charlotte, so I need to be sure that it's all sorted.'

Wearily Belle joined him and shut the door on them both. 'How did you know that I'd been to see him?'

'Oh, I called earlier and heard that Matt had borrowed a carriage for you. Did you twist Davenant round your little finger, sister mine?'

Actually, Edward, it was all rather a horrid surprise. I found out that I'd met him before. I let him kiss me. I made an utter and complete idiot of myself.

Belle gazed at her younger brother. What in the name of goodness would he say, if he learned Davenant had suggested just now that she be his mistress—then changed his mind?

Edward would splutter. He would spout about their family honour and Davenant's lowly background, and, dear God, Belle couldn't face that just now.

'It is indeed all sorted,' she said tonelessly. 'He's agreed to forget about those sheep you stole.'

'I didn't—' he began.

Belle just looked at him and his voice trailed away. But being Edward, he quickly recovered. 'Big of him to say he'd forget it,' grumbled her brother, 'considering those sheep were on land that should by rights be mine!'

She whirled round on him. 'Edward. You put me in an almost impossible position, by telling me he paid you only two hundred guineas for that land, when, in fact, he paid you two thousand. How *could* you?'

He flushed slightly. 'Whatever, Belle, the fellow's no right to give himself airs.'

'That *fellow* could have put you in a debtors' gaol!'

'He said that?' Her brother's voice shook a little. She nodded. 'The vindictive, low-born wretch,' muttered Edward. 'By God, he'd better not go around dragging our good name in the mud.'

'*What* good name, Edward?' she said in utter weariness. 'For heaven's sake, what good name?'

Her brother fiddled uncomfortably with his high starched collar. She thought again of Adam Davenant's severe but fashionable clothes and for some stupid reason a huge ache rose in her throat.

'Well,' Edward went on, brushing a fleck of dust from his breeches, 'I'll leave you to it, then, with your shop, and all your flummery—such fun for you.'

'I work hard, Edward. Very hard.' She spoke tightly.

'Oh, I know. But you enjoy it, don't you? What else would you do with yourself? You've been a widow for five years, so clearly you've no desire for a doting husband and children.'

'Clearly not,' echoed Belle as she escorted her brother to the back door.

Edward turned to her one last time. The light from the doorway threw the old puckered scar on his forehead into sharp relief. 'I'm glad it's all sorted, at any rate,' he said. 'Oh, by the way, you won't tell Charlotte about any of this, will you? I knew I could rely on you, Belle!' He adjusted his coat, put on his new hat and hurried outside. She closed the door and leaned against it.

I must be the biggest fool in London.

Davenant had spoken of Edward in tones of utter contempt and God help her, she understood why. But to tell him exactly why she protected Edward and would always do so would cause her far more pain than merely to let Davenant go on thinking her a fool.

She wasn't a fool. She knew that what had occurred today at Davenant's house was a burden she'd bear for the rest of her life. She'd never forget the coldness in his grey eyes as he'd put her away.

Gabby's voice penetrated her bleak thoughts. '*Madame. Madame*, are you all right?'

Belle scrubbed her eyes quickly with her handkerchief. 'Yes, I'm fine, Gabby. Did you want me?'

Gabby glanced along the corridor towards the shop. 'Well...I tried to deal with her at first. But—oh, *madame*, we have another complaint! It's Lady Jenkinson.'

Oh, no. Belle headed quickly for the shop with Gabby to see Lady Jenkinson pacing the floor with a cowed-looking maid in tow. The room was for the moment empty of other customers and it was as well.

'Disgraceful! Disgraceful, I call it!' Lady Jenkinson was declaring.

'Can I be of assistance, my lady?' asked Belle calmly. Gabby hovered anxiously.

'You most certainly can.' Lady Jenkinson swung round on her. 'You can give me my money back and an apology, too! You, girl—' she was addressing her own unfortunate maid '—stop lumping around like a good-for-nothing and show this hussy the result of her work.'

Belle felt every nerve tensing. 'I'm sure there's no need for wild insults, Lady Jenkinson.'

'Aye, and you think not, do you, madam? Well, look at *this*.' The maid was nervously spreading an apricot silk gown out on the counter and Lady Jenkinson started jabbing one fat, ring-smothered finger at it. Belle wished she'd followed her instinct when Lady Jenkinson first visited the shop and politely guided her towards another *modiste*, as far away as possible.

'Is there some kind of fault in the fabric?' Belle asked with forced calm. 'We usually check every length with the utmost care, but of course we can replace the panel...'

'No fault in the fabric, but in the sewing,' screeched Lady Jenkinson. 'Look!' She was holding up a split seam in the skirt, displaying an opening that ran for a foot or more.

Belle did look at it, frowning. 'I'm so sorry. Of course, we can repair it as a priority, and perhaps in the meantime you would like to accept one of these silk scarves to make up for your trouble? This light peach one will match the gown perfectly, I think...'

'Now, don't you be thinking you can buy me off. I know your kind! My money back, if you please. And all my friends of the *ton*—Lady Jersey not least of them— will hear about this, you mark my words!'

Belle pressed her lips together and went for the key to her cash box. Gabby caught her eye and pulled a face. The money refund wasn't so much of a problem; the worst of it was that the hideous Lady Jenkinson really would take great pleasure in spreading news of her dissatisfaction all around the town.

Yet Lady Jenkinson had been almost obsequiously keen to be dressed by Belle. 'All my friends tell me you are quite the thing, Mrs Marchmain,' she'd gushed. So—why this sudden turn-around?

Gabby opened the door for her ladyship and bobbed

her a tight curtsy. Then, as soon as the door was shut again, she turned to Belle and rolled her eyes.

'The cow,' Gabby declared. 'She must have been clumsy and torn it perhaps when she was climbing into her new town *cabriolet*...' Gabby mimicked Lady Jenkinson's mincing accent.

Belle smiled only briefly. 'Gabby, this wasn't an accident. The thread's been cut.'

'Cut?'

'Yes. Look.' Belle turned to where the apricot gown still lay on the counter. 'It's been cut so thoroughly—*here*, and *here*—that whoever did it has even nicked the fabric itself, with a sharp little pair of scissors.'

Gabby gasped. 'You're right. But why? Her ladyship absolutely loved the gown when she first tried it on!'

'Well, she's clearly changed her mind. Or perhaps one of her new friends was rude about the colour or style.'

'Impossible. She was so eager to be a client of yours, *madame*.'

'Things change rather rapidly in the world of fashion,' said Belle quietly.

For the moment, Belle's order books were full—but it would not take much for a business like hers, that depended on society's whim, to change overnight from minor success to a struggle for survival. Yet even that worry paled into insignificance in the face of the blow dealt to her today by Adam Davenant.

The hateful man had provoked her into offering herself to him. Had kissed her senseless—then turned her down. And every fibre of her being was throbbing rawly with the sheer, damned humiliation of it.

It's just your pride, she told herself bitterly. *Just your stupid pride that's hurt.*

In which case, she would get over her humiliation and forget all about that damnable man very quickly—wouldn't she?

Chapter Six

'Mr Davenant,' Adam's lawyer Turnbull pronounced in some amazement the next morning, 'your missing livestock were worth several hundred pounds. My dear sir, this was an act of deliberate theft, no doubting it!'

Adam had visited Turnbull's Aldwych office early, taking steps to erase the fact that he could have had young Edward Hathersleigh sent to prison.

'I've reason to assume it was an error on Hathersleigh's part,' said Adam. 'And I believe some of those sheep had strayed.'

'But your fences are inspected regularly, and your sheep were clearly marked—'

'They'd strayed,' Adam declared flatly. 'End of matter.'

He left Turnbull bemused. 'Never stops,' the lawyer muttered to his clerk. 'That man never stops.'

And indeed for the next few days Adam continued to be busy from dawn till dusk, meeting bankers and businessmen in a concentrated effort to make the very most of the fine Bath stone from the Sawle Down quarry. Finding a market would be no problem—London was awash with high-class building schemes like the grandiose Regent Street project being drawn up by the Prince and his friend the architect Nash.

But getting the stone to London was crucial and Adam knew everything depended on building his railway to the Avon canal, with its direct links to the Thames and thence to the capital. *Four miles.* That was the distance between the Sawle Down quarry and the canal, if he followed the obvious route past Midford. The first section of land was his and the next belonged to his ally Bartlett; no problem there.

But the last, crucial half-mile that led to the canal near Limpley Stoke crossed Jarvis's land. It was Jarvis's land, too, for at least a mile both up and down the canal. For Adam to take his railway route north meant making excavations that would be expensive as well as dangerous for his workers.

If Adam tried to avoid the barrier Jarvis presented by taking his route south, there'd be the expense not only of extra track laying, but of more land to be bought, from possibly unwilling landowners. Again and again he studied his maps alongside his chief engineer George Shipley, who'd come to London from Somerset for the sole purpose of helping Adam to devise a rail route.

But for the first time in his life Adam found his sharp brain wandering—to thoughts of an utterly provoking female called Belle Marchmain, who had come to him to plead in sheer desperation for her brother.

He felt nothing but contempt for Edward Hathersleigh. Hadn't Adam tried to help the young fool out already, by paying him far more for that land than it was worth? And Hathersleigh repaid him by lying about the price and stealing Adam's livestock! Yet still

Hathersleigh went round boasting of his blue blood, convinced that the world owed him as much money as he wanted. Aristocrats like him certainly helped to explain the French Revolution.

And mere money didn't buy happiness; witness Adam's own parents' miserable marriage. Adam's mother had once brutally told him that had it not been for him and his brother, Freddy, she could have escaped the living hell of marriage to their father. A fine encouragement to wedlock and parenthood, that.

'Look at you, Adam,' Freddy would point out, laughing. 'You'll simply have to cave in to the fortune-hunters some day. You're twenty-nine years old, good-looking and filthy rich, but you've no wife yet, let alone an heir to pass it all on to.'

'So?' Adam had answered mildly. 'Thanks to your three strapping young sons, there's no danger whatsoever of our family line running out, Freddy. And it won't be long before you've more brats on the way, I shouldn't be surprised.'

Freddy's pleasant face had coloured with happiness. 'Well actually, Adam, since you've mentioned it, Louisa's into her third month, but we're keeping it quiet for now.'

Adam had patted his brother on the back. 'Delighted for you. Means I can continue to repel the fortune-hunters with a clear conscience.'

Freddy grinned. Freddy was always grinning these days, like a cat who'd got the cream. So damned happy, he and Louisa both, with their rural home in Surrey where their three boys, the oldest only seven, could roam happily around the countryside on their ponies.

That sort of life wasn't for Adam. The responsibility of the family inheritance—the estates, the businesses and all the people they employed—was his. Though he outwardly bore it lightly, it consumed the majority of his time. And—marriage? To some top-lofty daughter of a noble house who would for ever be remembering that she'd married beneath her rank? *Never.*

Once, in the school holidays when Adam was ten, he'd heard his parents arguing after some lavish party they'd given at Hathersleigh Manor.

'My friends feel sorry for me—do you know that?' his mother had bitterly declared. 'To be married to the son of a *miner.* My God, everyone laughs at your manners, at the way you speak—'

Adam was aware of his father replying in a low voice, of his mother speaking more shrilly now. 'Don't walk away when I'm talking to you! Where do you think you're going?'

Then Adam heard his father clearly. 'Anywhere. I'm going anywhere, to sleep in the stables if need be, to get away from you. Go off with one of your lovers, why the hell don't you?'

So much for wedding vows. Always, when some eligible female sidled up to him with marriage on her mind, Adam remembered his mother's shrill voice that night. He'd sworn to avoid commitment, and his usually careful choice of mistresses had so far served him well. But—*damn it.* That woman, Belle.

He'd accused her of coming to sell herself in return for her brother's debts; indeed, after Jarvis's insinuations it was a natural assumption to make. But things had gone disturbingly wrong. Firstly, she didn't seem like a woman for sale. And secondly, to put it quite simply, she'd found a way past Adam's rather formidable self-control.

She was beautiful—that he'd already acknowledged—and so luscious to hold that his loins still tightened at the memory of her soft, slender body crushed in his arms. She'd been delectable and melting as golden honey, and just as sweet to taste. It had taken a huge effort on his part to pull himself away and tell her his offer no longer stood. And she'd looked absolutely stricken.

A muscle clenched in his jaw as he remembered it. Again, any normal woman out to trick him would have archly referred to the fact that his arousal was still very much in evidence, and would have tried to coax him into even more intimate activity. But Belle Marchmain had backed away at his words of rejection as if he'd struck her.

And she'd told him she hated Jarvis. Told him Jarvis had made an offer that she'd found obscene... Good grief, he'd found himself almost *apologising* for making his own offer to her in the first place!

Had she been right, to accuse him of deliberately punishing her for those insults she'd uttered at Sawle Down? Perhaps. And certainly as far as he was concerned his business with the Hathersleighs was concluded. He was damned if he was going to stoop to pursuing her feckless brother over a flock of sheep.

But—let Mrs Marchmain dwell on that kiss, because she'd revelled in it as much as he, no denying. Meanwhile it was time for Adam to find himself a new mistress and then, perhaps, he'd take her to buy a new gown or two from Mrs Marchmain's shop. Condescension, he'd found, was often the sweetest revenge possible.

A week after his encounter with Belle Marchmain Adam was hard at work by candlelight in the study of his Mayfair house. At ten he heard a knock on the door and his business secretary Bernard Lowell came in, laden with papers.

'Here are the letters you asked me to draft, Mr Davenant. And some bills for you to approve.' Lowell put the letters on the table; Adam looked at them quickly.

'Thank you, Lowell. It looks as if you've done an excellent job as usual. Anything else?'

'Two documents need signing tonight. And...' Lowell hesitated. 'Have you seen any more of Mrs Marchmain since last week, sir?'

Adam sat back in his chair and gave his secretary all his attention. Lowell was a thin, mild-mannered clerk whose gentle voice and habit of blinking behind his spectacles tended to disguise the fact that he was sharply intelligent and utterly loyal. Lowell didn't ask a question like *that* without good reason.

'You used to know her family, didn't you, Lowell?'

'I grew up in Bath, sir, as you're aware, near to her family home. And I remember her—Miss Hathersleigh, she was then—as a young girl, always tearing around the countryside on a horse too big for her, though she didn't mind how many times she fell off. She's got pluck, that lady. But her husband died, didn't he, in the war?' Lowell shook his head. 'A blow indeed. I hear she's still single, though from what I remember she could have had her pick of the Bath gentlemen. Now, if I could just ask you to sign this final letter, Mr Davenant...'

Adam signed and handed it back. 'Have you any idea why she's not married again?'

'There was no obvious explanation, sir. I believe the proposals came from perfectly eligible gentlemen. It is just possible, I suppose, that she loved her husband and still mourns him...'

'Lowell.'

'Sir?'

'Does Mrs Marchmain *look* as if she's a grieving widow?'

'I have to admit she does not, sir.'

Exactly. Adam leaned back in his chair. 'Do you know her brother at all, Lowell?'

'Master Edward? I know he's a year or two younger than she is. And the young gentleman...' Lowell cleared his throat '...is unfortunately haphazard, I hear, when it comes to matters of money.'

Adam's fingers tightened round his pen. 'Explain, if you please.'

'Edward Hathersleigh has debts at White's, sir.'

'White's!'

'Indeed. His debts are to the club itself. They are substantial, I believe, for anyone, let alone for a man of straitened circumstances.'

Adam's breath caught in his throat. *The fool. The idiotic young fool.*

'He incurred the debts during his recent stay in town,' continued Lowell steadily. 'Because of his family circumstances—he is imminently, I understand, to enter the state of fatherhood—the proprietor of White's has granted him a month to pay those debts. But someone else is planning at this moment to buy them up.'

'Who?'

Lowell hesitated. 'Lord Jarvis, sir.'

Adam heard the big clock ticking out in the hall, but there was no other sound in the whole of this house. At last he said, 'How much does Hathersleigh owe at White's?'

'In the region of five thousand guineas, I believe.'

Slowly Adam leaned back in his chair. 'Lowell,' he said, 'I'd like you to go there now and buy up that debt in my name.'

Lowell blinked just once. 'Buy it up, sir. Yes. Of course.'

Adam might as well have been telling him to pay for the weekly delivery of coal.

When Adam strolled into his club on St James's Street at three o'clock the next afternoon, he saw Lord Rupert Jarvis studying stock prices in *The Times*. On spotting Adam, he got languidly to his feet.

'So you wanted a meeting,' said Jarvis, a thin smile playing around his lips. 'But I'm not going to change my mind, you know, about letting you have my land for your railway.'

He sat down and Adam also eased himself into a chair. 'Not even you can halt the future, Jarvis. And some day your horses and carriages will seem as antiquated as the ox or the coracle.'

Jarvis poured them both brandy. 'Horses have been with us for centuries, Davenant, and will be with us for centuries more. Your damned new-fangled steam engines will blow themselves to bits within months.'

Adam gazed at him thoughtfully. Rupert Jarvis had once had a wife, but she'd died some years ago—a poor little thing, she'd always looked terrified. Adam said softly, 'I think you've already made your views on my railway perfectly clear, Jarvis. I've come to talk about something else. Your connection to the lady who visited my house on the day of our last encounter. Mrs Belle Marchmain.'

Jarvis looked startled, then smiled. 'Her?' He steepled his fingers. 'Ah, she's selling herself in her own way, flaunting herself round town in her gaudy clothes. What's she on the hunt for but a damned protector? Though she's choosy. She wants someone well born and rich, but she had the sheer arrogance to turn me down, Davenant!'

Just then a waiter brought the meal Jarvis had ordered and Jarvis started to attack his beef steak with greedy relish. 'You eating here, or not?'

Adam said, 'I'm not. But I'd like to know why you were trying to buy up her brother's debts at White's.'

Jarvis's head shot up from his food. 'Heard about that, have you? Yes, young Hathersleigh's got himself into a fine mess—and my thinking is *this*. I buy up Edward Hathersleigh's gambling debts—they've given him a month, I hear, but he hasn't a hope in hell of repaying them—and I then make it plain to him that he owes me *nothing* providing he sends his pretty sister in my direction.'

'But you've already told me you made her an offer and she turned you down.'

Jarvis put down his knife and fork and chuckled. 'This time, thanks to her brother's debts, she'll have no choice. I'm going to bed her whether she likes it or not. Spread stories about her until she's got little option, by the time I've finished with her, other than to sell herself on the street…'

'Before you get too carried away,' Adam interrupted, 'I'm afraid you're just a little too late.'

Jarvis frowned. 'Late? What the devil do you mean? I'm going round to White's later this afternoon—I've an appointment!'

'Then you'd better cancel it. Because *I've* bought up Hathersleigh's gambling debts.'

Jarvis's face turned red, then white. 'Why in hell—?'

Adam shrugged. 'A whim. A fancy.'

'Sell them to me.'

'Can you give me one good reason why I should?'

'Because I'll pay you double the sum.'

'I don't want your money. I want your land, Jarvis.'

Jarvis leaned back in his chair, breathing heavily. 'Give me the woman and you get it.'

Adam was very still.

'Or,' went on Jarvis, 'let's think this through, shall we?' He poured himself more brandy. 'I know that she loathes me. But *you*, now, Davenant. You can twist any woman round your little finger... I've got an idea.' A reptilian smile flickered round his thin lips. '*You* will have to do what I was going to do to that damned woman.'

Jarvis leaned forwards, wagging his finger; Adam realised he was more than a little inebriated. 'You'll have to enlighten me, Lord Jarvis,' Adam drawled.

'I mean exactly what I said. You, Davenant, have got the Marchmain woman and her brother utterly in your power thanks to that debt, haven't you? I also assume you bear neither of them any kindness?'

'About as much as either of them would show to me,' said Adam flatly.

Jarvis nodded. 'Damn it, I *did* want her, badly. Who wouldn't? But it strikes me she could be hellish difficult, that Marchmain woman, and I've got a far better notion. *You* do it, Davenant.' Jarvis swigged back another mouthful of brandy. 'Yes, you bed the woman, then ditch her—and I'll give you all the land you want.'

The club was filling up. A group of men were talking noisily nearby about a new opera singer who'd caught everyone's fancy at Sadler's Wells, but Adam was focused on no one, nothing but Jarvis.

Adam said evenly, 'An interesting proposal. But I'd like to think you were sober, Lord Jarvis, when you made it.'

Jarvis clenched his fist and thumped it on the table defiantly. 'Never more so, believe me. We'll get it written up. We'll do this *properly*. What do you say? Oh, I'd have enjoyed taking the woman down a peg or two myself, but on thinking about it, it would give me just as much satisfaction to see her with her fancy airs in thrall to *you*, because...'

His voice trailed away. His pale eyes gleamed. Adam could have finished that sentence for him.

Because you're Miner Tom's grandson. And Mrs Belle Marchmain rates herself above the likes of you.

Adam said nothing. Jarvis was speaking again. 'Another idea. On second thoughts, Davenant, perhaps your merely bedding her isn't enough.'

Adam waited, not a muscle of his face betraying any flicker of emotion. Jarvis, on the other hand, was agitated, toying with the brandy bottle, with his half-empty plate. At last he slapped his hand on the table.

'Betrothal!' he exclaimed. 'That's it! I want you to get her to agree to a betrothal with you. Then you'll jilt her publicly, Davenant—accuse her of something obnoxious, rutting with one of your servants, perhaps—so the whole of society will mock her humiliation. And after that—I'll let you have all the land you need for your blasted railway.'

Adam pushed back his chair and stood up. Jarvis became flushed with anger. 'You're not turning me down, damn it?'

'Far from it.' Adam gave him a chilly smile. 'I'm going to find someone to witness our agreement, Lord Jarvis.'

Within a short space of time Adam had written out two copies of that agreement in the club's library, with Jarvis eyeing every word over his shoulder. After that it was a simple matter of finding a mutual acquaintance—the uncurious Sir Gareth Blakeley—to witness their signatures on both documents while the contents were hidden from him; such arrangements were commonplace amidst London's clubs. Jarvis left with his own copy, but after he'd gone Adam stayed there in the seclusion of the library.

It was a game, Adam reminded himself. Yes, this was just another episode in the long game he'd played all his life, with every move finely calculated to win. Adam wanted his railway and Belle Marchmain was always going to be the loser one way or another. And didn't she deserve everything that was coming to her?

She despised him. She'd insulted him to kingdom come. She gave herself such airs, yet she'd swiftly offered to warm his bed in exchange for him forgetting the sheep business.

Well, now he was going to offer her marriage—or betrothal, to be more precise; he only had to remind her of her brother's debts to have her completely in his power. Then, once he'd got her to accept his proposal of marriage, he'd drop her in a matter of weeks.

Humiliate her, Jarvis had specified. Pictures suddenly seared his mind of the defiant widow melting in his arms. Of her soft, rosy lips parting beneath his questing tongue, her body sweetly pliant against his...

No doubt about it, Belle Marchmain still puzzled him. She'd struck him as vulnerable. Inexperienced, even.

Or very, very clever. And either way, what did it matter to him? It was a case of weighing up the affairs of that arrogant, conceited young fool Hathersleigh and his proud sister against the success of the massive future he envisaged for the quarry. It wasn't just a matter of pure financial gain either—that railway would create jobs and save lives, no doubt about it.

Adam left at last, with the signed agreement folded away in his pocket. It looked as if the next phase of the game was about to begin.

Chapter Seven

'*Pardieu, madame*, what is wrong with you?' Gabby teased merrily when Belle dropped her scissors for the third time. 'Best let me cut that ottoman silk, at four shillings the yard.'

It was two weeks since Belle's disastrous visit to Davenant's house, and now Belle had something else to worry about. Though the Strand was as full of shoppers as ever, her shop was virtually empty.

Gabby tried to reassure her. 'We are not as busy as we have been, perhaps—but do not forget that we had an extremely large order from Lady Tindall and her two daughters last week.'

They were the exception, thought Belle. Whatever Gabby said, their shop's order book should be much fuller than this. And what really worried her was that there had been another complaint only yesterday. A customer had come in to say that her new gown was an appalling fit.

'The tightness around my arms almost made me faint,' the customer had declared. 'I am going to tell all my friends *never* to use this shop again. My money back, if you please!'

Gabby was furious. 'She lies through her teeth. Look at this beautiful gown—the bodice has been taken apart and sewn up again—it was never *comme ça* when it left our shop. You should have argued with her!'

But Belle's suspicions were growing that this was a concerted attempt to ruin her business; so now, as she worked with Gabby on Lady Tindall's ballgown, she said nothing more, but applied extra care to cutting the precious silk...and tried to put the sardonic face of the hateful Mr Davenant firmly from her mind.

Easier said than done. Again and again the memory of her visit to him racked her. By proposing that she be his mistress then coldly withdrawing his offer, he'd made her feel quite sick with humiliation.

He despised her, no doubt whatsoever about that. He would by now have completely forgotten the incident and Belle only wished she could do the same. But every time a smart carriage rolled by outside in the Strand, she wondered if he was inside. At night it was worse, for she couldn't stop thinking about him. She couldn't forget his hands, his strong fingers, the way they had touched her. The way his hard lips and his tongue's possession had sent a surge of dark pleasure to every nerve ending.

Davenant's firm mouth on hers had dragged all semblance of sense from her body, implanting instead a sweet languor that flooded her veins. His caressing hands had urged her to surrender to the sensual and deliberately teasing strokes of his tongue and, to her eternal shame, it was he who'd drawn away, not she. Heat surged through her at the memory.

She'd expressed her scorn for his low birth, but he'd had enough of *her*, quite clearly. And why not, when his conquests of society beauties were legendary? When some of England's most aristocratic families were desperate to throw their marriageable daughters in his path?

His casual cancelling of the business of the sheep had underlined his contempt for her. That, as far as Mr Adam Davenant was concerned, was the end of it.

But it was very much *not* the end for Belle.

Somehow she was going to get together the money to pay him back for those sheep. Last night she'd resolved to tell Edward about her decision—but a letter from Edward had arrived this morning. The writing was haphazard and scratchy; several words had been crossed out.

My dear Belle, Charlotte has given birth to a baby boy. But you will be grieved to hear that the infant is extremely frail; I do not like to think what will happen if poor Charlotte loses this child...

Belle's hands had been shaking by the time she put the letter down. After two miscarriages, Charlotte had at last given birth to a living child—but this one might bring her even more grief than those earlier tragedies. Belle could imagine only too well the all-night vigils, the grave voices of the doctor and nurse, the scents of the sick room.

Great though the differences were between her and her brother, she could scarcely bear to think of the sorrow of that vulnerable little household.

'But I've said at least twenty times, we need another pleat of silk here— Oh, *madame*. Why don't you take a walk in the fresh air, down to the park perhaps?' Gabby gave a little sigh. 'As you were saying, we're not exactly busy— *Dieu!*'

Something out in the street had caught Gabby's keen eye and she hurried to the bow window. 'There's a carriage pulling up outside. It's being driven by the most wonderful-looking man…'

Belle sprang to the window to join her. *Oh, horrors.*

Gabby's wonderful man was letting himself down from the seat of a plain but expensive curricle, while his groom held the beautiful black horses. *Adam Davenant.*

Her heart was thudding sickly. Why was he here? Had he changed his mind, about those blasted sheep? Mentally she counted up the money she'd got together to pay him back. *Not enough. Not nearly enough.*

Perhaps they could come to some agreement. But wasn't 'an agreement' exactly what he'd suggested— then withdrawn? Oh, drat the man. Shivers ran up and down her spine.

She could see through the window that he was walking—no, striding—towards her shop door. A man with a figure like his didn't just *walk* anywhere. Belle found she was gripping her scissors defensively. 'Will you go out to him, please, Gabby, and find out what he wants?'

Gabby, wide-eyed, nodded and hurried out; seconds later she was back, her face alight with excitement.

'*Madame*, his name is Monsieur Davenant. He says to tell you that he knows you're in, he saw you through the window. He asks would you come out for a drive with him, in the park, because there are some matters you need to discuss.'

For a second Belle's blood froze in her veins. 'Tell Mr Davenant we have nothing to discuss, Gabby. Tell him a drive in the park is not at all convenient.'

Once more Gabby dashed out and in again. '*Madame*, he says he will stand outside on the pavement until it *is* convenient. Till nightfall if need be!'

And he damn well would. Belle bit her lip in frustration as Gabby rattled on, 'Oh, *madame*, I have heard about Monsieur Davenant. The fashionable ladies of the town, they fight to be his mistress—'

Perhaps a temporary, a tactical surrender was her only option. 'Please tell him,' Belle cut in tartly, 'that given the unexpected pleasure of his invitation, I'm sure Mr Davenant will quite understand that I need to get changed into something—*appropriate*.'

Over twenty minutes later Belle came down the stairs and Gabby's eyes opened wide with awe.

'*Madame.* Are you sure?'

Belle looked down at herself, a dangerous light in her eyes. 'This gown is striking, Gabby, don't you think?'

'But you made it for—someone else! For Mrs Sherville, who is not known, *madame*, for her subtlety in her manner of dressing!'

'*Absolutely* not,' agreed Belle. Harriet Sherville was, in fact, a well-known actress and courtesan. 'But the lady in question hasn't paid us for her last two outfits yet, so I've decided I shall wear this one myself.'

In Belle's eyes glittered a steely determination. Gabby opened her mouth to speak, then, thinking better of it, swallowed and hurried to open the door for her.

Belle was clad in a military-style carriage gown of crimson lutestring. Gold-braid frogging, lavish with knots and loops, adorned it from collar to toe. The crimson collar was high, emphasising her clear complexion; the stiffened bodice cupped her bosom tightly—and was slashed to reveal a tempting display of creamy cleavage.

If this gown embarrassed Adam Davenant, then so

much the better. As a finishing touch Belle set on her dark curls a crimson silk shako, with one long gold feather trailing to her shoulder.

Gabby looked stunned. *Thank you, Harriet Sherville*, muttered Belle under her breath. And swept out.

Mr Davenant was looking at his watch.

She expected him to take one glance at her and send her back to get changed again. Or to utter some pithy insult and drive off in his fancy curricle.

He did neither. Instead his dark eyebrow arched. 'Almost worth the wait,' he remarked casually.

Belle fastened her gold-satin reticule with something of a snap. 'I thought I might make you think twice another time, Mr Davenant, before issuing your peremptory summons.'

'Then I'm afraid you've failed,' he said. 'You're making me think I should have treated myself to your company earlier.'

Belle stared at him in astonishment. *Drat the man.* She glanced down and caught sight of her own daring cleavage. Touched, unthinking, her red hat with its trailing feather. 'You mean—you approve of what I'm wearing?'

'I like it very much. Though I'd rather you'd not taken so long over it all.'

'Oh, it's a woman's privilege, you know, to be as late as she chooses.'

'Not at the expense of my horses. My groom's had to unharness them and walk them up and down the Strand for almost half an hour.'

She bit her lip. Damn. She didn't mind making *him* suffer, but his horses were a different matter. She smiled sweetly up at him. 'Then perhaps on *another* occasion you might do me the honour of giving me a little more notice of your intentions.' Her smile vanished. 'My time is valuable, Mr Davenant. I hope you have good reason for this intrusion.'

He leaned closer—unsettlingly closer. Oh, Lord, her cleavage—he'd be able to see right down... 'I do,' he said softly. 'But I would prefer to discuss the matter in the park. We need to talk. Please climb up.'

He was holding out his hand. 'The park? Mr Davenant, you must know what people will think!'

'People will do more than think, if they see us together.' His eyes assessed her briefly. 'They will talk a great deal about us. And—it might be a good idea to look as if we're enjoying one another's company.'

'Enjoy?' She huffed with indignation. 'You are jesting.'

'Then *pretend* to enjoy being at my side. It's in your best interests, I assure you.'

She tossed her head, setting that long golden feather a-quiver. 'Very well. I'm told I'm quite good at acting.'

Ouch, Adam acknowledged. He helped her up—unable to resist relishing the slenderness of her waist—but he did try not to look at her *décolletage*. Then he told his groom to go and buy himself a pint of ale at the Red Lion nearby.

'Very well, guv'nor.' The little groom, who'd privately been admiring Mrs Marchmain's *décolletage* very much and was familiar with his master's methods of telling him his presence wasn't required, touched his hat cheerfully. 'A pint of best, then I'll find me own way back, eh? You enjoy your drive, now!'

Adam set off at a smart pace, but kept one eye on his companion to make sure she wasn't about to leap off, or perhaps stab him with those sewing scissors he'd seen her clutching rather desperately inside her shop.

If she'd hoped to deter him with that outfit, she was failing abysmally. Once you ignored the violent colour—which actually, he liked, he was fed up with insipid pale muslins—the neat military style rather deliciously hugged the alluring contours of her figure. And though she was clearly having second thoughts about the low neckline—she kept tugging the gold-braided edges of the gown together—the garment was really being remarkably stubborn and insisted on parting to display a tantalising glimpse of her smooth, rounded breasts.

She was nervous, he thought suddenly. Nervous, and also quite delectable. He found himself remembering how that pink mouth had tasted sweet and soft beneath his own...

Adam arrested his burgeoning desire rather grimly and concentrated on the traffic.

Time for business.

Belle sat upright at his side, almost shaking with fury and consternation. *Why?* Why had he sought out her company when he'd told her, at his Mayfair house, that they need never see each other again?

But—it was such a lovely day, and Hyde Park looked so beautiful. As Adam swung his carriage into the fashionable cavalcade, several of the gentry, riding fine horses or driving open carriages, nodded and smiled to Adam, though when they noted that he wasn't alone, many a head was twisted again in blatant curiosity.

The women watched Adam, too, with acquisitive glances; Belle herself couldn't resist stealing a look at her handsome companion as he concentrated on tooling his splendid horses, couldn't help but feel her breath catching in her throat. *Oh, my.*

She'd already noticed he was wearing a dark-grey coat that was unostentatious, but so well fitted that there was always a disturbing sense of his powerful male body beneath the elegant finery. His thighs, encased in skintight buckskins, were iron-hard with muscle—her own legs had brushed against them inadvertently as he seated himself and the heat had flared in her veins just at that touch. He held the reins without gloves; she saw that his hands were strong and firm and lightly tanned, with long, well-manicured fingers...

Stop it, Belle, you fool. She pushed the very physical reality of Mr Adam Davenant to the back of her mind to concentrate on the question—why had he talked just now, in a way that sent shivers down her spine, about the need for them to be seen in public together?

At their last meeting this man—whose grandfather began life as a penniless miner!—couldn't have made it plainer that he despised her thoroughly. She felt cold beneath her ridiculous finery. *So what did he want from her now?*

Clearly he intended to keep her waiting. He pulled up to talk briefly to some friends of his who were on horseback. Belle sat very primly, but she was aware that the men were eyeing her with frank appreciation. Wearing this startling red outfit was a huge mistake. She'd hoped to embarrass Davenant, but had simply succeeded in embarrassing herself.

Her second mistake was to have agreed to this *at all.*

'Well, Mr Davenant,' she said with icy politeness once his friends had gone, 'it will soon be all round town that I'm enjoying the dubious pleasure of your company—but I think we were both of us quite clear at our last meeting that this was something neither of us wanted. As to Edward and the unfortunate matter of the sheep—'

'His livestock thievery,' interrupted Davenant obligingly.

Her teeth clenched. 'It was a matter of only a few dozen, I believe!'

'Ah, yes. A hanging offence, merely,' he said politely.

The colour drained from her cheeks. *'Anyway,'* Belle pressed on, tilting her chin, 'I have decided the situation is far from acceptable to me and I'm well on my way to getting the necessary sum to pay you back.'

He turned to gaze at her. First at her cleavage—for long enough to make her cheeks flame—then at her face. Something in those hooded grey eyes made her stomach quail within her. 'Mrs Marchmain, one of the things I most respect about you is your honesty. Don't let me down. I have, in fact, heard that you've rather desperately been trying to raise money in the last day or so.'

'Y-you've heard? But how?'

'A single woman wearing outrageous clothes and trailing round London's banks inevitably stirs up gossip. I must say, I was a little surprised. I thought—in fact, you told me quite forthrightly—that your dressmaking business was doing well.'

'Oh, it *is*,' Belle said blithely. 'We're simply going through a temporary quiet spell.'

'I see. I gather,' he went on calmly, 'that you've had no success in your efforts to borrow money—otherwise you'd by now have thrust the filthy lucre in my face and told me to go to the very devil.'

She gazed at him, stricken. Adam staunched any

sneaking pity for the flamboyant little widow dressed in military red and went on, 'I thought I made it quite clear I do not *wish* to be repaid for those damned sheep. Especially as they were stolen by your brother, who, if he had an ounce of your spirit, would be bowing his head in shame for having sent his sister to me to plead for him.'

'He did not *ask* me to—'

'Then why?' he asked sharply. 'Why trouble to defend such a weak, shallow fool?'

She said tightly, 'Do you have to make everything so hateful, Mr Davenant?'

'I like to understand situations and people,' he rapped out. 'I flatter myself that I have some skill. But one thing about you puzzles me mightily, Mrs Marchmain. Your refusal to see your brother for what he is.'

She turned sideways to face him, and bestowed on him a glittering smile. 'La, Mr Davenant,' she simpered in a Somerset accent. 'How wonderful it would be, to find oneself as all-seeing as you!' Her green eyes glittered; her cheeks were now extremely pale. Slowly, deliberately, she took off her bright red shako with its single trailing feather and dropped it over the side of the carriage. 'Oh, dear,' she said sweetly. 'I seem to have lost my hat. Would you retrieve it for me?'

Frowning, he drew his black horses to a halt, looped the reins and jumped down.

The minute he bent to pick up her hat, Belle slid across into the driver's seat to take up the ribbons. 'Hup!' she called. The horses trotted off smartly. She heard his shouts.

She seethed. *Abominable, hateful man to insult her*

so! Serve him right if she just left him there. She tooled on a little, expertly holding the reins. Gentlemen she didn't know pulled up their horses and stared at her in open-mouthed admiration; she was hardly missable in Mrs Sherville's outrageous outfit. She nodded and smiled at them. By God, she would make Adam Davenant regret his high-handedness.

She made a skilful manoeuvre and returned to him at last, holding his mettlesome horses in a neat walk. He was just standing there, watching. No hint of a smile touched his finely shaped mouth.

She pulled up and slid sideways into her own seat. Swinging himself aboard, he handed her the shako without a word, took the reins and sent the horses on at a rather smart trot that nearly threw her off.

He said at last, in a decidedly cool voice, 'That wasn't a bad display. But you were holding the left rein a little too tightly—you should have made adjustments for the longer step of the leading wheeler.' He was irate, she could see. There was something about the set of his jaw that made her tremble a little inside.

No. Don't be afraid, Belle. That's the worst thing you can possibly do, you fool, with a man of his kind. At least—don't let him see that you're afraid.

She settled her bright red hat back upon her curls and tilted her chin defiantly. 'Were you scared that I might fall off?'

He turned to her, his eyes iron-hard. 'No. But I *was* afraid you might damage my horses.'

She did not reply, but clenched her hands together very tightly. When Adam turned to look at her he saw she was holding her head as high as ever, but—the devil, was that a glint of tears in her eyes?

He cleared his throat and looked straight ahead. 'I have come to offer you a new proposal, Mrs Marchmain.'

Her heart filled with dread.

'I thought we'd been through this,' she said carefully. 'You asked me to be your mistress. But when I agreed you told me you'd changed your mind.'

She kept her voice steady. But the humiliation of that day at his house—the memory of his kiss, to which she'd so raptly surrendered—was still an unhealed wound.

'This is different,' he announced.

'Oh?' She smiled up at him sweetly. 'You'll forgive me if I tell you that *any* kind of proposal from you, Mr Davenant, is unlikely to be received by me with rapture.'

'You'll at least hear me out, I hope. I've been thinking. You've referred often enough to my lowly background.'

She hissed in a sharp breath.

'You, on the contrary,' he pressed on ruthlessly, 'are related to a duke. And I've been told on many occasions that I should make a match into the aristocracy.'

'I hardly see why you're troubling to inform me of your matrimonial plans, Mr Davenant.' *Though I feel heartily sorry for the woman of your choice*, she added with feeling under her breath.

'Don't you?' He turned to her and raised an eyebrow. 'I've been thinking, believe it or not, that the great-niece of a duke might just suit my purpose.'

Belle could hardly speak. 'If this is your idea of a jest…'

'Not at all. Last time, at my house, we talked somewhat unsuccessfully about you paying for your brother's folly by becoming my mistress. This time, Mrs Marchmain—I'm suggesting a betrothal.'

Now the colour really did drain from Belle's cheeks; in fact, her world spun round. 'A betrothal? With *me*? You cannot be serious!'

He shrugged. 'Why not? You're penniless but blue-blooded. I'm a miner's grandson and rich. A good joke, isn't it?' He glanced at her—to check, perhaps, that she wasn't about to jump off his moving carriage and flee his detestable presence.

She'd whirled on him. 'Your joke fails to amuse me. And anyway, what could I possibly offer *you*, Mr Davenant? You talk of my blue blood, but I know how very little that counts with you!'

'You underestimate yourself, Mrs Marchmain. You could, in fact, be very useful to me.'

'How?'

'I'm only talking about a temporary betrothal—a matter of a month or two. You'll be well aware that during the next few weeks the London Season will reach its height, which is a matter of great inconvenience to me, since to be honest I can't stand the insipid heiresses who are thrown in my path day and night.'

'Leave London,' Belle said flatly.

'I can't. I have vital business here, which involves meetings with lawyers, investors and London bankers. I also have to socialise, or appear extremely rude. But I need a respite from the fortune-hunters, and a convenient fiancée would serve the purpose admirably. During that time you would, of course, enjoy the benefits of my protection as well as my money.'

Belle burst out, *'No.* This is ridiculous. To pretend to be betrothed to you—it's *unthinkable*!'

Too late she saw the dangerous spark in his eyes. 'I

have choices, but you don't,' he said abruptly. 'Were you aware that your brother gambled?'

He saw the colour drain from her cheeks. 'Yes, but that was long ago...'

'Not long ago at all. During his recent stay in London, he ran up large debts at White's.'

'No. Please, this cannot be true.'

The look, the unguarded look on her face as she turned to him with such dismay in those wide, dark-lashed eyes... Adam felt, not for the first time in this woman's presence, a sense of utter disquiet. 'Your brother,' he proceeded ruthlessly, 'has debts to the tune of five thousand guineas.'

'Five *thousand*...'

'But,' went on Adam remorselessly, 'I have bought them up.'

'You have bought—' *No. Please, no.*

Adam wondered if she would spend the rest of the afternoon echoing his words. But after that she became so still, so frozen that for a few moments he wondered if she would ever speak again.

Belle felt that the park was whirling around her. That she was clinging on to reality only by a thread. She said at last, very quietly, 'I know, Mr Davenant, that you cannot have purchased my brother's debts out of any sense of duty, or liking. I can only assume you have done this to further my family's humiliation.' She cleared her throat. 'No doubt you expect me to promise to pay you back. But I fear that such a sum is beyond me or my brother, for the present at least...'

'I've already explained,' he said without expression, 'how you can pay me back, Mrs Marchmain.'

'You—you have?'

'Yes. I will consider your brother's debts cancelled if you do as I asked and agree to a betrothal.'

The colour drained from her face; she looked suddenly fragile.

They'd entered a quieter area of the park, where trees sheltered them from the general throng. She realised he was pulling his horses to a halt. He gazed down at her, his eyes slate-grey, his mouth a thin line. 'I will try not to make your new position too detestable for you, Mrs Marchmain,' he went on. 'But I'd like you to appear in public as my fiancée, until mid-July when society retreats to the country. I think you're as aware as I am that such an arrangement can be easily ended.'

Oh, he would enjoy discarding her. Clever. So clever.

She said, at last, 'Am I going to be punished for ever, Mr Davenant, for those comments I made about you on Sawle Down?'

He shrugged. 'Punishment? Call it that if you like, but it's your chance to ensure I'll not serve notice on your brother for his debts. Do you or do you not accept?'

Oh, God. What choice did she have? She felt dizzy and sick. She twisted the ring she wore and drew a deep, deep breath. 'I fear you will find you have got yourself a bad bargain, Mr Davenant,' she answered quietly.

He was silent a moment. Then: 'I'll take you home, Mrs Marchmain' was all he said.

Chapter Eight

All the way back from Hyde Park to the Strand Adam had been aware of a restless tension simmering inside his powerful body. This woman was, quite frankly, turning his hitherto well-organised life upside down.

It wasn't just that she was strikingly attractive—he'd known that from the start. It wasn't just her outfit, that ridiculous military-red affair devised to put her breasts almost on full display. It was—everything. Her clothes, her dark curls, her figure—all combined in some incredible allure that made every man in the park snap his head round and stare after her with pure lust.

Adam was accustomed to mere beauty. The difference with Mrs Marchmain was that she was defiant—and vulnerable. She was a twenty-seven-year-old widow, a woman who had lost her husband in the cruel war, yet survived on her own with some success. A woman who despised him. But he felt himself aching to hold her, to protect her… *Face it, Adam, you long to get her in your bed and kiss every inch of her.*

Damn. He glanced down at her as the traffic at the corner of Bedford Street came to a standstill and saw how the bodice of that outrageous crimson dress had slipped apart again, showing the delicious upper curve of her breasts. Thanks to the motion of the curricle her slender legs beneath her gown kept unavoidably brushing his; he couldn't help noticing how some loose curls of her raven-black hair had escaped from her damned hat, trailing down the soft nape of her neck just where he'd like to place his lips...

She must realise the effect she had on any normal red-blooded male. Yet her name had never been associated with any man's since her widowhood; his secretary Lowell had told him so. Lowell had even suggested that she had loved her husband.

Adam had scornfully rejected the notion. Hadn't Jarvis said she was out for what she could get? Hadn't Mrs Marchmain herself offered her services to him, in return for those blasted sheep her brother had stolen?

He'd pulled the horses up a short way from her shop because a delivery dray made it impossible for him to draw up outside. 'Will you be all right if I set you down here?' he asked curtly.

She was clearly endeavouring to pull that gown together again. She said, in a voice that sounded more than a little distraught, 'Mr Davenant, I really think you ought to know that I am completely lacking in what—in what I realise you will require from me.'

'What are you talking about?'

She jerked her head up. 'I mean in the matters of the bedchamber.'

No. Was that another tear shining in the corner of her eye? Was this all part of her act? Adam offered her his pristine handkerchief as the disturbing urge to put his arm round her and simply offer her comfort unfurled again in his gut. *Stop it*. He said, 'I should, I think, have stressed from the very beginning that *you* will dictate the nature and the pace of our relationship, Mrs Marchmain.'

'What?' She was turning, white-faced, to look up at him.

'People will assume, of course,' he went on, his voice perfectly calm, 'that our relationship is an intimate one.'

She dropped his handkerchief.

'But their assumptions will be wrong,' Adam went on imperturbably, 'because you will *not* share my bed. Unless you choose to, of course.'

He wasn't even looking at her now, but was staring straight ahead. Belle felt her stomach pitch. *Oh, God. All this. Why?*

Because she'd insulted him quite lethally—and her brother had offered him the weapon of revenge that Davenant had probably been looking for ever since. She straightened her bonnet and uttered a light laugh. 'La, Mr Davenant, so you're not even going to pretend to be seduced by my charms? I swear, you put me to the blush!'

He turned to her and said, 'In the eyes of the general public, I'll play the perfect suitor, believe me.' He lifted his hand and very, very gently stroked the pad of his blunt forefinger across the smooth velvet of her cheek and down to her full lower lip. Belle hadn't known that a simple touch could be so sensuous.

She jerked her head away to avoid that intimate caress, but all she did was present him with the opportunity to trail his hand across the nape of her neck, his fingers briefly massaging her tender skin there in a way that sent shivers of incredible warmth fluttering through her veins to pool at the very pit of her abdomen.

She pulled away again and tugged her foolish gold-trimmed crimson gown tighter to stop him seeing how her breasts, with their tautening nipples, betrayed her body's treacherous reaction to his sinuous caress.

To this devilish man's touch. To his mere *touch*.

And he knew. Dear God, she felt sick with shame. He was watching her calmly like a hunter preparing to strike. Her pulse still raced tumultuously; her ribs ached with the need for air. He said, 'I repeat: I will expect nothing of you that you're not prepared to give, Mrs Marchmain.'

She moistened her dry mouth and answered, 'You may be quite sure I shall never freely offer you anything at all that I value, Mr Davenant. May I go now?'

But he wasn't quite finished with her yet. 'One last thing,' he put in. 'While you are—in name at least—my bride-to-be, I would prefer you not to live at your shop.'

That was straightforward. 'My shop is my life!' Belle cried. 'And I will need it, for when this ridiculous—*arrangement* is at an end!'

'I know that. But as my prospective wife I think you'll agree that for you to live there would not be fitting.'

This, from Miner Tom's grandson. She clenched her jaw. 'You surely cannot expect me to live with *you*?'

'I haven't asked you to,' he said cuttingly. 'But I have a house in Bruton Street that I think would suit the purpose. I would expect you to reside there and attend social functions with me for the remainder of the Season. After all, we have to make this convincing, don't we?'

He helped her out and she couldn't reply, because she wasn't able to. *Why was he doing this?* She somehow reached her shop, holding her head high as she negotiated the jostling crowds.

But inwardly she was shaking—because she guessed she knew the answer to her unspoken question. Why was he doing this? Because, quite simply, he was out to break her.

Adam drove thoughtfully away, the first part of his mission accomplished. He would announce their betrothal, then as soon as possible end it; Jarvis would be satisfied and Belle Marchmain would be a target for the gossips all over town and beyond.

She deserved nothing less for the insults she'd hurled at him. Meanwhile he'd saved her brother from ruin, hadn't he? So what was wrong? Why did he feel such a lowlife? She was proud and made no secret of despising him for his lowly background. Why, then, had his stomach clenched at the look of sheer desolation in her eyes when he revealed her brother's calamitous folly?

Adam tightened his jaw. Business bargains were tough and there were always losers. Some deserved to be losers. He'd pay her off well at the end of it all.

But revenge should have tasted a damn sight sweeter than this.

Belle could only be thankful that her shop was for once busy for the rest of the day. So although Gabby kept casting pleading looks in her direction that said, *What happened?* Belle was able to keep her at bay. And that evening, shy Matt had asked Gabby if she would go with him to the Vauxhall Pleasure Gardens, which meant Belle was by herself.

She tried to write to her brother, but her pen kept faltering. She simply couldn't understand how Edward could have left London with those awful gaming debts unpaid. Just as she could not understand why Adam Davenant could want to make such an outrageous proposition to her.

Yes, he'd explained he needed a convenient fiancée, but surely he could have thought up a less drastic solution? Found himself a new mistress, for example, or absented himself from the social scene? No earthly need for such a convoluted form of revenge. Unless it wasn't revenge at all... No. *No.* Such a man as he would never actually fall for a penniless, foolishly defiant dressmaker. Never!

She felt her lips, where his fingers had rested. Oh, Lord. She hated him for his arrogance, his cynicism. Yet—his mere touch filled her with dark, forbidden imaginings. She sat very still with her pen in her hand as the shadows lengthened.

In the end she just wrote, *I am so sorry, Edward, about your baby. Please let me know if there is anything I can do.*

Afterwards Belle tried to do some sewing by candlelight up in her sitting room. Anything to distract herself from her dark thoughts. At last she heard the back door opening, and Gabby ran up the stairs and came in.

'Did you enjoy Vauxhall Gardens, Gabby?' Belle knew that lovelorn Matt had hired sculls at Westminster to take the two of them across the river and had also booked a private box that would give them a prime view of the acrobats and the singers. He had even bought himself a new striped waistcoat. Belle fervently hoped Matt had made the most of the opportunity to press his suit and hadn't simply sat speechlessly watching Gabby with adoring eyes.

'Oh, yes!' Gabby eagerly pulled up a chair. 'We had a wonderful time. Matt danced with me and he talked extremely foolishly—oh, *madame*—about love!'

Good for you, Matt. Belle smiled. 'Why do you consider him foolish, Gabby dear?'

'For a grown man to talk of how his heart will be broken if I turn him down—*tenez*, it is absurd. But none of it as foolish as *you*, *madame*, sewing at this late hour when I hear that all your difficulties are at an end!'

Belle put her sewing down slowly. 'What are you talking about, Gabby?'

Gabby wagged her finger. 'Why, about Mr Davenant! I know, of course, that he took you driving in the park this afternoon. But this evening I met dear Lady Tindall at Vauxhall Gardens, and—well, it's all over town that you and he are betrothed!'

My God, Davenant works quickly, thought Belle rather dazedly. She drew in a deep breath. 'Listen, Gabby.' She tried to sound calm. 'There will be an announcement of a betrothal—' Gabby gave a little squeak of delight '—but it is to be purely a matter of convenience for both him and me, do you understand?'

'But he *must* have fallen in love with you, *madame*,' Gabby persisted. 'I thought, when you were so flustered by his arrival in his carriage this afternoon, that there was something going on—though I didn't even realise you'd met before!'

'We've met twice before.' *And both occasions were absolutely calamitous.*

'Well,' said Gabby firmly, 'it's not as if Monsieur Davenant is lacking female company—I told you before, he is well known indeed for the beautiful women he has escorted round the town. And they still talk, so longingly, of him. *Pardieu, madame*, they go on about his good looks. His fine manners. His generosity. When he bids a final farewell to his mistresses—ah, how they must grieve—he sees that they do not want for *anything*.' Gabby sighed, but then her brown eyes twinkled again with mischief. 'And, of course, there is all the talk of his *virilité*...'

Belle froze. 'What on earth do you mean?'

'I mean his—' Gabby shrugged in a very Gallic way '—his manhood, *madame*. His skill as a lover!'

Belle pretended to yawn. 'Oh, do you know, Gabby, I'm so tired. I think I'll have an early night. I'll just go and check that everywhere is locked up.'

'Madame!' Gabrielle was following her down the stairs. 'Don't you want to hear what they say? He keeps his mistresses at a lovely house in Bruton Street, Mayfair, and—'

Belle stood stock still. 'In Bruton Street? His mistresses?'

'Why, yes, *madame*. Are you all right? This betrothal—isn't it what you desire? If not, then why...?'

Belle struggled to compose herself. 'Dear Gabby, I'm not sure of anything just at the moment. But clearly it's going to be the talk of the town, so let everyone think I'm quite happy with it all, will you?'

'Of course.' Gabby pressed Belle's hand then turned to go to her room. Belle just stood there. *Not sure of anything*. It was true. She was no longer sure of anything at all—except that Adam Davenant despised her.

The next day, after Belle had spent a sleepless night, a note was delivered. It said simply, *The house is ready. I will call for you later this morning at eleven, to show you round. Davenant.*

The house where he kept his mistresses—his bits of muslin, his doxies. Belle wanted to weep with rage and vexation. He'd promised her he wouldn't touch her, but shivers of warning surged through her veins at the thought of being in that formidable man's power. He'd told her he needed her to ward off the husband-hunters—but Belle knew he was doing this to humiliate her. Had most likely bought up her brother's debts for the sole purpose of humiliating her.

Well, it wouldn't last long, he'd promised her that. And—Belle drew in a sharp breath at the sudden idea that smote her—wasn't it just possible that Adam Davenant could be persuaded to end this obnoxious false betrothal sooner rather than later?

Chapter Nine

Mr Davenant called at eleven exactly as he'd promised. Belle had dressed so loudly, so brashly that even loyal Gabby's eyes had widened with doubt.

But Adam Davenant did not bat one sleepy eyelid.

It was as if he was used, every day of his life, to escorting a woman dressed in a Spanish pelisse of raspberry-pink sarsenet trimmed with lime-green satin.

Belle adjusted her pink-kid gloves and beamed up at him. 'La,' she declared in her best Somerset accent, 'I be fair up in the clouds with the idea of being your ladybird, Mr Davenant, I be!'

He blinked. He gave a bow. 'My fiancée, to be precise. My carriage is waiting, Mrs Marchmain' was all he said.

She fluttered her dark eyelashes and put her hands on her hips. 'So you're going to show me round this big, fancy house you told me about? I declare, I cannot wait. But how I do happer on; you must tell me if my conversation is too much for you, Mr D.'

'Happer on?' he echoed, frowning.

'It's what they say in Somerset for someone who is a chatterbox. I can rattle away at quite a rate, you see.'

His jaw set, he held out his arm to lead her to his carriage.

It was a fine, warm day. And this time, she realised, he'd brought his open barouche, with a liveried coachman at the reins; it was even showier than yesterday's vehicle.

He said, as he helped her in, 'I want to make very sure we're noticed together. Clearly you've had the same notion.'

Belle glanced down at her dazzling attire—they would be noticed all right. 'Oh, gracious, Mr D.,' she simpered, 'I do declare, you're making my head spin with your flattery.' She crammed on her tall-crowned pink hat with its festoons of ribbons.

Mr Davenant jumped in after her and told his coachman to drive on.

The journey shouldn't have taken long, but at the corner of St James's Street and Piccadilly the traffic had come to a standstill because of some altercation between a dray and a hackney-cab driver. Adam's coachman was forced to hold in his fine bays while around them the occupants of other stationary carriages gazed around and grumbled—until they espied Adam with his new companion.

Belle could almost believe that the wretched man had *arranged* this.

A barouche had been forced to a halt just behind them. It contained two men and three fashionably dressed women who, irritated by the delay, were casting around them for a topic to relieve the tedium.

It didn't take long for them to find it.

'Look just there, in that carriage ahead of us,' murmured one of the women. 'That's surely the handsome Mr Davenant, with—who would have guessed it?—with Mrs Marchmain, the little *modiste* from the Strand! Goodness, have you ever *seen* such a very loud gown and bonnet? Quite outrageous, especially as I've heard she was once of good family...'

Belle trembled, a flush of anger spreading up from her throat to her cheeks. Adam was still looking straight ahead, as though he hadn't heard them.

'Of good family?' the chattering went on behind them. 'Really, my dear?'

'Would you believe, her mother was niece to the Duke of Sutherland?'

'Goodness! So perhaps Davenant hasn't entirely lost his wits in taking her up?'

'Taking her up? That's the least of it. They are to announce a betrothal any day, I hear! The little *modiste* must have quite a few tricks up her sleeve.'

'Or up her skirts,' edged in one of the men, sniggering.

Adam's strong hand was suddenly on Belle's. 'Take no notice whatsoever. Smile up at me and pretend we're having an amicable conversation.'

She shrugged. 'I warn you, Mr Davenant. This is just the start. You are going to find my company embarrassing, I assure you.'

'Embarrassing? Good God, not in the slightest,' he said calmly.

She gave her most glittering smile and tilted her chin. 'Then I shall have to work a little harder, shan't I?'

He bent his head low and murmured enticingly, 'Do your worst, Mrs Marchmain.'

Oh, my. The way he *looked* at her, with his dark head a little on one side and his eyes, slate-grey beneath those dark arched brows, crinkling with amusement. It made her lungs ache with the need for air. If she'd been standing, her legs would have given way.

Ahead the traffic blockage was easing, but they were still some way from the quieter streets of Mayfair. Adam's hand briefly tightened on hers. 'Remember we're supposed to be in love,' he said. Then he leaned forwards, to give new instructions to his coachman.

In love. Belle sank back against the seat and suddenly she was overwhelmed by memories.

When Belle was seventeen Aunt Mildred had agreed to take her to a summer gala night at Bath's Sydney Gardens, and Belle had been so looking forward to the illuminations and the music. But her delight had quickly faded when she became aware that she was dressed quite wrongly for the evening.

All the other girls—some of them her old school friends from the Bath seminary—were clad in delightfully wispy muslin gowns with fluttering white ribbons in their carefully curled hair. Belle wore a dress insisted on by Aunt Mildred, made of dull lavender silk and perhaps ten years out of fashion, with her hair scraped back in a bun.

She'd wanted to sink through the floor as the other girls giggled and stared.

Two weeks later she'd asked Aunt Mildred if she could go again. Her aunt had frowned at the frivolity of two outings within a month, but Uncle Philip had peered at Belle over his spectacles and said, 'Why not? Heaven knows the girl needs preparation for her London come-out next year. She has to marry well—she has no other future.'

That time as they travelled to the Sydney Gardens

Belle kept herself well cloaked-up, and only when they were there did she reveal what she'd done to her old silk dress. She'd altered seams to tighten the fit over her slender waist and hips. She'd lowered the neckline and cut off the unfashionably long sleeves to remake them into little puff ones. She'd sewn on some white satin ribbons which brought the lavender gown to life.

That afternoon she'd cajoled a housemaid into arranging her thick dark curls in a pretty cascade, all hidden from Aunt Mildred's inspection until they'd reached their destination and Belle handed her drab bonnet and cloak to a footman.

Aunt Mildred was horrified. Belle was the envy of all the girls there and was surrounded by young men. And that night, she fell in love with Captain Harry Marchmain.

'We're there,' Adam Davenant's deep voice said in her ear.

She jumped. 'So—so soon?'

'Indeed.'

They were outside a tall, elegant house. As they climbed the steps a manservant clad in black was there to greet them almost immediately.

'This is Mrs Marchmain, Lennox,' Adam said to him. 'Mrs Marchmain—my steward.'

'Mr Lennox!' Belle beamed at him. 'My, what a delight to meet you!'

Lennox was well trained; there was not a flicker of surprise in his eyes at her gaudy apparel as he bowed his head.

Then Lennox retreated and Davenant began to show her round himself. Every so often he stopped, his eyebrows raised quizzically. 'I'm waiting for your objections,' he said.

'Heavens above, I'm flummoxed! Give me time, Mr Davenant,' she answered in a merry Somerset lilt, pointing a jaunty finger at him.

But her heart was beating rather fast. This place was—exquisite. It was light, airy and spacious. Everywhere smelled newly polished; the brass and the woodwork gleamed. There must be servants galore under Lennox's direction; she saw them in the distance occasionally. All employed to maintain the house where Davenant kept his mistresses and where he intended to get his revenge.

A faint headache throbbed at her temples. She was feeling tired and somewhat daunted; a feeling not helped by the fact that Davenant once more looked remote, and forbidding, and utterly *male*.

She swallowed quickly on the sudden dryness in her throat as he turned round while leading her up the stairs and caught her staring at him. 'It's delightful, Mr D.,' Belle declared, looking around. 'Such a *pretty* abode.'

He was watching her carefully, his eyes assessing her. 'I sense a "but" on its way. I sense that *pretty* is not what Mrs Marchmain requires.'

'Lawks, Mr D.,' she announced with a sigh, following him airily into the first-floor drawing room, 'you've certainly hit the nail on the head.'

'I have?'

'Well, of course! These furnishings are hideously insipid, I fear. Pastels and beiges—the word "dowdy" doesn't *begin* to cover it, I'm sure you'll agree. This, this and this—' she swept her hand at various pieces of expensive furniture '—will have to go. I rather favour raspberry pink and lime green this season, you see.' She gestured at her own bold costume.

Not one muscle of his handsome face flickered. He said calmly, 'Raspberry pink and lime green it is.'

'And the overall theme must be Egyptian, of course,' she declared with sudden inspiration. 'I think the Egyptian style so—ennobling, don't you, Mr D.? Ah, the glories of a bygone age! So we will need plenty of black marble and gilding. And sphinxes—yes, I have my mind absolutely set on sphinxes.'

'Do what the deuce you like, Mrs Marchmain. Speak to Lennox and he'll tell the tradesmen to send the bills to me.'

Belle blinked. Then—a little faintly—'No financial limit?'

He shrugged. 'Spend as much of my filthy lucre as you like. Though I must admit I draw the line a little at livestock.'

His turn to take *her* by surprise. 'L-livestock?'

'Caged birds. Lapdogs and the like,' he answered. Just then Lennox appeared to ask if anything was needed and Adam said to him, 'Mrs Marchmain will require some refurbishments to the place, Lennox. You will, perhaps, draw up for her a list of tradespeople to whom she might like to give her instructions.'

'Of course, sir.' Lennox gave Belle a stiff bow, and Belle felt her stomach lurch with despair. He looked so *disapproving...*

'Lawks a mercy, Mr D.,' simpered Belle, 'I have heard that amongst the *ton*, you know, it is the latest thing to have all one's servants dressed in purple.'

Lennox almost choked; Davenant's dark eyebrows shot up. 'Really?'

'Oh, yes! Black is so *boring*. Like having dozens of gramfers crawling around one's house.'

Lennox looked horrified. 'Gramfers?' echoed Adam.

'Woodlice, Adam dearest. La, I thought you knew your Somerset!'

Adam Davenant never batted an eyelid. 'I will consider the matter.' He turned to his steward. 'We'll take tea in the ground-floor salon in ten minutes, Lennox, thank you.'

Lennox looked as if he was about to have an apoplexy as he made his way rather dazedly to the door. Belle mentally apologised to the poor man, then turned brightly back to Adam. 'Well? Are you going to show me the rest of my new residence, Mr D.?'

Really, the house was faultless. She'd been in many fashionable homes, but this was simply exquisite. She followed Davenant around in a state of rather helpless awe, though whenever he turned to her, she would wrinkle her nose in a frown and point, wagging her finger. 'I do declare, Mr D., we need brighter colours here—a touch of orange, I think—and oh, Lady Cattermole has some Egyptian-style onyx tables in *her* parlour and I am so wildly jealous of them, you know.'

'There's a sale of Egyptian antiquities at Christie's tomorrow afternoon,' he said. 'I'll arrange for you to attend.'

Yet again Belle was dumbfounded by this man's tolerance. She was behaving ridiculously. Monstrously. Why on earth was he putting up with her whims?

Rather dismayingly, Belle reminded herself that she knew the answer. He was a powerful, a clever man. He was waging a ruthless campaign against her, her

brother and, she suspected, the whole of the fashionable world that had once dared to question his right to
occupy his place in the upper strata of society.

She jutted her chin. Yes, he was using her—but she
would make sure he regretted it.

It was easy, of course, to keep up the image she'd
chosen to project while he was showing her round the
house. In every room Belle flounced about, excited,
silly, preposterous. She was momentarily floored when
he led her into the bedroom—*oh, goodness, the size
of that luxurious bed, with all its cream-silk hang-
ings*—but she very quickly regained her composure
by criticising the lack of colour in the expensive curtains at the windows and the dullness of the priceless
Aubusson rug.

It was not quite so easy to maintain her frivolous
mask when they retired to the exquisitely furnished
salon. Poor Lennox had brought teapot and cups and
also put coal on the fire; he glanced at Belle rather nervously on his way out, as if expecting her to demand
that he dress himself in purple livery that very minute.

As the door closed behind Lennox Davenant sat
in one of the satin-upholstered chairs and stretched
out his long, booted legs. 'Do you mind pouring?' he
asked Belle.

'Not at all.' She just hoped her hands wouldn't shake.
'Oh, my, this is all so exciting.' She pointed at the piano
in the corner. 'Just to think—of an evening, as your fiancée, I suppose you will require me to entertain you
by playing that piano, or singing, or some such delightful pursuit. I declare I cannot wait!'

'Then I must inform you that no musical duties will
be required. You see, I'm tone deaf.'

'In that case, Mr Davenant,' she declared brightly, thrusting his cup of tea at him, 'I could play a hand or two at piquet with you. What fun that will be!'

'It won't,' said Davenant. 'One gambler in the family is enough.'

Oh, no. Trust her to walk straight into that one. Damn the man and his superiority.

'Well,' he went on, 'now that it's just the two of us, Mrs Marchmain, can you tell me why you've been prattling like a drunken parrot for the last hour or so?'

Belle had just lifted her own tea to her lips. She put the cup down, too hastily; it shook in its saucer. 'Why, Mr D.—'

He cut in, 'If you're hoping to make me regret our temporary betrothal, then I assure you, you'll fail. I've explained to you quite clearly that I'm going to make use of your presence here to protect me from the marriage-hunters, so you might as well stop wearing yourself out with your inane chatter. And for God's sake, stop calling me Mr D.'

Belle had gone rather pale.

'And if you're intent on putting me off bedding you,' he went on, 'then let me remind you that I'm not going to touch you unless you beg me to.' *And then I'll think twice about it.*

Belle squared her shoulders. 'You will see me in hell first, Mr Davenant!'

'Oh, for heaven's sake,' he said irritably, 'stop behaving like some third-rate actress.' He took his tea cup. 'My God, anybody would think I was about to subject you to a torture chamber at the very least.'

Belle wasn't thinking of a torture chamber. She was remembering that kiss; unwise, because she was just putting down her own cup and missed the saucer so some of the hot liquid spilled on the table.

Davenant was on his feet. 'I will ring for one of the maids.'

'No. Please,' she said rather desperately. 'They will think me so *stupid...*'

He eyed her sharply. 'Then I'll fetch a cloth myself. Mrs Marchmain, you are perhaps finding all this more difficult than you thought.'

'No,' she said quickly. *Edward's debts. Oh, Lord, Edward's debts.* 'No. Please. After all—we *both* of us know this is only a matter of convenience, don't we? And my brother—he will want, I am *sure*, to find some way in the very near future to pay back his gambling debts to you—'

'Your brother hasn't a hope in hell of paying me back,' Davenant broke in curtly. He made for the door again. 'That cloth. I'll be back in a moment.'

She settled her cup back in its saucer, but her fingers were still trembling.

You'll marry again before too long, people had said. *You must. So very tragic, but you've your life ahead of you...*

No, had been her reply. *No, I'll never marry again. Not ever.*

Now she shivered, alone in the grandeur of that lovely house. Oh, God, she ought to be honest. She ought to say, *Mr Davenant, I thought I could play this game, but I find that I cannot.*

He was coming back in with a cloth in his hand, which he used to blot the tea neatly from the table. Then he said, 'Mrs Marchmain, unless I'm very much mistaken, you're about to spill more of that tea all over your gown, which would be a great pity.' Smoothly he moved her cup away from her side of the table.

'You mean—you actually like my outfit?' Earlier Lennox had taken her pelisse and bonnet, leaving her clad in a pink-muslin walking dress with long sleeves and copious cherry-coloured flounces.

He ran his eye over her as he returned to his chair and sat down. 'Very much so. But if you're hoping to disguise your charms, you're utterly mistaken. If anything, it enhances them.'

She was looking down at herself in dismay. 'How— what do you mean?'

'The fabric of your gown might be all-concealing, but it's nevertheless rather thin. You were cold, I think—fashed, as you'd say in Somerset—just now.'

Belle's eyes shot down to her breasts. Saw them peaking beneath the fine muslin, the nipples prominent... Oh, Lord. Resisting the urge to fling her arms across them, she sat very straight and said quietly, 'You are hateful to remark upon something so personal.'

'Just trying to help.' He smiled his sleepy smile that did something rather strange to her insides.

Belle said with icy sweetness, 'Perhaps you'd like to choose my wardrobe for me, Mr Davenant?'

'Whatever's happened to your Somerset accent? And choose your wardrobe? Good God, no. You have a reputation as a leader of fashion. Live up to that. Surprise me.'

She said bitterly, 'It's difficult for me to surprise you, since you know far too much about me and my brother already.'

'About your brother, yes. But not you.' His expression was suddenly grave. 'Although I do know that your husband died in the war.'

'He was killed at the Battle of Toulouse five years ago.'

Adam remembered Lowell suggesting that she might still be mourning her husband. *Dressed like that? Surely not.* But he said, 'I'm sorry.'

'It's something many women have had to bear.' She faced him without flinching, though just for a moment she'd looked vulnerable, almost afraid. 'But you did not invite me here to talk about my past.' She gave that forced smile again. 'I suppose I ought to be making light gossip, about the latest play, or some such thing. Or flattering you, Mr Davenant...' Her voice trailed away once more.

'Just give me a respite from the husband-hunters for a few weeks,' he said. 'That's all I ask.'

Her green eyes were glittering again a little dangerously. 'So—*inconvenient*, to be rich and eligible. I don't suppose you've considered a genuine betrothal as a solution, Mr Davenant?'

'Good God, no,' he remarked imperturbably. 'Far too much trouble.'

He saw her bite her lip; saw her eyes darken with emotion. Damn, thought Adam. Normally he had no trouble condemning the frivolity of all forms of sentiment. But just at this moment something that was almost uncertainty clouded his well-ordered thoughts. Up till now he'd found this woman infuriating, surprising and amusing in equal measure. Her Somerset accent was so impish that it had made him want to laugh out loud.

But he'd not missed the flash of pain that shadowed her eyes whenever her husband was mentioned. When she looked as she looked *now*, her vulnerability made him long to take her in his arms and…

Nonsense! All an act. She was tough; she'd had to be, to make a success of her business in a hugely competitive world. Holding her own in an upper-class milieu, clinging to the hereditary arrogance of her upper-class birth and thus avoiding the subservience of some of the other fashionable *modistes*, who only clawed their way up through sycophancy towards the rich.

And she was beautiful enough to make any man's blood race.

Adam got slowly to his feet, reminding himself that he didn't want to find his own emotions tangled up in Belle Marchmain's messy life…*bed the woman, then ditch her—and I'll give you all the land you want*. How Jarvis had grinned as he said it.

Well, Adam wasn't going to bed her, but Jarvis wasn't to know that.

And when the time came to do what he had to do, she'd hate him for it—but didn't she hate him anyway? Why, then, did the nagging thought keep lurking at the back of his mind that he rather *liked* her?

Ridiculous!

He walked over to the walnut bureau in the corner and unlocked a drawer. 'By the way,' he went on imperturbably, 'I've placed a notice of our betrothal in the *Gazette*. It will appear on Friday. And I believe that on an occasion such as this, a token of esteem is customary.'

He handed her a small, wrapped box and watched her open it. It was a ring he'd bought yesterday from Gray's in Sackville Street, made of sapphires set in gold. It was unostentatious, but exquisite, and he'd expected her—she was, after all, a woman—to be pleased.

She clearly wasn't.

Belle Marchmain just looked at it coldly and said, 'I don't want it.'

As she held it in a hand that trembled a little, something inexplicable tightened in his chest. She looked so vulnerable, so beautiful that, damn it, Adam wanted to take her in his arms and hold her. Kiss those full pink lips, and watch her eyes close in hazy desire. Make love to her until she whispered his name in reciprocated passion...

He said, 'It's simply a gift. I'm sorry if you're offended by it.'

She'd already put the ring back in its box and placed it carefully on the table. 'Presumably your gifts are usually welcomed with cries of gratitude?' she enquired brightly.

'God damn it,' Adam swore. 'But you're an awkward creature, Mrs Marchmain! Most people would not understand your damned reluctance to accept my offer of betrothal, especially as it's a...'

'A small price to pay for keeping my brother out of gaol?'

Adam was silent, watching the pulse that flickered in her throat.

She said at last, in a quiet voice that somehow twisted his gut, 'Mr Davenant. I have fought and fought for my independence. It is, perhaps, the one thing I most value above all. But please—*please* don't pretend that all this, your house, your gifts, are anything other than your attempt to express your contempt for me.'

He said, after a while, 'I have my pride, as you

surely know. Do you really think I would want to be associated with a woman for whom I felt contempt?'

She heaved air into her tight lungs and lifted her chin. Adam Davenant certainly couldn't be telling her that he *liked* her. 'La, Mr Davenant,' she retorted crisply, 'you are a strange creature, to be sure! But it's your time and your money that's being wasted.'

'Oh, I don't consider it a waste,' Adam said softly. 'Besides—I cannot resist a challenge.'

'A challenge? Ha!' Her brilliant green eyes were glittering again. 'You seem to have this picture of me as a virtuous paragon. But my five years as a merry widow have been full ones, I assure you! Why, I've had admirers by the dozen…'

'Name one of them.'

'What?'

'Your admirers. Name just one.' He folded his arms across his broad chest.

'Well—well, there are *so many*. Five years, Mr D.!'

'I'm waiting.'

'How could I possibly give you names?' Belle said a little breathlessly. 'That would be entirely shabby of me, would it not?'

'You've forgotten your accent again.'

'What?'

'Your Somerset accent.'

Belle went pale. 'Can I go now?'

He looked at his watch, meticulous over timing as ever. 'Lennox has instructions to provide a coach and driver in half an hour.'

Half an hour—oh, Lord, an eternity. Her eyes fell on the piano in the corner of the room.

'Then I have time for my music!' She put one hand

to her breast like an opera singer. 'I cannot *live* without my music—I told you so, didn't I?'

'And I told *you*...'

But she was already sweeping to the piano to pull out the stool. 'Every day, I absolutely *must* practise, for a *whole hour*, and I have to sing as well...'

'You'll have the house often enough to yourself,' he said swiftly. 'So the piano, surely, can wait.'

'But, Mr D., I have to play whenever the music takes me, and that moment is *now*!'

She began to attack the keyboard in a thundering cacophony of notes. It had been one of Aunt Mildred's ideas that she learn to play the piano, one of Belle's ideas that she *didn't*, and as a girl she'd deliberately driven her ancient music master to despair.

She smiled at Adam sweetly and began to warble, *'Cherry ripe, cherry ripe, Ripe I cry...'*

She sang in the ridiculously affected way she'd heard one of the Misses Pomfrey sing, to much applause, in the Upper Assembly Rooms in Bath. Trilling on the high notes, she gazed at Mr Davenant and simpered at him between verses, while her fingers continued to attack the keys with a quite extraordinary variety of wrong notes. *'Full and fair ones, come and buy!'* she sang to him one last time.

His broad shoulders were shaking. She realised he was laughing.

'Stop,' he was saying. 'In the name of God, *stop*...'

She did. She stood up and all trace of mischief had gone from her expression. Her face was rather pale.

She eased the dryness of her lips with the tip of her tongue. 'I warned you that you would quickly tire of me, did I not, Mr Davenant?'

'Will I?' he breathed. 'Will I, Belle?' He was on his

feet now, slowly coming towards her like a predatory animal. Something in his husky drawl made her heart race and her pulse thump. She swung away with a gasp, ever alert to danger—this was nothing less than danger!—but he came steadily nearer, the laughter still dancing in his watchful eyes, and captured her with one big hand around her waist. His fingers imprinted themselves through the skimpy muslin, sending pulsing warmth through every nerve ending.

'You are indeed making a mistake,' he said softly, 'if you think I am not the man to respond to your challenge, Mrs Marchmain.'

Chapter Ten

Oh, Lord. 'That was *not* a challenge!' she fired back in desperation. 'That song was to show you what an absolutely hideous fiancée I will be, Mr Davenant—convenient or not!'

'I'm not convinced,' he replied. His voice was strangely husky. 'I think I shall make you play the piano for me every night, wearing pink and lime green. And I shall definitely—most definitely—ask you to sing for me.'

Belle stared at him. 'I'm beginning to think you're mad,' she said flatly.

'No, I'm simply fascinated. I can't wait to find out what other skills you possess.'

Something was tingling through her veins. A kind of sweet intoxication at the sound of his husky voice.

'You talk of many lovers,' he went on, so close now that she could feel the heat of his big body. 'I wonder—did they touch you like this, Mrs Marchmain?'

He was using his lean finger to stroke the satin-soft skin beneath her earlobe and then, when her eyes flew up to his with utter shock, Adam cupped the back of her head and lowered his own.

His lips brushed gently over hers, slow but sure. Tasting. Exploring. At first she was rigid with fear. She felt the blood race through her veins, thundering to her heart. Then she was melting helplessly beneath that tender caress. Like his first kiss, but more of everything.

This was what she had dreamed a kiss could be like. This was what...

Still tenderly, he held her face with both his hands and tipped it up to allow his own lips fuller access. And she found she was yielding to the tingling, building need; aware, in a dark whirlpool of longing, of the searching pressure of his tongue, before she gave way to the hard thrust of it; harsh, yes, but she welcomed it!

Scarcely aware of what she was doing, she'd reached round him and under his coat, her palms gliding with a will of their own up over the crisp lawn of his white shirt to his shoulders, sensing, beneath her palms, those mighty muscles bunching. The feel of his hard body sent her imagination reeling into a realm well beyond kissing. As if to imprint what this was a precursor to, he'd drawn her so close in his arms that his powerful thigh was pushed between hers; she could feel his arousal, thick and taut, against her stomach and her soft breasts were crushed, their nipples hardening, against the broad wall of his chest. Deep inside her was a throbbing ache, a fluttering sweet pulse, needing something. Needing—*him.*

Dear God, she wasn't supposed to feel like this. She despised this arrogant, low-born man who'd forced her into a calculated, cynical betrothal. But his satin-textured lips were still tasting her, his slightly rough tongue teasing, then withdrawing and slowly teasing again, mingling with hers in dark insinuation as his arms held her close. And she felt a low moan of need escape her.

He continued to explore her with half-kisses and devastating strokes of his tongue until she found herself reaching to run her hands through the thickness of his hair. At the same time his hands were finding and cupping her breasts and the pads of his thumbs were circling each nipple, sending her spiralling in a delicious whirlwind of torment. She writhed against him, lost in his slow deep kiss.

He drew away just a little. She made an involuntary sound of loss and her eyes flew up to meet his heavy-lidded gaze.

'Belle,' he was saying huskily. 'Belle, there's a bed upstairs...'

Her breathing was agitated, the peaks of her breasts hot and hard. She was aching, they were aching, for his touch, for his big, strong hands to cup them again, to rekindle that delicious feeling...

And wasn't that what this man wanted? For her to *beg* him to make love to her, simply so he could reject her and utterly humiliate her? Wasn't that what he'd wanted ever since her words of insult that day on Sawle Down?

A tight pain seized her chest. All her senses felt raw. She breathed, 'I thought you said you would wait for an invitation.'

His grey eyes were hooded. Dangerous. 'By God, Mrs Marchmain,' he said with a gravelly edge to his voice, 'if that wasn't an invitation to bed you, then I don't know what the hell it was.'

She stared up at him in utter dismay. 'Yes. I'm sorry. I didn't mean...'

Adam gazed down at her, the painful throb of his

erection not even beginning to ease because with her lips swollen and her sweet breasts pouting beneath that pink muslin flimsiness, she looked more desirable than ever. A widow, a woman of the world; funny, clever and beautiful, yet with a little-girl-lost look that if he wasn't careful might just have the power to melt his hard heart. Except there was no way on earth that he would let it. And anyway, she hated him.

Remember the railway. His bargain with Jarvis had to come first. Using her? Yes, he was using her—just as she was using him, to save that contemptible brother of hers from ruin.

'Let's make things clearer between us next time, shall we?' Even as he spoke Adam was walking towards the door. 'As I said—I'm not going to force myself on you. But on the other hand, I won't be toyed with, do you understand me, Mrs Marchmain?'

She licked her dry lips. 'I understand,' she whispered.

He held himself very still for a moment, then said levelly, 'I think you should move in here as soon as you can. I've already told you it's not acceptable for my fiancée to live above a dress shop.'

Her cheeks whitened; she lifted her chin. 'I see. Yet it's acceptable for her to live in a house usually inhabited by your mistresses?'

Adam registered the scorn she flung into that word with a renewed flash of anger. *Damn her for her upper-class self-righteousness.* 'Oh,' he answered smoothly, 'as you're fond of pointing out, I wasn't bred to live by the rules of polite society. You'll move in, as soon as possible.'

Belle closed her eyes. She was condemned to spend the next few weeks under the protection of a man who despised her. Who could also—he'd just proved it yet again—reduce her to a molten heap of need with just one kiss.

And she could see no way out. Already he was auto-cratically leading the way into the hall where his steward rather warily stood holding her raspberry-pink and lime-green pelisse.

'My coachman will call for you tomorrow afternoon,' Adam told Belle curtly as he escorted her to the coach waiting in the street. 'As I said earlier, there's an auction of Egyptian-style furniture at Christie's. He will take you there.'

Oh, God. That Egyptian furniture she'd made such a song and dance about. Now, she simply felt an idiot for pretending to like such gaudy ostentation. 'Will you...?' she began.

'Yes, I'll be there waiting for you,' Davenant went on ruthlessly. 'And even if you feel you're not quite ready to move in here yet, people will observe that we are together, and will guess that we're preparing this house for your occupation. What with that and the announcement in the newspapers, no one can doubt that you and I are serious about our commitment.'

Deadly serious. Belle swallowed. 'Very well. But I will dress in my own attire, as usual!'

'By all means. I expect you to make an impact, Mrs Marchmain. And I trust your taste.'

'You—you *do*?'

'I do.' A hint of gentleness in his voice now. Mis-leading, dangerous even, because this man bore her no kindness.

He was holding open the door to the carriage for her. At the last moment she turned, the pink and green ribbons on her tall hat fluttering, and said in desperation: 'I am not *sure*. I really cannot be sure about all this and you, too, in your heart of hearts must doubt the wisdom of what we are entering into...'

His eyes were unreadable. 'In my heart of hearts? Clearly you haven't listened to enough gossip about me. You see, it's rumoured that I simply don't possess a heart, Mrs Marchmain.'

He was already giving her his hand to help her inside and the beautiful bay horses moved smoothly off. Despite the warm afternoon sun, Belle found she was shivering.

Adam returned to the parlour, dragging his hand through his cropped dark hair. Damn. Damn it to hell. The room was still imbued with the delicate lavender scent of her clothes and her skin. Her sweet, soft skin...

His body throbbed at the way she had opened to his kiss, at the memory of her low moan as his hands cradled her breasts. He'd known what she was ready for, and so did she. But hell, he'd sworn that he wouldn't touch her unless she begged him to. And hadn't she just done that?

No.

That was the trouble. She'd reacted divinely to his kiss, to his caresses—but as far as she was concerned he was breaking his damned promise. Taking advantage. Hell's teeth, that was the way women *thought*. Even though she must have felt his goddamn arousal burning against her, even while she clutched him close begging for more, it was all his blasted fault.

Adam cursed again. If he wasn't careful, this could go badly wrong. Before this latest, dangerous stage of their relationship, Adam had to admit he'd been enjoying her company far more than he'd have thought possible. He'd found her amusing, original and outrageous. And as for her piano playing—he was grinning just at the memory of it.

Yes, *outrageous* was the word for Mrs Belle Marchmain. But underneath that sparkling veneer he guessed she was as fragile as hell.

He reminded himself that it was her own damned arrogance that had made her vulnerable. *That, and her loyalty to her brother*, a little voice inside him said. Normally Adam let his mistresses down gently; always they were regretful, but he was careful not to upset their pride.

He knew that with Belle Marchmain there could be no gentle parting. No sweet words of regret followed by a handsome payout. He had to humiliate her. That was the price Jarvis had demanded for his land. And Adam needed to get started on his railway before the autumn set in—so this counterfeit betrothal could be for only a few weeks at most.

Grimly Adam suppressed the memory of the taste of her soft pink lips, the feel of her sweet firm breasts that had peaked to his touch, the almost overriding urge he'd experienced to carry her slender body upstairs and make powerful love to her.

Damn it to hell—there must be no more of these kind of riotous thoughts. Pity was a sentiment he definitely couldn't afford, and besides, if she didn't hate him now, she surely would before too long.

Back at her shop Belle swiftly took off her pelisse and bonnet, trying to look calm when inside she felt sick. *To have let him kiss her again...* 'Has everything been all right while I've been out, Gabby?'

Gabby hesitated. 'Oh, *madame*, we have been so quiet that I sent the girls home.'

Belle's stomach pitched. Adam Davenant was forgotten. 'No customers at all?'

'No one, *madame*. But you look so tired, I will make you a cup of tea. And there is a letter for you.'

Belle opened the letter and this time went cold with utter dismay.

It was from her landlord, giving details of the next quarter's rent—and the amount was double what it used to be.

She could not pay it. She simply stood there frozen, while the letter dropped from her hands.

Gabby came back in with the tray of tea things, making an effort to be bright and cheerful. 'And so, what is it like, the house Monsieur Davenant has provided for you? Is it very grand? Is it—?'

Belle cut in. 'Gabby, I'm afraid this shop will have to go.'

Gabby put the tray down rather shakily. 'But—what about Jenny, and Susan, and Matt?'

'I will find us *something* else,' Belle assured her quickly. 'A smaller shop, in a less expensive area. But I doubt if I can keep paying the girls and Matt.'

Gabby's voice trembled a little. 'Matt and I—we are going to be married!'

'Oh, Gabby.' Belle hugged her. 'But this won't stop you, will it? Matt will still have plenty of work with his brother, surely?'

Gabby was dabbing her eyes. 'His brother says times are hard also. *Madame*, we all like working here for you so much—' She broke off with a small sob.

Belle paced the floor. 'I will ensure, then,' she said almost fiercely, 'that I find somewhere that makes enough profit for me to employ you all. Though as I said, it will have to be in a less fashionable district.'

'But if you do that,' Gabby cried, 'we will surely lose the rich customers we have left! Why not ask Monsieur Davenant for help?'

Belle shivered. 'He's not a charity, Gabby. In fact, I'm not even sure he particularly *likes* me. He just wants me to fend off the hordes of society beauties he seems to imagine are clamouring for him.'

'But they are!' pointed out Gabby. 'I told you so, remember? He is—'

'Yes,' interrupted Belle, 'I believe you've already told me quite enough about Mr Davenant's—attributes, thank you, Gabby!' She picked up the letter from her landlord and read it again distractedly, then thrust it upon the table.

Gabby sighed. *'Ma chérie,'* she went on tenaciously, putting her hand on Belle's arm, 'Monsieur Davenant is going to a great deal of trouble and expense just to set you up for his convenience. He must have regard for you, and why not? You are so brave, so beautiful.'

He thinks me an utter fool. And no wonder. Belle felt a very strong desire to cry. But she pulled herself up, blew her nose and said, 'I'm going to look at my account books and see how we can cut our losses when we have to close this shop.'

'But—'

'Please don't argue, Gabby. We will have to search for another shop, you and me, *without* Mr Davenant's help, and there is an end to it.'

When Gabby had gone Belle put her palms to her cheeks, drew a deep breath then walked round rather agitatedly amongst the lengths of silk that gleamed at her cruelly.

She was afraid, because her life was collapsing around her.

She simply couldn't go on with her arrangement with Adam Davenant. What a fool she'd made of herself today—and that was just the *beginning*.

But if she refused to fulfil her part of the bargain, then Davenant might immediately demand that Edward reimburse him for those gambling debts. And as for those dratted sheep…

She felt rather sick. Clearly she'd have to confide in Edward, however distressed he was about his poor baby. There had to be some way out of this, there had to be.

Belle had no other relatives to turn to; Aunt Mildred and Uncle Philip had washed their hands of her nine years ago, when Belle told them she had fallen in love.

After several months of secret if brief assignations in Bath, Harry Marchmain asked Belle to marry him. Harry had been so handsome, so gallant in his army uniform, and Belle had felt so sure of their love that she earnestly told him she would defy not just her family but the world for him. But though Harry was of good family he had no money apart from his army pay. 'It's a totally unsuitable liaison,' Uncle Philip had told Belle sharply.

Together Belle and Harry arranged to be seen passionately kissing in a deserted conservatory at a ball in the Upper Assembly Rooms one night—and the ensuing gossip that spread like wildfire changed everything, just as Belle and Harry had intended. When, a few days later, Harry came once more to ask for her hand in marriage, Uncle Philip had no choice but to stonily agree.

Belle had thought it would never happen again. Thought that she would never let her life be turned upside down by any man. But dear heaven, the feel of Adam Davenant's hands, the taste of him, still coursed through her veins and tightened her tingling breasts. And between her thighs a tender pulse throbbed sweetly, achingly.

She remembered Gabby's awed words with a fresh thud of anguish. 'Monsieur Davenant is well known indeed for the beautiful women he has escorted around the town. And of course there is all the talk of his *virilité*…'

She was as big a fool as any of his conquests, because he'd melted her with just a kiss. Sheer dread had her in its grip again. Her business faced ruin. She would have to start up a new shop in far less elegant, far less profitable surroundings—and surely Adam Davenant would no longer want her as his fiancée. So— oh, Lord, what would happen then to Edward's debts?

She would find out tomorrow, when she told Davenant of this latest blow. And then, next morning, another letter arrived from Edward.

'So you see,' Belle said brightly to Adam Davenant, 'I have decided to close my shop in the Strand and set up a new one. Of course this means a *complete* rethink of my plans and I must end our betrothal, but I will, instead, arrange to repay my brother's debts to you in instalments. And you will save a fortune, Mr D., in not having to spend money on my vastly expensive refurbishments of that big house of yours in Bruton Street. La! The thought of you paying out for all those Egyptian antiquities I was set on acquiring—what a lucky escape you have had, to be *sure*!'

They were at the back of the auction room the next day. The place teemed with the fashionable crowds who'd been eagerly assessing the Egyptian items on display and were now intently watching the auctioneer as he climbed his rostrum.

But Mr Davenant had eyes only for her. And those eyes were hard as flint. 'I've told you,' he said through gritted teeth. 'Do *not* call me Mr D. Where are you opening this new shop?'

'Well, at first I thought of Bath...'

'Bath is full of old maids and dowds,' he said dismissively.

'I haven't *finished* yet. And then I thought of Soho,' she said airily, smoothing down her walking dress of pink-and-white striped percale, over which she'd thrown an emerald cashmere shawl.

'Soho?' said Davenant dangerously.

'Yes, I shall rent a stall in the Soho Bazaar, it will be such fun—oh, look at these lions' heads, Mr D., aren't they quaint?'

He ignored her attempt at distraction. 'To set yourself up in the Soho Bazaar,' he pronounced, 'is little better than crying your wares from a stall in Cheapside, and you must know it. Which of your fashionable clients do you think would be moon-dipped enough to follow you there?'

She tilted her head, setting the feathers on her emerald bonnet a-bobbing. 'Oh, women will *always* want gowns, you know. And...' Her voice trailed away suddenly.

'You might as well tell me what's gone wrong,' said Davenant.

'It's the rent,' she said in little more than a whisper. 'The landlord has doubled my rent and I cannot afford it.'

He was silent a moment. 'I thought business was flourishing.'

'It was, until recently!' she uttered. 'But then there were problems. Complaints.'

'I see. And how the deuce, Mrs Marchmain, do you intend to pay off your brother's debts and thus rid yourself of my obnoxious presence—from a *market stall*?'

Belle fought for words as well as for breath. 'Oh, you are so *arrogant*. I will work night and day; I will not stop until I've...'

Suddenly she realised she was being drowned out by the piercing voice of the auctioneer. 'Nineteen guineas, ladies and gentlemen—any advance? Twenty guineas now, and a bargain. Twenty-one! Twenty-two!'

Belle waved her catalogue in frustration. 'I will *borrow* the money, Mr Davenant,' she cried, 'rather than be bound to you a single day longer...'

'Sold!' cried the auctioneer in triumph. 'Sold for twenty-five guineas to the lady in the green hat with feathers standing at the back of the room.'

Oh, no.

'You've just bought yourself a pair of gilded sphinxes,' Davenant told her flatly. 'You were about to tell me how you're going to pay off your brother's debts. And don't forget that the auctioneer will also need paying—*today*.'

She could have wept. She gazed at him, utterly stricken.

Davenant went on, 'Have you even *told* your brother what's been happening? If he had any decency at all, he would be dealing with all this himself instead of skulking in Somerset. What the hell is he thinking of?'

'His baby died,' she whispered. 'I got a letter from him this morning. The baby was born two weeks ago. It was very ill, and now it's died. And his wife has been told that for the sake of her health, she must not bear another child...'

She tried to swallow down the huge lump of grief that was blocking her throat. This morning as she'd read that letter Belle had felt quite numb with sorrow for the little life lost and for Edward and Charlotte's agony. Her brother, whatever his faults, adored Charlotte and had shared her desperate longing for children.

The auctioneer's voice started to rise again as bidding began for the next item.

'Let's go outside,' Davenant said abruptly, 'before you end up with a six-foot-high marble elephant. I'm sorry about your brother's child. But I am determined our original plan will go ahead.'

'No! I cannot *possibly* accept your charity.'

Adam Davenant clenched his teeth.

Just then a porter came hurrying up. 'Two gilded sphinxes—was they for you, sir?'

Davenant handed him his card after scribbling on it. 'Deliver them to this address in Bruton Street and send me the bill.' Then he guided Belle into the empty hallway beyond the noisy auction room. 'Mrs Marchmain, I've already told you how you can pay me back—by appearing in public with me as my fiancée. And I've a new idea. Yes, you will reimburse me, but we will do it properly, in a businesslike way. I'll invest in your shop. And it won't be in some damned rookery in Soho, but in Piccadilly.'

Now, where the hell had that idea come from? Simple, really; he couldn't let her break off their betrothal. He had to keep his bargain with Jarvis. But damn it, that piece of land for his railway was getting more expensive by the minute.

Belle's hand had flown to her throat. 'Piccadilly! But—'

'I happen to know,' he pressed on relentlessly, 'of a jeweller's shop close to Hatchard's that's becoming vacant shortly. You'll like it—big glass windows for your displays, a workshop at the back for your staff. I'll tell my secretary Lowell to acquire the lease.'

Just like that. 'I will not put myself further in your debt!'

'My intention is that you *won't*,' he said abruptly. 'I will be extremely disappointed, in fact, if I don't make a healthy profit. I'll expect you to become all the rage.'

'But our betrothal is only temporary—'

'This need have nothing to do with our betrothal. This, Mrs Marchmain, is business.'

The porter was trundling past them with the two sphinxes on his wheeled trolley; Davenant gazed at them and said, 'Do you know, I've rarely seen anything quite so hideous in my life. By the way—I assume you'll agree now to move into the Bruton Street house?'

He saw her hesitate. Damn it, she was still desperately trying to wriggle her way out of this. *How she must detest him.*

'You'll do so as soon as possible if you've any sense,' he said. 'After all, the gossip about you and me will do no end of good for your shop.'

A few days before the expiry date of her old lease, Matt and his brother moved all Belle's stock to her new Piccadilly premises. Bernard Lowell had approved the legal work, the shop sign had been painted and hung, and Belle had elegant cards printed and sent to all her clients.

Secretly she was awed by the shop's prestigious situation, its airy rooms. Adam told her to order the furniture she needed, and so she did—no gaudy ornateness, but counters of polished walnut and floor-to-ceiling shelves in pale oak, fitted by Matt to display her valuable rolls of fabric.

Adam's contributions—though he claimed to know nothing about the dressmaking trade—were invaluable. It was he who suggested that she continue with her eye-catching designs, but make them available also in softer colours to appeal to women of less adventurous tastes. He displayed, in fact, a remarkable knowledge of fabrics and styles, and Belle tried to stop herself sharply reflecting that he'd probably visited rather a lot of *modistes* with all his previous mistresses.

There was accommodation above the shop—a small but pleasant bedchamber and sitting room—and when Gabby and Matt told Belle their marriage date was set, Belle offered the rooms to them.

'How convenient,' Adam had approved when she told him. 'Your staff living on the premises means you have security as well as commitment. Well done, Mrs Marchmain.'

'You think I planned it?' Belle flashed. 'You are so cynical! Sometimes love just *happens*!'

'So I'm told.' He shrugged.

On the opening day she was at the shop at dawn. Matt, Gabby and her two assistants Jenny and Susan were there, too; Matt as usual was the odd-job man and furniture mover while Gabby and Belle put finishing touches to the striking fabric displays they'd set up for passers-by to view through the plate-glass windows.

The shop was to open to selected clients at midday. Invitations had been sent out and the champagne was ready. As the minutes ticked by there was one last delivery—dozens of beautiful flowers in shades of cream, ivory and palest yellow. Belle opened the accompanying note with slightly unsteady fingers. *I wish you luck today. You deserve it. A.D.*

Something caught in Belle's throat as she gave her staff their final instructions. 'As from now,' she told them, 'Gabby will be in charge of this wonderful new shop. But I will still come *every day*, and believe me, your welfare and this business will always be uppermost in my mind.'

Gabby's eyes twinkled. 'We can manage here without you, you know, *madame*. I'll keep you very well informed. All you need to do is call in two or three times a week, perhaps meet our most important clients.'

'Two or three times a week?' Belle was scandalised. 'I assure you, I will do a good deal more than that. I'll be here every morning!'

'Every morning?' Gabby said softly, merrily. 'And what will Monsieur Davenant think of that, for goodness' sake?'

Belle coloured slightly. 'My plans have his full approval, since he is well aware I have a business to run.'

'But when he makes you his wife, which surely he will…'

Again Belle felt a sharp lump in her throat. 'Gabby. Please say nothing to anyone else, but I do know that I may well need this shop to come back to. It's my refuge, it's my life. Look after it for me.'

'Of course,' said Gabby softly. 'Oh, *madame*, do not

cry. And Mr Davenant—I hear things, so does Matt, and Mr Davenant is said to be a good man, honest and fair.'

Except to those who have mortally insulted him, thought Belle rather desperately. Oh, if only she'd never met him at Sawle Down. If only… Regret was pointless; she had to deal with her life as it was now. Taking a deep breath, Belle went to open the doors to her new shop.

Chapter Eleven

There followed a hectic time in which Belle reached the startling conclusion that—if she pushed aside the precise reasons for her present situation—she was actually enjoying herself.

She'd moved into Adam's house in Bruton Street. The London Season was in full swing, her new shop thrived, and Adam's businesslike advice was invaluable. As for the house, Belle continued to add an outrageous piece of furniture here and a gaudy Egyptian antiquity there. The gilded sphinxes were a damned nuisance—she knocked her shins or caught her gown on them at least once a day. But even so she would find herself wandering around thinking, *This is beautiful.*

Her bedchamber was perhaps the loveliest room, light and airy with pale lemon wall-hangings. Even a huge old Egyptian-style chair she'd insisted on installing in one corner—made of heavily carved black wood with an overarching canopy—failed to mar its beauty.

She saw Adam most days, sometimes in meetings about her new shop together with his secretary Lowell; more often in the evenings, when he would escort her to some of London's most fashionable venues such as the theatre or the ballet. After taking her back to Bruton Street well before midnight, he would leave for his own house in Clarges Street nearby, doing nothing more than nod his dark head in polite farewell.

Some sense of rebellion in Belle—or fear, perhaps, at the obligation under which she found herself—made her seek again and again to shatter Davenant's calm demeanour with her bright clothes or with some outrageous remark. But it was like charging against a brick wall. Or bumping into one of the hideous sphinxes and sarcophagi that littered the corridors of her new house.

He was imperturbable. Indifferent, most likely, thought Belle with a strange little stab. She would be his fiancée for a while—oh, many were the congratulations she was offered on her engagement, and even more frequent the sly glances of envy—but in private he couldn't have made it plainer that this was simply a business arrangement. She would give him respite from the marriage mart till the Season ended in July, then that would be the end of their betrothal. She would eventually pay back Edward's debts to him through her profits, but doubtless that would be all sorted through Lowell.

Yes, a business arrangement.

Belle tried everything to annoy him. She wore a purple pelisse sewn with silver frogging to the theatre and a bonnet adorned with purple-dyed feathers. She flirted and joked outrageously with his men friends, interlacing her conversation every now and then with Somerset dialect, hanging on to his strong arm and calling him *her Mr D.*, but he coped with all her public eccentricities with amused ease.

There was just one evening when she thought she caught some flicker of emotion in his hooded grey eyes. They were at the opera; Belle had insisted on being taken there, largely because he'd told her he loathed it. Indeed so secretly did she, and once in their private box her own heart sank at the tedious hours which lay ahead.

But then she began to realise that the story was about doomed love. The music, even though she didn't understand the Italian words, was actually incredibly beautiful. And as the heroine sang her dying farewell to the hero Belle felt a huge lump in her throat.

Don't be a fool. It's sentimental humbug.

It made her want to cry. Oh, Lord, she *was* crying…

'Are you all right, Mrs Marchmain?' Adam at her side asked quietly.

She hid her handkerchief and smiled up brightly from behind her purple fan. 'Oh, indeed, Mr D., I swear it is *so* diverting!'

He gritted his teeth, but didn't remind her not to call him Mr D. They were due to join his friends for a supper party after the performance, but he said instead, 'You look tired. I'll take you home. You've been at your shop almost all day today, haven't you?'

Belle was silent a moment, still struggling with her emotions. Then she said, 'Does that spy of yours, Lennox, tell you everything?'

'Yes,' he answered imperturbably. 'Do you really have to be there so often?'

She flicked her fan. 'But of course,' she said gaily. 'Only think of your investment, Mr D.!'

And I need to be independent, she vowed. *I have to be. I cannot rely on any man, let alone you.*

She'd quickly realised that she now had considerable status in the eyes of the *ton* because she'd been picked out by one of London's most eligible bachelors. But there were disadvantages. Again and again she argued with Adam over the number of staff at the Bruton Street house. 'There are maids and footmen everywhere and I do not need them.'

'You need the maid I hired, don't you?'

'Simmons? Well, yes, I suppose...'

'Do you object to her?'

'No,' said Belle. 'No, I don't.' She was, in fact, used to dressing herself, but she had to admit that Simmons was invaluable in looking after her new and extensive wardrobe.

But it irked her that at Davenant's insistence she couldn't go anywhere by herself and had to either travel in the coach he'd provided, or, if she chose to walk, be accompanied by one of his grooms.

Davenant would always answer her protests with, 'I have a certain position to uphold in society, Mrs Marchmain. And so do you.'

In other words he was as formal, as correct as ever. But that look in his eyes at the opera, when he'd asked her if she was all right, had fractured something in her carefully maintained defences. And every night when he left her alone in that big house, some part of her ached for him to stay. Not just to stay, but to kiss her again, with those firm warm lips that had set her pulse racing and her insides clenching with forbidden heat...

No. That would make things simply impossible. That would be the ruination of their civilised companionship, which Belle was coming to value more than was remotely wise. *Why* was he going to all this trouble and expense? At first she'd feared he wanted to exact revenge for her insults; now she assumed he was eager for her shop to do well because he'd invested money in it and was expecting some return in order to can-

cel out Edward's massive debt. But to spend so much
time with her...

Could it be possible that he was actually starting
to care for her?

No. Belle found the blood pounding hotly in her
veins. That was the last thing on earth she wanted.
She absolutely *detested* Adam Davenant—didn't she?

Adam, meanwhile, had matters of his own to attend
to. One night he invited Lord Jarvis to dine with him at
his house in Clarges Street and when the main courses
had been removed and the servants gone, Adam poured
Jarvis more wine and said calmly, 'You'll acknowledge, I hope, that I'm fulfilling my side of our bargain.'

Jarvis's pale eyes gleamed. 'I thought we'd arrive at the business of the widow sooner or later. I assume you're eager to be getting on with that railway
of yours?'

'My engineer, George Shipley, has advised me that
the excavations ought to be well on their way by Au-
gust.'

Jarvis drank half his glass of the rather fine burgundy in one go. Then he said, 'You're being presump-
tuous, Davenant.'

'Am I?'

'Yes.' Jarvis helped himself to more wine, then sat
back in his chair and watched Davenant narrowly.
'You've got to break with her. Humiliate her. Remember?' He suddenly leaned closer. 'She should be
counting the days—and nights—to your wedding. She
should be beside herself with joy. But people are saying that the pair of you look more like friends than
lovers—dear God, man, given your reputation with
women, she should be swooning at your every touch!'

Adam looked at him steadily. 'She's a mature widow, Jarvis, not a lovesick girl. We're seen almost every night around the town together and are officially betrothed. But you know that I've absolutely no intention of meeting her at the altar. Isn't that enough for you? I take it you don't expect a ringside view of our more intimate moments?'

'Now, *there*'s an idea,' said Jarvis. 'What's she like in bed, I wonder? Does she squeal, Davenant, when you take her? Is she docile, or does she beg you for more, like—'

Adam put one fist on the table, though he kept his voice calm. 'I don't remember it being part of our agreement that you have leave to insult her. I repeat— when are you going to give my engineers access to the land you promised me?'

Jarvis scowled. 'As soon as I'm sure Mrs Marchmain is head over heels in love with you and is convinced you'll marry her very soon. But devil take it, you've not even introduced her to your family yet!'

'Good God, man, I've little enough family, as you know.'

'You have a brother in Surrey. Has he even met your so-called fiancée?'

Adam laughed. 'That's hardly your business.'

'But this agreement's my business,' said Jarvis softly. 'I want to see her humiliated, if you want that damned land. As for the shop you've set up for her in Piccadilly—I take it that's just a temporary affair also? That you'll pull out from your investment as soon as you break off this sham betrothal and so leave her ruined?'

Adam said nothing. Jarvis frowned down at his glass suddenly. 'Damn it, Davenant, have you nothing stronger than this burgundy? You used to have some fine brandy—or is that reserved for your friends?'

Adam stretched his long limbs and rose to fetch the brandy and two glasses from the sideboard. He started pouring. Said, in a deceptively soft voice, 'You hate Mrs Marchmain, don't you, Jarvis? Did you by any chance contrive to destroy her shop in the Strand as revenge for her rejection of you two years ago?'

Jarvis's hand froze over his glass. 'I don't know what you're talking about.'

'I think you're lying. Someone arranged a succession of complaints, then instructed her landlord to double the rent.' Adam gazed at Jarvis with steely eyes. 'I think it was you.'

Jarvis laughed. 'Dear God, I wouldn't dirty my hands with such a lowly matter. Just remember, Davenant—I want to see her broken if you're to get your land, understand?' He drank down his brandy and stood, straightening his coat. 'Time on that note for me to go.'

Adam had risen also, towering over him. 'I think you *did* try to ruin her business, Jarvis. Be careful. I don't remember anything in our agreement about you being allowed to harm Mrs Marchmain in any way whatsoever. Do you understand?'

Jarvis let out a hiss of surprise. 'Are you threatening me? My, my—a mistake, that, showing your hand too early. Maybe you *are* starting to get a little too fond of her.'

'I've no intention of continuing my relationship with her beyond the terms of our agreement,' said Adam curtly. 'And don't forget we've each got a copy of the details, signed and witnessed.'

'Maybe so. But there's no way I'm letting you have

access to the land you need until you've given me a little more proof of your commitment—and until the town is full of the news that you've broken with her. *Ruined* her.'

'You're a bastard, Jarvis.'

'So are you,' said Jarvis calmly. His hand was already on the door. 'And wouldn't the lovely Mrs Marchmain be interested to be told of what we agreed? Because that's what will happen if you try to wriggle out of this in any way at all. Understand?'

Adam saw him out. Off his property. Damn it. *Damn it.*

The next evening Adam escorted Belle as usual back to Bruton Street after a night at the theatre. But—and this *wasn't* usual—he followed her into the house.

She was untying her bonnet, a delicious little affair of sage green and claret that matched her figure-hugging pelisse. Her eyes, Adam noted, were still sparkling with laughter from the comedy they'd both enjoyed. Her lips were full and rosy, and as she took off her bonnet some soft coils of black hair fell enticingly to her shoulders.

Tonight she'd turned to him in the interval and put her small, warm hand impulsively on his. She'd said, 'Oh, I'm enjoying this so much—thank you, Adam, for bringing me!'

'My pleasure,' Adam had said. And that was the trouble. It was. He found her intriguing, amusing and damnably arousing.

He liked her. He wanted her—no use denying it. His weeks of celibacy, and her nearness, were wreaking havoc with his self-control. At this moment, his body was throbbing with need, and he wanted to lead her upstairs and make love to her until they were both giddy with sensual delight…

'Such a lovely evening,' she was saying with innocent pleasure as he followed her into the parlour. 'I'm becoming quite an expert on the playwrights. The merits of Mr Sheridan, as opposed to those of Mr Goldsmith—I did enjoy our literary discussion with all your friends.'

She turned to him with such a sweet smile that Adam sucked in a betraying breath at the way her soft cheek tempted him to press his lips there. At the way the faint, delectable scent of lavender drifted from her body…

He forced himself to smile back lightly. 'I'm sure they enjoyed talking to you. But I fear their attentions weren't entirely on the finer points of the discussion.'

'What do you—?'

'They were enjoying being close to you, Belle,' he said, going to pour her a glass of ratafia from the tray of drinks Lennox had left and using the moment to fight down his uncomfortable erection before she spotted it. 'At this rate—' he turned back to her '—you'll have half of London's male population at your feet. Perhaps as your fiancé I should show my mettle and drive off some of the more persistent of them.'

She gasped, her smooth brow furrowing. '*Oh*. I really hadn't thought—I mean, especially as we are only pretending…'

Pretending! Good God, she clearly *hadn't* noticed. He clenched his teeth. 'I know you can fend them off,' he said. 'But you should be aware of their interest.'

She blinked. 'Is this why you've come inside with me tonight? To warn me that I'm not behaving correctly?'

'Partly,' he said, 'though with my lowly origins I'm hardly a suitable person to lecture you on the manners expected of the *ton*.' He handed her the glass. 'But chiefly it's to tell you I've got a proposition for you.' He put his hand on the mantelpiece and turned to face her directly.

Belle's stomach unaccountably pitched.

It was a long time since the matter of his so-called lowly origins had even crossed her mind. And something about him tonight—was it the way he'd brushed his hair in a slightly different style? The way his plain but perfect cravat set off the sculpted features of his strong face? Something, somehow, made her feel quite shaky whenever she looked at him. Made her wish…

Oh, Lord. *That this was for real.* And now just being in the same room as him had started to make her feel a kind of aching longing that bewildered and frightened her. She *knew* he felt nothing for her. That he was merely extracting payment for her insane insults.

But it was as if every time she saw him her yearning body was disconnected from her brain. Every time he said goodnight and left her—so politely, so damned politely—she would totter away to her bed with her pulse thumping and her mind a whirling morass of emotions. Of desire—yes, pure, trembling desire—for him to take her in his arms.

Damn Edward and his debts. Because otherwise she could have pretended that this man was falling in love with her.

Tonight she was wearing a sage-green silk dress that demanded a tight corset. But the corset, which ended just below her nipples, had been chafing her breasts all evening, making them so sensitive she'd wanted to scream. Wanted, even more, to feel his cool hands on them or, dear God, his lips, drawing those burning peaks into his mouth…

'Are you listening to me, Belle?'

'Yes. Yes, of course. I'm sorry.' She fixed him with a bright smile, but her heart lurched. His lean cheek was already shadowed with evening stubble; his mobile mouth looked more tempting than ever as it twisted in a slight, wry smile.

'You looked miles away,' he remarked. 'I was saying, I need to ask a favour of you.' He was pouring himself brandy, only a small glass. His father had often sought refuge from his wife's vitriolic tongue in alcohol; Adam had no desire to follow him down that path.

'My brother,' Adam went on, 'has come to stay in his London house for a few days with his family; it's his son's eighth birthday, and they're going to visit Astley's Amphitheatre as a treat. Would you come with me and join in the celebrations?'

'You have a nephew?'

'Three, in fact. The birthday boy is the oldest; his name is Joshua.' Adam sipped his frugal brandy. 'He and the two younger boys are delightful little rogues and my brother and his wife are quite charming. You'd enjoy it, I'm sure.'

She twisted her wedding ring, giving herself time to think. She needed to remind herself that everything Adam did was for business, not pleasure; but why he should require *this* of her she couldn't fathom. 'Have you told your brother—Freddy, isn't it?—about the particular nature of our betrothal?' she ventured at last.

'That it's temporary, you mean? I scarcely think it's relevant to him, do you?'

Belle was silent a moment then said, 'Don't you mind deceiving your brother?'

'Freddy knows me well enough,' he answered. 'Please come. I'd enjoy your company.' Then he smiled. 'Any ideas for a birthday present for an eight-year-old boy?'

They talked a little more, while he finished his brandy. She followed him to the door, where he took her hand in his and let his firm lips just brush her fingers. Then he was gone and she sat down again.

Freddy knows me well enough. Belle felt as if he'd just flattened her. He might as well have said, *Freddy knows I pick and discard women as I please.*

And yet, just the touch of his lips on the sensitive back of her hand had sent such a torrent of raw hunger for this man thudding through her veins that she felt real despair.

Adam set off home, opting to walk so the night air would clear his head and dampen down the rather dangerous racing of his pulse that started up whenever he was too close to Mrs Belle Marchmain. Whenever he as much as touched her hand, for God's sake.

He'd spoken to Freddy earlier today, about Belle.

'Another of your beauteous *chère-amies*, Adam?' Freddy had queried.

'No—my fiancée, in fact.'

'Fiancée!' They'd been dining at Adam's club and Freddy almost spilled his wine in surprise. 'Good God, Adam, you vowed you'd never let yourself be leg-shackled. In fact, you've told me repeatedly that our parents' sad marriage was enough to put you off for life. You're not actually serious about this Belle, are you?'

Silence fell. At last Adam said softly, 'If you're

wondering whether she's fit company for Louisa and the boys—'

'No. Dash it, Adam, it wasn't that!'

'I think you'll be pleasantly surprised,' finished Adam.

And that was that. Freddy had looked amazed. No doubt there were a hundred questions he'd wished to ask, but he'd enough sense not to bother. And if honest, kind Freddy knew exactly why Adam was so insistent Belle be introduced to them all, Freddy would think his brother the biggest villain in London.

Well, as Adam walked steadily through the night-time streets of Mayfair with the silver moon shining overhead, he felt he probably *was* the biggest villain in London. Even worse than Jarvis. No one in their right mind trusted Lord Jarvis.

But Belle Marchmain, he feared, was beginning to trust *him*.

Chapter Twelve

It was a bright summer's afternoon when Adam called to take Belle over the river to Astley's Amphitheatre. Outwardly Belle was ready for him, with her light smile and defiant air. But as ever these days, just one look at him had her thoughts tumbling into complete disarray.

She'd watched him from the window as he climbed down from his chaise with long-limbed ease, dressed with devastating simplicity in his caped driving coat and shining top boots. Belle met him at the open door; he bowed over her hand then assessed her swiftly.

He frowned a little.

She stiffened, her heart missing a beat; Lord, how sensitive she was to his every gesture, every look. 'La, Mr D., you look as if you'd swallowed a spider. Is something wrong?' she queried with a jaunty smile.

Amusement gleamed in his dark eyes. 'Since you ask, yes. Your clothes disappoint me a little.'

'Disappoint you?' she gasped.

A muscle quivered at the corner of his jaw. 'Indeed. They're almost—conventional.'

She glanced down quickly at her dove-grey pelisse.

'But I thought—since we're meeting your family—I decided you would be embarrassed if I dressed in my usual foolish way...'

'*Not* foolish,' he said quietly. 'Please don't change yourself, Belle. For me, or anyone.'

Dear God. If she didn't have more sense she'd be head over heels in love with this man. But she *did* know better, so she plastered on her bright smile, stilled her shaking heart and hurried inside, to come out very soon in a cherry-pink walking dress with navy ruffles and a wide-brimmed straw hat trimmed with pink-silk ribbons galore. 'Better?' She tilted her head jauntily and waved a cherry-coloured fan.

Adam grinned. 'Oh, *much* better. Shall we depart?'

He held out his arm so she could rest her fingers daintily on it and led her to his carriage.

After driving the chaise over Westminster Bridge, Adam left the vehicle in the tender care of his coachman Joseph and led her towards the vast amphitheatre that was Astley's. Such a throng had gathered for the popular attraction that she wondered they'd be able to find anyone at all, but soon there were gleeful shouts of 'Uncle Adam! It's Uncle Adam!' and two little boys were running towards them.

A moment later a cheerful-looking man—Adam's younger brother, it *had* to be—was striding eagerly forwards to grip Adam by the hand.

'Out of the way, you hooligans!' Freddy commanded. 'Is that the way, brats, to greet your esteemed uncle?' The grin on his pleasant face completely counteracted the severity of his words. He had the same thick dark hair as Adam, the same chiselled jaw, but was just a little less tall and looked as though he spent most of his time smiling. 'Adam, good to see you. And—' his gaze had fastened on Belle '—Mrs Marchmain? Your servant, ma'am!' His eyes were widening considerably. 'Come away, brats, and give the lady some space.'

The oldest boy—he must be Joshua—was gazing up at her, frowning. 'Papa, is she one of Uncle Adam's *petticoats* that you and Mama were talking about at breakfast when I came in?'

'Oh, Lord. Joshua, you little imp, that's quite enough!' Freddy turned to Adam and Belle in rueful consternation. 'So sorry, so very sorry. Joshua, no more London treats for you, if you don't remember your manners!'

Joshua, the birthday boy, looked crestfallen. 'Please,' said Belle quickly. 'I don't mind at all—I know my appearance is a little *unexpected...*'

She heard her voice trailing away. *This is awful. I'm not going to be able to cope with this. I should have refused to come...*

'I like her,' said the smaller boy, Tom, stoutly. 'I like her pink dress and her ribbons. I don't see why Mama and Papa were so worried 'bout her coming with us today.'

'Good grief,' exclaimed Freddy, 'my apologies *again*, Mrs Marchmain, you can see that parental discipline is totally lacking here. I've told Louisa many times, we should have tutors and footmen with us on outings like this to instil some kind of order on our brood—but she just won't have it! Oh, here comes Louisa now, thank goodness, with our youngest...'

They were joined by one of the prettiest women Belle had ever seen, holding a curly-haired four-year-old boy tightly by the hand. She was, to someone of Belle's experienced eye, wearing a gown that allowed for her state of pregnancy, and Belle saw how Freddy's face lit up at her approach. 'My wife,' he said to Belle, with all the love and pride in the world.

Caught unawares, some emotion—some old pain, long-buried—smote Belle with such intensity that she shook. *No children for her.*

The lovely, charming Louisa took Belle's hand with her own free one. 'How delightful to meet you, Mrs Marchmain.'

'It's extremely kind of you,' Belle said steadily, 'to include me in your party.'

'Why on earth shouldn't we, my dear?' Louisa smiled. 'You are, after all, very special to dear Adam... Josh darling, what is it now?'

'It's my *birthday*!' Josh announced importantly to Belle, having pressed his way between his mother and her. 'My birthday, and I'm *eight*, you know.'

With much chattering and laughter, Freddy and Louisa got their lively family to their seats in the huge tiered amphitheatre. The show wasn't due to start for twenty minutes, but the excited audience had packed the place early and kept the vendors who moved around selling sweetmeats more than busy.

Belle saw how the boys fought to sit next to their uncle Adam. He'd bought them each toffee apples and Belle found herself wincing for him as they clambered all over his pristine clothes with their sticky fingers, but he seemed completely unconcerned, laughing with them and telling them about the spectacle they were shortly to witness. *A family. He should have a family of his own...*

'Mrs Marchmain?'

It was Louisa's voice. For a while, in the merry exchange of seats that seemed to be an essential part of the family outing, Adam's sister-in-law was next to her. 'Mrs Marchmain,' Louisa went on rather breathlessly, 'I so envy you your life in London! And your clothes are so beautiful.'

Belle smiled. 'I'm afraid some consider my clothes a little outrageous.'

Louisa stopped her by putting her hand over hers. 'Adam clearly doesn't,' she whispered. 'Adam is completely smitten. You've made quite a conquest, my dear; Freddy and I thought it would never happen. We are so glad for you.'

With that Louisa turned back to her little boys; just as well, because Belle couldn't have spoken a word. *She shouldn't have come here.* She'd made herself stupidly vulnerable by coming here.

The noise around them was rising as the lights were dimmed for the opening ceremony. The blood had rushed to her cheeks at Louisa's words; she fumbled in her reticule for her folded fan and realised Adam was leaning close, his dark face shadowed.

'Are you all right, Belle?' he asked quietly.

A simple question, but after Louisa's comments it floored her. *Adam is completely smitten.* No, he wasn't. No, she was *not* all right, she was a stupid fool and this false betrothal was tearing her in two.

'Oh, absolutely!' she answered with a merry smile and wafted her fan in the air. 'I'm so excited, I must declare. And as for you, Adam—you've kept all *this* quiet. You have a family that dotes on you! Do you secretly dream of a place in the country, where you can rusticate, as your brother does?'

He gave her an answering grin. 'Oh, I leave that sort of thing to Freddy. He's good at it.'

'Adam.' She heaved air into her tight lungs and her

smile vanished. 'Adam, I hate these lies. I hate these deceptions.'

His face was suddenly devoid of good humour. 'Then let's take a look at these *deceptions*, as you call them. For example—have you even told Edward yet that you know about his gambling debts? Have you told him what you've *done* for him?'

He saw a pulse flicker in the slender column of her throat. She breathed, 'I—I didn't want to trouble him.'

'Trouble him!' His voice was rich with scorn.

'Not until his wife is recovered—at least a little— from her grief.'

'Your brother surely hasn't imagined his debt of five thousand guineas would vanish into thin air?' He sounded incredulous. 'You realise I could enforce that debt at any time?'

Belle breathed, 'You can't seriously think you need to remind me? Isn't my being here proof enough of the hateful power you hold over us *both*?'

Some latecomers were pushing their way in front of them, causing loud protests. After that Belle had an excuse to turn from him because Louisa was asking her something about her gown.

Adam watched her talk to Louisa, his eyes narrowed. She looked as vulnerable as he'd ever seen her, despite her defiant words. He felt something twist in his gut as he realised how pale, how forlorn she looked in her gaudy finery.

Suddenly it was as though Jarvis was at his shoulder. Jarvis, saying to him, *Devil take it, you've not even introduced her to your family yet. I want to see her broken if you're to get your damned land, understand?*

Adam gritted his teeth. Jarvis would only be satisfied if he ended the betrothal in public, indicating to the whole world that he no longer considered her a suitable match. Usually it was the woman's privilege to curtail a betrothal; for the man to break it was a fate reserved for females who'd shown themselves to be liars, libertines or worse.

Adam reminded himself grimly that the livelihoods of hundreds of men and their families depended on him. He was doing the right—the only—thing, wasn't he? She would survive it, as she'd survived so much else, and, God's teeth, she'd insulted him to kingdom come that day on Sawle Down.

But as he watched her, looking calm and steadfast but guessing very well that wasn't how she felt—as he watched her, Adam wasn't so sure.

He wasn't sure at all.

When the show began at last the boys were clearly thrilled beyond words by what they saw. They shrieked with delight as the tumbling acrobats made way for a troop of gorgeously apparelled horses, whose riders—clad in Saracen robes—galloped around the ring in breathtaking feats of horsemanship.

The noise from the applauding crowd, seated in tier upon tier around the covered amphitheatre, rose to deafening levels as a troop of gallant Crusaders suddenly rode out to a fanfare of trumpets and put the Saracens to flight. But that was only after much swordfighting, during which Freddy's youngest, four-year-old Oliver, crept on to Belle's lap for a better view, his eyes round with awe. A parade of all the horses and their riders was followed by the return of the acrobats, who to the wild applause of the audience crowned their act by leaping on one another's shoulders until they'd formed a huge human pyramid.

* * *

The boys were still quite breathless with excitement as they left the arena and emerged with the crowds into the afternoon sunshine.

'That was *wonderful*,' gasped Josh, awed. Adam had gone ahead to find the carriages, so Freddy shepherded the remainder of the party to an agreed rendezvous while the boys chattered away. 'I'm going to ride a horse like that when I'm bigger.'

'You couldn't, silly!' That was six-year-old Tom. 'You have to be a—a Crusader! Don't you, Papa? Tell him!'

Freddy said tactfully, 'You could join the cavalry, Josh. When you're a bit older, of course.'

'The cavalry!' Josh's eyes widened. 'Yes, Papa, can I join the cavalry?'

'Me, too!' cried Tom. 'I'm joining, too! Where's Uncle Adam? I'm going to tell him!'

'He'll be back soon, darling,' said Louisa, laughing. 'Oh, here, Oliver, let me wipe your sticky face! Watch Tom a moment, will you, Belle?'

But somehow—*somehow*, though Belle was sure she'd got little Tom's hand tightly in hers—Tom got away. Within moments—that was all it took—he was quite lost, amidst all the people still pouring out of the amphitheatre.

'Belle?' Louisa's voice, sharp with panic. 'Belle, where's Tom?'

'He was here. I had him here…' Belle could barely speak for the panic thudding in her chest.

Louisa had gone quite white. She was already rushing towards her husband. 'Freddy. Tom's gone.'

Freddy, taller than they, was urgently scouring the crowds. 'Josh—Ollie—hold your mother's hands, *un-*

derstand? Look—Tom's over there, I can see him. He's spotted Adam!'

It was true, Belle realised. Tom had somehow through the throng seen Adam returning and had run off to meet him, quite oblivious of the busy thoroughfare he would have to cross. Belle was the first to fly after him, panic and dread weighting her every step with lead.

For a second the little boy stood frozen amidst the horses and carriages. Belle ran on, knowing sickeningly that she'd be too late. Then—Adam was there. Adam was scooping Tom up and out of the way in his strong arms, just before the wheels of a heavy town coach rumbled over the very place where the child had stood.

Tom was unharmed. He cried a little in his fright, and once Adam handed him to his mother Louisa hugged him to her, kissing him over and over again. Freddy gathered his precious brood together and told them sternly that they must stay close, at all times.

Belle could barely breathe. *She* had been in charge of Tom; *she* had let him slip away from her grasp.

'Belle. Are you all right?' Adam's voice; he was at her side.

She whispered, 'Please will you take me home?'

Adam had lifted her hand; she was shaking. 'No one blames you, Belle.'

He saw how her lips were quite white; her hands trembled as she shook her head. 'Everyone thought I was holding him safely. If it wasn't for you—oh, Adam, if you hadn't got there in time, he'd have been terribly hurt...'

'But I *did* get there in time. And Belle, he slipped away from you—boys will be boys, you know that!'

'I know that it was my fault,' she breathed, her eyes dark with distress. 'Please, Adam. Take me home.'

An hour later Belle was alone in her bedroom in Bruton Street when there were strong footsteps on the stairs, a familiar knock at her door. She jumped to her feet as the door opened.

Adam, of course. He'd left her here—at her insistence—then gone on home to act as host to his brother and his wife, who were dining with him that evening.

He came inside, his face unreadable in the shadows. He said, 'You've not even lit any candles. I'll send for a maid—'

'*No.*'

'Belle, Lennox told me you've had nothing to eat and nothing to drink. You're sitting here in the dark. You should have come with me to Clarges Street.'

'I—I cannot face your brother and his wife. I cannot.'

'I told you. Nobody blames you.'

But she blamed herself, more than he or anyone could ever know. She sat on the bed again with her head bowed, her arms folded tightly across her breasts. Adam sighed and went to light two candles above the fireplace. Then he seated himself on the big bed beside her, took hold of one of her hands and turned her gently to face him. 'Accidents happen,' he said. 'It wasn't your fault that Tom did something he knew very well was wrong. And he is *all right.*'

'Only thanks to you!'

'Perhaps, but even so you will not hide up here, as if you've done the child a grave injury—do you hear me?'

She was still trembling. 'Perhaps not *this* time. But I did, years ago...'

'You did what?' His arm was round her now, holding her. 'What, Belle?'

'My brother,' she whispered. 'Adam, my brother nearly died. Because of me.'

And so it all came pouring out. 'He was only six, Adam. The same age as Tom. I was almost eight and—and we were in the house my father once owned, in Bath. Our maid was meant to be looking after us, but I heard a troop of cavalry coming up the street and so I led Edward outside to watch them…' Her hand went to her throat.

'Take your time,' Adam said. 'I'm listening.'

Somehow, she told him the rest. How Edward, escaping from her hold, had run excitedly towards the trotting horses. How the one nearest to him, taking fright, had reared up and Edward had been knocked over by those plunging hooves.

'My little brother was badly injured,' she went on, her voice scarcely audible. 'His arm and wrist were broken, and his face—oh, Adam, a hoof caught his forehead. He was in terrible pain and was an invalid for a long, long time. I often think it's why he's—not as strong in other ways as he should be. He almost died and I shall never forgive myself.'

She was shivering, but she refused to cry. Adam kept his arm round her and felt raw emotion punch him in the gut. If she'd cried—damn it, yes, if she'd *cried*, as most women would have done—he'd have offered a few terse words of comfort then backed off as quickly as he could.

But she was the one backing off. Pulling away from him, hastily brushing her dark curls back from her face and saying in a fractured voice, 'There. You know it all now. You should go back, to your brother and his lovely family. I will be *quite all right*.'

But Adam wasn't all right. Adam was finding that all his safe and sure convictions—that he was a tough man, that the weakness of indulging in sympathy for others was not for him—were falling apart around him.

He said in a voice that was almost harsh, 'Belle. I understand that was a terrible thing to happen. But for you to let it tear at you like this, to let it scar your whole life, cannot be right. Are you really saying that the accident to Edward is why you sacrifice yourself for him? Do you think that *helps* him, for God's sake?'

She'd got up to walk distractedly up and down the room, still in that cherry-pink dress in which she'd looked so radiant when he'd picked her up to take her to Astley's. She was always beautiful, damn it; even more so now, because she looked so damned vulnerable.

She turned to him, her green eyes wide and translucent in the whiteness of her face. 'Whatever I do for Edward,' she breathed, 'can never be enough. *Ever.*'

Her low self-worth—her *despair*—tore at his gut. He stood up to grasp her hand and make her sit again, next to him on the edge of the bed. 'By God,' he said, 'it's more than enough. Listen, Belle. You should *not* spend your whole life feeling guilty for your brother. You were only a child yourself. Surely your parents—your mother at least—realised your grief, your remorse? Surely the maid who was supposed to be watching you was as much to blame—if we are apportioning blame—as you?' Adam saw one silent tear trailing freshly down her cheek and yearned to kiss it tenderly away.

She dashed that tear aside with her own hand and

said flatly, 'My mother died when I was two. My father never forgave me for Edward's accident.'

Adam sighed. He was holding both her hands in his; they felt small and cold. 'Oh, Belle. None of us are blessed with everything we want in our lives, but you deserve so much more than you have. Than you *allow* yourself to have.'

Her face flew up to his, her expression one of surprise and almost fear. 'No! You are just saying this, because of the accident to poor little Tom. I am really quite happy with my life and my shop...'

His arm was round her shoulder, warming her. He affected her—oh, that touch!—in a way she would not have believed possible. And it simply would not *do*, because she knew that in Adam Davenant's life everyone and everything had a purpose—including her. He was using her to keep the husband-hunters at bay and was making her pay sorely for her brother's debts and her own insults.

He despised her, of course. Yet as his long, lean fingers fondled her shoulders through the thin fabric of her gown, she could scarcely breathe for the pleasure of it.

He was murmuring, 'So stubborn. So *determined* to exclude yourself from the kind of life most women long for. Yet you were wonderful with those children today. Belle, why didn't you have children of your own?'

She paused, gathering her thoughts. 'I was told I could not have them. I did hope to become a doting aunt to my brother's children, but Charlotte—she...' Her throat was suddenly too tight to speak.

'Charlotte's baby has just died,' he put in quietly. 'Belle. Tell me. Why didn't you marry again? You surely must have had suitors...'

He saw her stricken expression and stopped. He went on, even more softly, 'Did you love your husband so very much?'

'There has been no one else,' she whispered. *'No one.'* Until now...

Then she rose to her feet and smoothed down her skirts, making a desperate attempt to pull herself together. 'To exist on one's own,' she declared, 'is perfectly feasible, as you so often declare, Adam. Families tend to be over-rated, don't you think? Though *yours*— gracious me, your brother and his family are quite delightful, as one might expect!' Another tear was rolling down her cheek; again she dashed it away. 'You'll forgive me for my slight exasperation, I hope, you—you wretchedly perfect man! Does *nothing* ever go wrong for you?' She was fumbling for a handkerchief; more tears were brimming over her dark eyelashes.

Suddenly Adam was on his feet, too. He strode across to her and was holding her. She lifted her hand in some half-hearted gesture of resistance, but that was actually worse than useless, because he caught her fingers and pressed a kiss to the delicate skin of her inner wrist that sent shivers pulsing through her. Gathering her remorselessly into his powerfully muscled arms, he lowered his head to hers and kissed her.

The sweetness of his tongue slipping between her parted lips, silkily tasting and touching, made her feel quite faint with desire. She was aware of his arousal now, throbbing darkly against her abdomen; her hands had instinctively twined around his powerful shoulders.

A physical reaction, her pleasure-besieged brain told her. Nothing more. Nothing at all more. That was why she didn't stop him when his strong hand moved to gently caress her breast. That was why, at the juncture of her thighs, she felt an ache of sheer, sweet longing that was almost a pain...

Yes, it was wrong, all wrong. But, oh God, she *wanted* this man. So badly.

Adam's emotions, too, were in roiling tumult. He was taking advantage of her and he hadn't damn well meant to. As his lips possessed hers, as his tongue explored the satin recesses of her exquisite mouth, he fought to stop a great surge of desire pushing reason out of the window.

Lowell had been right, he'd been wrong. For all these years she'd been faithfully grieving her lost husband. He'd exploited that grief. He'd also exploited, just now, her remembrance of childhood horrors for which she unfairly blamed herself.

He knew he ought to take his hands off her, now. But he wanted her. He wanted her with an urgency he couldn't ever remember feeling in his entire life, and that big bed was too damned close...

He forced himself away. 'Tell me to stop, for God's sake,' he gritted. 'Damn it, Belle, tell me to stop now, for I swear if we carry on much longer, I will not be able to do so.'

'You mean—this is real?' she breathed. 'You actually find me desirable?'

What in hell was she talking about? He gave a harsh, incredulous laugh. 'Can't you tell?' He was brushing his lips along her cheek and throat, his arousal nudging hard at his breeches.

'Adam—we'd agreed there would be no intimacy!'

There was an edge of panic to her voice that made him freeze. Cupping her face with his hands, he gazed down at her. His blood was pounding, his loins thudding just from her being near, this beautiful woman whose full, tremulous lips he longed to kiss again.

'Belle,' he said quietly. 'You loved your husband very much, I realise that—'

He broke off, feeling her tremble in his arms. 'But it's five years since he died,' he went on, 'and I want to kiss you, Belle. I want to do more than kiss you—I think you want it, too. And if you don't want me to take this further, then say so, now. Say, *Adam, I want you to leave.*'

A soft sound—a moan, a plea—escaped from her throat. Once more she was lifting her sweet face to his, her full lips parted with desire. Adam found that his strong hands were shaking more than a little as he slid the shoulders of her cherry-pink gown almost reverently down her slender arms, then bent his head to trail kisses from her throat down to the sweet curve of her breasts. She wrapped her hands round his waist, gasping as he cupped one creamy globe with his hand and took its peak very gently into his mouth.

Belle shuddered as his warm lips enclosed her coral nipple, his strong tongue sweeping to and fro across its taut crest. Her body was hot and alive, throbbing to his touch, and the most sensitive part of her was aching for more. His mouth had gone to her other breast, then he kissed her again. That bed beckoned. Adam stepped backwards to swing her up in his arms and carry her towards it...

'Damn!' The back of his head had encountered something hard and unyielding.

'Adam?' Her lips were swollen from his kiss, her voice hazy.

Still holding her, he moved away from the wall. 'It's

all right. That blasted Egyptian thing—I knocked my head against it.'

She gave a hiccup of laughter and tightened her arms around him, glancing quickly at the black Egyptian throne she'd insisted on buying, with its overhanging wooden canopy. 'I hate it, too,' she breathed.

'Good God. You mean…'

'I loathe it. I—I only said I wanted it, to annoy you.'

'You hussy,' he murmured. 'You wicked, delightful hussy.' And to Belle's joy, he strode on towards the bed, where he laid her down.

Belle was blind to everything except this man's ardent caresses and her own desperate need. All she wanted was for him to join with her, fulfil her. Adam lifted one hand to carefully sweep her hair back so he could lean forwards and kiss the sensitive skin below her ear. She was breathing rapidly, scarcely able to bear the glorious sensations he was creating as he ran his cool palm along her thigh, stroking up it towards the most sensitive part of her being, seeking the throbbing core of her arousal, until…

'Adam.' His name burst from her lips as his fingers caressed her pulsing centre, the pleasure tearing through her. She reared against him, her own clothes in an impossible tangle, her emotions haywire as his faintly stubbled jaw brushed her breast while he tongued her taut nipples. Her whole body tingled with the impossibly delicious sensations shooting out from where he stroked her.

For a moment he went perfectly still, taking his weight on his strong arms, gazing down at her with dark hunger gleaming in his hooded eyes. Then he made his move, all masculine power and grace. He'd slid his breeches down; she could see the flatness of his taut belly, the dark silken line of hair leading down to his pulsing manhood; she felt her lips part in an involuntary cry at the sight of that silken, steely shaft, but he stopped her cry with his kiss, his tongue thrusting deep. She clung to him, her body shaking.

'Belle,' he murmured thickly, lifting his mouth from hers. 'My beautiful Belle.'

The endearment rocked her. Her hands were clutching at his muscled back beneath his shirt, her slender thighs falling helplessly apart to welcome his intimate possession. Needing his possession, as she'd needed nothing before.

She cried his name again in soft joy as he slid his lean hips forwards and she felt his hard shaft sliding smoothly inside her. A wave of rapture engulfed her and she clutched his shoulders, then lifted her hips urgently, welcoming him deeper still. He paused a moment, leaving her taut with anguish, then he began to move again, steadily, strongly driving his length deep into her. She clung to him, clasping him with her thighs, flying higher and higher, while her own breathing came in shallow, moaning gasps. His hand had slid downwards again to touch her there, to urge on her pleasure, and suddenly her back arched, her inner muscles clutched tight round his hardness and her world exploded into a rapturous vortex of sensation.

Moments later, she heard Adam's harsh breathing as he stormed his way towards his own climax and spilled his seed deep within her. Joy pulsed again in splintering ripples at the core of her being as he enfolded her in his arms and she lay with her head against his broad, warm shoulder.

She thought she could hear his steady heartbeat. His eyes were closed; she tried to move a little, but his arm tightened round her. A disturbing surge of exhilaration swept through her from her toes to her fingertips as she gazed silently at his perfectly sculpted features.

It was swiftly followed by anguish. This was *wrong*. She wasn't supposed to feel like this—safe, and warm, and vibrantly alive. As if the most wonderful man in the world had just made incredibly powerful, incredibly tender love to her...

Love?

The cynical words he had spoken long ago echoed through her reeling mind. *It's rumoured, Mrs Marchmain, that I don't possess a heart.*

She'd been an utter fool to let this happen. How could she have allowed her already vulnerable defences slip so badly?

Adam didn't want to move. He wanted to hold her and remember the cries of ecstasy rippling from her throat; to relive the exquisite sensuality of her sweet body as she enfolded him... What was he thinking?

Conscious of her starting to draw away from him, he pulled her back into his arms. No doubt she could feel him hardening anew, for she gave a little gasp as he eased his aroused body against hers. Hell, he wanted her again, badly. His hand was sliding down gently to touch her hip; her flesh there was smooth, delicately rounded...

He'd sworn not to do this. He'd vowed that whatever else his agreement with Jarvis led him into, he would *not* seduce her. *I will expect nothing of you that you're not prepared to give, Mrs Marchmain.*

Had she offered herself to him? The point was debatable, the result beyond doubt. He had damned well broken his word and he was furious with himself.

Sighing he raised himself on one arm and gently brushed a lock of hair back from her cheek. 'Belle. This doesn't really make things between us so very different, though we have to talk, to get everything clear...'

Belle froze. Not different? To have shared such rapture with him, such intimacy—and he was saying—*nothing had changed*?

She lay very still in the crook of his muscular arm. The afterglow of her orgasm was still glimmering inside her, spreading a wondrous sense of fulfilment through every fibre of her being. His lean, muscled body still warmed her; her slender legs were still twined with his...

Not different? She sat up and smiled brightly at him. What a silly fool he would think her, were she to try to play the love-struck innocent. Her, a widow, twenty-seven years old. 'Goodness me, Adam,' she said. 'We're mature people, both of us. And the world assumes we're lovers anyway.'

He looked at her. 'So are you suggesting that we continue to enjoy intimacy—as we just have done—for the duration of our betrothal?' He'd leaned back against the pillows again, his muscled torso gloriously bare, and was reaching to pull her back into his arms, with an expression of pure desire that simply scorched her.

Belle felt something stop in her throat. She had to survive this. Had to be strong, even though she was melting already at his nearness, at his husky voice. 'Gracious,' she said lightly. 'Why not? It was a pleasurable experience, no denying.'

'Then let's repeat it,' he said calmly.

And to that Belle could give no reply. With his indomitable strength he pulled her down beside him, his hands already roving her breasts, his lips brushing her cheek. He made love to her again, darkly, passionately, absorbing her husky cries as she shattered into a thousand pieces in his arms.

Afterwards he settled her head against his shoulder, drifting his fingers along her ribs, soothing her until her breathing returned to normal. He knew the moment she fell asleep. But Adam didn't sleep.

Jarvis had expressed doubt as to whether Adam had actually bedded her. Well, he'd done it. And damn it, he could still hear the cries of ecstasy that had rippled from her slender throat. He still reeled from the sheer sensuality of her sweet body as she shook with pleasure in his arms.

But his bargain with Jarvis wasn't completed yet. Next, he had to break with her. Publicly, Jarvis had said, with maximum humiliation. And then, by God, Belle Marchmain could feel free to hate him for the rest of her life.

Chapter Thirteen

A week later Adam called for her in the evening at seven. They'd been invited to a charity ball at Lord Horwich's grand house in Eaton Square; Adam wore a coat of dark-blue superfine that was designed and cut by Weston of Old Bond Street and bore all the quiet perfection that was the prestigious tailor's hallmark.

But Belle, now—she took great pleasure in defying convention. With a half-smile curving his strong mouth, Adam watched her coming down the stairs of the house in Bruton Street.

Her ballgown was some frothy concoction in shimmering yellow and blue. But he wasn't really seeing her clothes. He was seeing—Belle. *The way she moved*, he was marvelling. So innately graceful, yet somehow so sensual. Everything about her made his pulse kick in sudden warning. Made his physical desire for her throb into life. *Careful.*

Yes, indeed. Careful. Or he would be gathering her in his arms, sweeping her up to her bedroom and making delicious love to her, as he had every night for the past week. Her passion amazed him; aroused him anew time and time again, as if both of them were storing this up, for when…

For when it was over.

Adam's mistresses had always been sophisticated women who could arouse and satisfy him. But he'd never before been with someone who caused sheer desire to surge through his veins every time he damned well saw her. *Learn to cope with it, you fool.* Yet the way she was gazing at him now made something tighten warningly in his chest because she looked vulnerable and almost afraid.

Afraid of *him*, if she'd any sense.

She treated their relationship lightly in public, just touching his arm now and then, teasing him or bestowing a mischievous smile. But it was as if she was two people, for in bed at night she was tender, giving and wildly passionate. Sometimes at moments like that he felt as if he saw her soul laid bare.

Now he must have frightened her with just his look, because that natural joy had fled from her eyes and her usual sweet smile was uncertain as she declared, 'Gracious, Mr D., how you stare! Is my gown too much for you tonight?' She was coming towards him, hips swaying enchantingly beneath her full skirts.

He shook himself mentally. 'It's dazzling enough to frighten my horses…. No. I'm jesting,' he teased her gently. 'It's absolutely perfect. As always, Belle.'

He was always stunned by just how ravishing she was, with her curling black hair and tip-tilted nose and full, rosy mouth. Was amazed as ever by her startling raiment—this time a jonquil-yellow ballgown tiered with layers of gauze and trimmed with turquoise-blue satin. It made him blink, step back then think: *Yes. I've never seen such an outfit before—but she has got it perfectly right.*

'Are you sure it's suitable?' she asked hesitantly. 'I don't want to look stupid or showy. I don't want the *ton* to laugh at me, Adam.'

He drew her into his arms and kissed the tip of her perfect nose. 'They won't laugh,' he said steadily. 'Firstly, because you'll be with me. And secondly, because your taste is unusual but faultless. Everyone's aware that your shop also caters for those with quieter tastes—but what disappointment there would be if Mrs Belle Marchmain *didn't* wear something spectacular to a grand ball!' He pressed his finger to her soft lips. 'Don't be nervous. You look beautiful.'

Her smile wavered a fraction. 'You are always so calm at these society affairs. They all look up to you.'

'Money talks amongst these people.' There was a trace of harshness around his mobile mouth now. 'But just remember you're as worthy as any of them, Belle. You are, after all, the—'

'Great-niece to a duke,' they chorused together and laughed. He fought the urge to put his arm round her— fought the demands of his body, and the overwhelming impulse not to go out *anywhere*, but lead her upstairs and take off her clothes piece by piece, and...

'My carriage is waiting outside,' he said softly. 'Will you accompany me to the ball, Mrs Marchmain?'

She made him an elegant curtsy. 'With the greatest of pleasure, Mr Davenant.'

As his carriage took them the short distance to Eaton Square, a shadow of premonition was stealing through Belle's veins. *Careful. Guard yourself.*

Because soon it would be over.

Sultry July had ushered in the closing days of the London Season. Lord Horwich's ball was one of the final events. And any time now Adam would come to her and tell her she'd paid off her brother's dues. He would cancel Edward's gambling debt, inform her she'd kept him safe from the husband-hunters for long enough and tell her their betrothal was at an end.

He'd always reassured her that he was fully committed to the shop as a business venture; she did not doubt that he would retain his stake in it, for trade there was flourishing. But more and more she'd noticed that Adam was using his secretary Bernard Lowell to deal with the financial side and this surely was the shape of things to come.

Belle guessed with sudden bleakness that he'd found it more amusing than he'd thought, perhaps, to parade her round town as his intended. Besides, the cries of rapture he'd extracted from her night after night in his skilled arms must surely have obliterated for ever those insults she'd hurled at him on Sawle Down.

She'd always known she was merely a pawn in this powerful man's finely calculated day-to-day activities, in his balancing of enjoyment, his consolidation of his position amongst the *ton* and the all-important business of making money.

Yes, she was a mere pawn; so what a fool she was to let her pulse race so every time he came near. To feel her heart jolt each time he paid her some light, meaningless compliment. She shook a little inside every time his fingers so much as brushed hers. And as for the dark, ravishing pleasure she experienced in his arms at night…

She was a stupid fool, because all this was for him simply a matter of extracting sensual enjoyment from a situation he'd initially designed as revenge against her family.

Pleasure and convenience combined.

'If it weren't for Adam Davenant,' she scolded herself fiercely as they entered the grand house of Lord Horwich, 'your brother would be a bankrupt and you would be struggling to make *any* sort of living from a stall in the Soho Bazaar!'

She lifted her head. She was Belle Marchmain, proprietress of one of the most fashionable shops in town, and at her side was one of the wealthiest, most eligible men in London. Yes, soon it would be over. But until then—she was going to enjoy herself.

There were hundreds of candles in each of the main reception rooms, reflected everywhere in the silver plate and gilt mirrors. Liveried footmen hovered with fine wines; a group of musicians were already playing in the ballroom and all the guests were wonderfully dressed. Everyone seemed to know everyone else...

Belle found herself clinging a little tighter to Adam's strong arm.

He smiled down at her. 'Lift your head up. You look superb.'

She needed the compliment. Because soon they were surrounded—*he* was surrounded—by beautiful women trying to catch Adam's eye; by beady-eyed matrons still hungry for gossip about Davenant's unexpected betrothal and by the many male friends of Adam's who seized yet again the chance to eye up Davenant's prize.

Belle shrank instinctively back. But then the crowds parted because someone whom everyone knew, Lady Jersey, doyenne of Almack's, was making her stately way towards them.

'My dear Davenant!' she exclaimed. 'Here you are, you heart-breaker, looking, as usual, too wickedly handsome for words!'

Adam bowed over Lady Jersey's hand with a smile; she looked at Belle. 'So this is the beauty who's at last broken your resolve never to marry, Davenant. Mrs Marchmain, is it not?' Everyone watched and waited in breathless suspense—a mere comment from this woman could make or break her.

At last Lady Jersey clicked her pearl-encrusted fan and gave a little sigh. 'I hate to admit it, but you've done yourself proud, Davenant. Not only a beauty, but a superb *modiste*, I hear.' She turned back to Belle. 'I am wary of new sensations in the fashion world—but you are building up such a reputation! And your gown—a truly unusual colour—is it made of silk?'

'It's actually made of *faille*, my lady—just a little softer, as you'll see, than grosgrain.'

'I do see. Wonderful! And the lace?'

'Nottingham lace, my lady. I use English-made goods whenever I can.'

'Excellent. I must call in at your shop—in Piccadilly, isn't it?' She gave something that was almost a wink. 'They've been talking about you, you know, all the gossips, and not a single one told me how beautiful you are. But women being women, they wouldn't, would they?'

Lady Jersey tapped Adam's chest with her fan. 'I'm holding a rout next week, Davenant. A last flourish, before I escape to the country for the rest of the summer. I'll send you and your delightful fiancée an invitation.'

Adam bowed low again, a smile lurking at the corners of his mouth. 'I'm sure we'll accept it with pleasure, Lady Jersey.'

A cluster of eager women immediately surrounded Belle, anxious not to miss out on this latest sensation who had won the approval of Lady Jersey herself. But what meant most of all to Belle was the sight of Adam looking outwardly as calm as ever, yet in his sleepy grey eyes she thought she saw a flash of—pride.

And desire. Oh, God, *desire*.

She thought she was strong, but the sudden bolt of emotion that shot through her made her gasp for breath.

She ought to resist him. She should never, ever have submitted to him.

Because now she could not imagine life without him.

The dancing came next and Belle was overwhelmed with offers, though it was the cotillion she danced with Adam that she enjoyed most of all. Then came supper—but on their way Belle heard a piercing female voice just a few yards away.

'Adam, darling. How *are* you?'

Adam had turned swiftly. 'Lady Farnsworth. This is my fiancée, Mrs Marchmain.'

Belle froze inwardly at the sight of the beautiful Lady Farnsworth, who had once been Adam's mistress. 'Lady Farnsworth,' she said coolly. 'How do you do?'

'Oh, *I*'m well enough,' said the blonde beauty. 'But I hear things. I hear, for example, Mrs Marchmain, that your brother is too fond of the card tables—but that you, my dear, have found a novel way to pay off his debts!'

Belle felt her pulse hammering. She moistened her lips to reply; Adam was there first.

'You always were one for idle mischief-making,

Lady Farnsworth,' he said coolly. 'But you're rather scraping the barrel this time—even for you.'

Lady Farnsworth coloured, shot a look that held daggers in it at Belle and marched off.

Belle felt cold. She'd just been accused of selling herself to Adam for money—and wasn't it true? The magic had suddenly gone out of the evening. She whirled on Adam. 'If *that woman* knows about Edward's debts, there'll be more who will.'

'And so?' Something in Adam's face frightened her. He guided her into a corner and said, 'Listen. The last thing you do is run away from this, do you hear me? Someone's been talking, yes, but you must face the gossips out with boldness. You're not a whore, but she is.'

'But she was your mistress!'

'Believe me,' said Adam grimly, 'I got out of her clutches very quickly. Wait here—there's someone I need to speak to, and meanwhile you can have a few moments of peace. You're doing marvellously, Belle. I'm proud of you.'

He was gone for a long time. The minutes ticked slowly by; Lady Jersey and some of her friends came to talk to her, but all Belle wanted was to find Adam again. Seeing his tall figure on the far side of the crowded room, she started to make her way towards him.

Only to pull to an abrupt halt a few feet away when she saw he was deep in intense conversation with— Lord Jarvis. Jarvis looked furious and was gesticulating wildly. Adam appeared rigid with anger. Cold fingers of fear were for some reason travelling up and down Belle's spine.

'Getting rather too fond of the little widow, aren't you, Davenant?' she could hear Jarvis snarling.

Adam spoke more quietly than Jarvis; Belle couldn't hear him. But whatever he said made Jarvis clench his fists in utter rage.

'Everything's at stake—do you understand?' she heard Jarvis hiss. 'Yes, you've seduced the Marchmain widow, you've coaxed her into a public betrothal, but you're damned well not playing by our rules. And until I see you doing so you can't expect me to keep my side of the bargain!'

Bargain? Rules? Belle's world was spinning dizzyingly around her. She couldn't hear anything else. She didn't need to.

'Why did you leave the ball without me, Belle? God damn it, I was worried sick...'

Belle had left Lord Horwich's house immediately, asking a footman to summon a hackney. By the time Adam reached Bruton Street twenty minutes after her, Belle was in her bedroom and had packed half her clothes. He'd pounded up the stairs and flung the door open without knocking, only to look at the piles of clothes in disbelief.

'You were *worried*?' she breathed, turning her face to him. 'Yes, I suppose you *must* have been anxious that Lord Jarvis might withdraw from the bargain you made with him. What was it—a wager?'

He'd run his hand through his hair. His white neckcloth was rumpled and he looked utterly, heartbreakingly handsome. 'How much did you hear?'

She dragged air into her aching lungs. 'Enough to know that he'd offered you something—no, I don't want to know what!—to parade me as your fiancée.'

Dear Lord, she'd opened to his embraces as hungrily as a whore. 'Would you mind leaving me on my own, Adam?'

Adam's shoulders were rigid. 'You didn't hear anything else?'

Oh, God. This was bad. This had to be just about the worst moment of her life. 'I'm heartily glad I didn't,' she answered. 'I dread to think what else you had planned for me.'

'Belle…'

She turned back to the pile of clothes on the bed, throwing them into the valises set out there; now she whirled to face him. 'Do you really think I want to hear any more, Adam?' Her voice was etched with pain. 'Haven't you put me through *enough*?'

He was silent a moment. Then, 'What are you doing, Belle?' he said softly.

Just his voice tormented her in a way she hadn't believed possible. 'I'm packing some things, so that I can go and live above the shop.' Once more she faced him. 'I know that these clothes and the shop are partly yours, but, my God, Adam, I'll buy you out just as soon as I can. If I fail to raise the money, I'll sell up and move out of London. *Anything*, believe me, rather than live under the falsehood of this *arrangement* any longer!'

He went very still. 'Not everything was a falsehood, Belle,' he said.

The blood rushed to her cheeks. She couldn't answer. *The incredible sweetness of his kisses. The tender power of his lovemaking, night after night.* All an act. Oh, God…

'Listen,' he went on, gripping her arms and forcing her to face him. 'Let me explain. I wanted some of Jarvis's land. *Needed* it, for a railway I'm building in Somerset. He wouldn't be bought with money. The railway means jobs and prosperity for my men.'

She was quite white. She breathed, 'And Jarvis said he'd let you have that land, if—if you seduced me?'

'What you heard at Lord Horwich's tonight was only a part of it. Things changed between you and me. You know how very much they changed, Belle.'

'Stop,' she cried. '*Stop*. You mean you were to display me as your infatuated fiancée as part of a *business* agreement...' Her voice suddenly faltered. 'Those complaints,' she whispered. 'My landlord, suddenly doubling the rent...'

'Not me, but Jarvis.' His voice was tight; she saw he was clenching and unclenching his fists.

Her hands flew to her cheeks. 'Then why didn't you tell me? I think you're lying again. I think you've lied to me from the day we met. Oh, there's no need at all for you to suggest we end our betrothal—I'll save you the trouble. I'm going to take myself completely out of your life.'

'No, you won't,' he said. He'd started picking out the clothing she'd put in her valises.

'What the hell are you doing?' she cried.

'You can't take these clothes. As you observed, I've paid for most of them. And I have to inform you it's essential that you stay on here—at least for the time being.'

Her green eyes flashed with defiance. 'No. Oh, no. That is impossible.'

'I'm afraid you must make it possible. I will not force my company on you, but it's essential for your own safety that you reside here under my protection for at least the next few weeks.'

'*Protection?*' She was almost laughing at the savage irony of this. 'Protection, when as far as I can see the only person I'm in danger from is yourself? Anyway, how can you *make* me, without keeping me under lock and key...?'

Suddenly Belle needed to sit down, because her legs felt as though they wouldn't hold her any more. 'My brother. My brother still owes you all that money. And you will use his debt to force me to stay on, in this hateful situation.' She gazed up at him steadily. 'You've seduced me. You've humiliated me. You've used my brother's debts—all for a railway. A damned railway. Get out. I know this is your house, but please get out of here. Yes, I will stay. But—you cannot make me endure your company!'

His firm jaw was clenched. 'There's just one more thing.'

She wasn't sure how much longer she could control her shaking limbs. 'More orders?' she queried caustically.

'I'm afraid so. I've already told you not to go anywhere around town alone—but I've reason to believe you've been disobeying me.'

She said bitterly, 'My God, your spies have certainly been busy.'

'Call them that if you must. Nevertheless you will oblige me by not going anywhere, unless one of my men attends you.'

She closed her eyes briefly. 'For how long....?'

But he'd already left her.

Belle sat on her bed and stared into blackness. Oh, God. So cleverly, so subtly he'd entrapped her. She'd tried her damnedest to resist. But Adam had worked his dark magic on her until she had been desperate for him. She'd abandoned herself completely in his arms to his powerful yet tender lovemaking.

And all he wanted was—land for his damned railway.

The tears began to fall at last and this time she let them, though she told herself it was the very last time she would allow herself to cry for Adam Davenant.

Adam returned to his big house in Clarges Street. He went to his study and paced the floor. If only the night could be relived. If only Belle Marchmain had trusted him. Then he might have been able to make her listen to the truth.

For tonight, Adam had told Lord Jarvis to keep his damned land, because their bargain was off.

Adam had heard several days ago that Jarvis had taken up with Lady Farnsworth. So, when she'd come up to them at Lord Horwich's house, Adam knew it signalled trouble. Indeed it did, for she'd blurted out what Jarvis, the fool, must have told her about Edward's debts. Adam had cuttingly silenced her, then had gone in search of Jarvis.

'We had an agreement,' Adam had challenged him bluntly. 'But I *don't* remember an agreement giving you permission to give details of our private deal to your latest mistress.'

'Getting rather too fond of the little Marchmain widow, are you?' Jarvis had growled. And had proceeded to utter the warnings, the threats that Belle, God damn it, must have overheard. 'You're damned well not playing by our rules.'

'That's because I've changed my mind, Jarvis.'

'You've…'

'I've decided I'll manage without your land for my

railway. Understand? I'm not going to make a public spectacle of Belle Marchmain just for you.'

Jarvis's mouth had worked furiously. 'Then I will!' he got out at last.

And Jarvis, in a fury of rage and more than slightly drunk, had proceeded to issue specific threats against Mrs Marchmain. Spat out obscenities as to how Adam could damn well whistle for his railway land, and that he, Jarvis, would take Belle for himself—by force, if necessary—then turn her over to his grooms once he'd finished with her.

Jarvis only stopped when Adam seized him by his lapels, thudded him up against the nearest wall and warned the man that he would take pleasure in pummelling him to kingdom come if he so much as harmed one hair of Belle Marchmain's head.

Now Adam paced his study. Belle's pale, vulnerable face as she accused him of nothing but the truth— *You've seduced me. You've humiliated me. You've used my brother's debts—all for a railway!*—would haunt him for the rest of his life.

He sat in the chair beside his desk, its surface scattered with maps and quarry plans. His efforts to remedy the damage done had come far too late. He should have warned Belle much earlier that it was Jarvis who'd endeavoured to ruin her Strand shop, but now that his treacherous bargain with Jarvis had been exposed she trusted Adam about as much as she'd trust a venomous snake.

She'd made up her mind that Adam was the villain in all this and who could blame her? He *had* agreed to Jarvis's initial, vile proposition and there was no getting round that fact. He remembered her face just now.

Pale, defiant, proud. But underneath, he guessed, so hurt. So desperately hurt.

For five years, she appeared to have kept herself away from men in honour of the memory of her dead husband—but Adam had broken through her defences. Quite possibly he'd broken *her*.

He cursed Jarvis, cursed that damned agreement, and most of all cursed himself.

Adam went to only one social engagement that week and wished he hadn't. He missed Belle at his side. Missed her outrageous clothes, her humour, her mixture of defiance and vulnerability. He cancelled all invitations for the next fortnight—there were mercifully few anyway since the Season was all but over—and spent his days in meetings with bankers and businessmen, discussing the Sawle Down quarry's prospects, negotiating contracts for this new and valuable supply of Bath stone.

Already he'd sent orders to George Shipley, his chief engineer in Somerset, to hire men and begin excavations for the railway through his and his friend Bartlett's estates. But Jarvis's land still barred the way to the canal, and two weeks after the momentous ball at Lord Horwich's house Shipley arrived from Somerset at Adam's home one sultry night in late July with the ominous news that threats were being made against the neighbouring estate owners who'd offered to support Adam's railway.

'There's damage been done to fences and crops by night, Mr Davenant,' warned Shipley, who was tired from his two-day journey. 'Threats against tenants and families by anonymous bully-boys who ride into the local villages, then ride off again, setting up the kind of fear that sticks. And at the actual site, around the excavations your lads have begun digging, there's been accidents that look more like sabotage.'

Adam handed him a glass of wine. 'You look like you need this. Is it Jarvis?'

'He would seem the obvious culprit, sir, and I reckon he's got quite a few of the Somerset magistrates in his pay. What can you do?'

'A considerable amount, I think,' said Adam grimly, 'if I travel to Somerset myself.'

Shipley appeared heartened. But something else worried Adam. Could it be Jarvis's intention that Adam be lured away from his rigorous watch over Belle? Only this morning Lennox had told Adam he'd seen suspicious characters lurking around the Bruton Street house at dusk.

A warning had hammered in Adam's chest. 'You're ensuring she's never alone, Lennox?'

'The maid Simmons keeps an eye on Mrs Marchmain in the house, sir, and of course I send a groom with her whenever she sets off for her shop.'

'She still goes there?'

'Every day, without fail—she insists on it. I send a man to bring her home as well. Though I wouldn't put it past her to give one of them the slip some day soon, sir.'

Adam wouldn't either. He *had* to keep her under his protection, but he also had to go to Somerset. There was only one answer and Belle would absolutely hate it.

She would have to come with him.

Chapter Fourteen

It was true; Belle went into her shop every morning and worked till late, because work offered the only respite from the pain that engulfed her whenever she thought of Adam's betrayal.

Gabby and the others asked no questions, but just once Gabby had found Belle sitting alone in the work-room, with a single garment spread out before her on the sewing table. It was the crimson carriage gown she'd worn during that drive in the park with Adam. A customer had asked for one in a similar style and Belle had brought it in here to measure out the fabric, but the memories it evoked savaged her already raw emotions.

'*Madame?*' Gabby's whisper was full of concern. 'Are you all right, *madame*?'

Belle jerked her head up. 'Perfectly, thank you, Gabby!'

'*Madame*, I do not like to pry. But Monsieur Davenant—he cares for you, I am sure of it.'

Belle stood up, smiling brightly. '*So* much work to do, Gabby—now, I need a length of red lutestring and some gold braid…'

Gabby sighed and proceeded to help her.

After Lord Horwich's ball Belle had spent night after sleepless night agonising over her dire situation. What if Adam had meant what he'd said—that, yes, he'd made his agreement with Lord Jarvis, but things had changed? *You know how very much they changed, Belle.*

She was a fool to search for any kind of hope. He was a ruthless businessman. How could she ever forget that he'd used her brother's debts to force her into that betrothal? He'd bartered her, in effect, for the railway land he was so desperate for.

Adam never visited her now in the Bruton Street house, but sometimes she heard the servants talking about him. One morning Joseph, Adam's coachman, was speaking with Lennox in the hallway when she was about to descend the stairs.

'I've come to pick up the master's travelling clothes,' Joseph informed Lennox.

Belle froze. Adam had got into the habit of leaving items of clothing here—some coats and changes of indoor garments—because of the nights he used to spend there so often with her. *Oh, those nights. Those magical nights.* After their lovemaking he would stay in her bed all night long, holding her in his arms as he slept…

'Going away, is he?' Lennox asked Joseph.

'Aye, to Somerset. To see about that railway of his…'

Belle stole back to her room, feeling shaky. So he was going away. She, too, should get away. From this place and from him—but his absence changed nothing. Edward's debts still kept her his prisoner.

After that she'd gone into the shop escorted by one of Lennox's men as usual, but that particular morning it was quiet—not only because the fashionable elite had left for the country, but also because of the rain that had been falling since dawn. Belle was so busy arranging some new rolls of silk on a back shelf that she didn't hear Gabby coming up behind her.

'*Madame.*' Gabby was tapping her on the shoulder. 'Someone is here for you.'

Something in her voice made Belle's pulse rate hitch. She turned from her silks, and saw that Adam was there.

Two weeks since she'd seen him and something surged in her veins. Shock, and more. Sudden heat, instead of cold. A shameful racing of her blood, just at his presence. *Breathe, Belle, you fool.* Somehow she dragged air painfully into her lungs and felt her heart jolt back into action.

He was a tall, almost threatening figure. She'd forgotten in just this short space of time how big he was. His magnetic presence somehow filled the shop. His exquisitely cut coat of grey broadcloth glistened with the soft rain that fell outside; his dark hair gleamed with beads of water. She'd hoped she could hate him, but oh, God, fresh pain lanced her just at the sight of him.

Gabby emptied the shop still further by shooing out the assistants. 'You naughty creatures, *mon dieu*, what do you think you are playing at? We have four gowns to complete by tomorrow and you stand around doing *nothing*?' She followed them out after one swift, anxious glance at Belle.

'Mr Davenant,' Belle managed to say at last.

He bowed his head a fraction. 'Mrs Marchmain. I have business in Somerset that requires my immediate attention and I've come to ask you to accompany me there.'

That was it. As simple as that. Oh, Lord. She'd hoped she was prepared for him—this meeting had to come sooner or later—but she wasn't.

There was no hint of remembered pleasure in his flat remark. Her pulse was thudding as she reminded herself that this man had calmly used her as a pawn against Jarvis. Squandered her dignity, her reputation, in exchange for some *land* he wanted for his money-making. And it wasn't over yet.

He said he had business in Somerset. Could it be with—Jarvis?

She said, with a brilliant smile, 'Gracious me, Mr Davenant, what an invitation! And so charmingly expressed!' She let her smile drop. 'My answer is no.' And she turned back to the rolls of silk she was arranging.

'You'll have to pack. It's almost ten and I want to leave by eleven,' he said imperturbably.

She swung round. '*No!* How many times do I have to say it?'

'It doesn't matter how many times you repeat yourself; I'm not leaving you here.'

'Why?'

'Because I think you might be in danger.'

'*Danger.*' She put her head on one side, pretending to think. 'Now, what kind of danger might present itself? I know—someone might decide to use me as a *commodity* in one of his devious business deals. Yes, I must by all means be protected from such a heinous villain! Oh, and Mr Davenant, *please* don't let me delay you in your urgent journey.'

Her silks once more engaged her attention. *Damn,* thought Adam. He knew her well enough to realise that beneath that usual calm exterior she was trembling with emotion. With distress. What the hell had he expected?

'I'm not actually giving you an option,' he said flatly. 'You are coming with me. Perhaps, on the way, we might be able to come to a better understanding of our present situation.'

'Oh, now, that *is* impossible,' Belle broke in airily.

His dark eyes were ominous. 'I have an important meeting in Bath in two days' time. I need to be on the road before noon and you're coming, too.'

This time the colour had left her face. 'I take it that if I were foolish enough to argue, you would refer yet again to my brother's debts?'

'If it will stop this pointless argument, then, yes, I will. Joseph is outside; he'll take you in the coach back to Bruton Street, where you can pack your things accordingly. I expect to be in Somerset for a week or so; you could use the opportunity to visit your brother and his wife. I'm sure Gabby and your assistants can look after your shop admirably for a while. I'll collect you from Bruton Street shortly.'

With that, he left.

It should be easy to hate him now. But Belle felt every fibre of her body hurting in a way she wouldn't have believed possible. Oh, this was bad. She hadn't realised that the cruellest of emotions—hope—still lurked somewhere in the recesses of her heart. Until now.

After flinging on a cloak against the rain, Belle went outside to tell Joseph that she'd be with him shortly. And from him she found out some rather interesting details about Adam's planned journey.

They would arrive in Bath tomorrow evening. Joseph was driving the carriage as far as Chippenham, which they should reach tomorrow afternoon; but at Chippenham, Joseph told her, Mr Davenant kept a light curricle which he would drive himself to Bath while Joseph followed more slowly in the coach with the luggage.

Belle's mind raced. She went back inside to speak to Gabby. 'I'm going away to Somerset, Gabby, just for a few days.'

'To visit your brother and his poor wife?'

'I may do so, yes. Actually, I'm travelling with Mr Davenant.'

Gabby's eyes lit up. 'Oh, *madame*, I'm so glad—'

'It's not a cause for celebration,' Belle cut in. *Though I intend to make the event just a little more eventful than Mr Davenant has bargained for.* 'Is Matt around?'

Matt was out in the yard now that the rain had stopped, sawing up wood to make some new shelves for her silks. Matt's talents knew no bounds. At least, Belle fervently hoped so. She gave him his orders swiftly, ignored his protests, then turned to go back into the shop, feeling as tight as a coiled spring at the thought of the ordeal to come.

Half an hour later there was nothing more that needed her attention in the shop. She'd gone over everything with Gabby at least three times. Now for Bruton Street, to await Adam Davenant's autocratic, hateful presence.

Gabby was ushering her to the door. 'Oh, *madame*, I will miss you!' They hugged one another. 'I'll miss Matt, too,' Gabby went on. 'He's told me he's going away on a most important errand for you.'

'And I'm really grateful to him, Gabby. You have—the extra item?'

'It is here.' Carefully Gabby picked up a large wicker basket with a strap to hold its lid in place. 'But I would never have guessed that Mr Davenant—'

'Oh, Mr Davenant is full of surprises,' cut in Belle lightly. 'As am I.'

The basket wriggled a little. From within came the faint sound of scuffling. Then—silence.

Gabby carefully handed it over and stood at the shop door to wave as Belle climbed into the waiting carriage, to be taken by Joseph to Bruton Street.

Belle hoped that Adam might waver over taking her with him when he saw how much luggage she had. Even the ever-obedient maid Simmons had blinked at her travelling outfit, a tight purple jacket over a pale blue gown sprigged with purple daisies.

Casting Adam a challenging stare, Belle clutched her big straw hat on her head and with her other hand the wicker basket. Joseph held the horses while Lennox and a footman struggled to squeeze her valises into the luggage space at the back.

'I hope that's all you're taking,' Adam said. 'You'd oblige me by getting in. I'd like to make Newbury by nightfall.'

She tilted her chin to meet his hard gaze. 'Perhaps I'd oblige you most by not getting in at all. May I remind you that you've hauled me away from my shop with hardly a moment's notice?'

He glanced pointedly at his watch. 'Mrs Marchmain, you've already delayed my journey by ten minutes and—'

'Oh, fie, Mr D. You and your timekeeping!' Ignoring

his proffered hand, she climbed in, placing the wicker basket on the seat beside her.

'That could have gone on the back with your other luggage,' he said.

'No, it couldn't.'

He pressed his lips together and climbed in to sit opposite her, somehow finding space for his long, heavily muscled legs. He was dressed, she reluctantly noticed, as immaculately as ever for their journey in buckskins and top boots, with a light-coloured greatcoat that was exquisitely cut...

She jerked her head away to look quickly out of the window, pretending utter absorption in London's streets as the chaise moved off.

'I think you'll be pleasantly surprised,' he said after a few moments, 'by how well your business manages to run without you.'

'I sincerely hope so,' she answered briskly, turning back to him with a steady gaze. 'Because soon, Mr Davenant, I intend to buy you out. After that, let me assure you that I will owe nothing to anyone.'

Adam said, 'It's a pity that your brother didn't learn the same lesson.'

Belle snapped open her latest edition of *La Belle Assemblée* and began to study the fashion plates without speaking another word.

The silence lasted hardly longer than five minutes. Adam was studying the basket at her side. Then he was saying, in that dangerously quiet voice of his, 'Unless I'm very much mistaken, that basket beside you is starting to move.'

'Why, yes,' she acknowledged coolly. She turned to

start undoing the straps of the basket. 'Since I acquired him, I never travel anywhere without dear Florizel.'

His eyebrows shot up as she opened the lid, pulled out a squirming puppy and cuddled it in her lap. 'He's an absolute darling,' she chattered on. 'Let me show you…'

His eyes were fixed with steely grimness on the small, fluffy white creature with ribbons round its neck and a little bell that tinkled. 'Precisely *when* did you acquire—Florizel?'

'Oh, recently!' she answered. *Just after Adam's visit, to be precise, thanks to Gabby.* It was Gabby who'd told Belle of the pups which were up for sale and who had been only too delighted to go and get one for her.

'Strange,' he said tightly, 'that Lennox never told me…'

'Florry lives at the shop. And I'm so very relieved to have *some* secrets from you, Mr Davenant.' Belle soothed the tiny dog tenderly. 'Florry is such a little darling,' she went on, 'and you will soon grow to love him, just as I do.'

'You think so,' he breathed. 'What kind of name is that for a dog?'

'Florry? Short for Prince Florizel, Mr Davenant! Fie, have you never seen Shakespeare's *Winter's Tale*?' He gritted his teeth, as he always did at any supposed reference to his lack of culture. 'It is all the rage, you know,' Belle blurted on, 'to carry a little dog. With ribbons that match the colours of my gown—see? Purple and green today. Isn't he a sweet little thing? He will sleep in my room, of course, when we have to stop tonight…'

'He's most certainly not sleeping in mine,' Adam said. 'And you'll have to deal with his bodily functions yourself. Don't expect my coachman to. He'd most likely throttle the thing.'

'Mr Davenant—really!' She pouted with indignation, but she bent to fondle the little dog with a rare sensation of triumph and went back to reading her journal.

But it didn't take long for her temporary optimism to dissipate. Adam Davenant exuded self-control; she tried to match it, but every time he moved—every time he breathed, even—she remembered how he'd made love to her and her wretched heart turned over. To be in such close proximity to this man—trapped, in fact, for hours—was going to be torture.

That he was powerful and rich she already knew. But who else would have his own horses kept at every posting station on the road to Somerset? 'Mr Davenant makes the journey so often,' Joseph told her at their lunchtime stop, 'that it makes sense, it do, to keep his own teams. The master don't want some hired nags that are fit only for the knacker's yard.'

Belle reckoned Adam probably wished he could consign *her* to the knacker's yard, because she was deliberately making an absolute pest of herself. Every time they stopped and the ostlers came running to change his horses, she would make a great show of taking Florizel for a walk round the inn yard using his ribbon-plaited lead. But Florizel wasn't the problem, Adam was. Just the touch of his lean hand, or the inadvertent brushing of his hard male body against hers, made her senses throb and her breath catch in her throat.

Most of the time as they journeyed westwards, she buried her nose in her journal or played with Florizel in her lap, but her mind was miles away. What was his meeting in Somerset about? Why had he said he needed her with him? *Because Jarvis would be there?*

During the journey Adam had intended to address the vital documents he'd brought with him in preparation for his meeting. But all too often, as Belle read her journal or petted that absurd little dog, he would find his eyes drawn against his will to the alluring curves of her bosom, to the creamy softness of her cheeks and her full, rosy lips.

Damn. Even the faint lavender scent of her skin caused the familiar arousal to surge through him. He wanted to slip his hands inside that ridiculous little purple jacket, caress her luscious breasts, feel her melt in his arms again...

Ridiculous. Apart from the fact that the dog would snap his fingers off, he'd noticed that her hostility to him never wavered. She shrank away from him even when he was merely offering her his hand to help her down from the coach.

She despised him for making that bargain with Jarvis for his railway land—hell, he despised *himself.* He'd tried to tell her he'd cancelled the agreement, but she wouldn't even listen. He couldn't blame her and she clearly hated him even more for making her accompany him on this journey. But he'd been truly afraid at the thought of what Jarvis might try to do to her if Adam left her in London.

It would be interesting to know, he found himself wondering bleakly as the miles rolled by, which of the two men—himself or Jarvis—she hated more.

He felt as though during the past few weeks she had hurled his whole existence into a disturbing state of tumult—so much so that he was just beginning to wonder if his iron-hard heart wasn't as impervious to stripes and brightly coloured ribbons as it damned well ought to be.

And he had something else to worry about. He guessed they were being followed.

They dined that night in the private parlour of a Newbury inn; the yappy little dog had fallen asleep in its basket in the corner, thank God, but now Adam almost wished it would wake up and distract her because he'd quite forgotten that the dark-panelled walls in here were hung with old regimental prints and battle scenes.

Seeing her glance at them, then turn quickly away, he chose a chair for her that meant she wouldn't have to stare at them all through this damned meal. 'I'm sorry,' he said, after the deferential waiter had brought in the food, then departed. 'You must find reminders of the war painful.'

'Such a terrible waste of so many lives,' she answered quietly.

And that was it, though he thought he saw her hand tremble a little as she put down her fork. He'd already noted that Belle barely ate enough to keep a bird alive. As soon as the waiter had cleared their plates away she rose and went over to the basket where the dog lay. 'Come, Florry,' she trilled. 'It's time to go up to our room!'

But Adam asked her to stay with him, just for a few moments.

She sat down again on the edge of her chair, clutching the dog. 'Yes?'

'I've reason to believe, Belle, that we are being followed.'

'Followed...?'

'When I've looked back at the road behind us today,' Adam explained, 'I've sometimes seen a lone horseman come into view, only to disappear again. Have you noticed anything?'

She gazed at him blankly. The little dog yapped in her arms. 'Why would anyone wish to follow us? Hush, Florry, it's all right…'

'I've no idea. But will you make sure your bedroom door is locked and bolted tonight?'

'Most definitely,' she asserted, with the most spirit she'd shown all day.

No doubt she meant she would bolt it against *him*. Adam clenched his teeth and said, 'That's all. Goodnight, Belle.'

They set off early the next morning and Adam got out some business documents which clearly absorbed him. He didn't mention their follower again.

He's getting ready for his important meeting. Belle shivered. They stopped for an early lunch; by mid-afternoon, Joseph reminded her, they would reach Chippenham and would transfer to the curricle Adam kept there, which he would drive himself.

Belle was sitting as far as she could from him with her nose jammed in her fashion journal. But after a while she realised that he was leaning over to look at it.

'That violet day gown would look marvellous with your hair,' he pointed out.

Too close. Oh, Lord, he was too close, she could feel the warmth of his body. 'Violet is not considered fashionable at present, Mr Davenant!' she declared breezily. Florizel, in his basket at her feet, woke up and started yapping. Belle leant over and stroked his fluffy ears. 'Hush now, Florry, Mr Davenant is trying to be nice to me.'

She heard the hiss of his indrawn breath. 'It's a business suggestion. You should *make* violet fashionable,' he observed. 'Only the waist should be tighter. With your figure, it would look wonderful.'

How could he talk so lightly? When he planned… Lord knew what he planned, but one way or another he seemed bent on destroying her. Florizel whimpered; she pulled the puppy up on to her lap and said, in as smooth a tone as she could manage, 'I thought, Mr Davenant, we were agreed on one thing at least—that nothing personal, of any kind, would pass between us ever again. Compliments, insults, or anything else for that matter.' She looked directly at him, her eyes burning. 'You could do me that kindness, at least.'

'Belle,' he said. His voice was different. Something in his eyes made her heart shake. 'I know you will find this difficult to believe. But I would give a great deal, if we could only start again from the beginning, you and I.'

Something broke inside her. He was her enemy, he had to be, just as Lord Jarvis was; Adam was using her, and she… Florizel chose that moment to start whining for attention; quickly she bent to fuss over the little dog. Adam went back to reading his damned papers and said no more.

For Belle the next few miles went by in an agony of apprehension. When they stopped at the busy Chippenham coaching inn just after two, Adam prepared to transfer the two of them and a single valise each to the light curricle he kept there, leaving Joseph to follow on with the coach and remaining luggage at a slower pace.

Belle walked with Florizel round and round the inn yard, desperately watching every traveller, every horseman, until Adam fetched her and made her get on board. 'We can leave the dog,' he said icily, 'but I'm not leaving you.'

She jutted her chin, but said nothing. Adam took the reins, so Belle was left to sit inside with just Florizel and *La Belle Assemblée* for company. But to be honest she hadn't read a thing for the past few miles. Suddenly, with a clattering of hooves, the horses swerved violently. She could hear Adam shouting a warning to her; her heart hammered. The horses neighed frantically as the curricle, with a dreadful creaking sound, lurched sideways and settled itself at a lopsided angle halfway over the right-hand ditch.

Belle stumbled outside. The horses reared and fretted in their traces. And Adam lay very still, on the road. Oh, *no*. She'd only meant to make him miss his meeting. Not this. Please, God, not this.

Chapter Fifteen

Feeling sick, Belle crouched at Adam's side in the mud to check beneath his coat for his heartbeat. He was still breathing, but his eyes were shut and there was a livid bruise on his forehead. Her own pulse was hammering. She had to get help. The two horses were terrified, pulling at their harness, tossing their heads, and no wonder; just ahead of them a sapling tree lay right across the road.

Hurriedly she went to tie Florizel's leash to the curricle's wheel and tried to soothe the horses. *Adam must have swerved to stop them crashing into that sapling. But Matt had said…*

She ran back to kneel at Adam's side; he still lay prone, helpless. The curricle needed righting and the horses might try to bolt any minute. Should she unharness them? Walk for help? But where? Her stomach lurched again. This had all gone so horribly, terribly *wrong*.

Just then the sound of a horse and rider coming up fast set her pulse thudding anew—especially when she realised that the rider galloping up was her brother.

She scrambled to her feet. 'Edward. Oh, God, Edward—what are you doing here?

Edward was jumping from his horse and staring at Davenant. His face was pale. 'I meant to make the arrogant bastard stop, that was all.'

Oh, no. 'You don't mean—oh, please, you're not saying... Was it *you* who caused his curricle to overturn?'

'Damn it, Belle, I didn't mean to hurt the man! But I couldn't think how else to make him listen to me. I just *had* to have this out with him when I heard he was on his way here with you!'

Belle was white-lipped. 'For God's sake, *what* did you have to have out with him, Edward?'

He was bracing his shoulders now, with that look half of fear, half of defiance in his eyes that she remembered so well. 'Why, I was defending your honour, Belle. I'd heard you were betrothed to him and I knew he must have somehow forced you into it!'

She found she was trembling with shock and distress. Yes, he had, but...

Belle cast another anguished look back at the unconscious man. Whatever he'd done, whatever his plans for her—she couldn't bear to see him hurt. 'For God's sake, Edward. We can't waste time talking. Tie up your own horse and see to Adam's pair. Calm them down, will you?'

She was down at Adam's side again. *Please don't be badly hurt. Please.* She called out to Edward, 'We passed an inn a mile or so back. If I can drive him there, they will surely know of a local doctor—'

She broke off at the sound of more hoofbeats coming along the road. A solitary rider was drawing near. Belle scrambled to her feet. It was Matt.

'Mrs Marchmain. And Mr Hathersleigh...' Matt jumped off his sturdy horse and took in Edward, the curricle and the frightened horses. Suddenly he saw Davenant's prone figure and looked horrified. 'What's happened here? I thought you wanted me to follow you, ma'am, and make Mr Davenant late for some meeting of his—'

Belle broke in sharply. 'I did, Matt, yes. But my brother's taken some action of his own, you'll observe, and he's been rather over-thorough... Please. *Both* of you. Help me!'

For Belle the next few minutes passed in a haze of anxiety. While she held the horses Edward and Matt together hauled the curricle upright—it was still roadworthy, thank goodness—and got Adam's prone body inside, laid awkwardly out along the seat. Belle put Florizel back in his basket and into the curricle while Matt climbed on to the driver's seat to take the reins.

Her brother still looked stunned. 'Honest to God, Belle, I didn't mean to actually harm him. But—I still don't understand why you let yourself be betrothed to him...'

'Edward. Mr Davenant bought up your gambling debts. Five thousand guineas, wasn't it? What else could I have done, when my getting betrothed to him was what Davenant required in return for keeping you out of prison?'

'Prison? He didn't say that, did he?'

For heaven's sake. 'Where else did you think your debts would lead you?'

'But—to *force* you...'

'Edward, I'm not wasting any more time discussing this. Whatever's happened in the past, you've only made things a thousand times worse. I must get him to a doctor.'

Matt drove the curricle back towards the little roadside inn while Belle sat beside Adam's body and tried to cushion his head against the jolting. Edward followed them on his own horse, also leading Matt's mount.

Adam had not opened his eyes. Belle watched his drawn white face and felt as wretched as she'd ever felt in her life. When the inn finally came into sight half a mile away, she called to Matt to stop and said to her brother, as he drew up alongside, 'It's best if you go now, Edward. We don't want *anyone* to know you had anything to do with this, least of all Mr Davenant. You, too, Matt.'

Matt looked stubborn. 'But, ma'am—'

Edward was running his hand through his hair; she saw the old childhood scar on his temple. 'Belle. You won't actually tell Davenant, will you, what I...?'

Her throat tightened with emotion. 'Heaven help me, Edward, I'll protect you as ever,' she'd said with bitter resignation. 'Now *go*. Both of you. I can drive the curricle at least as well as you, Matt. You, Edward, go home to your wife; Matt, go back to London. Oh, and Matt, will you take Florizel? You can strap the basket to the back of your saddle, can't you?'

Matt looked prepared to argue, but she said, rather desperately, *'Please.'*

Matt and Edward rode off together. Belle drove at a steady pace towards the little inn, but her mind was in utter turmoil.

She'd been terribly afraid that Adam might have

been taking her to Somerset to use her to bargain with Jarvis over that land he so desperately wanted. So she'd ordered Matt to follow them and use his ingenuity to delay Adam once he was driving his own curricle—loosen a wheel, perhaps, or tamper with the harness a little. Just enough to make Adam miss his vital meeting and give herself the choice, perhaps, of making her own decision as to what to do next.

She'd never intended such harm to him. Whatever he'd done to deceive her, he didn't deserve *this*.

Within half an hour of their arrival at the inn a doctor had arrived and was giving Belle his verdict in the small parlour where she waited, tense with anxiety. 'He's got a bruised head from his fall, but no bones broken,' said the doctor in his calm voice. 'Your husband came round as I examined him and I gave him some powders to soothe him. He's sleeping calmly now. I would advise him to rest for the night before you travel onwards, of course, but there's really nothing to worry about, ma'am.'

From their arrival at the inn it had been assumed they were married; Belle nodded, outwardly calm, but the relief she felt at the doctor's words frightened her with its intensity. 'What else can I do, doctor?'

'You should go to him now,' he encouraged. 'He'll sleep a while, but he'll be relieved when he wakes to see you at his side, ma'am.'

Oh, wrong there. If Adam knew everything—about Edward, about Matt—he would not be relieved in the slightest. But she nodded. 'Thank you. I will go up to him.'

She thought she had her emotions under tight control. But she stopped with a low cry when she entered the room. *The doctor had said he was all right.*

Well, he wasn't. Any fool could see that. He just— wasn't. His eyes were closed and the dark stubble on his jaw emphasised the pallor of his face. His shirt had been ripped apart—to allow the doctor to examine him, presumably—and Belle could see that his muscular chest was gleaming with perspiration. To witness this strong man so helpless clawed at her insides like some almost unbearable torment.

If he caught a fever, had a relapse… Oh, she should have asked the doctor for more advice before he left!

Seeing a jug of cold water on the wash stand, she quickly dampened a clean towel and sat on a chair beside the bed to carefully bathe his face. She could see the bruise on his temple, already darkening.

His breathing had become easier, but Belle felt helpless and wretched. She sat there at his side, her mind in turbulence, until as the sun started to sink over the Somerset hills the innkeeper's wife knocked and came in with a tray of soup and bread rolls.

'Oh, is he still asleep? So shocking, your accident. But Dr Molloy said your husband'll be all right, don't you fret now, ma'am.'

Belle let the soup go cold. Instead she tried to smooth his pillow and stroked the damp towel once more over his temples and hard cheekbones. *Oh, my.* How very sensual his mouth was; how well-shaped those firm lips that had kissed her to distraction, and more…

He stirred. His slate-grey eyes opened, but they were burning now with dark-gold flecks as he gazed at her. 'Belle. What…?'

Her chest tightened. 'You were hurt,' she whispered. 'In an accident.'

His intent gaze never wavered. 'Don't go,' he said quietly.

'Of course I won't go.' Her voice sounded ridiculously calm and normal. They were—supposedly—man and wife, so she'd have rather a lot of explaining to do to the innkeeper if she *did*. She pulled herself away from him. 'You need to rest, Adam. I'll take a pillow and a blanket—there's a sofa there that I can sleep on...'

'No,' he said sharply. 'I'm afraid someone is after us.' His hand closed around hers. 'You must stay next to me, so I know you're safe. There's a pistol under my coat, on this chair just here. If I can't get to it, you must use it.'

'But Adam—' *Now was the time to tell him. Now.* But she couldn't, because his powerful, heavy arm had curled tightly around her.

'Use it,' he repeated.

His eyes had closed and his grip relaxed a little. She undressed over in the corner—she could not sleep in her shoes or in her stays, for that matter, and God knew she had to have her sleep tonight; she'd need all her wits around her to deal with tomorrow.

The innkeeper had brought her valise up here; she delved in it for a huge white nightgown. If Adam had any lingering intentions towards her whatsoever, the garment would extinguish his ardour.

So *that* was all right. Except—why was her pulse starting to beat so hard when she scrambled into the bed, at the very far side from him? *You're completely safe—he's scarcely able to move.* And whether or not he'd meant what he said in the carriage about wishing they could start again from the beginning, she was surely justified in hating him for making that loathsome bargain with Jarvis?

But she *couldn't* hate him. Just the opposite.

She lay in utter despair, listening to his breathing, slow and deep. Then she slept, too, at the far side of the bed, bone-tired from the events of the day. Yet she woke up in the dead of night. Not because of any intruders, but because she'd become aware that she was curled snugly in his arms, her back against his broad chest.

Her white shroud of a nightgown wasn't much protection *here*. His breath was falling warm on her neck, his body was hard and solid against hers and a honeyed warmth made all her flesh languorous. Dear Lord, how long had she been lying like this in his arms? There was just one answer to that—*too* long.

Adam wakened in time to see Belle jump out of the bed and grab her shawl, her dark curls tumbling round her shoulders. Hell, he thought. What was she doing in his bed, dressed in that white shroud? Come to that, where in damnation was he?

Gradually the memories crowded in, prompted by his aching head. The curricle. The tree in the road followed by blackness, until he'd come round to the sound of the doctor's calm voice in this unknown room. Then Belle had joined him. Willingly? Damn it, no—he'd practically forced her to sleep in his bed, to keep her safe. And here he was, he thought bitterly, practically preparing to ravish her luscious body in his dreams…

Good work, Davenant, he reprimanded himself.

He tried to force down his painful arousal. But it wasn't easy with her standing so near, her dark curls

framing the perfect oval of her face and her delicate
lavender fragrance haunting his senses. Damn it, she
even made that old-fashioned high-necked nightgown
somehow sweetly enchanting.

'I'm sorry,' he grated. He'd raised himself on one
arm. 'For a while I couldn't even work out where I was.
But now I remember. I had to swerve to avoid something in the road and was flung off, wasn't I? And the
doctor told me this is a roadside inn.'

He saw Belle shivering as she stood facing him.
'That's right. There was an accident…'

He swung his legs abruptly off the bed to sit on its
edge facing her. He was still wearing his breeches; that
was something to be grateful for. He only prayed that
in a few minutes he'd get his body—to be specific, his
mighty erection—under control. He said, '*No*. It wasn't
an accident, Belle.'

She went to sit on a chair by the empty fireplace.
She looked—haunted. She whispered, 'Then what—?'

'I told you,' he said grimly, 'that I'd thought since
we left London someone was after us. And I believe
that sapling was laid deliberately across the road to
make my curricle overturn.'

She took a deep breath. 'It could have been some
highway thief, perhaps, who saw us coming.'

'I would be inclined to agree, if I didn't know you
already had an enemy.' He was on his feet now, going
to find tinder and flint to light a candle.

'Enemy?' Belle said brightly. 'Gracious, how you
do overdramatise, Mr D.'

He reached for his white shirt and eased it over
his powerful shoulders. His eyes were deadly serious.
'Belle,' he said. 'Your enemy—and mine—is Lord
Jarvis.'

The colour left her cheeks, but she still managed to tilt her chin in that defiant way of hers. 'Lord Jarvis? But Adam, he's your ally. Don't I know, only too well, how you would do anything to get his land for your railway?'

'I didn't get his land, Belle,' he interrupted quietly, 'because I didn't keep *my* side of the bargain.'

Her hand flew to her throat.

He was buttoning up his shirt with lean fingers, but his dark eyes never left her face. 'I *did* make a hateful bargain with Jarvis—something for which I shall never forgive myself. I said that I would persuade you into a betrothal, then end it, in return for the land I needed from him. But I found I couldn't carry on with the bargain...'

His words in the carriage drummed through her head. *I would give a great deal, if we could only start again from the beginning, you and I...*

Belle whispered, 'You—ended it?'

'Yes. I tried to tell you that night after Lord Horwich's ball, but you wouldn't listen and how could I blame you?'

He *had* tried to tell her. Oh, Lord, she remembered it now. *What you heard at Lord Horwich's was only a part of it, Belle. Things changed...*

'I told Jarvis it was over and he was angry,' Adam went on. 'He made threats against you.'

She swallowed. 'What kind of threats?'

Adam remembered Jarvis's brutal warnings—how he'd sworn he would bed Belle himself, with force if necessary, then turn her over to his grooms if Adam didn't give up his entire railway project. 'Believe me, you're better not knowing. But I told him in no uncertain terms that you would *not* be leaving my protection.'

She could barely speak as understanding poured through her. 'You ordered me to stay at Bruton Street. You told me I must not go anywhere without one of your men to accompany me...'

'Exactly. Then I realised I had to go to Somerset to deal with some problems for which I believed Jarvis was responsible. But...'

'You couldn't leave me,' she breathed.

'I couldn't leave you, because Lord Jarvis is still in London.'

She sat down, her legs suddenly weak.

'I knew, of course,' he went on, 'that my men in London would be keeping you under close guard. But the thought of Jarvis getting anywhere near you was intolerable.'

And something in his eyes burned so fiercely that Belle felt her ribs aching with the need for air.

She didn't know what to say. She felt shattered with emotion and bleak despair. He'd told her, after Lord Horwich's ball: *It's essential for your own safety that you remain under my protection.* She'd not believed him. She'd flung his words back in his face. Now she put her palms to her temples.

He'd wanted that land—*needed* that land, because he cared for his workers. But he'd lost it now. He'd lost it, because he wasn't prepared to sacrifice *her.* Yet on the road from Chippenham Edward could have killed him; she herself was almost as culpable, for hadn't she ordered Matt to follow them from London and tamper with his curricle, to delay him?

Matt—quite rightly—had been unhappy with the

whole affair. *Messing with those vehicles is a chancy business at best, Mrs Marchmain.*

How could she tell Adam all this now? Her fresh despair must have shown, because Adam sighed and started pulling on his boots. 'I'm going to find the landlord and ask him for a second room.'

'But—he thinks that we're...'

'I'll tell him you have a bad headache after the shock of the accident,' he said abruptly. 'Or something. Anything. We both need our sleep. In the morning—which isn't far off now—we'll try to sort out this mess.'

She nodded, feeling sick inside. 'Very well. But I've been so foolish, Adam. Dear God, you just don't know how foolish.'

She turned away from him suddenly. He saw her trembling.

Adam was capable of immense self-control, but just at this moment his emotions were in tumult. She thought that hideous nightdress protected her. Well, it didn't, because all the time they were talking he could see it softly outlining the surprising fullness of her breasts, the long, slim length of her shapely legs. He was aroused—more than aroused. He was also full of anger at Jarvis and anger at *himself*, for thinking he could get away with accepting Jarvis's blasted proposal without hurting anyone.

'Damn it,' he said aloud. He strode across the room to her. She still had her back to him and was doing something with her long dark hair to tidy it, as women did. He put his hands on her shoulders and turned her round abruptly.

Her face was very pale, her eyes huge and vulnerable; one tear slid like a diamond from beneath her dark lashes. All Adam's anger melted away. He felt, instead, something gripping his insides. Something he couldn't identify, but it burned hotly in his veins.

'Belle,' he said softly. 'Sweetheart. Please forgive me.'

He thought he heard a sob escape her. Quickly he pulled her into his arms, her cheek against his chest, against his heart. He eased his grip just a little and wordlessly she lifted her face to his.

'Adam,' she whispered. 'There's something I have to tell you.'

'What?' His whole body had tensed.

'You seem to think that you were guilty of seducing me.'

Dear God. 'And wasn't I?'

Instead of answering straight away she lifted her face to his, her expression full of anguish. 'Adam. Do you remember our first kiss?'

His fingertips caressed her silken cheek. 'When you came to my house—into the lion's den?' He smiled. 'How could I *forget* our first kiss? But you detested me.'

'No. No, I didn't. In fact, ever since that kiss, Adam, I longed, so much, for—'

'For what, Belle?' Tenderly he cupped her face with his hands.

'For you to make love to me,' she whispered. 'I want you to know that and not to reproach yourself, because…'

'Hush, sweetheart. Hush. Why talk of blame?'

Why talk of anything at all? He was already kissing her. She let out a low moan; her eyes were closed, but her soft, full lips opened so deliciously for him that desire almost got the better of him. He was ready to pull her on to the bed, and…

Slowly. Be sure, this time.

'Adam. Please…'

Was it a protest? An endearment? He couldn't be sure, but he kissed her again and her tongue, like a flame, was mingling with his, drawing him deep. With a groan he lifted her, featherlight, in his strong arms and carried her to the bed. He kissed her again, then started pulling away his own clothes; she was already lifting her nightgown and her breasts fitted his waiting hands so very perfectly.

He bent to kiss them, sucked each nipple in turn, heard her soft sigh as his own arousal throbbed thickly, darkly; he saw how her skin was flushed, her lips swollen with desire.

He'd missed her in his arms. It frightened him how much he'd missed her. He ran one palm slowly over her breasts and down across her abdomen—she quivered with need, moaned his name—and then his fingers were lower, rubbing back and forth at her tender core.

Her dark lashes flew open to reveal the brilliant green of her shimmering eyes. He leaned down to kiss her mouth.

She suddenly shivered. *'Adam.'*

'What, sweetheart?'

She moistened her lips. 'You were hurt. You shouldn't…'

'Ah, but I've made a miraculous recovery,' he breathed. His lips touched her breasts again. Then Belle gasped because he was moving *downwards*. Easing her slender thighs apart. Letting his skilled fingers trail again in the honeyed heat, the silken folds of her most intimate place, stroking her, tantalising her.

She trembled with desire. She shook, at the sensations pulsing through her. Then—dear God, he bowed his dark head and his tongue was there, caressing her furls of flesh, pleasuring her. Bolts of rapture shot through her again and again at the sensual onslaught. She cried out his name; she lifted her hips for him, offering herself. She gloried in the spasms of delight that shook her. 'Adam. Please...'

He was moving up her body to kiss her mouth again, his eyes dark with desire. Taking his body's weight on his bent arms, he eased his hips between her parted thighs so that the head of his erection was poised at her core.

He was kissing her lips again, tasting her, licking her, his tongue lazily thrusting. She clutched his strong shoulders almost helplessly, her body trembling with acute need. He cradled her bottom as his mouth moved down to one breast, suckling it gently at first, then harder until she began to cry out, and his heavy shaft was nudging its way between her slick folds. Finding her, sliding into her, as she opened to him, calling out his name.

'Belle. My beautiful Belle,' Adam was murmuring.

She clenched her legs round him, opening even more to his sweet caresses, finding his rhythm in fresh astonishment and delight. When he withdrew just a little she whimpered with loss, reaching to clutch him to her again; he smiled darkly and kissed her fevered cheek.

He buried his free hand in her raven curls. He drove himself into her again, slowly, deeply, filling her. She had never felt anything so shatteringly beautiful. She was crying out now with his every incredible move, frantically running her hands over his muscled back, needing more.

'Come with me, Belle,' he was murmuring, his lips warm at her throat, his fingers caressing that most sensitive part of her. 'Come with me, sweetheart.'

Wave after wave of ecstasy was building inside her. Her lungs were at the point of bursting. Every part of her strained with need and just when she felt she could bear it no more, the pleasure engulfed her; her world exploded and she soared. And still he was holding her, kissing her, as he drove himself to his own powerful release.

She lay sated in his arms, her heart thundering. Every part of her was stupidly hoping this beautiful dream would last for ever—but like all dreams it was surely made to be shattered.

She could feel him holding her tightly until gradually his breathing became deep and steady. When he was asleep at last, she eased herself away from him and curled herself in the big chair near the embers of the fire so she could just watch him. Remember him.

Pain squeezed her chest. This could never last— but he'd shown her how very beautiful love between a man and a woman could be. She twisted the ring on her finger. The *hateful* ring. Adam thought Belle had loved her husband. He was wrong.

They'd told Belle she'd looked like a fairytale bride on the day of her wedding and indeed that night Belle had felt like a princess, waiting in the bedchamber for her handsome young officer husband to come to her. She'd been so shy. So—anxious.

Because since their betrothal, her doubts had assailed her thick and fast. Oh, Harry Marchmain was witty and charming, but he'd been so very angry when he'd realised how small her dowry was.

Belle, only eighteen years old and an innocent, had no one to talk to, no one to confide in, about her secret worries that Harry was disappointed with her wedding portion and also spent a little too much time drinking with his friends. He was a recruiting officer and unlikely, he'd told her, to see service abroad; she'd been glad, of course, that he wouldn't be caught up in the terrible battles of the Peninsula, but she didn't like the way he and his friends spoke scornfully of the men being sent off to war. She'd even seen him flirting with other women, but she told herself everything would be different, everything would be perfect once they were married.

Disillusionment set in swiftly. On their wedding night, in fact.

Harry had come staggering into the bridal chamber at, oh, it must have been one in the morning. He'd been downstairs with friends and as he pulled her into his arms he smelled of brandy. He'd mauled her with his hands and thrust his tongue into her mouth. Then he'd pushed her away with a snarl.

'Come on, girl, show some eagerness. What in hell's name are you wearing? Looks like a goddamned shroud...'

After unbuttoning his breeches he'd rucked up her nightdress, pulled her legs apart and roughly forced himself into her. She'd tried to tell Harry he was hurting her, but he wasn't listening. She'd felt nothing but pain for a few moments, the fierce pain of male possession. One harsh deep thrust as he spent himself—and it was over. He'd gone to sleep instantly.

He'd tried to take her again the next morning, but she'd been frightened at the thought of more pain and flinched from him. Harry never forgave her after that. 'God, woman,' he'd exclaimed, 'I knew you weren't going to make me rich, but I thought at least I'd get some bed sport out of you!'

Her fault, Belle had thought. She'd learnt to tolerate his lovemaking—but that was all. Other women sighed with pleasure over the mysterious prowess of their husbands, so it must be that she was simply unable to please a man in that way.

Adam had revealed to her the intensity of her own sensuality and she had misjudged him sorely. He had been trying, in this journey to Somerset, to protect her, not harm her; fresh agony seared her as she lay in his sleeping arms, filled with the sweet warmth of his lovemaking, yet totally full of dread.

As it happened, Harry Marchmain's plans had gone wrong. He'd been sent to join Wellington's army in 1814 and during the fighting at Toulouse he'd met his death. God help her, she'd tried to miss him, she'd tried to mourn him, but her marriage had been a disaster.

Now she'd found someone who really cared; someone she loved. But all through the long hours of the night her thoughts were turbulent with despair. *Tell him, you fool. Tell him everything. About your husband, and about Edward and the awful accident to the curricle...* But then she would have to tell Adam about Matt and her own plans to delay him, which had been so stupidly reckless.

Adam drew her to him in his half-sleep and murmured, 'Tell me. Whatever happened to that damned dog?'

Her pulse jolted. 'Oh,' she said lightly, 'he was taken up by some kind passers-by who promised to take him on to Bath for me. I knew that his barking would annoy you, Adam, and I feared you were very badly injured.'

And so the lies begin again. She started to ease herself away from him. 'It's almost seven. I really should get up now.'

'Clock-watching, Belle?' he teased. He was reaching for her sleepily. 'Mmm. How I love the scent of your hair. I can't say I'm sorry about the foolish creature...'

She was already on her feet.

He was fully awake now, raising himself swiftly on one elbow, grey eyes alert.

'You're regretting it already,' he said quietly. 'What happened between us last night.'

She nodded, closing her eyes so she wouldn't have to see his expression.

He, too, was on his feet, pulling on his clothes. He said in a set voice, 'Rest assured, this is the last time you'll be able to claim I made you act against your wishes.'

Oh, God.

'I'll go downstairs,' he said tersely, 'and order breakfast while you finish getting ready. I've still got my meeting to think of.' He looked at her sharply. 'What do you want to do next, Belle? Clearly you want to be rid of me as soon as possible. Shall I take you to your brother's house?'

'No!' Her denial was so emphatic that he raised his dark brows.

'That is,' she went on, flustered, 'I will call on Edward and Charlotte, of course, but I—I have no desire to put them to any inconvenience. If you could take me into Bath, perhaps, to some small hotel, I would be very much obliged.'

He was standing by the door, ready to leave. She felt quite sick with shame and loss. 'I still fear,' he said, 'that Jarvis might seek some kind of revenge on you.'

She met his dark eyes steadily. 'Not if I'm no longer in London. He'll lose interest in me very quickly, I imagine, if I'm living over a hundred miles away.'

'You're considering leaving London permanently? But what about your shop?'

She drew a deep breath. 'I have been thinking,' she blurted out, 'that I have had enough of London and London society. You will be anxious about your investment in the shop, Adam, I know, but Gabby can run it all. She is just as talented a seamstress as me and the clients love her. I will open a small dress shop in Bath, perhaps—after all, it is my home. And then I think it would be perfectly clear to Lord Jarvis that I am no longer under your protection. That, in fact, you have done exactly as he wished and so—and so you might even get your land from him—'

She broke off. She'd suddenly noticed the bruise on his temple and it smote her. Edward had done that. Her own brother. But it might just as well have been her.

His hand was on the door again. His eyes were like narrowed chips of flint. 'Whether you wish it or not,' he said, 'I'll make it clear to Lord Jarvis that you're under my protection wherever you are.'

Then he was gone. Belle felt as if every part of her—every fibre, every nerve ending—was hurting with the kind of pain she hadn't known existed. She sank into a chair by the window and put her head in her hands.

She wanted to lie on the bed where she'd slept in his arms and remember the warmth of those arms. She so desperately wanted to confess to him about Edward stupidly causing his accident and how she'd told Matt to delay his coach. But it was too late. She'd lied too much for him ever to forgive her now.

Adam paced the parlour downstairs. The landlord had served coffee, which was bitter and scalded his throat but also brought a measure of sense back to his tumultuous thoughts. Ensuring the safety of those who worked for him was Adam's first priority now. There'd been sabotage on the railway excavations and his neighbours had been threatened; he should have been there already.

Belle Marchmain wanted nothing more to do with him, that was plain. Every time they made love, she must feel she was betraying her beloved husband all over again. As for the bargain that Adam had made with Jarvis—Belle was right, it was unforgivable, whatever he'd tried to do to make up for it afterwards.

Time, for God's sake, to stop thinking about her. Time to prepare for the last stage of this journey. But at that moment he heard a chaise rattling into the front courtyard, then the voice of a young man talking in some agitation to the landlord outside. There were hurried footsteps and the door burst open. It was Edward Hathersleigh.

Chapter Sixteen

'Mr Davenant,' Belle's brother began. 'I've come to make a confession. I'm very sorry, sir, but it was me who caused your accident yesterday.' Edward's hand was nervously pushing back his dark hair and Adam found his eyes fastened on the puckered childhood scar at his temple.

'I only wanted to stop you,' Edward blurted on, 'because I thought that you were making off with my sister. At first I felt it best to keep quiet about—the accident on the road. But I can't do it, you see, because what I did just wasn't right, though I didn't mean to actually knock you senseless!'

Adam listened to him in stupefaction. Then he heard light footsteps on the staircase. *Belle.* She stood there frozen. Her brother, with his back to the stairs, had not seen her.

'I've come to say I'm sorry I misjudged you so, sir,' Edward went on. 'Thinking that you were after Belle and so forth. She told me yesterday—after the accident, I mean—that you've actually been more than good to her, setting her up in a fine shop in London, with no evil intentions to her whatsoever. And she told me I was quite wrong to stop you as if I was one of the High Toby; in fact, she tore a strip off me, I've never seen her so upset...'

Adam said, 'Your sister's behind you, Hathersleigh.'

And indeed, Belle stood there, looking as though her world was falling apart around her.

Edward let out a gasp of dismay. 'Belle. Belle, I just *had* to tell him...'

Adam said softly to Belle, 'So you knew all along that it was your brother who overturned my curricle.'

Her face was chalk-white. 'Yes.'

Edward stepped forwards again. 'I know I was wrong, sir. But I was only trying to protect my sister's honour!'

'A pity,' said Adam, 'that you didn't consider your sister's honour when you made her prey to every man in town thanks to your gambling debts.' He turned from Edward to Belle. 'We need to talk, you and I. We need to get a few things straight...'

But Belle was already hurrying upstairs. Adam looked at his watch. Damn it. Damn it, he had to get to his meeting today...

Edward was still protesting his apologies. 'Hathersleigh,' Adam said, 'do me a favour and stow it, will you, while I go and sort things with your sister?'

'But sir, my debts! Belle told me that you bought them up. Why haven't you called them in?'

Adam cast him a withering glance. 'If I've shown any clemency at all, Hathersleigh, it's been for your sister's sake, not yours. She's far, far better than you damned well deserve.'

And Adam turned, to take the stairs two at a time.

* * *

Edward went dejectedly out to his chaise, his head bowed so it took him a moment or two to realise that Belle was sitting inside it, with her valise.

'Belle!' he cried. 'How did you get here? What the...?'

'Take me to Bath, Edward. *Please.*'

'But what about Davenant?'

'I think it best,' she said in a voice that was taut with strain, 'if I never see him again. Oh, he's done me no harm, Edward, far from it. And as for *you*—he could enforce that debt and ruin you, any time. He could put you in prison for waylaying his carriage. Do you realise that?'

Edward was white-faced. 'Do you think he will?'

'I rather think that he's more honourable than either of us deserve.' Her voice shook a little. 'Take me to Bath.' *Away, from him.*

If hearts could break, hers was well and truly shattered.

Adam discovered too late that there was a back staircase. By the time he'd got downstairs again he'd realised she'd evaded him and gone off with her blasted brother. Should he go after her? He was pretty damned certain she wouldn't want him to, but he was furious and worried: furious with her, and furious with himself for driving her away from the shelter of his protection, when that protection was the one thing he could offer her now.

He hoped she would be safe at her brother's house, but her brother had the common sense of a flea.

The meeting at the Sawle Down quarry later that day didn't improve Adam's spirits. Shipley had ordered his workmen to press on with the excavations and none could have worked harder, but the weather had turned against them and, since mid-morning, it had been raining steadily.

Adam, on site again at dawn the next morning, found the excavations had been turned overnight into a quagmire. At least the attacks on the neighbouring villages had stopped, thanks to the night guards Adam had ordered Shipley to hire.

But there had been another accident—sabotage, his men suspected. One of the timber supports had given way and a man's leg had been broken in two places. It looked as if Jarvis was seeking other ways to destroy the railway.

Grimly, in spite of the rain that poured down, Adam threw himself into helping his men to clear away rock and soil from the site with an energy and strength that awed all of them. Now that a compromise with Jarvis looked impossible, Adam knew he would soon have to tell his men they would need to take the long and difficult diversion around Jarvis's land.

But then George Shipley came up to him with the news that Lord Jarvis had arrived in Bath that morning.

'His lordship's been heard muttering something about getting even, sir,' said Shipley worriedly. 'You, me and all of us had best be on our guard.'

Swiftly Adam dragged on his coat and flung himself astride his horse, apprehension tightening every sinew. 'I'll be back later, George,' he called. 'There's something—*someone*—I've got to see.'

For too long now he'd been trying to hide from himself the fact that Belle Marchmain had somehow found a place in the heart he'd believed to be cold as ice. Dear heaven, he missed her more every hour that went by. She'd become a vital part of his life, with her clothes and her teasing. He couldn't forget the passionate hours they'd spent in bed together. He couldn't even bear a grudge for the trickery over his journey here—who could blame her for thinking he really might be about to throw her into Jarvis's ugly hands?

She loved her dead husband, he knew; she could never love *him*, especially after the bargain he'd made with Jarvis. But damn it, he had still sworn to protect her. She'd gone with Edward and Adam had assumed she would be safe—but things had changed.

Did Jarvis know that Belle was nearby? And that her foolish brother was now her only protector?

A butler had opened the big door to Hathersleigh Manor two miles outside Bath, but almost immediately Edward himself was there.

'Mr Davenant!' Edward turned to his butler. 'Thank you, Turner, that will be all.' He turned nervously back to Adam once they were alone. 'What can I do for you, sir?'

'I came for your sister,' Adam began, 'not you...'

Just then another door into the hallway opened and a soft voice said, 'Edward?'

Adam saw a wraith—a young woman with pale hair and pale eyes—who whispered, 'Edward. Is it the doctor?'

She went to her husband and clung to his arm, her black gown hanging shapelessly from her thin frame. 'Has he come to tell us our baby is well again? Edward, has he?'

'No, Charlotte.' Adam saw Edward clutch his wife's hands to his in a kind of fierce despair. 'It's not the doctor. It's a man I need to see about some business, my love.'

'My baby,' whispered Charlotte. 'My...'

'Yes, I know, dearest—you'll excuse me a moment, Mr Davenant?' Gently Edward led his wife to another room, leaving Adam dripping water into the hallway. Adam remembered from his last visit how the place wore all the signs of genteel poverty. Everything—the floor tiles, the oak stairway, the plasterwork—had seen far better days. On the wall hung an old map showing the Hathersleigh estate as it had been fifty years ago; Adam turned from it as Edward came back into the hallway.

'I'm sorry,' Edward said. There was utter despair in his eyes 'My wife has not been well since our baby died. Will you come into my study, Mr Davenant?'

Adam indicated his soaking clothes and boots.

'No matter.' Edward opened a door quickly and ushered him into his study, where the desk was strewn with files and sheets of paper.

A mess. The whole estate, a mess. But all Adam wanted was to know that Belle was safe. To tell her— God, what *could* he tell her?—that he was here if she needed him.

Edward was looking at him squarely. 'Have you come to tell me that you're going to prosecute me for causing the accident to your curricle?'

What? 'Good God, no, I just came to... Has your wife had good medical care, Hathersleigh?'

Edward ran his hand through his hair. 'As soon as we realised she was pregnant again we hired an expensive doctor, who promised her that this child would live. She was desperate, Mr Davenant. I—I didn't have enough money to pay him, so I tried the gaming tables and at first it went well...' He gazed at Adam in despair. 'Those debts at White's that you bought up— you'll no doubt want me to repay you.'

'I'll give you time,' said Adam.

Edward looked overcome. 'This is good of you, Mr Davenant; in fact, more than I deserve.'

'I'm not doing this for you, Hathersleigh. I'm thinking of your sister.'

Edward drew a deep breath. 'Yes. Belle told me how you helped her so much with her shop.' He braced his shoulders. 'You'll have to forgive me for saying this, sir. But it's occurred to me that if anyone at all deserves my sister, *you* do.'

Those words of praise tore at Adam's gut. He shook his head bitterly. 'You must know as well as I, Hathersleigh, that she adored her husband and would never look at anyone else.' *Devil take it, a man would have to practically force her into his bed. Just as he, Adam, had done.* 'I've come because I'd actually like to speak to your sister about something rather urgent.'

'But Belle's not here!'

Adam felt the ground shift under his feet. 'Not here?'

'No! She absolutely insisted that I took her to Bath, that day we left you at the inn. She's staying at a small hotel in Trinity Street.'

In Bath. Where Jarvis was heading. Adam started to the door, but stopped because Edward was blocking his way.

'One last thing, Mr Davenant,' Edward said resolutely. 'Something you said just now. Do you really imagine that my sister *loved* that husband of hers?'

Emotion roiled in Adam's gut. 'Didn't she?'

'No, sir. No, she damned well did not!'

And Edward Hathersleigh began to tell Adam—everything.

Once in Bath, Belle had lost no time in looking for a suitable shop for rent and on the fourth day she found one, in a cobbled lane near the river. In anguish she forced herself to stop thinking about Adam and the wrecking of all her impossible dreams.

She would recover, she told herself, as the rain poured down and turned Bath's elegant streets into streams of mud. She might even stop some day imagining every moment that she could hear the husky voice of the man she loved. Might stop imagining that if she turned she would see his impossibly handsome face smiling down at her, in the way that he used to.

She would sell her share of the Piccadilly shop to Adam and Adam would keep Gabby and the rest of the staff on, if he had any sense. Then she would move here quietly and alone. Raw pain clawed at her heart. Yes—*alone*. Adam would be glad to forget her, after the tangled mess she'd made of everything.

The shop she'd found was a quaint little building with bow windows between a confectioner's and a hat shop—empty and a trifle dusty, but it took Belle's quick mind no time at all to mentally furnish it with shelves full of delicious fabric and knots of ribbons. *'Bath is full of old maids and dowds,'* Adam had once said dismissively.

Well, she was weary of thinking about Adam. Of remembering his kisses and his tender yet powerful lovemaking. *He doesn't care, you fool.* In fact, far from caring, Adam would be sick to the back teeth of her and Edward. Bad enough that he'd found out she'd covered up for Edward's stupid trick with the curricle, but if he discovered that she, too, had laid her plans for Matt to stop him reaching his vital meeting, he would despise her with all his being.

Best, by far, that she simply remove herself from Adam's life. But her heart seemed to split in two every time she faced up to the fact that she would never see him again.

One morning when a watery sun was trying to dry up the puddles, Belle walked briskly from her small hotel to the office of the lawyer who'd agreed to handle her purchase of the shop's lease. She thought she had just enough money of her own for the deposit and the lawyer had assured her that he would be able to deal with the sale of her share in her London business.

'You mean,' she'd said, 'that I won't even have to *meet* Mr Davenant?'

'Not at all, Mrs Marchmain,' Mr Cherritt, the lawyer, had told her breezily. 'There will be correspondence, of course—a document or two to sign—but I can handle it all, I assure you.'

So far, so good—but this morning, on her way once more to Mr Cherritt's office in Monmouth Street, something made her stop.

Bath was busy with traffic and pedestrians as usual. But she thought she'd seen a hateful face she knew amongst the crowds. Her heart began to thump rather sickeningly.

She'd started to feel strange sensations these past few days. A little dizziness, if she got up from a chair too swiftly, an unwillingness to eat. It was simply fatigue, she told herself; just as her belief that she'd seen

Lord Jarvis staring after her a moment ago simply must be a product of her tired imagination…

She turned this way and that, trying to find him again. But the familiar-looking figure had disappeared into the throng.

Impossible. Jarvis must still be in London. But she still felt afraid. She'd got so used to *not* being afraid, when Adam was with her. No good thinking of Adam. No good letting the pain of losing him claw at her stomach as it was now. Swallowing down the sudden tightness in her throat, she pressed on and entered her lawyer's office. But Mr Cherritt, normally so friendly, did not look pleased to see her.

'Mrs Marchmain,' he began, 'I regret to say the landlord of the shop you are after has been given some adverse reports about your business history.'

What on earth…? 'I run a successful shop in London's Piccadilly!'

'Maybe. But the landlord understands your previous business failed, due to your inability to pay the rent. He's also been told that custom had dropped away badly after a number of complaints.'

'How? How could anyone know all this?' Belle's voice trailed away as she remembered Adam's warning that Jarvis had been determined to ruin her shop in the Strand. *That hurrying figure she'd seen just now…* Her heart raced then slowed. She said, 'Do you—or this landlord—happen to know Lord Jarvis?'

The lawyer flushed a little. 'That is neither here nor there. Mrs Marchmain, I regret the landlord has decided against letting you have the premises in Bridge Street. And now, if you'll excuse me, I have other clients waiting.'

Cherritt had got up from his desk and was holding the door open. Belle didn't move. 'Lord Jarvis is in Bath, isn't he?' she said steadily. 'Tell me. Tell me where he is staying.'

'My dear madam, how should I know that?'

She wanted to hit him. Then it struck her. *Jarvis would, of course, choose none other than the most expensive hotel in Bath.* 'Is he at the York House Hotel?'

Cherritt said nothing. Belle whirled from the room, banging the door hard behind her.

It was raining heavily now. Unfolding her umbrella, she hurried to the York House Hotel in George Street and entered the spacious reception area where a liveried footman approached her. 'Can I be of assistance, ma'am?'

'Yes,' she began hurriedly, 'I want to know if...'

There was no need to say any more.

'Well, Mrs Marchmain. This is a pleasant surprise.' It was Lord Jarvis, strolling up behind her. Waving the footman away, Jarvis drew close—hatefully close— and was murmuring with a smile, 'Looking for me, were you? Of course, when you and I first met two years ago, I didn't offer you enough—I realise that now. How much did Davenant pay for your services? A generous amount, I guess, together, of course, with that elegant Bruton Street house. But I can do better, you know!'

Shivers ran up and down her spine, but she stood very straight. 'You tried to ruin me, Lord Jarvis,' she breathed. 'And are still trying. But you will not succeed.'

'I think you are a little late—I *have* succeeded. Poor Mrs Marchmain. Such weak judgement. Offering yourself to Davenant, of all people—he is a low-class upstart. But he's rich, isn't he?' Jarvis's face was twisted with malice. 'And money, even dirty money like his, buys power. Buys *women*.'

'Your money is the kind that strikes me as dirty, Lord Jarvis,' Belle said steadily.

A flush appeared slowly in his cheeks as he glanced around the crowded foyer. 'You and I have some talking to do. Come upstairs to my room.'

'I will never—'

'Come upstairs,' he repeated softly, 'or your precious Mr Davenant will be in an even worse mess than he is now.'

She froze. He pointed the way to the big staircase. 'After you. Oh, and I've sent for your things, from that shabby place where you were staying.'

'I will not stay here!'

'You're right, because you're coming with me to London. But first we must talk. In my room. And if I were you I wouldn't worry too much about your reputation. I told that footman I was expecting a whore.'

'You bastard,' Belle said quietly.

He bowed. 'After you, my dear Mrs Marchmain.'

All day Adam had searched desperately for Belle. After finding she'd checked out of the small hotel that Edward had told him of, Adam had set his men to enquire at every other hotel and lodging house in Bath for her. But she was laying low. At least, he hoped she was. The alternative—that Jarvis had found her—did not bear thinking about. After giving up temporarily on his search for Belle, Adam had hunted Jarvis down to the York House Hotel, but was told that he'd set off for London an hour ago in a hired post-chaise.

Then one of Adam's men came to him with news. 'Seems Mrs Marchmain's been visiting a lawyer called Cherritt, Mr Davenant. She was interested in the lease of a shop by the river and asked his advice.'

Adam knew Cherritt. Knew he'd worked in the past for Jarvis, damn it.

It was pouring with rain again by the time Adam reached Cherritt's premises. A clerk in the reception area flinched at his rain-soaked, formidable figure, then blustered and said the lawyer was busy. Adam pushed past him and went straight into Cherritt's office.

The little lawyer jumped to his feet like a nervous rabbit when he saw who it was. Adam wasted no time.

'I believe you've recently had business with a lady from London. Mrs Marchmain.'

Cherritt shook his head. 'I can't say I recognise the name *at all*, Mr Davenant, sir...'

Adam drew nearer. 'I think you're lying to me, Cherritt.' Then he saw it. A document lying on a sheaf of other papers. Cherritt was already grasping for it, but Adam was quicker by far.

It had Belle's name on it and an address in Bridge Street.

'Sit down again,' said Adam. 'And tell me what exactly's been happening.' He was already glancing quickly through the document. 'This refers to the lease of a shop. Is Mrs Marchmain going ahead with this transaction?'

'No!'

'Why not?' Adam was still on his feet, hands resting on the edge of Cherritt's desk so his formidable figure leaned menacingly over the little lawyer. Outside, the rain drummed steadily on the windows and the very candles in the room seemed to shake with the force of Adam's scarcely controlled emotions. 'Tell me,' Adam breathed. 'Tell me everything you know about Jarvis and Mrs Marchmain, or I can make life very unpleasant for you—understand? I know damn well you've been acting for Jarvis. I know damn well—as I'm sure you do—that Jarvis has been breaking the law by sabotaging my land and workers. I can break you, Cherritt.'

'That particular shop is no longer available, sir,' Cherritt stuttered, 'at least not to Mrs Marchmain—because Lord Jarvis gave the landlord some information that made him halt the transaction.'

'Do you have any idea where Mrs Marchmain is now?'

'She—she's gone to London, sir! With Lord Jarvis...'

This time Cherritt cowered from Adam's formidable figure, from his clenched fists. 'You *knew* about this?' grated Adam. 'By God, he's as good as abducted her and you stood by?'

'Sir. Sir.' Cherritt was trembling. 'She went with him quite willingly, sir. It will soon be a matter of common knowledge, I believe, that—that she has agreed to be Lord Jarvis's mistress!'

The blood pounded in Adam's temples.

'Money will buy any woman, sir,' said Cherritt, anxiously trying to appease him. 'And she is, after all, only a dressmaker—'

Adam was round the desk and on him, his big hands round Cherritt's throat. 'You shouldn't have said that, Cherritt,' he said softly. 'You most definitely should *not* have said that.'

Cherritt quaked. 'Sir. Mrs Marchmain anticipated that you might call on me,' he stuttered. 'And I have a letter for you.'

He was already bringing it out from a drawer in his desk. Adam broke the seal and read it in dawning disbelief.

Mr Davenant.
I cannot repeat strongly enough that I want noth-
ing more to do with you. The money my brother
owes you will soon be repaid. My share in the
London shop is yours also. Now that I am under
Lord Jarvis's kind protection, I have better things
to do with my days and nights than to sew clothes.
Mrs Belle Marchmain.

No. *No.* Adam could not believe it. It might be
Belle's writing, but...

He put the letter down, breathing hard. Cherritt's
small eyes were flickering nervously between the letter and Adam's face.

'Cherritt,' said Adam, 'it strikes me that you know
rather a lot about Lord Jarvis's business affairs, don't
you?'

'H-his lordship is simply one of my many clients—'
The stuttering little lawyer broke off as Adam gave
him a warning look.

'Lock the door, so we're not interrupted. Then sit
down again. Do you have Jarvis's private papers here—
his deeds and everything else?'

'Yes!' Cherritt positively quivered with fear. 'Yes,
but...'

'Shut up. Where the hell are they?'

'I—in there.' Cherritt pointed with shaking fingers
to a door at the back of his office. 'They're locked in
a safe.'

'Then damn well get them out,' said Adam, settling
himself in a chair on the other side of Cherritt's desk.
'All of them. Or you're finished. In every way possible.'

Chapter Seventeen

On her journey to London with Jarvis Belle had been sick, literally sick, and that was what had saved her. Nausea had racked her as she was shaken in Jarvis's rough carriage and during their one overnight stop at an inn he'd made no attempt to force his attentions on her.

But she wouldn't be sick for ever. And she could not forget the agreement Jarvis had wrung from her in Bath. In the private sitting room of the York House Hotel he'd paced to and fro, his pale eyes never leaving her, while she stood defiant, refusing the chair he'd offered.

'I will not rest until Davenant is humiliated,' he told her softly. 'Suddenly that's become even more important to me than stopping his damned railway. Oh, I can carry on hindering his workers. Accidents, landfalls, faulty supplies—it can all drag on and on—and no one will trace it back to me. But he's as stubborn as me—he'll kill himself sooner than give up on his railway.'

'That is because he *cares*,' declared Belle. 'About his workers and their families.'

'Then he's a damned idiot,' said Jarvis curtly. 'As I said—building a railway's a dangerous business. And

Davenant's in the thick of it—did you realise? He's out there day after day with his men, trying to get those rails laid before the autumn rains really set in.'

Belle struggled to stay calm. 'Why are you telling me all this?'

He suddenly pointed a finger at her. 'Because it's up to you now,' said Jarvis softly. 'Davenant's been fool enough to fall for you, hasn't he?'

'No!' Her cry was from the heart. 'Absolutely not, I assure you—nothing could be further from the truth...' She was fighting the sudden, overwhelming tightness that had clenched her lungs.

'Good try,' he sneered. 'But all of London knows that stone-hearted Davenant has fallen for a little dressmaker... No, don't try lying and protesting, my pretty, you're too clever for that. Now, as I said, I'm getting a bit tired of Davenant's obstinate ways. And I might have to take drastic action against him very soon, in the form of a convenient accident.'

No. Dear God, no.

'But there *is*,' went on Jarvis, 'an alternative.' He paused, letting his eyes run over her in a way that made her feel cold to her stomach. 'I'll let him proceed with his railway without any further interference. I might even sell him that damned land, so he doesn't have to make an expensive detour around my boundaries. But only if you, my dear, will consent to be my mistress.'

What could she have done, other than say *yes*? During the journey to London she'd kept Jarvis at bay with her travel sickness; she hadn't needed to feign it either.

He'd threatened Adam's life and Belle could not bear it. She knew everything was over between herself and Adam, knew he could never forgive her for her stupidity in so many ways. But she knew also she would always love him.

He was proud and honourable. He'd been a wonderful, tender lover and proved himself to be a man who cared, really cared for all the workers who depended on him.

That Jarvis would carry out his threat to injure or even kill Adam by means of a so-called accident she didn't doubt. She'd heard Adam mention the mishaps that were already occurring as his men struggled to lay the new railway across difficult terrain. She also knew how Jarvis was accustomed to paying to get the law on his side.

No hope, no hope, the noise of Jarvis's carriage wheels taunted her as they retraced the journey she'd made with Adam. She would never see Adam again and perhaps it was as well, for he would think her beneath contempt once he'd read that letter she'd written.

In London Jarvis installed her in a drab little house somewhere in Whitechapel. They'd arrived there as darkness was falling, and though she strove to recognise some detail of the dirty, cobbled lane where his coach stopped, he'd gripped her arm and led her into the house so quickly that she had no chance to find out any more.

Adam would never find her here, she thought desperately. Then remembered—why would he *want* to? He would know she was Jarvis's from her letter. He wouldn't ever understand why. He would think himself well rid of her indeed.

For the first day she didn't move from her bedchamber and barely spoke to the two servants she saw, a surly maid called Tibbs and a man called Harris who had foul breath and a face that was as battered as an ex-boxer's. There was no bolt on her bedroom door so she had to suffer their frequent intrusions as they brought her food and other necessities. Most of the time she just sat by the window to gaze at the narrow but busy lane below—it was somewhere off Botolph Street, she guessed—and watched the people and horses go by.

Early in the evening she tiptoed downstairs to the front door, only to find it locked. And burly Harris was there almost instantly, wiping his nose with his sleeve.

'Now, I do hope you're not thinkin' of leaving us, my pretty,' he'd leered.

She'd hurried back upstairs and slammed her door. *You fool, Belle.* And how could she even think of escaping after the threats Jarvis had made against Adam?

The worst—the very worst of it was that Adam would never know that she'd done all this for him.

Two days after bringing her here Jarvis came up the narrow little staircase to see her. 'How are you feeling, Mrs Marchmain?' he asked, removing his hat and gloves.

'Sick at the sight of you,' she said.

He laughed. 'Indeed, you're looking pale. And your clothes—dear me, is this the Belle Marchmain who used to dazzle society with her daring attire?'

The maid Tibbs had shown her a wardrobe full of new gowns; Belle had deliberately chosen the drabbest of them and covered her shoulders with a grey shawl. She looked up at him steadily. 'My former life is over, Lord Jarvis. You must realise that.'

'It's by no means over,' he answered softly. 'You see, you're going to attend a party I'm giving in a week's time, and I intend to present you as my mistress. Yes,

London's quiet now the Season's over, but any event of mine will muster up quite enough prestigious guests to serve my purpose. And I can't think of a better way for the news of our happy union to reach Davenant in Somerset.'

Something in her expression must have altered when he spoke Adam's name because Jarvis leaned forwards to touch her cheek and laughed. 'Yes, your hero's still far away. Perhaps you hoped he might come running here looking for you? I'm afraid not.'

He reached out to touch her again, but she jumped back and spat out, *'Don't.'*

His mouth thinned. 'Oh, by the way,' he said. 'There was a nasty rock fall the other day above the valley where your former lover's labourers are digging and some stones missed Davenant himself by inches. Accidents, these accidents.'

'You said you'd *stop* this. You said you'd let him have the land he needs!'

'Oh, indeed. Once you're mine—once you're clearly, openly mine—I'll let him have his land at a price. Change your mind and he's dead.'

When he'd gone she sat down again because her legs were shaking. Jarvis hadn't tried anything more than touching her yet, but surely it couldn't be long. She pressed her hands to her cheeks.

For how many nights, how many weeks, would she have to endure—oh, God—Jarvis's possession? Not long, she suspected, her heart squeezing painfully against her ribs. Not long at all—once she told Jarvis she was pregnant.

It was true. After relinquishing all hope of pregnancy during her brief years of marriage, the miracle had happened. And Adam, her baby's father, would be convinced after reading her letter that she'd surrendered herself to Jarvis.

She would survive this, she *must*, for her baby's sake. But sometimes despair all but overwhelmed her. Jarvis called daily at the house in Whitechapel. If Belle tried to protest at her captivity or complain about the watch Tibbs and Harris kept on her, he would raise his eyebrows and say, 'I'd imagine Davenant will be working on one of the most dangerous sections of his railway excavations today. Gunpowder, rock falls—so very many risks, so many mishaps that might befall him.'

She guessed that Jarvis's forthcoming party—her first appearance in society with him—would mark a new stage of their horrifying relationship. He'd already told her that she must appear happy and relaxed at his side. After that, she feared very much that he would feel entitled to do whatever he wished with her.

The sullen maid Tibbs had clearly been ordered to make Belle appear more presentable, but because Belle had lost weight and was pale with inactivity, every item of clothing Jarvis had provided for her looked lifeless and dull. Jarvis, exasperated, told her he was ordering a *modiste* to attend on her. He wouldn't let Belle leave the house, so Madame Monique Tournier arrived to see her three days before the party with lengths of fabric and various fashion illustrations.

She was dark, French and saturnine. Jarvis seemed impatient as he led her into Belle's sitting room.

'Let her brighten you up, for God's sake,' he said to Belle. 'Or you know what will happen to a mutual acquaintance of ours.'

Belle couldn't help herself. 'Is he still…?'

Jarvis snapped to Madame Tournier to wait outside, then said, 'He's still working on his damned railway, yes. Coming up to the most dangerous stage now, when they have to lower the rails into place. And, by the way, he's still not given a second thought to your disappearance from Bath. But I really do want him to read in the news sheets about you looking radiant and happy—with me.'

Belle whispered, 'For how long do I have to endure this hateful captivity?'

Jarvis's lip curled. 'We'll discuss all that after the ball.'

She gazed at him. 'If you let anything happen to him,' she said steadily, 'I'll kill you. I mean it.'

He laughed. 'So you'd hang for him? I think not.' He stormed from the room.

Belle sat down, her trembling hands folded across her still-flat stomach.

Madame Tournier came bustling back in and Belle allowed herself to be measured and consulted over the fabric samples simply because it was easier than resisting. Just as the dressmaker was leaving she said to Belle in her expressionless way, 'You will have to come to my shop, *madame*, for the ballgown to be completed. I can make it up from these measurements, yes—but there are certain adjustments for which a final fitting on my premises is essential.'

'But Lord Jarvis won't allow—'

'You have to come on the afternoon of the ball in three days' time,' repeated Madame Tournier flatly. 'I will speak to milord.'

Just for a moment Belle's thoughts whirled. *A chance for escape?* But she was a hostage; the life of the man she loved was at stake, and the cruellest thing of all was that Adam would never know it.

* * *

The next day when Jarvis visited her as usual a little after midday he said, 'I gather you made some progress with the dressmaker. She says she needs you to go to her shop on the day of my ball for a final fitting.'

'And you'll let me out of here?' said Belle scornfully. 'Aren't you afraid that I'll tell Madame Tournier I'm your prisoner?'

Jarvis's pale eyes slid over her. 'She's in my pay and asks no questions,' he said. 'Anyway, you know what will happen to Davenant if you do anything stupid. Besides, I'll send Harris with you. He won't let you out of his damned sight.'

That was true; Harris followed her everywhere, his eyes mentally undressing her. Belle said bitterly, 'I can believe that.'

'As long as you behave during your outing, I'll tell Harris to restrain himself.' Jarvis's lip curled. 'If not—well, I think you know what the consequences will be.'

Belle braced herself against the sickness that shook her as she remembered Jarvis's long-ago words—*As a young widow you must be quite desperate for male companionship. I'll enjoy watching. I promise you won't be bored...*

Jarvis was already leaving. 'By the way—' he turned back '—I've ordered Madame Tournier to prepare a gown for you that's as flamboyant as anything you used to wear for Davenant. Only this time—' his voice was a lethal purr '—you'll be at *my* side. And I want news of your devotion to me to spread around town and further.'

* * *

On the day of the party Jarvis's carriage arrived for her at midday and the foul-breathed Harris bundled her aboard.

She heard him speak to the driver, expressing surly surprise. 'Who the hell are you? I don't know you, do I?'

'I'm new.' The coachman's voice was equally gruff. 'Usual man's ill.'

Harris curtly gave him directions, then sat opposite Belle and didn't take his lecherous eyes off her.

And for once, Belle didn't give a damn about Harris, because her mind was racing. Harris hadn't known the driver. But she thought, oh, she'd thought just for one wild moment that she recognised that voice…

Her heart wouldn't stop thumping. At Covent Garden the traffic was at a standstill because two carriages had collided—she could see it from her window—and coachmen and bystanders were getting embroiled in a noisy argument. Harris, cursing, called out to their driver to find some other way. The driver retorted, 'I'm doing my best. Drive the thing yourself if you think you can do better.'

Wild, surging hope riveted Belle. *Matt's voice.* It was Matt, just as she'd dared to hope.

Harris, swearing loudly, was already getting out. 'I'll give that damned fellow a piece of my mind as well as the feel of my fist.' He turned back to Belle. 'If you move from there you're finished—understand?'

Harris had thrust his way into the crowd of pedestrians and was elbowing his way to the driver. Belle, gazing tensely out of the window, heard him give an exclamation of angry surprise—and realised Harris was in the grasp of two burly constables.

'Make way, ladies and gents!' the constables were calling to the crowd. 'Just caught a pickpocket here— make way, while we take him to gaol where he belongs!'

Then the door on the other side of the carriage swung open just as it started to move and someone leaped in. 'It's all right, Belle,' a husky male voice said. 'It's all right.'

Adam. It was *Adam*. Her heart was suddenly full of joy—joy she thought she would never feel again. 'Adam—how...?'

'Those two constables are my men.' He smiled, settling on the seat beside her. 'And Matt is driving the carriage.'

'I knew it!' She was in his arms. 'I recognised his voice. But Adam, how did you...?'

'Find you? We've been searching for days. Jarvis was clever; he went to all sorts of lengths to conceal his visits to you, but he made a mistake. You see, Madame Tournier knows Gabby and she told her about you. But first things first.' He was holding her tightly; his eyes were full of fierce tenderness. 'Has Jarvis hurt you? Have any of his men hurt you?'

Oh, God, he looked divine. Her heart was thudding wildly at the sight of him. He wore a rough grey coat over breeches and riding boots; his neckcloth was rumpled, his thick dark hair just a little untidy and an unshaven beard darkened his jawline. No more the suave man about town. But—the look in his eyes. The raw *emotion* in his voice.

'I'm all right,' she said quickly. 'For some reason he's not touched me yet, Adam.'

'Good.' His voice was grim. 'I think he knew I'd kill him if he so much as harmed a hair on your head.

I guessed he held you prisoner, but he denied it, and I couldn't damn well prove anything until Madame Tournier appeared. I've got him now. But Belle, why did you leave Bath with him?'

'He said—' she tried to keep her voice steady '—he said he'd arrange an accident on your railway. He threatened you'd be badly hurt. He made me write that letter—'

'I guessed as much.'

'And he said he would let you have that land you need so badly if I stayed with him.'

'You would do that, for me and my railway?' he asked wonderingly.

'For you and your workers, Adam. And I've been so stupid. I've got to tell you what I did...'

He was still holding her. Now his fingers touched her cheek. 'Tell me if you must.'

'I got Matt to follow us to Bath. I'd told him, on the second day, to try to delay your journey.'

He put one finger to her lips. 'I know,' he said quietly. 'Edward told me.'

'Edward?'

'Edward told me a good deal. I'd been hateful to you, Belle—and I damned well deserved your plotting.'

'No. No,' she cried distractedly. 'I've been such a fool.'

He held her face between his big, warm hands and gazed down into her eyes. There was something in his expression Belle had never seen before and it fractured her heart. But she mustn't hope. Hope was cruel.

'You were going to give yourself to Jarvis. For me,' he said quietly.

'I think he would have tired of me very quickly.'

She was beginning to shake, try though she might to hold herself steady, to be strong.

'Belle,' he said. His arms were around her again. 'You're not going back to him ever, believe me.'

'But—'

He touched her lips with his finger. 'Listen. I have one last favour to ask you. Do you feel strong enough to come to Lord Jarvis's party tonight—with *me*?'

'To Jarvis's party?' she breathed. Her eyes were dark with emotion in her pale face. 'But how…?'

'He sent me an invitation. I imagine he hoped to see my face when I saw you standing at his side. Belle, will you do it?'

Slowly—incredibly—she began to smile. He'd always thought her beautiful, but *now*…

She looked radiant. 'Mr Davenant and guest,' she breathed. Her eyes sparkled suddenly. 'Adam, I don't see how I can refuse!'

He held her tightly and kissed her forehead. 'My brave, brave Belle. I promise you—everything is going to be all right.'

Despair engulfed her once more. All right? No— it could never be all right. She clamped down on the tight pain in her chest.

She ought to tell him. She ought to tell him right now, but she couldn't, not when he was holding her in his arms and his face was so full of caring. What would he say? How could she explain her own stupidity this time?

She had told him quite plainly that she was unable to bear children. And oh, what an old, tedious female trick that was, to entrap the man you wanted. If Adam had desired a family, he'd have married a suitable bride years ago. But he didn't, and how his beautiful eyes would narrow with cynicism—disgust, even—when she told him she was pregnant.

If she told him.

The carriage was swinging round towards Piccadilly; she turned to him, questioning. 'Adam, where...?'

'We're going to your shop, for a ballgown for tonight,' he told her. 'Madame Tournier's been paid for her efforts, but we don't want her gown. We don't want anything Jarvis has had a hand in. Meanwhile—Gabby's been busy, sweetheart.'

Adam saw her into her shop, then told her he was going with Matt to return Jarvis's carriage and horses. 'I'm not having him accusing me of theft,' Adam said. 'But finding his carriage outside his house with no driver, no Harris and no *you* will give Jarvis plenty to think about.' He hesitated. 'Belle, we've got so much to discuss. And that's what we'll do—after tonight.'

He took her hand and kissed it in the old, familiar way that tore at her already overburdened heart. Then he was gone and Gabby was there, hugging her; they laughed and exclaimed together.

'Oh, *madame*! Monsieur Davenant came here days ago looking for you! He's had his men searching all over London—he was so very anxious! We are overjoyed that you're together again!'

Something clutched at Belle's throat. 'I don't think it's for long, Gabby.' She wondered how much to tell her. 'I've been so foolish.'

'You *still* think he does not care for you?' Gabby looked astonished. 'Then—wait here, *madame*!'

A few moments later Gabby came out of the back room, carrying a frothy, gorgeous ball dress. 'For you,' she breathed, touching it tenderly. 'Yesterday Mr Davenant told us to put all else aside, so *this* was ready.'

'*Oh.*' Belle once more felt that lump in her throat. 'It's so beautiful.' The puff-sleeved gown was of ivory silk, its full skirt adorned with tiers of Vandyke lace trimmed with tiny turquoise satin roses and pearls.

'There is more, *madame.*'

Indeed, there were small roses made of ivory satin to wear in her hair, long kid gloves, ivory satin pumps and an exquisite pearl necklace. Gabby laid them all out for her joyously—then suddenly realised there were tears in Belle's eyes.

'There, there, he loves you, I'm sure!' Gabby was offering her a handkerchief and Belle scrubbed fiercely at her eyes.

Love her? No. He'd rescued her from Jarvis, yes—but he was still using her, by taking her to the party tonight. And why not? She'd stupidly destroyed anything he might have felt for her. He was thinking of far more important things than her: his quarry, his vital railway, his hundreds of workers and their families. Whereas she'd mistrusted him and insulted him, never realising how honourable, how brave he was, until it was too late.

After tonight—what would happen then?

She wouldn't let him kiss her. She must not even let him touch her again. Instead she would ask him if he would help her open a small shop in Bath and she wouldn't tell him her secret, ever. She simply could not expect him to provide for a child he had not wanted; a child he would feel he had been deceived into fathering.

She would never see him again. The thought was intolerable, but bear it she must.

* * *

Joseph and two more of Adam's men had come with a carriage to take Belle to Bruton Street and Gabby accompanied her, to dress her. Being back at that lovely house simply tore at Belle's heart, because everything reminded her of those weeks with Adam and their wonderful, passionate lovemaking. The sphinxes and the gilded Egyptian tables were still there—oh, Lord, how had Adam tolerated her wilfulness?—and Lennox and the servants were warm in their welcome. Belle felt that she did not deserve any of their kindness.

'We are delighted to see you here once more, ma'am,' said Lennox with a grave bow.

Even though she'd threatened to dress the poor man in purple. Belle smiled, but there was a stupid lump in her throat. 'Thank you, Lennox.' *But I doubt I'll be here for very long.*

Gabby must have spent almost two hours adjusting Belle's gown, arranging the satin roses in her dark curls and chattering nineteen to the dozen—which was as well, because Belle's emotions were in such tumult she could hardly speak. Gabby had only been silent once, and that was when she was starting to lace up Belle's stays. Almost instinctively, Belle had put out her hand. *'No.'*

Gabby stopped, frowning.

'Not too tight, Gabby.'

Gabby's brown eyes widened. *'Madame.* Oh, *madame,* you are…'

'Yes, Gabby, I am,' breathed Belle. 'But—I do not want Mr Davenant to know. Do you understand?'

'You are going to tell him later? As a surprise?'

Belle put her hands on her friend's arms. 'Gabby. I beg you to say *nothing.* Leave it to me. Please.'

Gabby gave a Gallic shrug. 'I promise.'

* * *

Adam called for her at eight, looking sensational. He wore black and his snow-white cravat emphasised the perfection of his hard cheekbones, his chiselled jaw. He looked—he *was*, quite simply—the man of her dreams. She remembered first seeing him on his big horse on Sawle Down that sunny March day, and her heart turned over with such pain that she had to catch her breath. If only she'd known what kind of a man Adam Davenant really was. If only...

As he handed her into the carriage, his dark eyes were full of something that made her insides melt. 'You look beautiful,' he said quietly as he helped her to arrange her full skirts. 'Are you ready?'

She nodded, with a smile. 'Fie, Mr Davenant, this is just like old times!'

'Almost,' he agreed, tenderly tucking her gossamer shawl round her shoulders.

Yes, she was ready for Lord Jarvis's ball. She felt she could face anything with this man at her side. But afterwards? Oh, it was going to take all her courage to face *afterwards*. When she would have to tell him she was leaving him.

Chapter Eighteen

Belle would always remember that party as a kaleidoscope of vivid pictures, a shimmering sequence of scenes darkly threaded with danger, because it took place at the home of her enemy Lord Jarvis.

As at any social event, she was aware of the music and dancing and loud chatter; aware, too, of the myriad wax candles and the scents of over-rich food and wine filling room after room in Jarvis's ornate mansion in Grosvenor Square. A mirage of opulent splendour in which—for her—the only reality, the only safety, was Adam's presence at her side.

Their arrival together caused a sensation. Adam ordered the footman to announce both their names, at which the great entrance hall, busy though it was, fell absolutely silent. As Lord Jarvis came towards them people moved back to watch. He'd fixed a thin smile to his face, but his voice was etched with vitriol and Belle drew instinctively closer to Adam.

'Davenant,' Jarvis said. 'You've been busy, I believe, one way and another. And—Mrs Marchmain.' He made a low bow, then turned back to Adam. 'You and I, Davenant, have a few matters of business to discuss.'

'Indeed we do,' said Adam smoothly. 'Here? Now? I'm all yours.'

Something in Jarvis's eyes flickered and he looked almost afraid as he glanced round his crowded hall. 'You shall *never* get my land for your damned railway,' he hissed in a low voice. 'Not now this woman here has broken our agreement.' But because people were still gathered around them, staring and whispering, he said, 'Perhaps later, Davenant, don't you think? Business can be so tedious.' He bowed his head tightly. 'I'm so very glad you could both avail yourselves of my hospitality.'

Adam and Belle were the sensation of the evening. The gossip had been rife, clearly about their departure to Bath, and now the tongues were wagging furiously. Enviously.

'Mr Davenant—so handsome! And he's with his widow again, Mrs Marchmain—my dears, did you ever see anything like her gown? It's incredibly pretty, and clearly she still has Mr Davenant tightly in her clutches...' The gossiping dowagers fluttered their fans; the younger women looked on enviously because Belle was easily the most beautiful woman there.

She knew, because Adam had told her so. It was he who made her beautiful, he whose presence kept her strong in their enemy's house. The two of them danced—oh, he was such a wonderful dancer, his hand at her waist making her want to melt into the lean length of him. Afterwards, as they circulated, Belle drew strength from him just being at her side. But all the time—all the time she felt the tension building in the room; saw how Jarvis kept glancing at them, like a serpent ready to spring for its prey.

The crisis, when it came, was sudden. Adam was

surrounded by a group of bankers and London businessmen who were eager to know about the progress of his railway; Jarvis kept casting him poisonous looks, but Adam ignored him.

At last Jarvis barged into the men gathered round Adam. 'Gentlemen,' he said, 'I'm going into supper. Coming with me?' He tried a sickly smile. 'I fancy that in this corner of the room the smell of quarry dust taints the air.'

There was a shocked silence. Belle felt herself freeze; then Adam's hand touched her gloved arm lightly, reassuringly. Keeping her by him.

'Jarvis,' he said smoothly, 'I've got something here that may interest you.'

'If it's a matter of business,' sneered Jarvis, 'save it for your quarry workers and country rustics.' But he looked afraid and his skin was sweaty beneath the flush of alcohol.

Adam said coolly, 'What I've got is quite fascinating. So fascinating I think I'll explain it to everybody. It's a document showing that the land I've been after for my railway never belonged to you at all.'

'*What?* You...' Jarvis had lunged towards him, but the cluster of men who'd gathered round Adam held him back, saying, 'Steady, Jarvis. Let Davenant have his say.'

Adam spoke quietly and calmly, but every single word filled the stark silence that had fallen.

'You and your lawyer Cherritt,' said Adam to Jarvis, reaching in his pocket, 'swindled the Hathersleigh estate out of that piece of land I need for my railway, many years ago. I have here the original map showing it belongs to Edward Hathersleigh. When Edward's father died, your lawyer Cherritt substituted a forged plan in the deeds and Edward—who was only a child when he was orphaned—had no idea where the exact boundaries of his estate truly lay.'

'No!' Jarvis had lunged forwards; several of Adam's colleagues held him back.

Adam gave Jarvis a look of narrow-eyed contempt, then coolly began to unfold the document. People gathered round to look.

'Edward Hathersleigh,' Adam went on, 'has agreed to sell the land to me. Care to face prosecution for your part in this fraud, Jarvis?'

Jarvis was shaking off the arms of those who held him, but he looked white and afraid. 'Your little widow's put you up to this,' he said loudly. 'She sold herself to you, Davenant. She's a whore and you've made all this up because you can't stand the way polite society has always looked down on you and your low-class family—'

'If you're an example of polite society, Jarvis,' interrupted Adam, 'you can keep it.'

And with one bunched fist he knocked Jarvis flying across the floor.

People applauded. People gathered round and cheered. Adam took Belle's hand and drew her very close. He gave an elegant bow to the delighted crowd. 'Ladies, gentlemen,' he announced, 'your sentiments are much appreciated, both by me and by my fiancée— the extremely beautiful Belle Marchmain, whom I hope to make my wife in the very near future!'

He kissed her full on the lips and the room was filled with happy sighs and murmurs of approval. He kissed her so thoroughly that her mind was in a daze, her insides melting at the honeyed warmth of his lips, the heat of his strong body.

Time enough. Time enough for her to shatter this beautiful dream and face reality. It would be over as soon as he realised the full extent of her unwitting deception.

The next few moments were filled with the kind of happiness she knew could never last. Amidst a storm of congratulations from well-wishers, Adam held her tight round her waist with one hand while with the other he seized a bottle of champagne and a glass from a nearby waiter. Then, his dark eyes still dancing, he led her outside and down the steps to where his coach was waiting, with Joseph up on the driver's seat.

'To us,' he said softly once he'd swept her inside the carriage. He pulled out the cork and poured the foaming liquid into the glass.

'Not for me,' she said quickly as he offered it to her. She forced a smile. 'Not just yet. Adam, tell me. Tell me how you came to learn about the land.'

He drank some champagne himself and told her, in a voice of taut triumph, how he'd seen an old map at Edward's house.

'You went there?' she broke in.

'I did,' he said softly. 'Looking for you, Belle. And I learned a good deal.'

'Edward's poor wife…' Something in his gaze was making her feel shaky.

'Yes. I met Edward's wife, and that wasn't all.' Adam's eyes were steadily on hers as the coach rattled along. 'Your brother told me about your marriage, Belle.'

'He shouldn't have. He had no *right*!' She was distressed now.

'I'm most glad he did,' Adam said gravely. 'We'll talk about your husband later. To finish my answer to your question—I tackled Cherritt about you in Bath, and I realised he was in Jarvis's pay. So I—*persuaded* him to show me Jarvis's deeds...'

And that was how he knew, marvelled Belle. As Adam's fine carriage swung down the street she listened to him with wonder and relief and genuine joy, because Edward had been able to help him. Edward had given him the land gladly, Adam told her, in return for the cancellation of his gambling debts, and now the Somerset railway line was forging ahead—indeed, would reach the canal within days.

She loved hearing him talk about it all; loved seeing his animated face, noting every detail of those dearly familiar features which she'd once thought so hard, so cynical. *He'd* not changed at all, but she had. She'd finally seen him for the man he truly was—honest and brave and in every way noble.

She'd refused champagne, but she grew heady drinking in everything about him as he talked to her in the coach: the thickness of his dark hair, which he'd rumpled with one careless hand; the beginnings of the stubble darkening his chiselled jawbone; the beauty of his strongly made body, accentuated rather than hidden by his formal attire.

Too late, she thought wildly, pain clawing at her insides. She'd misjudged him and insulted him from the fateful day she'd met him, on Sawle Down.

They'd arrived in Bruton Street. He got out first and was helping her down. Desire and despair burned her up in equal measure.

'Will you allow me to come in with you?' he asked, his eyes searching hers.

Her heart shook. She wanted to throw herself into

his arms, and tell him everything. 'I noticed earlier that the rooms are still full of sphinxes and sarcophagi.' She smiled. 'You enter at your own peril!'

He grinned—a gorgeous, wide, white smile—and went with her laughing up the steps. Lennox let them in, but very swiftly made himself scarce.

Belle took off her shawl and fiddled with her gloves. She felt sick again. He'd told everyone at Lord Jarvis's that he was going to make her his wife. Even if he meant it, he'd soon change his mind when he learned everything.

She had her back to him as she laid her mantle across one of the hideous sphinxes.

He came up behind her, his hands resting warmly on her shoulders, and said, huskily in her ear, 'Belle. May I stay with you tonight?'

She stood very still in her gorgeous ballgown, her heart thumping painfully against her ribs. 'Adam,' she said quietly. 'What you said earlier, about marrying me. I know you never wanted marriage, at any cost, and believe me, I quite *understand*…'

He lifted her hand and kissed it, his eyes burning into her. 'Don't you want to marry me, Belle?'

Oh, dear God. His lips sent blood pounding to her heart. *More than anything. Oh, Adam, my love.* 'It's not a question of that,' she said desperately. 'It's that I know you never wanted to be tied down, ever.'

'That was because I'd never met anyone like you.' He was still holding her hand, still fingering her sensitive palm.

'But…' she was floundering now '…you didn't want commitment. Children. You told me so.'

'Children?' He looked at her, his eyebrows slightly

gathered. 'Belle. My dear, practical Belle—why this sudden interrogation?'

She drew a deep, agonised breath. 'Adam...I'm pregnant.'

The hand that still enclosed hers had gone very still.

'It's true,' she went on in a low but desperate voice. 'I'm quite sure. And it's my fault, because I told you I could never have children. I truly believed it—in fact, the doctor told me so when I'd been married a year—but it seems he was wrong—*I* was wrong, so I've deceived you, yet again...'

He was frowning.

'So I've made my plans,' she went on steadily. 'I shall go to live in Bath and set up a shop there. Bath is such a lovely place to bring up a child, close to the countryside and—'

He gathered her in his arms, holding her close. 'My God. Don't *I* get any say in all this?'

She gazed up at him. 'But I didn't think you...'

'Our child,' he said steadily. '*Our* child, Belle.'

For the first time in his life, Adam was almost overwhelmed by the surge of emotions that pounded through his blood. After what he'd seen of his own parents' marriage, he'd dismissed all thoughts of fatherhood and a family. Had never thought he would say those words, *Our child.*

But with this woman, his life had opened up to new and wonderful horizons. He and Belle—surely they would be better parents than his own? If only because of the love, the hope, the honesty they shared...

He kissed Belle's pale forehead tenderly. 'All this means,' he said with hope in his voice, 'is that we have to alter our plans accordingly.'

She could hardly breathe.

'We have to get married all the sooner!' he said joyfully. And pulling her closely to him, Adam kissed Belle, with a slow, sensual kiss of ravishing intimacy.

Later, when they'd got upstairs and he'd removed her beautiful gown with such tenderness that she thought she'd die of it, he made love to her with a passion that reached new heights for both of them.

'It's all right, isn't it?' he'd asked tenderly, kissing her bare shoulders as her gown slithered to the floor. 'With the baby?'

'Oh, yes,' she breathed softly. Besides, she couldn't have said no to this wonderful man if she'd wanted to. Everything he did was amazing that night. His every touch melted her as he crushed her slender body to his, compressed her soft breasts against his hard chest and inflamed her with his kisses. Was it because she'd thought she'd lost him? Or was it because they'd finally found each other?

A combination of both, she decided deliriously as Adam, who seemed to know exactly what her yearning body and her ardent heart craved, aroused her to fresh heights of longing—teasing her and tormenting her until she cried out aloud, desperate for the silken strength of him inside her, completing her. Afterwards he cherished her, holding her steadily in his arms and kissing her flushed face as the aftermath of her pleasure rippled through her again and again, leaving her breathless, speechless, melting with joy.

He talked to her then, as the single candle burned steadily over the fireplace. He told her in his husky voice how he'd never thought he would meet anyone who could mean what she did to him.

'It was my stupid pride, Belle,' he told her, stroking

her cheek. 'I was so tired of being told I should marry and I'd seen what marriage did to my parents.'

'Your brother, Freddy, is happy,' she reminded him, stroking his deliciously stubbled jaw as the shadows fluttered around them.

'Freddy is *very* happy, yes, and Louisa is wonderful. Freddy wasn't as scarred by our upbringing as I was.'

'Because you protected him.' She laid her face against his chest.

'I tried to make sure he didn't hear what I heard. I hoped he didn't realise just how much our mother despised our father.' He drew a deep breath. 'Then, of course, I always felt the weight of the family inheritance on my shoulders. People assumed that all I cared about was money and I did—I still do. But in many ways I see wealth as a way in which someone like me can change people's lives for the better.'

'Like your railway,' she murmured, nestling into his strong arms.

'Like my railway. If you could hear, Belle, how people like Jarvis speak with such contempt of their workers. God knows I'm no saint, but I do have some desire to make their lives a little easier. I am driven, yes; I'll always be ambitious. Apart from early on vowing never to endure a repeat of my father's unhappiness, I never thought I'd have time for marriage and a family—until I met you. And then…' he cupped her face tenderly in one hand '…then I was smitten, not just by your beauty, but by your pride, your spirit. But I thought that you loved your husband.'

'No,' she breathed. 'No. He hurt me so much that I never wanted to be with another man. He told me I was—*undesirable.*'

'Do you believe that now?' He was holding her closer and pressing his lips to her cheek. 'Do you?'

'No, Adam.' Her eyes shone. 'With you, I feel the most beautiful woman in the world.'

'Which you are,' he chided softly, drawing one tender finger down her cheek to her lips. 'But I thought I'd lost you, Belle. That bargain I'd made with Jarvis was unforgivable. Believe me, it wasn't long before I began to regret it bitterly. I told Jarvis so at Lord Horwich's ball.'

'Though even when you tried to explain I wouldn't listen,' she breathed. 'I was foolish and proud.'

'No more so than me. And I paid for it. I almost lost the one thing that mattered most of all—your love.'

The pad of his thumb brushed across her trembling lips, and she was pierced by the raw emotion in his eyes. She caught his hand and kissed it. 'I've made mistakes, too, Adam. In so many ways.'

'You've been brave, my love,' he whispered. 'Brave and selfless. You were willing to give up so much for your brother, and then you would have sacrificed yourself for me. My God, I nearly lost my mind when I realised Jarvis had taken you from Bath.'

'You never believed—' her voice was racked with anxiety now '—that I would have gone with him *willingly*?'

'Never,' he assured her. 'But I didn't realise you were prepared to go so far, for my sake. We will work everything out now, sweetheart.' His voice was husky, his breath warm against her cheek as he whispered, 'I love you. Never leave me again, Belle. Promise me.'

'I promise. Oh, Adam, I love you, too, so very much!'

'We must get married very soon. If our baby's a girl

I'll love her and spoil her terribly, to make up for all the love that you didn't have as a child.'

'If it's a boy?' she teased, stroking back his hair.

He was silent a moment, then, 'If we have a son, I'll teach him never to lose sight of all the things in life that really matter.' He caught her hand and kissed it. 'There's an exciting new world ahead of us, Belle. Steam railways are only the beginning. Our sons—and daughters—will see it all.'

Belle smiled mischievously. 'It sounds as if you're planning on a whole brood.'

Adam grinned back. 'I don't see why we shouldn't have a try at outnumbering Freddy's family. But...' and he paused, a mischievous glint in his eyes '...no lapdogs.'

'And no Egyptian furniture.' She spoke emphatically.

Adam held her very tightly. 'Hussy,' he said. 'Shameless, wilful hussy. To force me into buying that hideous stuff—how am I going to extract payment from you for *that* little trick?'

Already the familiar surge of heated desire was flaring inside her as her fingertips drifted across his hair-roughened chest. She nibbled at his ear with her lips and murmured, 'I can think of *several* ways you might like to be paid. Only it will be instalments, Adam my love. Night—after night—after night...'

He held her close, his eyes burning darkly. 'This is really for ever, sweetheart.'

Just a day ago, she faced despair. Now, she was the happiest woman alive. 'For ever, Adam my love,' she breathed.

Epilogue

June, ten months later

Speedily Adam climbed the wide staircase of the Clarges Street mansion and strode into the light, airy sitting room that was now a nursery. Settling himself on the sofa beside Belle, he gazed down at the sleeping baby in his wife's arms.

'How is she?' he breathed.

'Exactly the same as she was two hours ago, when you went out,' Belle teased. 'Well fed and happy. Adam, how was your meeting?'

'Absolutely fine,' he told her, putting his arm round her shoulders and drawing her close. 'The shareholders of the Sawle Down quarry want to invest in more equipment and there's interest in our stone from builders and architects all over the country.'

'Which means more jobs, more prosperity for Somerset. I'm so glad.' Belle hesitated. 'Adam, I had a letter from Charlotte this morning. She and Edward want to come and stay with us next week for a few days. I think she has some news.'

'Really?'

'I don't think she's pregnant,' Belle said quickly. 'I don't think she ever will be, sadly. But you know, don't you, that she's been helping at the church orphanage in Bath? And she and Edward—they may be able to adopt.' Her face softened. 'There's a baby girl called Sophie—I think they've fallen completely in love with her. You don't mind, do you, if they visit us? You'll remember how entranced Charlotte was with Clara when she first saw her. And I'd be really happy if she had a baby of her own.'

Adam leaned over to kiss her cheek gently. 'I'll be glad to see them.'

'It was so good of you to make Edward a shareholder in the Sawle Down quarry, Adam.'

'Not at all. Your brother's proved himself an asset in promoting our Bath stone and I'll be able to discuss some new contracts with him when he arrives in London. Meanwhile—on to more important things.'

Belle looked anxious as he reached in his coat pocket to pull out a news sheet. 'Here you are,' he said, his eyes dancing. 'Forget your brother, and Bath stone and railways; now for the *real* news of the week. Remember Lady Causton's ball last Friday? Well, here's a piece about it.' He unfolded the paper and started to read aloud. *'Mrs Adam Davenant looked sublime in a ballgown of violet sarcenet adorned with rouleaus of cream silk. A headdress of pale pink gauze and feathers completed an outfit that took the fashionable world by storm...'*

'Oh, no!' Belle laughed and pretended to hide her face blushingly against her husband's shoulder. 'Adam, you know very well that Gabby and I practically threw that outfit together in about two hours when you told me I just *had* to leave Clara with the nursemaid for the evening and come with you to that ball!'

'And baby Clara was none the worse for it,' said Adam softly, touching his daughter's tiny curled fist. As if recognising her father's touch, Clara opened her eyes—eyes of green—and her perfect little fingers fluttered against Adam's big palm.

Belle, on seeing his expression, felt her heart overflow with joy.

'There's more.' He picked up the news sheet again. 'Listen. *Mr Davenant's wife was once famous...*'

'*Once* famous!' she protested indignantly.

'*Was once famous for the avant-garde styles she created in her fashionable Piccadilly shop. She is believed to still have a hand in the designs sold in the shop, though it is now run by her former assistant, Mrs Gabrielle Bellamy.*'

'Oh,' breathed Belle, 'this means dear Gabby will be busier than ever. That shop means so much to her.' She paused a moment. 'As it did to me,' she added quietly.

His arm was tightly round her again. 'Do you miss it, sweetheart? Do you miss your independence?'

Belle gazed down at their baby sleeping again in her arms, then looked up at Adam, her eyes shimmering with happiness. 'Well,' she said carefully, 'I suppose I'll always want to stay in touch with Gabby and the latest fashions. After all, I would *hate* my husband to grow bored with me...'

'No danger of that,' Adam said very softly. 'No danger of that whatsoever.' He turned her face to his, his eyes searching hers. 'I owe you everything, Belle, from the day you rode into my life on Sawle Down.'

'You accused me of trespassing.' She laughed. 'Oh,

you were so arrogant! And I was so unforgivably rude to you, Adam.'

'You were,' he agreed. 'But you were the most beautifully *rude* trespasser I'd ever seen. From that day to the day you agreed to marry me, you've thrown my life into a state of expenses, turmoil, unpredictability...'

She looked distressed. 'Adam, please don't remind me!'

'I haven't finished. And great, great happiness, my darling. Happiness I never expected and never deserved.'

'You deserve every happiness, Adam,' Belle breathed. 'Oh, my love, you deserve everything I can possibly give you.'

He touched her lips with his and the familiar pulse of heated desire flared inside her as she reached up to explore and cherish the lean contours of his face. Just then baby Clara gurgled softly and waved her tiny fists in the air.

'I love her so much,' Belle whispered as she cradled her baby close. 'But Clara and I—we have thrown your life into disarray, haven't we? You used to have everything running so smoothly, but now...'

'Don't worry,' he laughed. 'We simply have to adapt, you and I. Like we did this morning.'

'This morning? *Oh!*' Belle blushed suddenly, remembering how she'd woken in her husband's arms an hour before daylight, only to find Adam was awake, too, and...wanting her. Desiring her. As she desired him, would always desire him. Their lovemaking had been slow, delicious and achingly sensual, yet full of love. She smiled up at him as Adam's strong hand caressed his tiny daughter's cheek. 'Adam, shall we have an early night?' she whispered.

Adam's eyes were tender as he took their baby from her and revelled in the wonder of life and love that was theirs. 'As early as you like.'

Belle reached to kiss her husband's cheek. Sheer joy and contentment filled her heart. They had love to last a lifetime—and more.

* * * * *

MILLS & BOON®

The Regency Collection – Part 1

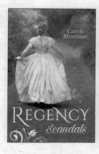
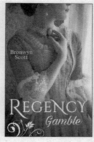

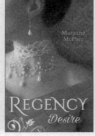

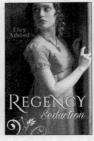

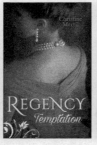